# PRAISE FOR JAMES HANKINS

"This outstanding crime thriller from Hankins . . . grabs the reader by the scruff of the neck and never lets go."
—*Publishers Weekly* (starred ~~~ ~~ *Shady Cross*

"[A] fine, offbeat novel . . . ~~~~ ogue and characters who are . . . all t~ ~~~~
*ady Cross*

"One thing about James Hankins—you are always surprised—having read all his books, each one is unique, creative, and different. He always hooks you from the beginning, keeping you in suspense—you never know what's coming . . ."
—*Must Read Books* on *The Prettiest One*

"*The Prettiest One* engrosses readers with enough twists and turns to keep them on their toes . . ."
—*Wicked Local: Gloucester*

"A thrill ride that takes you on a journey that is not for the 'faint of heart.' Wonderful character development, believable storyline, a true page turner, with an ending that I was not expecting . . . Five stars!"
—*Poised Pen Productions/Authors on the Air* on *The Prettiest One*

"A prosecutor and a homeless man team up against a murderous conspiracy in this rollicking thriller . . . The two settle into an entertaining dynamic as . . . Hankins surrounds them with a crackerjack cast of bristling thugs, weaselly lowlifes and beady-eyed feds, and he ties the story together with pitch-perfect dialogue, mordant humor and action scenes poised exquisitely between menace and chaos . . . A complex, entertaining thriller."
—*Kirkus Reviews* (starred review) on *Brothers and Bones*

# THE
# INSIDE
# DARK

# OTHER TITLES BY JAMES HANKINS

# THE INSIDE DARK

## JAMES HANKINS

THOMAS & MERCER

Published by Thomas & Mercer, Seattle

www.apub.com

Amazon, the Amazon logo, and Thomas & Mercer are trademarks of Amazon.com, Inc., or its affiliates.

ISBN-13: 9781477819906
ISBN-10: 1477819908

Cover design by Rex Bonomelli

Printed in the United States of America

*For Susan, Rick, Barbara, Chris, and John, who have been there for me from my very beginning.*

# CHAPTER ONE

*Death.*

There had been plenty of time for Jason Swike to think about it since awakening five days ago chained to the wall of an old horse corral in a deserted, ramshackle stable. And there were things he now knew.

*Death is cruel.*

It hadn't given him anything to eat; not a morsel in five days. And nothing to drink but a single bottle of Dasani water on each of the last four days, left for him while he slept.

The water was drugged. He knew that. He could tell because every time he drank it he passed out shortly thereafter. He didn't want to drink it. He would prefer to appear defiant and stronger than he was, but it was stiflingly hot in the stable and he was so damn thirsty. So he drank it. Every day. And the drug stayed in his system a long time, first knocking him out and then keeping him groggy for hours—neither necessarily a bad thing, given his horrific situation. And whenever the inevitable finally occurred, perhaps his foggy state of mind would spare him the worst of it. He was woozy even now. If he was lucky, he would be asleep when Death arrived.

*Because Death is terribly cruel.*

He knew that for a fact, because . . .

*Death enjoys what it does.*

He could hear it working, not far away, enjoying itself. He knew that to be true because . . .

*Death likes to whistle while it works.*

Though he had yet to see it, he could hear it whistling an old tune while doing what Death does. The song was "Take Me Out to the Ball Game."

And when the whistled tune reached the point where the familiar lyrics were "Buy me some peanuts and Cracker Jack," Jason's darkest fears were confirmed.

*Because Death has a name.*

At least *this* Death did. It had been all over the news for nearly a year. Headlines and magazine covers screamed it. And though it was known around the country, it was most feared in Massachusetts, where Death had been hunting lately. Latching on to the grisly details of the slayings, the media had dubbed Death's latest human incarnation *Crackerjack*—because serial killers with catchy monikers grab more viewers and sell more papers than ordinary killers do. And from what Jason had read about him, the name fit him like a tailor-made suit. Men—for some reason, only men—turning up broken, literally broken, with numerous bones in their bodies cracked, snapped, twisted, or crushed . . . bones in their hands, legs, feet, arms, chests . . . and finally, after what must have been hours of agony, the death blow . . . a blunt instrument to the head, caving in the skull. So the name *Crackerjack* seemed fitting. The killer himself seemed to approve, as he apparently had taken to whistling the old song while he tortured his victims—not caring, it seemed, that the media spelled his name as one word rather than two, the way the popular snack food was spelled. The whistling was something the world at large didn't know about him, Jason realized, because the only people who ever heard him do it were dead. And Jason realized something else.

*Death has a sense of humor . . .*

. . . because when the song reached the *one* in "For it's one . . . two . . . three strikes you're out," the whistling stopped abruptly and Jason heard a loud thump, followed by a scream. And he knew with terrible certainty what would follow, with the *two* and again with the *three*: each strike would be punctuated by another sickening thump, and another scream. Yes, Crackerjack had clearly taken his media-given nickname to heart, incorporating it into his work. What a funny guy Death was, Jason now knew. And he knew something else, too, something the public had learned over the past eleven months.

*Death has an odd sense of whimsy . . .*

. . . because in addition to broken bones and fractured skulls, Crackerjack's victims had all been found with their faces adorned with skillfully rendered designs, like the ones folks paid for at amusement parks and carnivals—superheroes and fairies, wild animals and cartoon characters.

The whole nasty, twisted business sold a lot of newspapers.

It was sad.

And creepy.

And terrifying for Jason, because there was one more thing he knew for certain: When the screaming not far away stopped . . .

*Death would come whistling for him.*

# CHAPTER TWO

Jason knew who was screaming not far away. His name was Ian Cobb. Sometime earlier that day, while Jason had been dozing, Crackerjack had brought the man in and chained him up in the horse stall next to Jason's. He'd probably been unconscious, the way Jason had been upon his arrival. When he had woken up, he'd sounded loopy. And even though Jason's own mind was fuzzy, as it was most of the time now, he'd tried his best to explain the situation to the new captive.

At first, Cobb cycled through the same range of emotions that Jason had—confusion, anger, and fear. There was a brief moment of something resembling panic, but he'd calmed himself down soon enough and they'd started talking.

Which wasn't easy for Jason. Twelve ounces of water per day was far from enough to keep his throat from becoming a desert road. His tongue felt too large for his mouth. But he talked anyway, pushing past the curtains of fog in his mind to describe his four long, hot, hungry, thirsty, sweaty days in this stable before Cobb had arrived. Jason listened, too, trying to pay attention as Cobb talked a little about his life and asked questions about Jason's. But it was difficult to concentrate. His brain felt like sludge.

"I heard all about you on the news," Cobb had said. "There were a lot of stories about you."

"Is there a reward?" Jason had asked in a voice that cracked like dry twigs.

It was a weak attempt at a joke. He didn't imagine there would be a reward in connection with his disappearance. Not like there had been for the killer's fourth victim, the handsome, charismatic twenty-four-year-old lead singer of a popular local Boston band that some music magazines had predicted was on the verge of breaking out. The one whose father had become a celebrity in his own right, the owner of a succession of hip and trendy and wildly successful restaurants that boasted a virtual who's who of the rich and famous as a clientele. When it became clear the young man was truly missing and not simply sleeping off a bender somewhere, the father offered $100,000 for information leading to his safe return. When the poor kid was found at a rest area off 91 North with a crushed skull, twenty-two broken bones, and a face painted to resemble a Teenage Mutant Ninja Turtle, the reward doubled . . . though, with a safe return no longer an option, the money was offered for information leading to Crackerjack's arrest and successful prosecution.

And Crackerjack became a household name.

"No reward," Cobb had admitted to Jason, "but the media talked all about you . . . and your wife and son."

Mention of his family had caused a tightness in Jason's chest. Sophie and Max were the main reasons he wasn't more hesitant to drink the drug-laced water left for him every day. The foggier his mind was, the less he could think about them . . . about how much he missed them, about how they might be handling his disappearance. He blinked and felt as though tears wanted to fall, but there didn't seem to be enough moisture in his body to produce them.

"Your wife's in a wheelchair?" Cobb had asked.

"Yeah."

"And your son has some sort of—"

"I'd rather not talk about my family."

A pause. "Sure. Sorry. I just . . . sorry."

They were quiet for a moment, and sleep was threatening to drag Jason into its dark depths again when, finally and inevitably, talk turned to their captor. Neither man had gotten a look at him. The last thing both remembered before waking up in the stable had been walking to their cars in deserted parking lots. Then . . . nothing.

"It's him, isn't it?" Cobb had asked. "Crackerjack."

"Has to be."

"How many guys has he killed?"

"He's up to ten, right? In less than a year, I think."

Neither of them mentioned the shattered condition of the bodies discovered in landfills, ditches, and dumpsters around Massachusetts.

"When he comes for me," Cobb had said, "I'll be ready. The bastard won't kill me without a fight."

Jason had told himself the same thing for the first few days, but he knew he wouldn't put up much of a struggle at this point. He was too weak. The muscles in his arms and legs had been cramping and erupting into spasms nearly nonstop for days. A relentless pounding assaulted his head from inside his skull. He hurt . . . everywhere. And he was tired. God, he was so very tired.

"I'll be ready," Cobb said again.

Jason had nodded then, knowing the gesture couldn't be seen, and let his chin drop to his chest. He couldn't hold his head up anymore.

He'd closed his eyes and was asleep when Death came for Ian Cobb.

———

It was the whistling that had awoken him . . . that and Cobb's screaming.

That tune—"Take Me Out to the Ball Game"—floating through the stable. The lyrics had come unbidden to his mind. "For it's one—"

That terrible thump, that scream.

"Two—"

Another thump, another scream. *Two strikes.* Jason rose to his knees, grabbed the chains tethering him to the stable wall, and yanked with every ounce of strength he could muster. It wasn't close to enough.

Too soon came the third thump—*three strikes you're out*—and this time Jason heard a bone snap. Bile filled his throat. Screams filled his ears. Then the screams died away.

Jason slumped to the floor. For some reason he couldn't fathom, Crackerjack had held him for nearly five days without touching him, without even showing his face, but had begun his torture of Ian Cobb within hours of taking him. Had he forgotten about Jason? But no, a bottle of water appeared every day.

Not far away, Cobb moaned unintelligibly. No, wait . . . there were decipherable words. Mumbled, pleading words. "No . . . more," he said. "Please . . . no more . . . no more . . . no more . . ."

Jason closed his eyes. Cobb was still moaning and pleading, so Jason put his hands over his ears. And though he wasn't a religious man, and he doubted anyone was listening, he prayed for Ian Cobb.

And himself.

And he prayed for his wife and son.

What else could he do until Death came for him, too?

# CHAPTER THREE

With his hands over his ears and his eyes closed, with fever-charged blood pounding through his head, Jason didn't hear the sudden commotion. But he felt it, felt the vibration in the stable wall as something slammed into it. Then a crash and a desperate, animal grunt. He opened his eyes as two people hurtled into his corral, one almost carrying the other over his shoulder as he charged forward, legs pumping, propelling him like a linebacker driving a receiver out of bounds. Jason barely had time to blink before they landed on him in a heap. Something banged painfully off his knee and clattered to the stained cement floor.

A hammer.

Cobb's desperate voice came from the top of the pile. "Help me, Jason." Sandwiched between them, on his back atop Jason, was the second man. He wore a black ski mask pulled down over his head. Jason tried to crawl out from beneath them.

"The hammer . . ." Cobb gasped as he fought.

It was happening so fast. The writhing bodies. The blood roaring in his ears. Cobb pleading for help.

"Please, Jason . . ."

One moment, Jason had been huddled in a ball, his eyes and ears closed, and the next a life-and-death struggle with a serial killer was taking place literally on top of him.

"Hurry . . ."

The hammer had come to rest not far from his hand. He reached for it, falling short for a moment as the chain on his wrist snagged on something and became taut. He strained and the chain slipped free, at last allowing his fingers to close around the hammer's smooth wooden handle.

"I don't know how long I can hold him," Cobb screamed. "*Hit him.*"

Without considering what he was about to do, Jason flung his arm out to the side, the hammer clenched in his fist.

"For God's sake, Jason . . . *put him down.*"

He swung the hammer hard and heard a sharp crack as its blunt tip connected with the ski mask. It was a sickening sound, but without hesitation he swung again, another crack, this one sounding a little less sharp and a little . . . wetter. He might have swung again, he wasn't sure, before the struggle ceased. The man was still.

Jason dropped the hammer. A warm stickiness touched his cheek and he knew blood was dripping through the mask even before he smelled its coppery scent. He turned his head and tried to shove the man off, but his dead weight, combined with Cobb's, was too much. Finally, Cobb rolled off the pile and Jason slithered out from beneath the man, his motion causing the mask to slide from the face. He dragged himself away from the body.

Because that's what the man was now. Nothing more than a body. Lifeless as a stone. Jason looked down into staring, empty eyes. The side of the man's head beneath the wiry, penny-red hair was caved in. Blood pooled beneath it.

Jason had killed someone. It was a strange feeling. He tried to work up some guilt over it, perhaps a shred of sympathy for the man whose life he had taken, but he felt nothing for Crackerjack, the sadistic serial killer who whistled as he tortured his victims. No, that wasn't quite true, because he did experience a moment of hatred, pure and intense, for the man who had torn him away from his family and would have killed him eventually had he not died first.

Jason looked over at Ian Cobb, got his first good look at him, and the first thing he noticed was his face. Around each of his eyes was a hand-painted butterfly with delicately filigreed green-and-gold wings. There was glitter in the paint, so the butterflies sparkled as they caught the sunlight filtering down through one of the many holes in the raftered ceiling. Jason couldn't help but notice the skill in the rendering of the insects. In the drab, run-down stable, the splashes of color were striking . . . but not unexpected—after all, each of Crackerjack's victims had been found with similar designs. Dead men whose faces had been painted to look like Spider-Man, or a tiger, or Frankenstein's monster.

Cobb was on his back, his right arm lying awkwardly across his stomach, cradled by his left. He'd been watching Jason stare down at the lifeless body, his expression unreadable, perhaps in part because of the bright butterflies around his eyes. Jason felt uncomfortable, naked and exposed, as though the hot hatred he'd felt toward Crackerjack a moment ago was blazing in red neon on his face. He sucked in a deep breath, blew it out, then nodded toward Cobb's arm.

"Are you okay?"

"Did you hear him whistling?" Cobb asked. He coughed, which made him wince and grunt in pain. "The son of a bitch was whistling while he did it to me, for God's sake."

"I know. Are you all right?"

"I've been better, but I'm okay." He nodded toward the man lying with his head in a puddle of red. "He's dead, right? He's definitely dead?"

Jason looked at the blood, the depression in the head, the vacant eyes.

"Yeah, he's dead."

Cobb rolled onto his side, then struggled to sit up, grimacing and groaning as he did. He kept supporting his right arm with his left.

"You sure you're okay?" Jason asked.

"I just want to . . . get away from here."

Jason looked down at Crackerjack again. What struck him was how ordinary the man would have looked without the crushed skull and dead eyes. If this man passed by on the street, no one would have suspected the darkness raging inside him. Average size, medium build, plain face. Nothing remarkable about him . . . except that he liked to break men to death after painting cheerful designs on their faces, snapping their bones one by one before caving in their skulls with a hammer. And there he lay, killed by hammer blows to the head, possibly delivered with the same tool he'd used to send at least ten other men to their graves. Irony abounded. Payback is a bitch.

Jason gingerly patted the dead man's pockets, looking for the keys to the manacles on his wrists. No luck.

He turned to Cobb sitting a few feet away. "I need you need to find a key to these chains, okay? Then we can get out of here together. Can you stand?"

Cobb nodded, then labored to his knees, still awkwardly supporting his right arm. Every movement elicited a pained groan expelled through gritted teeth.

"He broke your arm?" Jason asked.

"Maybe some ribs, too."

"It's amazing you were able to . . . do what you did . . . escape from him and . . ."

Cobb shrugged.

"You were fortunate," Jason added.

"Not as fortunate as you," Cobb replied, smiling weakly.

Jason smiled back, probably even more weakly. He was reminded again of how very tired he was, how depleted his reserves were. "Can you walk?" he asked.

Cobb nodded. "I'll look for keys."

He shuffled off. There was nothing for Jason to do but wait. His eyes drifted to the body of the man who used to be Crackerjack, to the ugly, bloody depression he'd made in the man's head.

Jason had killed him. It had been self-defense, but still . . . he had killed another person.

"Any luck?" he called. His voice was fragile and raspy and he wondered if his words had carried beyond the walls of his corral, but Cobb answered from not too far away.

"No handcuff keys yet, but I found some car keys here in a box on a workbench. Maybe a dozen sets. Cell phones, too, including mine. Some of these things may be yours."

"Call 911," Jason rasped.

"I already turned it on . . . waiting for a signal . . . dialing now . . ."

Jason closed his eyes. After what seemed an eternity, Cobb returned, jingling softly as he walked.

"Found these," he said, dropping a ring of keys beside Jason. "Maybe one of them will do the trick."

The fourth key opened the iron manacles. God, it felt good to be free of the chains. Now he needed—

"Water," he said in a dry whisper. "Did you see any water anywhere?"

Cobb shook his head. "Sorry. I should have looked. I know how thirsty you gotta be but I wanted to get you out of those chains."

"Let's look now."

Using the wall for support, he made it to his feet. He tottered for a moment, then shuffled out of the corral that had been his prison for almost five days. He saw that he was in a long building with horse stalls lining both sides. Some still had doors just tall enough to rise to a horse's chest. Others were missing their doors, like the one in which Jason had been imprisoned, and the one he was passing now . . . inside of which he saw a wooden table, long enough for a man to lie on. Its tan surface was scarred and stained dark brown in several places. Leather straps hung from brackets secured to each of the table's legs. A smaller table sat near the larger one. Arrayed on its surface were two incongruous sets of items. The first consisted of little jars of paint and delicate brushes while the second featured a small variety of blunt instruments: a wooden mallet with a round head, a mini sledgehammer, a mallet with a square head, a—

Cobb's voice came from not far away. "Here's where I found the keys and phones."

Jason turned away from the stall and, on leaden legs, followed the voice toward the far end of the stable where a big set of doors was set into the stable wall.

Doors. The outside. Freedom.

He found Cobb standing beside a workbench, its surface littered with numerous items, none of which was a bottle of water, the only thing Jason wanted at the moment. He wouldn't even have minded if it were drugged.

"You okay?" Cobb asked.

"No water here."

"Maybe they'll have some with them."

"They? Who—"

Then he heard them, too. Sirens. He leaned back against the wall, allowed himself to slide slowly to the floor, and waited. While he waited, he started to cry. Apparently, he had enough water in his body for tears after all.

# CHAPTER FOUR

Jason opened his eyes and saw white. White everywhere. Hazy, as though he were floating in a cloud. Slowly, he made out shapes. Ceiling tiles, walls, a curtain . . . Then the curtain started to slide into focus and he could make out little blue flowers on it.

At first, he thought he was back in the stable, hallucinating. Then he remembered the escape, and the police, and the ambulance. He smiled weakly. His mouth felt strange. He licked his lips and found them cracked, along with his tongue. He raised his hand to touch his mouth and felt an unfamiliar sensation on his forearm. He looked down and saw an IV line running from a spot near the crook of his arm to a pole beside the bed in which he lay. Movement caught his attention and he turned his head, gritting through a painful stiffness in his neck, and saw a woman standing near the foot of his bed. A nurse in pale-pink surgical scrubs writing on a clipboard. He blinked and his vision became clearer, the clearest it had been in days.

The nurse looked up, saw him watching, and smiled. Before she could say a word, Jason croaked out one of his own. "Water?"

"I'll be right back."

She left, returning a few long minutes later with a cup of ice chips. She spooned a few into his mouth, and the sensation on his cracked tongue and parched throat was wonderful, though the amount she gave him was far, far too small to provide much relief.

"More?" he asked in a dusty voice.

"I'm afraid that's all for now." The nurse was short and round and had a kind smile. "You'll have to take it slow."

"Just . . . a little?"

"Not yet. Soon, I promise. After the doctor sees you. My name is Maryann, by the way."

Jason marveled at Maryann's cruelty.

"My wife?" he whispered. He swallowed, wincing at the discomfort it caused. "Did she call?"

"Ms. Swike did call, and I told her what the doctors told me, that you're going to be fine."

He nodded again and watched her leave the room. Just outside the door, a man in a dark suit stopped her. They spoke for a few seconds. Maryann shook her head and walked away. The man in the suit watched him from the doorway until Jason turned his head and closed his eyes.

———

Dr. Silberman told Jason that he was lucky. He'd suffered moderately severe dehydration but was otherwise in fair health. His initial blood work had shown traces of a benzodiazepine—a drug used to treat anxiety and insomnia. The one that had been in his system was particularly long acting, meaning that its effects had lasted longer than those of many other sleeping aids. Subsequent tests confirmed that his blood was now clear of the drug. His muscles, which had spent days cycling through painful cramps and spasms, would be sore for a day or two, but there would be no long-term ill effects from his time in captivity, at least no physical ones. And Jason had to admit he was starting to feel a bit better. His muscles hurt less already. The ointment they applied regularly to his lips soothed them, and the oral fluids he'd been allowed in moderation did the same for his tongue. He was going to be okay, which was more than—

"What about the other guy?" For a moment, he couldn't come up with the name. "Cobb?"

"Mr. Cobb suffered a few injuries," Dr. Silberman said, "but he'll be fine. You were both lucky, it seems. Especially considering what you went through."

Silberman listened to Jason's heart and lungs, checked his eyes with a penlight, wrote a few things on a chart, then told him that he'd be able to leave at the end of the day if he felt up to it. Jason decided that he would definitely feel up to it, even if he didn't. He wanted to get out of there. He wanted to see Sophie and Max.

No sooner had he closed his eyes than he heard the rumble of a throat clearing nearby. He looked up to see the man in the dark suit standing a few feet from his bed. Six feet tall—maybe six one—and physically fit for a man who looked to be in his late fifties. His eyes were clear and sharp.

"Mr. Swike, I'm Lamar Briggs, a homicide detective with the Essex County State Police." He flipped open a black wallet, flashing a badge. "Feel up to answering a few questions? There are a lot of people who want to hear what you have to say."

Jason cleared his throat and said, "I'll bet. I doubt many people have escaped that guy."

"You and Mr. Cobb are the only ones we know of."

Jason nodded but he wasn't thrilled about having to recount his time in Crackerjack's stable. He wasn't certain how much he'd even be able to recall. The only thing he remembered well was beating a man to death, which he doubted he'd ever forget. He could almost feel the bone give way under the hammer in his hand. He could still hear the wet crack as the tool crashed through the man's skull. He could almost smell the tangy scent of blood, feel its warmth on his cheek. He closed his eyes for a moment, took a small breath, and opened them again.

"What can I tell you, Detective?"

# CHAPTER FIVE

Half a dozen news vans were parked in front of Ian Cobb's house, with two dozen people in and around them, waiting for him to arrive home, evidently hoping for a statement. They were going to be disappointed. They'd already heard from him coming out of the hospital yesterday, and that was enough for Cobb.

He pulled past them into his driveway and they followed on foot toward his house, microphones in hand and cameras on shoulders, shouting questions. He half expected them to duck under the garage door as it descended, but they remained outside.

He was already tired of it all, and it had just begun. He didn't want to be famous. He just wanted to be left alone. That would happen eventually. Soon enough another killer would come along who would grab the headlines and, thankfully, the attention away from Cobb. But he knew he'd have to put up with his sudden fame for a little while at least.

———

As on most days, Carolyn, the one who was almost but not quite pretty, was on duty with his father today. And as she did on most days, she appeared downstairs within seconds of Cobb's arrival home. It seemed to him that the moment she heard movement on the first floor, she left her post in his father's room upstairs, gathered her things, and hustled down, ready to bid him a quick good night before disappearing out the door. He couldn't blame her. It must be a long day for her here, stuck in an old man's room with no one to talk to in any meaningful way. Cobb felt lucky to have her. She was the best of the nurses in the rotation he employed, competent and caring. Like the others, though, she wasn't cheap. None of it was. The expense of keeping his father at home rather than in a long-term-care facility was significant. The older man's insurance benefits were too meager to help much, and Cobb's mother's life-insurance payout was long gone. Cobb estimated that more than half of his own income went to nursing care, doctors' visits, and medical supplies and equipment. But it was worth it to Cobb to be able to keep his father close, to see him every day.

He hadn't even put his wallet and keys on the kitchen counter when Carolyn appeared in the doorway. But this time, rather than issuing a perfunctory report on his father's never-changing condition before bolting for the front door, she stood there, one hand nervously massaging the other.

"Hello, Mr. Cobb," she said. "Um . . ."

"Hi, Carolyn. How is he today?"

"Your father? Um . . . the same."

Of course he was.

"Um . . ."

"Yes?"

"How are you, Mr. Cobb? Are you okay? Uh . . . I heard about you on the news. I mean, who hasn't? I didn't see it last night but then the news vans started showing up today, so I turned on the TV and, well . . ."

"I'm a little banged up," he said, nodding at the cast on his right forearm, "but I'm fine."

"I can't imagine what you—"

"I'm okay, I promise. Don't really feel like talking about it, though. You understand."

She had been about to say something else but closed her mouth and nodded.

"I'm in for the night," he added, "so you can head on home."

"Okay."

"And Carolyn? Don't talk to the reporters out there, okay? They're like pigeons. You feed them, they'll just keep asking for more. I don't want my life to become more of a circus than it already looks like it's gonna be for a while."

"Sure thing."

"Thanks. Have a good night."

At the top of the stairs, Ian walked to the second door on the right, which was open, and entered the room without knocking, as he always did.

Arthur Cobb was right where he'd been the last time Ian had seen him. And the time before that. And the ten thousand times before that. He hadn't moved a muscle, at least not of his own volition, in eight years; the occasional twitch, nothing more. He was lying in bed, staring at the ceiling. He blinked involuntarily. Tubes ran to and from various parts of his body. One through which he received nutrients and fluids and medicine ran from his arm to an IV pole beside the bed. Two corrugated plastic tubes—one white, the other blue—upon which he depended for his life's breath, were attached to a smaller tube protruding from a surgically made hole in the front of his throat and ran to a ventilator machine in the corner of the room. A trickle of urine flowed down from under the bedcovers through a catheter tube to a collection bag that hung from the bed frame. The bag would need to be emptied soon. Ian frowned. Carolyn should have done that before clocking out for the night.

"Hey, Dad," Ian said.

His father's only response was a small whoosh of air, then another—first in, then out—through his tracheal tube. In the corner, the ventilator thumped and clicked and whirred softly in time with the patient's breathing. Though many people in persistent vegetative states—perhaps even most—are able to breathe on their own, Arthur Cobb had been unfortunate enough to have suffered traumatic injury to his respiratory system in the same accident that caused such devastating damage to his brain, so his days of breathing without mechanical assistance were gone forever.

Ian leaned over his father and looked closely at the site of the tracheotomy. No sign of infection, which was good. Carolyn would often smile and say that Ian's father just might live forever. The old man's primary physician, Dr. Howe, said the same thing, though to him, that wasn't necessarily a good thing. It was good to Ian, though. He wanted his father around for as long as possible.

He sat in the chair near the head of the bed—it was still warm from Carolyn's recent presence—and regarded his father's profile. The man's skin had gone gray long before, having not been touched by direct sunlight in years. He could use a shave soon; the white stubble had been sprouting for nearly a week. Ian would mention it to Carolyn and Rose, though he shouldn't have to, he thought with irritation.

"Feel like talking a bit, Dad?" He waited a few seconds for an answer that would never come, eyeing the tubes connecting the man to the hissing-humming-clicking machine in the corner. "Not tonight, huh? Okay, I'll do the talking then."

He sat back and crossed one leg over the other.

"I broke my arm. The ulna. It's the smaller bone in the forearm, on the side with the little finger. Broke three ribs, too. Spent two hours in the hospital last night. Got this cast," he said, raising his arm a little. "Nothing they could do for the ribs, though. Just gotta try not to take deep breaths."

*Whoosh, whir, click, whoosh.*

"I coughed on the drive home and nearly screamed."

*Whoosh. Whir.*

"Carolyn said she saw me on the news." He looked at the dark screen of the small television mounted high on the wall opposite the bed. Its blank face was as empty as his father's. "I guess Rose probably did this morning, too," he said, referring to another of his father's regular nurses.

*Click, hum, whoosh.*

"Sorry I haven't seen much of you the past day or two. I've been busy, unfortunately. You'd know that if you watched the news . . . and could understand it. All they're talking about is how I escaped from Crackerjack. This other guy and me. I'm a little famous right now. I have no desire to be famous, Dad."

*Whoosh. Whir.*

"The other guy—Jason Swike—he seems like a decent person. Since he went missing last week they've run a lot of stories about him on the news. He's got a wife in a wheelchair. And a kid with Down syndrome, like Stevie had. I assume you remember Stevie, Dad. Anyway, his kid has some rare blood disease on top of that." Ian shook his head. "This guy, Jason, he's had things tough the last few years."

*Whoosh. Click.*

"He reminds me a lot of Johnny. A *lot*. You wouldn't believe it." A pause, then, "I can't stop wondering whether you remember any of us, Dad. Any of your sons. Me, Johnny, Stevie."

Nothing.

"Anyway, him reminding me so much of Johnny—he has red hair, like Johnny had, but there's other things, too—I started to feel sorry for him. A wife in a wheelchair, a sick kid with Down syndrome like Stevie had. I felt sorry for all of them. I miss Johnny and Stevie."

He watched his father breathe through his tubes for another few minutes, then he stood.

"I guess I should empty that catheter bag."

After he'd hung the empty bag on the side of the bed again and washed his hands, he headed for the door. Before he left the room, he flicked a wall switch, turning off the lights. He had no idea whether his father knew the difference between light and dark at this point, even though, by pure chance, his eyes were open at the moment, but it saved electricity to turn them off, so he did.

"I'm heading down to eat some dinner, Dad. I'll come and say good night later."

# CHAPTER SIX

"Just a few more questions, Mr. Swike," Detective Briggs said. "And really, I'm sorry to make you go over all of this again. I know you answered a lot of these questions yesterday when you first came out of that stable, but as you know, this case is a whopper. Gotta have all our i's dotted and our t's crossed."

"That's okay," Jason said. "I barely remember going over it the first time."

It was true. When the authorities had swarmed the stable the day before, Jason was in rough shape. He could hardly keep his eyes open. When someone started asking him questions, he'd done his best to answer, hoping that he was being helpful. Eventually paramedics arrived, and the next thing he remembered was waking up in the hospital.

Briggs was sitting in the chair by the door, where he'd been sitting for the past half hour, asking questions with a ballpoint pen in one hand and a little notebook in the other.

"I'm sorry I can't remember more," Jason said. "But everything is just so . . . hazy."

"I realize that. Again, I appreciate your trying."

"I just want to get out of here. I want to see my family. I haven't even talked to my wife yet, my son. I was barely awake before you started interviewing me."

"We're almost done for now, I promise. Then you can call your ex-wife."

"She's my wife, not my ex."

Briggs paused, flipped back a few pages in his notebook. "Of course. Sorry. Anyway, I know you work as a copywriter . . ."

"At the Barker Creative Agency, yeah."

"But I understand you're also an author."

Jason nodded.

"Crime novels, right?"

"Crime, mystery, suspense . . . the lines tend to blur."

"That's pretty cool."

*It's cool when you're selling books,* Jason thought, *when editors know your name, when people are talking about turning your crime thriller into a movie, when you still have an agent. It's not quite so cool when the film deal disappears and the only book you wrote that anyone read went out of print two years ago and is harder to find than a copy of the Gutenberg Bible, and even the digital version of it doesn't sell enough copies each month to buy you a tank of gas.*

"Mr. Swike? Did you hear me?"

"Oh, sorry. I'm still a bit . . . What was the question?"

"How many books do you have out there?"

"Just one. So far," he added quickly. He didn't count the two self-published thrillers—if that term actually applied—that he'd tried unsuccessfully to peddle to the masses. He didn't think there was anything wrong with self-published books generally—he'd read some good ones—but there must be something wrong with *his*, as virtually no one bought them.

"Got another one coming out soon?"

"Not that soon," he said, thinking about the dozen or so pages of notes he'd jotted down a few months ago, random thoughts on a vague idea he'd come up with for a murder mystery that had seemed marginally intriguing back then. But the concept hadn't held even his own interest for more than a week; he couldn't imagine it holding anyone else's for the time it took to read an entire novel. So he'd stuffed the notes in a drawer and hadn't glanced at them since. "I'm working on a new one, though."

"I imagine this would make a pretty good story. What you went through the past few days."

"I suppose."

"Be a good one to get your career back on track, I bet. 'Real-life crime writer kills serial killer.' I'd sure buy that one."

Jason shouldn't have been surprised that Briggs had done a little homework on him, and that would be all it took—a *little*—to learn that his writing career had stalled.

"I haven't had much time to think about my writing the last couple of days," he said.

Briggs nodded and looked down at his little notebook. Flipped back a few pages. "So, when Mr. Cobb and the suspect—"

"What's his name?"

"Excuse me?"

"The guy that I . . . the suspect. What was his name?"

"Wallace Barton."

Jason nodded.

Briggs continued. "So, when they crashed into the corral where you were being held . . ."

The questions kept coming and Jason did his best to answer them. The events of yesterday afternoon were jumbled in his mind, like snippets of Super 8mm film dropped in a pile on a table and spliced back together in random order. He saw images, flashes of movement. He heard sounds: whistling, screaming, a skull cracking. And though his mind knew the order in which they must have occurred, it took some effort to assemble them that way. He recounted how Cobb and Crackerjack landed on him, with Cobb on top and Barton on his back between them; how they were fighting; how Cobb sounded panicky, saying he wouldn't be able to hold the guy for long . . .

"How is he, by the way?" Jason asked. "Cobb."

"Broken arm, a few busted ribs. Spent a couple of hours in the ER. He'll be okay. Might have some bad dreams for a while, but he'll be all right."

Jason figured he had some nightmares ahead of him, too.

"You were saying?" Briggs prompted.

"Oh, yeah, just that Cobb was screaming for me to help, sounding scared and desperate now, so I grabbed the hammer from the floor."

"With which hand?"

"Excuse me?"

"Which hand did you grab the hammer with?"

"Uh, my right, I guess."

"And?"

"And . . ." He paused. He could still feel the worn-smooth wooden handle in his grip. "And I hit him. Crackerjack. I mean, Barton."

"How many times?"

Jason closed his eyes, thinking. "Twice maybe. Could have been three times."

"Where'd you hit him?"

"His head."

"His head? His whole head?"

"The side of his head." When Briggs didn't reply, he added, "The right side, I guess."

Briggs made a few notes.

Jason asked, "How did Cobb get free?" The detective looked up. "One minute, I heard him screaming not far away"—unbidden, a snapshot popped into his mind, an image of the wooden table in the corral, with its leather straps and the dark stains on its surface—"and the next, he tackled Crackerjack on top of me. How did he get loose?"

"Apparently, the suspect left one of the restraints binding him a little loose and Mr. Cobb was able to free one hand long enough to grab a mallet from a nearby table and strike the suspect's hand. During that distraction, Mr. Cobb got loose from the other restraints. Then the two of them went at it, fighting each other through the stable until Mr. Cobb forced the suspect into your corral."

*With a broken arm and three broken ribs*, Jason thought. *Wow.*

Briggs glanced down at his notes again. He asked several more questions to fill in some holes, sometimes repeating ones he'd already asked. At last, he said, "So, Mr. Swike, Wallace Barton held you for the better part of five days but didn't harm you, other than his failure to give you food or enough water. But he started his torture of Mr. Cobb the same day he brought him to the stable. Strange. And you say he never spoke to you?"

"Barton? No, not once. I never even saw him until . . ."

"So why keep you prisoner for several days but torture Mr. Cobb almost right away?"

"Maybe he had a better face for painting?" It seemed unlikely, but Jason couldn't think of a better explanation.

Briggs wrote something in his little book.

"I'm glad he's all right," Jason said. "Cobb, I mean. I'm glad he's okay. He saved my life."

The detective closed his notebook and slipped it into the pocket of his suit jacket. "That's funny. He says you're the one who saved him. According to him, you're the hero."

*Really?*

"No hero. I was just trying to stay alive."

"Well, a lot of people would disagree with you. Including the media. Have you watched the news yet?"

Jason shook his head.

"They're calling you both heroes."

He didn't feel like a hero. "I'm just happy that Barton is . . . that Crackerjack won't be killing anyone else."

Briggs stood and walked over to Jason's bedside. "Glad you're okay, Mr. Swike. I'll be in touch." He pulled a business card from his pocket and placed it on the nightstand. "If you think of anything else before then, give me a call."

Jason nodded. "Again, I'm sorry I can't be more helpful right now."

"Maybe more will come to you over time."

"No offense, Detective, but I hope not."

Briggs nodded. "Understandable. Have a good night."

Before the detective's shadow on the floor outside his room had even slid from view, Jason had the telephone receiver in his hand and was dialing Sophie's number. When he heard his wife's voice on the line, he couldn't speak for a moment. Finally he said, "It's me."

# CHAPTER SEVEN

He'd had to wait to be discharged until the doctors had completed their evening rounds, but shortly after 7:30 p.m., Jason glided through the hospital hallway in a wheelchair, feeling a bit silly. He was perfectly capable of walking out on his own two legs, but hospital regulations required that he leave the building in a wheelchair, so there he was, rolling along with Ben Britton pushing from behind. It wasn't like Sophie could have picked him up. Her driving days ended on a dark stretch of wet road a little more than two years ago. And Jason would never consider asking his mother-in-law to do it. So Ben Britton, his closest friend since the seventh grade, was the obvious choice.

"I think people are looking at me," Jason said when they were halfway across the semicrowded lobby, heading toward the hospital's front doors.

"Well," Ben said, "I noticed more than a few stares, but I think they're looking at *me*. This is a brand-new suit."

God, he was glad to see Ben. It had taken his friend no more than five minutes to get a laugh out of him.

"I just thought maybe they'd seen something on TV about me. The nurses kept telling me it's practically the only story on the news."

"Oh, get over yourself. You think you're my only friend who took down a serial killer lately?"

"I'm not?"

"Third this month."

With a few dozen eyes trailing them, they exited through a set of automatic doors. Jason spotted Ben's blue RAV4 at the curb in a patient loading-and-unloading zone, and they were soon pulling out of the hospital lot.

Jason looked over at Ben behind the wheel. It struck him that he had come close to never seeing his friend again. "I have to admit," he said, "that's a pretty sharp suit."

"I appreciate the honesty. I know that can't have been easy for you. And in the same spirit, I'll admit that it's possible, however unlikely, that those people were looking at you and not me. The Crackerjack story's a big one, I confess. And I hesitate to say this because you won't be able to fit your swelled head out of the car again, but a lot of people are calling you guys heroes."

Detective Briggs had mentioned that, too, so Jason wasn't surprised. He wasn't sure how he felt about that.

Neither of them said anything for a few moments before he again looked over at Ben, who had taken his eyes off the road for a moment and seemed to be scrutinizing him. "You're okay, right?" Ben asked.

"Yeah, I'm okay."

"Good. I don't want to get weepy and drip tears all over this suit—twenty-two hundred bucks, can you believe it?—but I have to say . . . if that guy had killed you, I would have been peeved. Want to talk about it?"

"Not really. Not yet anyway."

"Damn. I wanted you to talk about it."

"Maybe in a couple of days."

After a few minutes of forced small talk about how bad hospital food is and how embarrassingly revealing those johnnies are, Jason asked, "Did you talk to Sophie at all while I was . . ."

"I called her a couple of times to check on her."

"Did she . . . was she . . . upset?"

"Hmm, not that I could tell. Seemed fine to me. Hey, did you hear the Sox are thinking of bringing that kid up from Triple-A? The guy supposedly throws a hundred five miles an hour."

"Seriously? She wasn't at all—"

"Of course she was, Jason. Her ex, the father of her child, was missing for days. How could she not be upset?"

He hated when people called Sophie his ex, because she wasn't, not technically, and Ben should have known better. But he let it go.

"Did you talk to my mother-in-law?" he asked.

"Yeah, she answered the phone both times. Now, *she* didn't seem too upset about you."

Sophie lived in the house that she and Jason had bought in their second year of marriage, and which Jason still co-owned. After the accident, she'd asked her mother to move in with them. For Jason's good, she said. To help with Max. Two months later, when Sophie came home from rehab and asked Jason to move out, Janice stayed. Though Sophie had never been a needy person, her restriction to a wheelchair forced her to realize she would need help. And Janice, who had been a widow for more than a decade, was more than happy to take Jason's place.

He wondered how much Sophie had told her mother about the night of the crash . . . or the way she insisted on remembering it anyway.

Unconsciously, he touched the slight depression on his scalp under his hair, a few inches above his left temple, a reminder of the head injury that left him unable to remember the accident clearly. He could recall things leading up to it, flashes of motion, snippets of sound, but most of what he knew about that horrible moment came from Sophie—and he simply could not believe her version of it.

He'd never have done what she believed she'd stopped him from doing. Maybe he'd let the car drift a little rounding that bend, but if she hadn't jerked the wheel to avoid the stranger on the shoulder—the action that cost them control of the vehicle and caused the crash—he certainly would have steered away from the man himself. It was beyond frustrating that she didn't believe that. It was inconceivable.

That night had cost them their marriage.

And it had nearly cost him his relationship with his son. For the first few months after he'd moved out, Sophie had tried to keep Max away from him.

*I saw your face, Jason. I saw your eyes. You were heading right for that man.*

*You're wrong, Sophie. Why in hell would I do that? I'd never hurt anyone on purpose. And I'd sure as hell never hurt you or Max.*

Over time she seemed to grow a little more comfortable with Jason spending time with their son, though she never allowed him to take the boy out of the house. And she always stayed close by, no farther than the next room. He'd thought about taking her to court, but though her feelings toward him had so obviously changed, he'd never stopped loving her and didn't want to fight. All that mattered was that he saw his son. He hoped she'd come around someday and see him the way she had in the early part of their marriage, but in the meantime, at least they'd stopped talking about it. They'd reached a place where the issue or disagreement or whatever it was, while unlikely to ever go away entirely, was at least relegated to subtext.

"Home sweet home," Ben said as they pulled in to the service alley behind Jason's apartment building, derailing Jason's train of thought, for which he was thankful.

"What are we doing back here?"

"You feel like talking to reporters right now?"

"Not right now, no."

"That's why we're back here."

"There are reporters in front of my building?"

"There were when I came by to feed your fish this morning."

"My fish died months ago," Jason said.

"Yeah. I guessed that from the empty tank. You could have told me."

"Reporters, huh?"

"You're big news, remember, hot stuff? You want to talk to them, I'll drive you around front and you can make a grand entrance."

"I'll get out back here, thanks."

"That's what I figured. I'll come up after I find a spot on the street."

"Nah, no need for you to hang around."

"It's not even eight o'clock. I figured we'd crack a beer and watch some mindless action flick, something with fast cars and sexy women and absolutely no serial killers in it."

"Not tonight." Before his friend could protest, he said, "You don't need to stay, Ben. I'm all right. I just need some rest."

"You sure?"

"Yeah. Thanks again for the ride."

———

Jason's keys hadn't been found at the stable, so he entered his apartment using the spare he'd given Ben long ago. Inside, he flicked on the living-room light and crossed to a window that overlooked the street. He edged a curtain aside and looked out. Sure enough, there were several news vans out there with media personnel milling about, waiting for him to make an appearance. No one seemed to have noticed that a light had turned on in his apartment.

In the kitchen, he grabbed a bottle of water from the fridge and downed two-thirds of it in a long series of gulps. From his pocket he pulled his cell phone, which the authorities had recovered at the stable along with the phones of many of Crackerjack's other victims. It had been processed and deemed fit for release back into his possession. But the battery was dead so he plugged it in to a charger he kept in an outlet near the toaster. Then he noticed that the little green light on top of the cordless phone receiver was blinking, indicating that he had a message on his home line. He hit the "Speakerphone" button and a robotic voice told him that he had 213 messages.

*Whoa.*

The first several were from Sophie, starting five days ago. In the earliest one, she sounded annoyed that he was late visiting Max. In the next, she sounded both annoyed and a little concerned. Finally, late that first night, she was nothing but concerned—which, given all of their issues, he found a bit gratifying. She said she was giving up on his cell phone, figuring that its battery had died or he'd lost it somewhere. He glanced at it on the counter and wondered how many messages waited for him there. Meanwhile, the speakerphone had moved on to messages from the following day: a couple more from Sophie, one from Megan at work asking why he hadn't shown up, and two from Ben, who said that Sophie had called him because she was worried about him, and now Ben was worried, too—which must have been true because his messages contained no wisecracks. She and Ben alternated messages for the rest of that second day. Then there were no more messages until yesterday morning, after Jason had come out of Wallace Barton's stable.

The first reporter to call was from the *Boston Globe*. The next was from the *Herald*. Then Channel 4 had left a message, followed by the local Fox affiliate, then the *Boston Beacon*, then the *Globe* reporter had checked in again, then . . .

Jason turned off the machine. He'd listen to the rest of the calls tomorrow. Right now, all he wanted to do was rest.

That was what he told himself anyway. But he was lying and he knew it. What he wanted was to see his family: his son and his wife, from whom he was technically estranged—a word he hated—but with whom he was still irrevocably in love, despite her feelings toward him.

# CHAPTER EIGHT

The first indication that things were somehow different was the absence of a scowl on Janice's face. Jason was aware that their frosty relationship was the setup for a hundred mother-in-law jokes, and he'd seen it in just as many TV sitcoms. He'd never found it terribly funny before he was married, and it was even less funny now that he was living it. But he'd become accustomed to Janice's perpetual frown, and he almost didn't recognize her without it. He had no idea if it was there when he wasn't around, but in his presence it never slipped from her face, as permanent as the age lines carved in granite on Abraham Lincoln's face on the famous statue in his memorial in Washington, DC.

But when she opened the kitchen door tonight and saw Jason standing on her back porch, there was barely a trace of it—despite the fact that the presence of news vans in front of the house had made him come to the back door. Moreover, he'd arrived completely unannounced, which usually made the perpetual scowl deepen even more, something that seemed impossible unless seen with one's own eyes. But not tonight. She wasn't smiling, not even remotely, but she didn't frown when she saw him, either, which was practically a hug from her.

"Jason," she said, "I see you noticed the vultures out front. Come in."

"Yeah, sorry about that."

He stepped inside and immediately removed his shoes and lined them up neatly to the left of the door. It galled him to have to do that in his own house—well, the house he used to live in and still co-owned—but Sophie asked him to do it to please her mother, so he did.

"How are you?" she asked. Another first. He wondered if he should try to get abducted by a serial killer more often.

"I'm okay, thanks."

"You look like you lost a little weight, but otherwise no worse for the wear."

Not surprisingly, he had dropped a few pounds while starving in that stable. But he'd been a little overweight when Crackerjack had snatched him, so he could afford it. He was down to about what he weighed when he and Sophie had gotten married. With a little effort, maybe he'd be able to keep the love handles from coming back.

"Like I said, I'm okay."

"Well . . . good. You . . . you did the world a favor ridding it of that . . . person."

He shrugged.

"Max will be happy to see you," she said, and she actually seemed to mean it, as opposed to the way she usually said it, which somehow contained subtext implying that the boy would be better off if he never saw his father again.

"And Sophie?"

"I assume she'll be pleased to see you, too."

"I meant, how is she? How did she hold up while I was gone?"

The older woman thought for a moment, most likely trying to decide whether to be honest or disingenuous, to respond with something resembling kindness or with snarkiness. Finally, Janice 2.0 said, "After a day or two she seemed concerned. When she heard you'd turned up unharmed, she was relieved."

"I'd like to see her."

"So turn around." It was Sophie's voice.

He did, and there she was, rolling her wheelchair across the kitchen, stopping in front of him. Her honey-gold hair, usually thick and wavy, hung a bit limply, as though it had dodged a few shampoos. Dark circles surrounded her soft brown eyes. And though she typically went light on makeup—her natural beauty needing little enhancement, in his opinion—at the moment, she wore none. It might have surprised her then to know that, to him, she'd never looked more gorgeous.

He wasn't sure what to do next. They'd been separated for two years and had taken to greeting each other the same way every time—exchanging polite smiles devoid of depth or meaning, the kind of smiles you give a neighbor you run into in the supermarket. Like her mother, though, Sophie surprised him tonight. She reached up, took one of his hands, and pulled him down into a hug. It didn't last long, but it was the first one she'd given him in two years, so it felt nice.

"I was worried," she said. After a moment, she added, "I'm glad you're okay."

"It's good to see you, Sophie. I wasn't sure I ever would again."

"You look . . . thinner."

"I know."

"It's not bad on you."

*A compliment?*

They looked at each other for a moment, into each other's eyes, and to Jason, hers looked a little different to him. Like something was missing. A tiny coldness, maybe. That gently simmering animosity, bubbling far, far below the surface, but always there since the accident. But tonight, in this moment, a little of the iciness in her eyes seemed to have melted. He wondered if maybe—

"Something to drink, Jason?" Janice asked.

The spell, if indeed there had been one, was broken. He glanced at his mother-in-law and was about to decline but decided that if she were here in the kitchen fixing him something to drink, she wouldn't be hovering around them if Sophie invited him into the living room, which he hoped she would.

"That would be great. Maybe an espresso," he added, glancing at the machine on the counter. It would be more time consuming to make one of those than it would be to pour a soft drink. He didn't even like espresso. "Thanks, Janice."

She nodded curtly and turned away to fire up the espresso machine.

"Where's Max?" he asked.

"He was feeling tired after dinner so he's lying down," Sophie said. "Last I checked, he was still asleep. I can only imagine how much you want to see him, but I'd like to give him just a little longer, okay? He hasn't been sleeping well the past few days."

That was okay with Jason. As eager as he was to see his son, he wouldn't mind a little more time alone with Sophie, something he rarely, if ever, got these days.

She executed a neat turn and rolled out of the kitchen, across the hall, and into the living room. Jason knew better than to offer to push her. She came to a stop beside the sofa and he took a seat on the end closest to her. In the kitchen, the espresso maker *whooshed*.

Suddenly he heard Janice say, "Oh, for the love of God. Not another one."

Jason said, "What was—"

"Another reporter calling, I assume," Sophie said. "We finally turned the ringer off but a light flashes on the phone base when a call is coming in. It's driving my mother crazy."

"They've been calling a lot?"

"You have no idea."

Actually, he had some idea, considering the number of unheard messages still waiting at home for him.

"Max is okay?" he asked. "How did he hold up while I was . . ." He trailed off. "Was he scared?"

"Yeah, he was. I tried to shield him from it as best I could, and he didn't understand exactly what was going on, but he could tell I was worried, and that made him anxious. And like I said, the phone won't stop ringing. Friends, reporters, the police—and they were here a few times, of course, the police, which I imagine could be a scary thing for a six-year-old boy."

"It could also be exciting for a six-year-old boy."

"Not when he sees his mother . . . upset while talking to them."

He shouldn't have been remotely pleased that she'd been upset, but he was. "I suppose not."

They said nothing for a moment.

"Wanna talk about it?" she finally asked. He shrugged. "You don't have to, Jason, but if you want to, you can."

"Not tonight."

He'd tell her all about it eventually, if she really wanted to hear. How hungry he'd been. How scared. How hot during the day and how cold at night. How much he had thought about her and Max. Wondering how Max would handle it if his father never came home. Wondering if Sophie would feel—

"Oh, for the love of God," Janice said in the kitchen. "Another one? Why don't they stop calling already?"

"Seriously," Jason said to Sophie. "Sorry about the reporters."

She shrugged. "I understand it. I do. Ex-wife of a local hero, one of the men who finally took down Crackerjack."

*You're not my ex-wife,* he wanted to remind her. Instead, he said, "I'm no hero, Soph."

"That's not what everyone is saying."

*The feel of the hammer in his hands, sinking into Wallace Barton's skull. The man's dead, vacant eyes. His caved-in skull. The way it felt to end the life of another person . . .*

"I'm not."

She searched his eyes for a moment and he felt a little uncomfortable. At last she said, "Well, let's see, shall we?"

She picked up a remote control from the coffee table, turned on the flat-screen TV above the fireplace, and flipped to a local news station.

Then there he was, on TV, in full color and high definition: Crackerjack. Jason's only prior glimpse of Wallace Barton's face had been after his mask had slipped off, after Jason had smashed in his head with a hammer, leaving him bloody with empty, staring eyes. The eyes on the screen, though, were full of life, even crinkled a little at the corners because he had been smiling whenever this photo had been taken. He looked so . . . alive.

Sophie must have seen something in Jason's face because she said, "Sorry. Want me to turn it off?"

He shook his head. With his eyes on the screen, he barely noticed Janice coming into the room and trying to hand him an espresso in a tiny cup, and Sophie taking it for him and placing it on a coaster on the coffee table, and Janice sitting at the far end of the sofa, as far as possible from Jason, and Sophie asking if she wouldn't mind leaving them alone for a little while, and Janice leaving with the beginnings of her generally ubiquitous scowl creeping onto her face. Jason barely noticed these things because he was watching footage from the stable where he'd been held prisoner for nearly five days. And listening to a newscaster with a pleasing timbre to his voice and flawless diction—and no doubt perfect hair and teeth—recounting yesterday's dramatic events . . .

"The killing of a killer," the newscaster intoned.

Jason knew some of the facts. Detective Briggs had shared them with him.

Wallace Barton, aka Crackerjack, was fifty-two years old at the time of his death. The dilapidated stable was in a remote, overgrown corner of his forty-six-acre property. Three decades ago, when his parents were alive and the stable was still in use, a wide, hard-packed dirt road ran to it from the family's farmhouse. But then Wallace's mother passed away, and when Wallace Sr. followed two months later, Wallace Jr. inherited almost a hundred acres, along with a horse stable and apple and peach orchards. With no head for business, he sold the horses and more than half of the land, let the orchards die, and lived off the proceeds of the sales of the land and the animals. He had no remaining family. There was no indication that he'd had a single friend in the world when he died.

In the final decades of his life, Barton was a recluse, rarely leaving his property . . . or so everyone thought. It was now known, of course, that he must have left long enough to hunt for victims.

On the screen, the video footage of the stable changed to still photographs—of the stall where Jason had been held; of another stall, which he assumed had been Cobb's; and still another, this one containing the table Jason had seen, with the leather restraints and the dark-stained surface.

He was no longer listening to the newscaster. He could imagine the words. He'd lived the words.

"I shouldn't have turned this on," Sophie said. "I'm sorry. You don't need to see—"

"It's okay," he said.

On the TV, a cop was now describing the crime scene. Jason thought he recognized him as one of the first to arrive at the stable, but he couldn't be certain. He'd been so confused then. Eventually a photograph of Jason's face appeared on screen. He looked ragged, his face pale and thinner, his hair hanging limp over his forehead, sweat darkening its typical strawberry-blond color. Someone had to have snapped the shot while he was outside Barton's stable, waiting for an ambulance to take him away. Then his photo was replaced by one of Ian Cobb, obviously taken at the stable, as well. Though he'd had his arm and ribs broken, he'd spent only a day in captivity, so he looked healthier than Jason did. He also had bright green-and-gold butterflies painted around his eyes. A moment later, a series of brief person-on-the-street clips began as ordinary citizens opined on the big story of the day.

A middle-aged woman: "I think he got what he deserved."

A young man: "It's a relief, you know? That guy was crazy."

A young woman with a toddler on her hip: "It's about time someone got him. The police sure didn't do much to stop him."

A middle-aged man: "I'm just glad it's over. He liked to kill other guys, so I could've been his next victim, right? Or one of my buddies."

Another young woman: "Thank God those two men got away. And killed him. They're heroes."

Then the newscaster was on-screen briefly—Jason had been right about the perfect hair and teeth—saying, "And what does one of those heroes have to say?"

And then Ian Cobb's face, without the butterflies this time, was on the screen again, only this time it was video. He was walking away from the hospital, its entrance visible behind him. Several microphones were thrust toward him as he walked. He moved at a casual pace, not running away, not even hurrying, but he seemed to have no interest in being interviewed. He looked uncomfortable, unused to being the center of so much attention. Which made perfect sense. One minute he was a quiet nobody, and the next he was a screaming headline.

"Like I keep telling people," Cobb said, "I'm not the hero. I didn't do much. You should talk to Jason Swike. He's the one who killed Crackerjack. I owe him my life. Without him . . . well, he's the real hero."

Finally, Jason took the remote control from Sophie's hand and turned off the TV.

Was that true? Was *he* the real hero? It was still so hard to remember exactly what had happened. There was fighting, Cobb screaming for help, and Jason hitting Barton. But it was *Cobb*, not Jason, who had gotten loose, who had started their escape . . . but then again, he'd been screaming for Jason to help him, saying that he couldn't hold on. He had a broken arm, after all, not to mention broken ribs. It had sounded like he'd been on the verge of losing the fight. And it *was* Jason who had ended it, after all. That much was true. If Jason hadn't acted when he did, Barton probably would have regained the upper hand, which would have left Jason and Cobb to become his next victims. So maybe it was true. Maybe he really was . . .

He turned to Sophie and again saw something in her eyes that he hadn't seen in a long time. Maybe a little compassion, which didn't surprise him—she was a kind person, after all—but there might have been more. It was clear that she was relieved he hadn't ended up in a dumpster, a skin bag full of broken bones. But it was almost as though she saw him just a little differently now. Was she . . . impressed? Proud? He wasn't sure what it was, but he liked it.

"I know you don't feel like talking about it right now," she said, "and that's okay, but you can't be a big hero and not tell me the story. So sometime soon, you have to fill me in."

She took the remote control back from him. When their fingers touched, he tried to let his linger for a moment but she gently pulled her hand away.

"Okay, hero. Want to look in on Max?"

————

The house had two stories, but Sophie and Max now slept on the first floor, in bedrooms that had once been an office and a family room, respectively. Janice had claimed the master bedroom upstairs.

Jason and Sophie moved down the hall toward Max's door, which was ajar. Soft, blue-green light spilled onto the hallway floor, which used to be carpeted but was now covered with smooth tile. Jason knew the source of the glow: a night-light in the shape of a globe as large as a full-size lamp on his son's nightstand. Max loved it. He said he could see the whole world right from his bed. Jason stopped outside the door and peeked in at his sleeping son.

"We can wake him," Sophie said as she rolled up beside him.

"You said he hasn't been sleeping well lately, right?"

"Not so great the last couple of days, no."

"Let him sleep then. I'll see him tomorrow, if that's all right with you."

"Of course."

He nudged the door open a little farther and walked softly to his son's bedside. He loved to look at Max while he slept. The features of his face that some considered less than handsome—those common in children with Down syndrome—were beautiful to him. Everything about the boy was beautiful, from his appearance to his disposition. Any room he entered instantly grew brighter the second he set foot in it. Jason found himself smiling. Then the smile faded as he thought about how close he'd come to never being able to stand here again, watching his son sleep. And now he was frowning. Someday Max wouldn't be here. When that day came, Jason would no doubt wish he had indeed left the world before the boy did.

He turned and saw Sophie watching from the doorway. There was no mistaking the look in her eyes then. Despite any disagreements they might have had, she didn't seem to doubt—at least not any longer—that he loved Max. That he would never hurt their son.

"We don't know that he can't beat it," she said for what must have been the hundredth time since Max had been diagnosed five months ago with a rare blood disease—atypical hemolytic-uremic syndrome, or aHUS—that causes the formation of dangerous blood clots throughout the body. "He's not even experiencing symptoms," she said. "Maybe he never will, right? Don't you think that's possible?"

"Sure," Jason replied without conviction, because they both knew how extraordinarily unlikely that was. "Tell him I was here, okay?" he added before leaving to spend yet another night alone in his apartment.

# CHAPTER NINE

Ian Cobb had all five shopping bags hanging from his left forearm. His right one was broken, of course, but that wasn't much of an inconvenience, seeing as he was left-handed. He put the bags on the kitchen table, then stepped into the bathroom right off the kitchen. He had just lifted the toilet seat when he heard Carolyn's voice outside the door.

"Mr. Cobb? If you're home, I'm going to take off, okay?"

Seriously? She couldn't even wait for him to step out of the bathroom?

"Okay, Mr. Cobb? Can you hear me? I'm heading home now."

"That's fine," he called through the door. When he left the bathroom less than a minute later, she was already gone.

He emptied the grocery bags one by one, placing the various items on the table and countertops. He left a box of spaghetti and a jar of sauce on the counter but put the rest of the groceries away, everything in its place, whistling softly to himself as he worked. When he was finished, he turned on the small TV beside the microwave and found a news station. Then he boiled water to cook the spaghetti. He struggled one-handed with the lid on the jar of sauce but finally managed to get it open. When his meal was ready, he sat at the table and dug in as a weather report gave way to the top story of the day.

The face of Wallace Barton, known now to the world as the infamous Crackerjack, filled the screen. Cobb ate and watched the segment. He saw various photos and videos of the crime scene, then his own face, followed by that of Jason Swike, which immediately made Cobb think of his brother Johnny, of course. Then he heard interviews and facts and opinions given by police officers and average citizens relieved to see an end to Crackerjack's crimes. He saw himself again as he left the hospital yesterday, telling the camera that he owed his life to his fellow captive.

He frowned. He didn't want to be famous, even though he was now. He just wanted to be left alone.

After dinner, on his way up the stairs to the second floor, he passed framed photographs on the walls. Pictures of his parents, his mother smiling years before her tragic death, his father still healthy and vegetative-state-free. A family photo with aunts and uncles on his father's side of the family, including one man in his police uniform—Uncle Joe, who used to live two houses down and who had dropped dead from a heart attack ten years ago, an end too quick and easy for the hateful son of a bitch. And then there was Cobb's favorite picture. It was of himself with his two brothers, as children—Ian, the oldest at eight years old, with Johnny a year younger and Stevie just five. They stood next to one another, smiling in their own ways. Cobb always saw his own smile as a little cockeyed. Johnny, the all-American kid in his ubiquitous Boston Celtics cap tipped back on his mop of red hair, smiled slyly. And Stevie, the facial characteristics of his Down syndrome evident, smiled with carefree joy. The last photograph in the row was of Johnny and Stevie taken one Christmas morning. Cobb could still see Johnny racing across the living room to get to the presents under the tree. It was the last year Johnny would be able to run like that. A few months after the photo was taken, Uncle Joe said that the boy had fallen down the stairs at his house. His leg had broken in eight places. It wasn't the first time he'd fallen at Uncle Joe's.

It wasn't even the last. But it was the worst time. He'd walked with a profound limp after that.

Cobb had been heading for the second door on the right, his father's room—which had been his old man's office when Cobb was growing up—but found himself, as he often did, standing outside the first door. He looked into the room he had shared with his brothers so many years ago. The Boston Bruins pennant on the wall. On the dresser, Cobb's Little League trophy surrounded by Johnny's Star Wars action figures. Cobb's single bed against the left-hand wall, and the bunk beds his brothers shared against the right wall. Stevie's stuffed panda, which he'd called simply "Panda," was on the bottom bunk. Taped to the ceiling above Johnny's top bunk was the last thing he looked at every night before he went to sleep—a poster depicting the best-known of the celestial constellations. If it had to do with the night sky, Johnny loved it.

After Ian moved out years ago and Johnny followed a year later, when it was just Stevie in that room, it looked different. One bed and none of the older brothers' things. But a few years after Ian moved back in, he dragged all their old stuff down from the attic, including their beds, and with painstaking care recreated the bedroom of their youths. So now, everything was as it had been when they were children . . . long before Stevie, along with their mother, died in the car crash eight years ago, and before Johnny died in a different accident almost three years ago—one Cobb couldn't bring himself to consider truly accidental. Johnny had dealt with too much pain in his short life. He'd carried it with him from the time he was a young boy until the day he died. He talked about how he hurt all the time, sometimes physically but always mentally and emotionally. Since Johnny's death, Cobb had carried his brother's pain for him. It was a heavy burden. He didn't know how Johnny had been able to bear it for as long as he had.

The day after Johnny's funeral, Ian brought his father home from the long-term-care facility.

He missed his brothers.

He missed his mother.

He didn't have to miss his father because he saw him every day.

He moved to the next door down the hall and looked into the old man's room.

"Hey, Dad. Did you have a good day?"

His father didn't answer but Ian felt comforted by the steady *whoosh, whir, click* of the respirator. If Ian had his way, Arthur Cobb would live forever.

# CHAPTER TEN

Jason awoke with an undefined and highly uncharacteristic sense of optimism, and for a moment he didn't know the cause of it. And then he did. It was the slight thaw he'd seen in Sophie's eyes. And her calling him a hero. It was the news story he had watched with her, which he hadn't enjoyed seeing last night but which seemed different to him today. What stuck with him weren't the images of the stable that had been his prison, or the table with the leather restraints, or the photograph of Wallace Barton. No, it was the people interviewed on camera who called Jason and Ian Cobb heroes. It was Sophie hearing Cobb tell the world that *Jason* was the real hero.

Yes, the sun streaming through his window seemed a bit brighter this morning to Jason Swike.

He noticed it as he ate his toast at the breakfast table, listening to the messages from reporters and media outlets. And his world brightened even more when he heard the message from Elaine Connors, the famous cohost of the nation's number-two newsmagazine show, *The Real Scoop*—second only to *60 Minutes* in ratings share—stating her desire to come to Boston to interview him personally. She asked him to call her back on her personal and private number and pleaded with him not to share his story with anyone in the media before they'd had the chance to speak. He jotted down her number.

And then he heard the 204th message. It was from Howard Burrows, his old agent. Howard had been busy in the forty hours or so since Jason's escape from Crackerjack because he already had a low six-figure offer in hand from a major publisher for a nonfiction book about Jason's ordeal and his eventual escape. And he expected to parlay that into an even sweeter deal with another publisher. Jason had never written nonfiction, but for six figures he thought he'd be able to manage. And there was still more. Two Hollywood producers to whom Howard had leaked word of the book offer had left messages for him. And good old Howard had managed all this unburdened by the inconvenient fact that he had dropped Jason from his client list two years ago. Fortunately, Jason wasn't one to hold a grudge, at least not when book and movie deals were at stake.

He unplugged his now fully charged cell phone, ignored the forty-one messages on it, and pulled up Howard's office number from his list of contacts—a number he'd almost deleted from his phone. He dialed, knowing his call would go to voice mail because it wasn't even 5:00 a.m. in Los Angeles, and left a message. Then he left one for Elaine Connors saying that he would be happy to sit for an interview. After that, he finished getting ready to head into the office. It was going to be an interesting morning.

———

Normally, Jason hated going to work. Writing copy for a small marketing firm wasn't a horrible way to make a living, but for an author who had just missed making the *New York Times* bestseller list a few short years ago with a novel that had very nearly been turned into a movie starring two white-hot Hollywood A-listers, it was soul crushing. And though his last two manuscripts hadn't found a home with a publisher, every hour Jason spent churning out lifeless copy at the Barker Creative Agency was an hour he wasn't writing another book that just might get published.

Walking into the office felt different today, though. He knew he might have been imagining it, but it seemed to him that everyone looked at him differently. He certainly wasn't imagining the nods and small smiles from people who had barely noticed him before that day, or the clap on the back from Greg Norwood, or the awkward fist bump from Todd Cleaves.

In his cubicle, a small stack of files sat perched on the corner of his desk. Another occupied his chair. Several Post-it notes were stuck to his computer monitor. A quick glance told him that there was a theme, which essentially was "Welcome back, hero!"

He hadn't been imagining anything after all.

He didn't bother to clear his chair of folders. He was never going to sit in it again. He had a six-figure book offer in hand from a major publisher. He didn't have the particulars yet, and he'd never been a math whiz, but that was *at least* $100,000, which was more than twice his current annual salary. And who knew? Maybe the offer was for two hundred, even three hundred thousand. And there could be a film option, which he had learned the hard way was never a sure thing, but which would mean another nice chunk of change if all the stars aligned.

He couldn't wait to speak with Howard.

There was someone he needed to talk to first, though. He walked down to Ms. Landry's office and rapped his knuckles on her open door. She looked up, and if she was surprised to see him, she didn't show it.

"Jason, good morning. What do you think of this?" she asked as she held up a sixteen-by-twenty-inch poster board and turned it so he could see the ad design for a new frozen-yogurt chain.

"Honestly? I can't stand it," he said, wondering only vaguely which of his coworkers he had just shoved under a bus.

"I feel the same way," she said as she set the mock-up down on her desk. "It's good to have you back. I'm glad you're okay."

"Thanks, but . . . I'm not back. I'm only here to say goodbye."

"You're quitting? Are you sure? That's a big decision, and you've been through a lot. Maybe you should take a week or two to think about it. I think we can spare you for that long."

He almost told her that he'd been thinking about it every hour of every day since the moment he had first walked through Barker's doors, that the job had been slowly sucking the life out of him.

"No thanks, Ms. Landry. I appreciate the offer but I really need a change."

He smiled and left. He stopped by his desk for his personal effects, which amounted to a photograph of Sophie and Max and a copy of *The Drifter's Knife*, his only traditionally published book, which he kept next to his computer as a reminder to himself that he was an author.

Walking out through Barker's doors, knowing he'd never have to pass through them again, felt damn good. *He* felt good. Better than he had in a long while.

# CHAPTER ELEVEN

Detective Lamar Briggs stared down at the dark stains on the surface of the wooden table on which they believed Wallace Barton had tortured and killed most, if not all, of his victims. The stains were blood, of course, and laboratory technicians were already at work trying to match it to the victims. There wasn't much of it to work with, though, given that Barton's chosen method of torture was the cracking and smashing of bones with heavy, blunt objects. Each victim's wounds had been largely bloodless except for the coup de grâce—a blow to the head, crushing the skull. The evidence suggested that the deathblow had been delivered after the victim's head had been wrapped tight with multiple layers of clear plastic, which reduced excess spatter, leaving only a few dark-brown stains behind. A roll of Saran wrap had been found on the floor in the corner of the stall.

Briggs looked now at the smaller table that had once held Barton's instruments of torture. Incongruously, it had also held a veritable rainbow of face paints, along with several delicate, fine-bristled paintbrushes and a how-to book on face painting. Crime-scene technicians had already taken away the tools, though, along with the painting supplies and book.

Briggs imagined picking up a mallet, turning to a man bound to the table in front of him, and bringing the heavy tool down. He tried to imagine the sound the bone would make as it cracked. And he couldn't help but imagine the sound a man might make as his bones snapped.

He shook his head. Some people were absolutely crazy. Some were just plain evil. And some were a whole lot of both.

He stepped out of the stall and took a moment to watch the techs working the scene in the stable with admirable efficiency, taking photographs and videos, measuring distances, dusting for fingerprints. This work had begun not long after Ian Cobb called 911, and between the stable and Barton's house elsewhere on the property, there was a lot of ground to cover. That didn't even include the grounds themselves, which at that moment were being searched square foot by square foot by cadaver dogs—canines specially trained to sniff out human remains. Barton tended to dump the bodies of his victims in secluded public places, but that didn't mean there weren't more victims, as yet undiscovered, that might not have made it off his property. There were forty-six acres in all to cover, though Briggs had directed the search teams to start looking in the woods nearest the stable.

"Lamar?"

He turned and saw Dusty Owens, his frequent partner—and, after decades of Briggs rubbing people the wrong way and not giving a damn about it, the closest thing he had to a friend on the force—walking toward him. Detectives with the Massachusetts State Police didn't have regularly assigned partners; rather, if they worked with a partner at all, it was one with whom their superiors teamed them for a specific case. In Essex County—which drew the case because Crackerjack had dumped his first known victims there—the superior making such decisions was Lieutenant McCuller. He was the one who had assigned the case to Briggs initially, and he was the one who had teamed him with Owens, as he often did, intimating yet again that no one else wanted to partner with him. Briggs wasn't overly troubled by that. He had stopped caring long ago what anyone else at work thought of him. Those worthy of Briggs's respect seemed to respect him in return, even if they didn't actually like him. And those who weren't worthy of his respect didn't matter.

"What's up, Dusty?"

"The dogs found one."

Less than half an hour later, they found a second one.

# CHAPTER TWELVE

With his seven-year-old Toyota Camry still in possession of the state police, Jason had taken a taxi for his final trip to the Barker Creative Agency. He'd received a call on his way there, though, informing him that his vehicle had been fully processed for investigative purposes and was now available for him to retrieve. On his way to pick up the car after leaving the office—his second cab ride of the morning—Howard returned his call. Nine forty-five a.m. Not even seven in the morning in Los Angeles. Jason smiled.

When he answered, Howard gave a little lip service to having been concerned for Jason's welfare but moved on quickly to the fact that he'd been able to pit two publishers against each other and had the offer for a Crackerjack book up to $300,000, with hopes of raising it even higher. Moreover, Paramount—interestingly, the studio that had optioned the rights to *The Drifter's Knife* before ultimately scrapping the project—was offering $150,000 for a twelve-month option against a total purchase price of $400,000 if the movie entered production. The studio even hinted that it might want to revisit the idea of making a movie out of *The Drifter's Knife*, to which it still owned the film rights. As Jason recalled, the payout on the first day of principal photography on that project would be $250,000. And to top it all off, Howard had been trading messages with executives at both 20th Century Fox and Universal Studios.

Jason's head was swimming. Last week he was writing marketing copy for an annual salary of $42,500. Today, he had offers already totaling ten times that amount from major publishers and Hollywood studios, and the possibility of another $250,000 or more.

He suddenly remembered exactly how good he'd felt a few short years ago, when *The Drifter's Knife* was briefly a hot property before flaming out and descending into the oblivion of Development Hell, as it was known in "the Industry." But now, that project actually might rise like a phoenix from its own ashes . . . carrying a sack of cash in its beak.

They chatted a little more about the possibilities. Jason mentioned Elaine Connors and the opportunity for a newsmagazine show.

"Fantastic," Howard said. "Can't buy that kind of publicity. It will generate even more heat. Might add twenty percent to our offers."

Jason wasn't greedy. Personally, he'd jump at the offers already on the table. But Howard knew what he was doing.

"I'm going to keep working it, Jason. See what I can milk out of everyone. There's no need to rush it. This will stay hot for a while still, especially if you give a few interviews, get your face and your story out there. But don't give too much away for free. Save something for the book."

"Okay."

"And speaking of which, you might want to get started organizing your thoughts, considering your approach to it. Whichever offer we take, they're going to want an outline, and maybe even a few sample chapters, on the sooner side."

Before Jason could respond, his phone beeped, signaling another call coming in. He snuck a peek at the screen and recognized the number.

"I hear you, Howard," he said. "I have to go now. Talk soon."

He flashed to the incoming call and said, "Hello."

A voice he recognized immediately replied, "Jason Swike? It's Elaine Connors from *The Real Scoop.*"

A few minutes later, Jason ended the call with the famous television-show host. Twenty minutes after that, he was behind the wheel of his own car again.

And, for the first time in years, he felt behind the wheel of his own life.

# CHAPTER THIRTEEN

The phone rang on the desk in Ian Cobb's cramped home office, from which he ran the plumbing business he had inherited from his father. He pressed the "Speakerphone" button.

"Cobb and Sons Plumbing," he said.

"Hi, this is Elaine Connors."

Cobb said nothing.

"Mr. Cobb, this is Elaine Connors." Silence. "Um, of *The Real Scoop*."

"Okay."

"I left a message at this number but you didn't return my call."

She didn't need to tell him that. He was aware of it.

After a pause, she continued. "Mr. Cobb, as I said in my message, I'd love to interview you about . . . well, you know what it would be about. And I'd even come to you. How does that sound?"

"I'm not interested in being famous, Ms. Connors."

"Elaine, please." She paused, as though waiting for him to invite her to call him by his first name. After a moment, she added, "And who doesn't want to be famous?"

"Me."

She chuckled. "Well, I'm afraid the toothpaste is out of the tube, Mr. Cobb. You're already famous."

"Well, let's say that I don't wanna be more famous, then. I just wanna forget about all this and move on."

"That's totally understandable. You've been through a lot. But the thing is, as you must realize, this story isn't going away for a while. It's big news. Crackerjack killed ten men, one of them a budding rock star and son of a fabulously wealthy, jet-setting restaurateur."

Yes, Cobb knew. Crackerjack's fourth victim had certainly cranked up the public's interest in the case.

"And then two would-be victims escape from his clutches?" Connors was saying. "And kill the bad guy, no less? That's a fantastic story, my friend. And like it or not, you're one of its heroes."

"I'm not really," he said. "You should talk to Jason Swike."

"I have. And he's in."

"He is?"

"Sure is. And I want you to be in, too. It wouldn't be complete without the both of you. And it would give you the chance to tell the story your way. In your own words. Wouldn't you like that?"

Jason Swike was going to be interviewed? That changed things.

"We'd pay you an appearance fee, of course, Mr. Cobb. Five hundred dollars."

"Okay. I'll do it."

# CHAPTER FOURTEEN

"Let me get this straight," Ben said. "Television interview. Book deal. Movie deal. Possibly another movie when they dig *The Drifter's Knife* out of mothballs. Hundreds of thousands of dollars."

Jason was driving with one hand and holding his cell phone to his ear with the other. "That's what Howard says."

"Next time a serial killer starts grabbing victims, sign me up."

"Will do, Ben, because it was loads of fun. I wasn't scared for my life at all, and I sure wasn't worried about the possibility of Max growing up without a father."

"Too soon for levity?"

"A little."

"Fair enough. I'm just saying that if you had to go through something horrible like you did, at least you're getting something out of it, right? You got knocked off course a couple of years ago when they decided not to make a movie out of your first book, and your next couple of books . . ."

"Sucked?"

"I was going to say that they didn't sell. But who cares now? You're back on track. You've got money. You're on your way."

"Well, I'll be able to take care of my family, at least. That's what matters most. We've got some expensive issues, as you know."

"I know," he said as sincerely as was possible for Ben. "That's really good. I know you've been worried."

*Worried* didn't come close to describing the level of Jason's anxiety about his financial situation over the past year or so. After the accident, Sophie had shut down her business as a massage therapist, which she loved, and become a per diem medical-record transcriptionist, which she didn't. But at least she could do the job from home. In addition to being unfulfilling, though, it paid quite a bit less. Janice couldn't help much, living as she was on a modest stipend from a modest portfolio Sophie's father had left behind when he succumbed to lung cancer a few years ago. But providing for his family was Jason's responsibility. *He* wanted to support them, at least as much as he could.

But he'd been failing. His salary went only so far. After paying his own living expenses and most of his family's, there was little left to replenish the savings they had chewed through after the car accident. The fact was, their bank accounts were nearly empty and they were probably only a few months away from having to sell the house.

But money wasn't the only reason he'd slaved away at Barker. Because Sophie had been self-employed for years now and had no insurance coverage of her own, the agency's insurance plan was the only one their family had. And even after she had made plain that the accident had changed her opinion of Jason, that she needed him to move out, both realized that her physical condition and Max's medical needs made divorce impractical. So they remained married but not a couple. Betrothed but apart. And while that wouldn't necessarily change, other things had. Jason no longer needed Barker for a paycheck or health coverage. He'd be able to afford private insurance. And more. He could finally take care of his family. He could give Max what he needed most in life—as expensive as it was. And while he wasn't naïve enough to think that anything would change with Sophie, that things could ever go back to the way they were, he was thrilled that he'd be able to give his son and the woman he still loved whatever they needed.

He pulled over on the street parallel to Sophie's. He'd walk through backyards and knock on the kitchen door again, as he'd done last night.

"I gotta go, Ben. I'm at Sophie's. I'm gonna tell her about all of this. Let her know we'll be okay."

"Enjoy that moment. And make sure the Wicked Witch of the West hears, too."

———

Janice answered the back door without warmth but also without attitude, which Jason considered a good compromise. He removed his shoes and found Max and Sophie in the living room working on a puzzle. They were less than halfway finished, but he could tell it was going to be an underwater scene. They'd already completed a sea turtle and a stingray.

Jason sat on the floor next to his son, who was kneeling beside the coffee table, a puzzle piece in each hand, staring intently at the incomplete picture before him.

"Hey, Max," Jason said.

The boy—who hadn't seen Jason since his harrowing experience—looked up and, as he so often did, gave his father the sweetest smile.

"Daddy!"

He threw his arms around Jason's neck, squeezed briefly, then leaned away, put the puzzle pieces carefully on the table, and hugged him again, squeezing harder and for longer before releasing his hold. Jason felt tears threatening.

"How you been, buddy?" he asked.

"I been okay." It wasn't always easy to understand Max. His Down syndrome contributed to unclear diction. But where others might have difficulty, Jason understood every word. "You were gone," Max added.

"Just for a while. But I'm back."

"Mommy was sad."

Jason resisted the urge to look over at Sophie.

"No way. We don't do sadness. Happiness is what we do around here, right?"

"Not always."

"What?"

"We don't always do happy here." He picked up his puzzle pieces and focused on the puzzle again.

Jason glanced at Sophie, who frowned slightly, as though she hadn't heard Max say anything like this before.

"Mommy doesn't draw anymore. She used to be happy when she did that. But she put away her easel thing. It's downstairs."

"Her easel's in the basement?" Jason didn't like hearing that. Sophie had always liked to sketch. She'd never tried to sell anything, didn't think she was good enough—though Jason honestly disagreed—but she didn't care. She just loved to draw, and for years, her easel had been a fixture in her life.

He loved her sketches. Looking at them allowed him to see the world through her eyes. She always added some surprising, interesting detail, something someone else might not notice when looking at the same scene, or maybe something that wasn't even really there. A bird with ruffled feathers in the window. A crack in the glass on the table. A picture on the wall hanging slightly askew in the background. Her drawings were wonderful. And those of Max were her best. That she was no longer drawing was profoundly sad to him.

"She says she doesn't feel like it lately," Max said.

Jason turned to Sophie. "Since when?" *Since we separated?*

She shrugged. "I stopped five months ago."

Right around the time of Max's diagnosis.

"Well, Max," Jason said, "things are pretty good here for the most part, aren't they? Lots of reasons to be happy. You've got your mom, and your toys, and . . . your grandmother."

"Not you. You should be here, too."

A tiny jab to his heart. Little more than a poke, but it stung. He had to admit to himself, though, that it felt a little good to know that he was missed. This was the first time Max had hinted that he wished his father were around more, and it both pleased and saddened Jason.

"I'll try to come around more often, okay? How does that sound?"

Max was trying to fit a puzzle piece into a spot where it clearly didn't belong, turning it several times and trying again and again, and Jason suspected that Sophie had done most of the work on this one. He smiled as his son worked at it, getting nowhere but showing no frustration. Simply enjoying himself. Eventually, he put the piece down and chose another.

Jason gave a quick rub to Max's close-cropped hair—strawberry blond, like his father's—and moved over to the sofa.

"I have some news," he said.

She rolled herself closer. "Good or bad?"

"Good, for a change." He smiled. "Really good."

He told her about the book deal, and the movie deals, and the television interview, and the money he was being offered for all of it, and about how they'd be able to afford the best care for Max now, and, in general, how much better their lives were going to be.

"The best care?" she said. "Does that mean what I think it means?"

Three specialists had given them a bleak prognosis for Max because of aHUS, his blood disease, which could damage vital organs like the kidneys, heart, and brain. Max was very possibly facing a future of dialysis and even kidney transplants, both of which might address damage caused by the disease, but neither of which would actually treat or cure the underlying disease itself. Moreover, aHUS presented Max with a substantial risk of pulmonary issues, as well as neurological

James Hankins

and cardiovascular problems. It was only two years ago that the FDA approved a drug called Solizen, which had proven in extensive clinical trials to be effective in treating those afflicted with aHUS, reducing clotting issues, improving kidney function, and dramatically improving their quality of life. But no insurance company in the United States yet covered the medication, which currently cost patients more than $200,000 per year. The hope was that the cost of the drug would decrease over time, and that insurance companies would eventually agree to cover it, but that wouldn't help people in the short term. And the disease could do a lot of damage—possibly even fatal damage—in the short term.

Jason nodded. "We'll be able to afford Solizen, at least for a few years. And if I can keep things going, for as long as necessary."

Sophie cried. She turned away from Max, not wanting him to see. Because he might not understand what Jason did . . . that they were the good kind of tears. Her hand found his and squeezed for the briefest of moments before pulling away. He smiled.

# CHAPTER FIFTEEN

In all, they found six bodies buried in the woods behind Wallace Barton's stable, raising the killer's death toll to sixteen—that is, sixteen about which they knew. Each of the bodies had been wrapped in thick black plastic, which the medical examiner opened after photographs had been taken from every conceivable angle. Inside, the victims' heads had been completely covered with clear plastic wrap.

No one working the scene in those woods—least of all Lamar Briggs—needed the ME to explain how the dead men had likely been murdered. Each of their skulls had been caved in by a blunt object. Neither was someone with extensive medical training needed to explain how the victims had suffered, because limbs were bent at unnatural angles and a few jagged bones actually protruded through skin. And, of course, no one needed to be told who had killed these men.

"Eleanor?" Briggs said, addressing the medical examiner, whom he knew didn't like being called by her first name. He couldn't pronounce her last name well, though—it was something long and Hispanic—so he'd decided a few years ago to stick to Eleanor, and she no longer bothered to correct him. "Any idea how long these guys have been here?"

The ME stood, wiping the dirt from her hands on her blue jeans. She was attractive—dark hair pulled into a ponytail, pleasant face, slender figure—and if he were twenty years younger, he thought he might have had a shot with her. He'd had only three relatively brief affairs in more than forty years of marriage, and he didn't regret any of them, but the sneaking around was a pain in the ass. He thought Eleanor probably would have been worth it, though.

"Best guess?" she said. "One to two years. I'll be more certain when I've had the chance to examine them more thoroughly."

"Anything else you can tell me now?"

"See the holes in their skulls? All those broken bones? They pretty much tell the story."

"That's what I figured."

He looked at his watch. There wasn't much more for him to do here at the moment. If he headed back to the unit soon and banged out the day's paperwork, he could probably be home in time for dinner in front of *Jeopardy!* with Bonnie. She was terrible at *Jeopardy!*, and he suspected that she only watched it because he liked to, but he could live with that.

"If I learn anything else," Eleanor said, "you'll be the first to know."

"Thanks," he said, though he doubted she would learn much else. He wasn't sure it even mattered. The victims were dead. Wallace Barton was dead. Once they had identified the remains and notified next of kin, the rest was mostly paperwork and administrative tasks. Case nearly closed.

# CHAPTER SIXTEEN

Elaine Connors apparently didn't like to waste time. *The news stops for no man*, she had told Jason when she'd called a little while ago on her way to Boston, *and for a woman trying to make it in the news game, it won't even slow down.* Her interview with Ian Cobb and Jason was just two hours away now, scheduled for 10:00 a.m. It wouldn't be broadcast live; Connors said they would tape it while another camera unit traveled around and shot video to supplement what was already available on the web. Then they would beam all the footage back to New York, where editing and tech wizards would turn it into a segment for the live taping of tonight's episode of *The Real Scoop*. Connors, of course, would be on her way back to the Big Apple by early afternoon, well in time for tonight's broadcast.

As Jason was getting dressed, Sophie phoned to wish him luck. She hadn't called for something so light and breezy in a long time. Usually it was to tell him that Max wasn't feeling well so he'd have to cancel his visit with Jason, or to inform him that some bill was past due.

"I hope you're not thinking of wearing that black-and-white checked shirt you should have thrown out last millennium," she said.

He was wearing it at that moment, along with a pair of tan khakis that were a little loose in the waist, given the weight he'd lost this week. "Of course not."

"Good. Wear the burgundy shirt and Hermès tie we bought you in Chicago. Now, how about your pants? Anything but your tan khakis. Still have those gray pants?"

"Already have them on."

"Perfect." They said nothing for a moment before she added, "Well, good luck, Jason."

While Jason was eating breakfast a few minutes later, Ben called to add his own good-luck wishes. A little while later, as Jason was nearing the Taj Boston, the ritzy downtown hotel where the interview would take place, Howard called to do the same and to tell him that he had decided to hold an auction early next week for publishers.

"You really think the story will stay that hot?" Jason asked.

"With this television appearance, and maybe another few I'll set up for you, it will. And don't forget, Crackerjack was already a big story before you ended him. Killing a man almost every month for nearly a year, including a rich-kid rock-star wannabe? Painting their faces? And then you and the other guy not only escape, but you kill the bad guy? And you're a crime writer, no less? That's *big* stuff, Jason."

Howard reminded him that he should get to work on the book, and Jason said that he already had. He ended the call as he pulled up in front of the hotel, which sat at the end of fashionable Newbury Street. He turned his dented Camry over to a valet, a little self-consciously, and headed through the brass revolving door and into the glamorous hotel . . .

. . . to meet the beautiful, famous Elaine Connors . . .

. . . who would interview him for a national newsmagazine program. Incredible.

And soon he would see Ian Cobb again, with whom he shared a unique bond. He wasn't sure how he'd feel when they came face-to-face again. It had been only a few days since Jason had seen him, since their escape, but it felt like much longer. So much had happened. And Jason hadn't been in a clear frame of mind at the time. He didn't remember

Cobb well at all. To him, the man was a voice on the other side of a wall, a body on top of the pile as they fought for their lives, and a face on the TV news. Jason was interested in meeting him under more normal circumstances—if one could call being interviewed for a national network show normal.

He climbed half a dozen black-and-white marble stairs, crossed an elegant lobby, and pressed the elevator call button. When he reached the proper floor, he was met by a young woman holding a clipboard. She introduced herself as Karen, a production assistant, as she ushered him into an elegant suite, tastefully decorated in pale yellow and white. Three luxurious armchairs, upholstered in a rich gold-and-white floral pattern, were arranged in front of a fireplace. Three cameras on tripods faced the chairs from different angles.

"This is where the interview will take place," Karen said.

Jason stepped over to one of several windows that looked out over the city. The skyline was impressive under a clear, blue, spectacular midmorning sky. And below, right across the street, lay the beautiful Boston Public Garden.

She politely gave him a moment to take in the view, then said, "If you'll come this way, Mr. Swike."

"Jason," he said as they retraced their steps to a room they had passed when first entering the suite. Karen nudged open the door to a bedroom that had been temporarily converted to a makeup room. A man sat with his back to the door while another, tall and slender, stood before him, appraising him, dabbing at the man's face here and there with a tiny makeup sponge.

Karen directed Jason to a plush chair against a wall, where he sat. He looked at Ian Cobb's profile as the makeup person worked on him.

"Andy will be with you as soon as he finishes with Mr. Cobb," Karen said. "In the meantime, can I get you anything? Coffee? Tea? Water?"

"Water, please."

She smiled and left.

"Still thirsty, huh?" Cobb asked, without turning his head.

"Can't seem to drink enough."

Karen returned with a cold bottle of Dasani. *Seriously? It had to be Dasani?* Jason set the bottle, unopened, on an end table beside him.

Andy declared Cobb camera-ready and politely asked the men to switch places. They stood and, for a moment, regarded each other.

Cobb was bigger than Jason had remembered—a few inches taller than Jason and probably thirty pounds heavier—but otherwise looked like he had in the television news stories Jason had seen. He didn't seem to feel the same way about Jason, though, as he frowned and said, "I thought you were a redhead."

"Strawberry blond. Looks redder sometimes. In the right light or when it's wet."

"Or sweaty, maybe."

"Uh . . . I guess."

"That's how I remembered you. A redhead. But it's still red, right? Strawberry blond is kind of red, isn't it?"

"Yeah, it is."

Cobb nodded again, his frown slowly disappearing. It was an odd moment, on the verge of becoming an uncomfortable one, before he gave a small smile and said, "Good to see you again."

"Yeah, you, too." Jason smiled back and everything seemed normal enough now. He nodded toward the cast on Cobb's arm. "You doing okay?"

"Not that big a deal. A broken arm. A few ribs. I'm okay."

Andy cleared his throat discreetly and Jason slipped into the chair so the makeup man could get to work.

"Well," Jason said to Cobb, "I hope you don't shrug it all off so easily during the interview. Elaine Connors is probably hoping for more drama than that. After all, it's for prime time."

"I know." Cobb shifted uneasily in his chair. He couldn't look more uncomfortable if he were sitting on a thumbtack.

"You ready for this, Ian?"

"Not really. I don't like all the attention."

"Me, either," Jason said, knowing that it wasn't true. He wanted to be famous. He wanted to do interviews one day that weren't about his escape from a serial killer but, rather, were about his latest in a string of bestselling novels. He wanted to see his name in movie credits. *Based on the novel by Jason Swike.*

"If you don't want attention," Jason said, "why are you doing this interview?"

"Because you are."

"Really?"

"Yeah. We're a team."

"A . . . team?"

"Well, on this we were. That's what I mean. We did . . . what we did . . . together. It wouldn't be right if we didn't give our story as a team."

For a moment, Jason wondered if Cobb had heard about the book deal, and the potential movie based on the book, and was annoyed that Jason was planning to tell their story alone. He hoped not.

Karen's voice came from the doorway behind Jason. "Ms. Connors will be here in five minutes. We'll start taping in fifteen."

# CHAPTER SEVENTEEN

To Jason, Elaine Connors looked nearly like he had expected, as he'd seen her countless times on *The Real Scoop*, except for the tiny lines around her eyes and at the corners of her mouth, beneath her makeup, that weren't visible on television. But she was undeniably attractive, her beauty likely enhanced by her fame. And she seemed to have developed the ability, probably through years of practice, to slip on a smile that seemed friendly and disarming and entirely genuine. There was a reason, after all, that audiences had eaten her up on *The Real Scoop* for more than a decade.

They were seated in their chairs, Jason and Cobb side by side and Connors across from them. Technicians checked the cameras and adjusted the lighting. Karen approached and said, "We'll start in two minutes, Elaine, if you think you're ready."

Connors nodded and looked at Jason and Cobb. "How are you feeling? Not nervous, I hope."

"A little, I guess," Cobb said.

"I'm okay," Jason said.

"Well, you have nothing to worry about," Connors said. "I'll take care of you. Just try to relax, forget about the cameras, and let's have a good conversation." She graced them with a thousand-watt, million-dollar smile. "Ready to go?"

———

She started by asking them general questions about their lives, alternating between them. Jason discussed his childhood a little, then his marriage to Sophie and their life with Max. Connors didn't press about their current familial situation; perhaps someone's research had convinced her not to. She didn't broach the subject of Max's Down syndrome, though Jason would have been fine if she had, but he was thankful she didn't mention his blood disease. And she touched only briefly and very gently on the car accident that had tossed their lives into a shredder.

As the interview progressed, Jason heard some of Ian Cobb's life story, and it certainly hadn't been a fairy tale. Three years ago his brother John had died in an automobile accident. In a terrible coincidence, five years before that his parents and youngest brother had also been in a car crash, one that killed his mother and brother and left his father in a vegetative state from which he hadn't emerged.

*Holy hell,* Jason thought. He knew all too well the devastation a car crash could visit on a family, but to suffer *two* of them . . .

Mercifully, Connors spent little time on that part of Cobb's life, moving quickly on to present day. Cobb said he owned and operated a plumbing business, which his father had started and which he had shared with his brother John until the latter's death.

"I'd like to talk about Wallace Barton a bit now, if that's all right," Connors said.

Over the next half hour, she skillfully guided them through their respective stories. The last thing both men remembered was walking through virtually empty parking lots, late at night. Then . . . they woke up in Barton's stable. No, they hadn't known Barton before that, didn't recall ever meeting or even seeing him.

"We'll add some stuff in here about Barton," she said in a voice that was slightly less formal, less like that of a newscaster. Turning her "camera voice" back on, she said, "Jason, you were taken by Barton before Ian was. What was it like to wake up in an unfamiliar place, in a run-down stable, no less . . . and you were chained to the wall, weren't you?"

She paused, waiting for him to answer. And here's where things got tricky, because he could remember very little of his ordeal in that stable. But if he broadcast that to the world, what editor in his right mind would pay him to write a book about it? And so much was riding on a book deal—the possibility of jump-starting a career that, only a week ago, had seemed permanently stalled; a movie deal or two; and, of course, the money being dangled in front of him and all the good it could do for his family.

"Jason?" Connors said.

He was now acutely aware of the presence of the cameras, and the heat of the lights on his face, and everyone looking at him, waiting for him to say something . . . anything.

"Are you okay, Jason?" Connors asked. "Do you need to take a minute?"

If he answered honestly, he could lose it all. And given that he'd quit his job yesterday, he'd be worse off than before this all started. No book deal. No movie deals. No money, not even the modest biweekly paycheck from Barker, unless he crawled back to the agency.

"Maybe we should take five, everyone," Connors said, and Jason thought he detected a hint of frustration, the first time she had projected anything but friendliness and professionalism.

Sophie's face floated into his mind. More specifically, her eyes, the way they looked at him when she first saw him after his escape, and when she told him he was a hero, and above all, the look in them when he told her that their financial problems were behind them, that she and Max would have all that they needed, that they would be able to afford the $200,000-per-year miracle drug that was Max's best hope for a long and reasonably healthy life.

Then Max's sweet face replaced Sophie's.

What if he stretched the truth, embellished a bit—no more than he had to, just enough to get the job done? He didn't have to worry about being caught in a lie. The only person who could contradict his version of much of what his time in that stable had been like was Wallace Barton, and he was dead. Would it be so wrong to lie a little? When he had a wife in a wheelchair and a son with expensive medical needs? He didn't think so. And even if it was wrong, he thought he could live with it.

"Sorry, everyone," he finally said. "I zoned out for a second. I'm okay, though. No need for a break."

"Are you sure?" Connors asked, looking relieved.

"Positive. Let's keep going. Won't happen again."

Connors smiled, and the tension that had begun to settle on the room like a winter blanket lifted.

Jason was ready to lie.

# CHAPTER EIGHTEEN

"What was the question again?" Jason asked.

Connors smiled. "What was it like to wake up in that stable? Chained to a wall?"

"Right. Got it. Okay . . ."

He tried to remember his confusion, anger, fear, and desperation. He did his best to paint a vivid and emotional picture for the camera. And when he couldn't remember—which was often—he added a few brushstrokes from his imagination, filling in the empty white spaces with what he thought sounded plausible and, when he could manage it, dramatic.

No, he didn't know right away that he'd been taken by Crackerjack, but he figured it out soon enough. Correct, he was given no food and only a single bottle of water a day. Yes, Elaine, it was lonely and frightening.

When she had wrung from him what she could, she covered similar ground with Cobb, though this part of the interview took much less time, given that his stay in the stable was far shorter than Jason's. While he seemed to be doing his best to answer, he was clearly uncomfortable on camera and his responses tended to be brief and without much detail or color, so Connors seemed happy when they were able to move on.

Finally, she turned to the meat of the interview. Up until now, they'd been noshing on hors d'oeuvres. It was time for the main course. She directed her first questions at Cobb, who was the only one of them unfortunate enough to find his way onto Crackerjack's table. He described, in far less vivid detail than Connors probably would have liked, how he had woken up on a hard wooden table, his wrists and ankles bound to the table's legs. Above him stood a man in a black mask.

"That must have been terrifying," Connors said.

Cobb looked at her as though she were an idiot for stating something so obvious but had the good sense to reply simply, "It was."

Ignoring the look, Connors said, "Did he say anything to you?"

"No."

"Is that when he painted your face?"

"The butterflies? No, that was already done. Must have painted them before, while I was knocked out."

"I see. And what happened next?"

"Well, he picked up a wooden mallet, looked pretty heavy . . . There was a table there with a few tools on it, hammers, mallets . . . blunt, heavy things like that . . ." He trailed off.

"And then?" she prompted.

He shrugged. "Then he raised the mallet and brought it down on my arm." He raised his broken arm a little for the camera.

"That must have been painful."

He threw her that look again but said only, "Sure was. I think I screamed. I must have, right?"

Connors looked at Jason. "Did you hear any screaming?"

That part, he remembered. "I did. It sounded . . . terrible. But Ian, what about . . ."

"What?" Cobb asked.

"What about . . . the whistling?"

"Whistling?" Connors said, and she leaned forward slightly, eagerly, probably sensing something new here, virgin snow not yet trod upon by the media's first responders.

Cobb nodded, as if he'd just remembered it. "Right. Before he hit me he started whistling an old tune. That baseball song. I'm not sure exactly what it's called."

"'Take Me Out to the Ball Game,'" Jason said. It was another thing he was able to remember. He doubted he'd ever forget it.

"Right," Cobb said. "That's it." Then he recited some of the lyrics, not singing them but bobbing his head along with the words as if simultaneously hearing the tune in his mind. "'Take me out to the ball game . . .' You know the one, right? Then there's something about buying peanuts and Cracker Jack, which . . . well, you know . . . is what everyone called him. That seemed a bit twisted to me, you know?"

He went on to describe how Crackerjack whistled the famous tune and, at the appropriate moments, struck him with the mallet. Three times. *One . . . two . . . three strikes you're out.* Broke his arm in three places. Then he whistled the tune again, this time using a mini-sledgehammer and breaking three of his ribs.

"How horrible for you," Connors said, though the gleam in her eyes made it clear that it was great for her interview.

She spent another couple of minutes on the torture, really getting her money's worth from the whistling angle and the fact that the words *Cracker Jack* appeared in the lyrics of the song. This was her job and she was good at it, but it seemed a bit gratuitous to Jason. Cobb certainly made her earn it, though. He offered little without prompting and never seemed to say more than the bare minimum necessary.

After she had milked every last drop from the torture, she walked Cobb through his escape from his restraints and his fight with Barton.

"I was really starting to lose steam," Cobb said. "My arm was broken and I was having trouble catching my breath—because of the broken ribs, I guess. It was blind luck we stumbled into Jason's stall. If we hadn't done that, we'd both be dead, I think. Jason and me. Because I was about done."

Connors nodded and shifted her gaze to Jason. "And what happened then, Jason?"

Things were particularly fuzzy here. He took a moment to collect his thoughts. "They fell right on top of me. Literally. Ian was on top, Barton was between us, and I was on the bottom. One minute, I was sitting there on the floor; the next, I was lying on my back with two guys fighting it out on top of me. Ian yelled that he couldn't hold on much longer, and I grabbed the hammer off the floor—"

Cobb cut in. "Crackerjack pushed me off him and started to stand up."

*He did?*

Jason looked over at Cobb, who had locked eyes with Connors.

"I knew that if he made it to his feet," Cobb said, "it was all over for us. Jason still had chains on his wrists running to the wall, and I was hurt and just about useless by then, and Crackerjack still had that hammer in his hand."

Jason felt a confused frown threatening to appear on his face, and he couldn't have that, not if he wanted to appear to have a complete, unbroken, unvarnished memory of the event, so he beat the frown back. But still . . .

"And the son of a bitch—sorry, can I say that?" Cobb asked.

"Seems appropriate enough," Connors said.

"Okay, yeah. So the son of a bitch straightened up and raised his arm to hit me with the hammer again . . ."

Brief images from those moments three days ago flashed through Jason's brain in seemingly random order, and though he knew his recollection was hazy, none of what he saw in his mind matched what he was hearing. But he knew how faulty his memories were of that day, and Cobb's seemed strong and clear, so maybe . . .

"And I was sitting there just looking up at him," Cobb was saying, "watching that hammer, waiting for it to put an end to me . . . when

Jason here dove forward and grabbed him around the legs. The guy fell, right back on top of Jason."

Connors looked back at Jason. "What then, Jason?"

He wished she had kept the focus on Cobb . . . because he had no idea what happened next, at least not in this version of events, which seemed similar to but different from the version in his mind. But he had to say something.

"I picked up the hammer . . . which had fallen out of his hand, I guess . . . and I hit him with it and—"

Cobb interrupted again. "The first blow must have hurt like hell, but it wasn't enough to take him out, and Crackerjack reached around and got his hand on the hammer, and he and Jason were fighting for it . . ."

*We were?*

"And Jason looked like he was in trouble, I have to admit, but there wasn't anything I could do to help. I was totally spent and in pain and it looked like Crackerjack was starting to win. And again, I thought we were goners. But somehow—and I have no idea how he found the strength for it, seeing as he hadn't eaten in days—somehow Jason managed to tear that hammer away from that asshole—sorry, I know I can't say *asshole*—and it fell to the floor."

Connors was riveted.

So was Jason, frankly. Cobb, who earlier had seemed so reticent to offer much in the way of details, had grown downright chatty. Jason tried to catch his eye and succeeded only long enough for Cobb to give him a tiny nod that Jason had no idea how to interpret before the man immediately returned his focus to Connors.

"Crackerjack spins around," Cobb said, switching to present tense as he grew more animated, "and things are happening real fast now . . . he's choking Jason with one hand, staring down at him, and I see his other hand groping around the floor, trying to find the hammer, I figure. Meanwhile, my arm is throbbing and I can't seem to even move anymore, not a muscle. Maybe I was in shock; I don't know. And Jason's hand is flopping around, looking for the hammer, too, I guess, but he's having a tough time because he's chained, remember, and Crackerjack's choking the life out of him, and just when I thought it was over for Jason . . . somehow he comes up with the hammer."

He paused and looked over at Jason. Naturally, Connors looked his way, too. Both clearly expected him to pick up the story.

"I hit him with it again," he said after a moment. "And . . . he was looking down at me . . ."

"Through the mask," Cobb added. "He still had that on at the time."

"Right. That came off later."

Connors gave him a gentle nudge. "So he was looking down at you . . ."

"Right. He was looking down at me. And I hit him again. And that seemed to . . . do the trick."

He glanced at Cobb, secretly seeking confirmation.

"It sure did," Cobb said. "The bastard went limp. Fell right on top of Jason."

"He was dead?" Connors asked.

"Well, he wasn't moving. And his mask had slipped off as he fell, and his eyes . . . well, there wasn't anyone home anymore. I have to say, Elaine," Cobb said, his voice cracking a tiny bit, "if it weren't for Jason, I'd be dead right now." He reached his good left arm across his body and patted Jason's forearm. "I can't thank you enough for my life, Jason."

This was just too much. "You're the one who got free," Jason said. "You're the one who started our escape."

"But you had to finish it. I wasn't able to, but you did it. You saved us both."

There wasn't much else Jason could say. Connors skillfully let that emotional moment drag on for what she, as a veteran of these kinds of interviews, no doubt knew was the perfect length of time. At last, she

83

said, "And how did you feel this morning when you heard about the discovery of six more Crackerjack victims?"

"What? I hadn't heard," Jason said.

Cobb said he hadn't, either.

Connors filled them in briefly, then paused for a moment, looking very serious, before saying, "A truly incredible story of survival, gentlemen." After another pause, she smiled. "Now, I have a surprise for you."

Inside, Jason cringed. He'd had enough surprises already.

# CHAPTER NINETEEN

"Are you ready, boys?" Connors asked. "It's a big surprise."

Jason nodded, though he was far from ready. Ian Cobb had already sprung a few too many surprises on him for his liking, and his reactions to them all would be seen that evening by millions of people. And now Connors was threatening him with another.

She stood, and Jason and Cobb followed suit, the cameras tracking their movements. A moment later, from around a corner walked a man Jason recognized instantly. He had been on the news a lot a few months ago, pleading for the safe return of his son, Michael Sanderson, the rock musician on the verge of breakout stardom. Leonard Sanderson had said more than once in the press that he would give up everything he owned—an extensive list of possessions that included a number of ridiculously successful restaurants, three mansions, and numerous other extraordinarily successful businesses—if it would bring his son home safe. But Michael's broken body had been found a week later, Crackerjack's fourth victim.

Connors introduced Sanderson to Jason and Cobb and, in case they had recently emerged from a lengthy stay under a rock, explained who he was and his tragic connection to them. They all shook hands.

Sanderson cleared his throat. "Seven months ago I lost my son to that monster. My wife passed two years ago, and Michael was all I had left. And then . . . he was gone, just like that. I miss him every day, every hour of every day, and I've been unable to find a moment of peace since his disappearance. Until three days ago, when I learned that Crackerjack was dead. Thanks to you."

His voice had grown shaky at the end, so he cleared his throat again.

"You may recall that I had offered a reward for my son's safe return. But to my everlasting sorrow, he never came home again. When his body was found, I offered the money for information leading to Crackerjack's arrest and conviction."

He cleared his throat a third time. His eyes, which had started to look soft and moist, grew hard.

"Well, gentlemen, because of you, Crackerjack won't have to be arrested. He won't have to be tried in a court of law, where some slick lawyer or a confused jury could set him free. No, because of you, Wallace Barton, the monster who killed my son and numerous other men, is someplace where he can't harm anyone ever again. And I hope he roasts there for eternity."

Jason nodded. He didn't know what else to do.

"You have put me at peace," Sanderson said, "at least to the extent that I can be, without Michael in my life. And for that I thank you. And now"—he paused for effect—"I want you to share in the reward I had offered back then. You performed a great service. For me, for my wife, God rest her soul, and for the world."

At that, Sanderson held up two personal checks. Jason could see that each was written in the amount of $100,000. He felt his eyes start to widen but regained his composure quickly, remembering that millions of people would see his reaction in this moment. He needed to project the proper image, and greedily eyeing a huge check wasn't the right one.

"That's a hundred thousand dollars for each of you," Sanderson said. "I hope you can use it. I hope it makes your lives a little better. You deserve that."

Sanderson handed the first check to Jason, who took it and humbly thanked the man.

"Mr. Cobb?" Sanderson said.

Jason glanced at Cobb, who was staring down at the second check, shifting uneasily on his feet.

"I don't want it, Mr. Sanderson. I'm not trying to be noble or anything, but I wouldn't feel right taking it."

*Ah, hell,* Jason thought, realizing he should have done the same thing. But it was too late now. He'd already accepted his check. Rejecting it now would be transparently insincere.

"Mr. Cobb," Sanderson said, "I truly appreciate the gesture, but I promise you that I have far more money than I know what to do with, and what you and Mr. Swike did—"

"Don't get me wrong," Cobb said, cutting in. "I'm not saying no because I think it's wrong to accept your gift. If you've got the money to spare—and from what I hear, you do—and you want to say 'Thank you' with it, that's your right. But I'm saying 'No thank you' because I don't feel like I really deserve it. Jason's the one who does. He's the real hero."

Jason couldn't stop his eyes from widening that time, but he got them under control quickly.

"He's the one who killed Wallace Barton," Cobb said, "not me. I was useless in the end. He saved both our lives. I'd rather he get all the money, if that's okay with you."

"It sure sounds to me like you did plenty, too, Mr. Cobb," Sanderson said, "but if that's how you feel, I'm not going to argue with you. And it's commendable. It truly is. Are you sure?"

Cobb nodded. Sanderson smiled and held the check out to Jason, who simply stared down at it. He was at a total loss.

"Well, Jason?" Connors said, apparently feeling as though the spotlight had been off her for long enough. "What do you say?"

The money Sanderson was offering wasn't for the writing of a book, like the deal Howard was negotiating, money that Jason would earn by spending months in front of a computer screen applying a skill he'd developed over many years and many drafts. And it wasn't for the movie rights for books he'd written or would write soon. No, it was being offered in exchange for a service already rendered: killing a man. Sure, Wallace Barton was evil, but to be paid $200,000—in front of the entire world—for killing him? It now seemed wrong. Why the hell hadn't Jason looked at it like this when Sanderson gave him the first check?

"Jason?" Connors said. After a moment, she smiled. "I think he's in shock, Leonard."

Maybe it would be wrong to accept the checks, but his family needed the money. He might have some coming in soon from a book publisher and Hollywood producers, but he didn't have it yet, and they were already behind on the mortgage and several bills and were eager to get Max started on his horrendously expensive medicine.

Unable to come up with a better course of action, he took the second check—another $100,000—and said, "Thank you, Mr. Sanderson. This will mean a lot to my family. I appreciate it. I'm just sorry that . . . that Crackerjack wasn't stopped in time to save your son."

He turned to Ian. "And thank you, Ian. I don't know what to say. If you change your mind, let me know."

Cobb nodded again, and Sanderson shook everyone's hands again before disappearing around the corner.

"Incredible story," Connors said as she returned to her seat. Jason and Cobb did the same. "So what's next for you, Ian?"

"Back to plumbing, I guess."

"That was a lot of money you turned down."

"I do okay, though. And Jason has a family . . . They're . . . well, he needs it more than I do."

Jason looked at him. He wasn't sure how much Cobb knew about his family, but many of the details of his private life, including Sophie's and Max's various medical conditions, had become public.

"And hell," Cobb added, "the guy saved my life."

Jason was on the verge of protesting again, of trying to shine some of the light back onto Cobb, but he was growing weary of this dance. He just wanted it to end now.

"And how about you, Jason?" Connors asked. "Did I hear a rumor about a book deal in the works? You're a writer, after all. That would seem only natural."

"Well, if everything works out . . ."

He avoided making eye contact with Cobb . . . again, in case—

"A book deal, Jason?" Cobb said. "Good for you. Let me know if I can help."

He met Cobb's eyes and saw nothing but sincerity in them.

"Well, put me down for a copy," Connors said. "And I'll expect an autograph, of course."

She smiled and Jason smiled back. And finally, it was over.

———

Five minutes later, Connors shook their hands, told them they'd done a wonderful job, then was off, presumably on her way back to New York for tonight's show. The crew was already packing up the gear. Andy offered to remove the makeup he'd applied to their faces earlier, but Cobb said he'd wash it off in the bathroom, so Jason said he'd do the same.

As the two men passed through the short hall toward the bedroom that had served as their makeup area, heading for the marble-tiled bathroom there, Jason said, "Listen . . . what you did . . . with the check. It was really generous of you."

Cobb shrugged.

"But are you sure? There are no cameras around. No one would know if you changed your mind. I wouldn't tell anyone."

They stopped outside the bathroom.

"I meant what I said," Cobb said. "I owe you my life."

"Yeah, but . . . the way you described . . . was that really . . ." He trailed off, and Cobb waited for him to continue. Finally, he said, "Well, thanks again. That was a hell of a nice thing you did for me and for my family."

Cobb shrugged again. "How about you buy me a cup of coffee and we'll call it even?"

"You drive a hard bargain but I'll take that deal."

"Got time right now? For coffee?"

"I guess. Do you?"

"I just might." He checked his watch. "Gotta get out to Tewksbury later today. We're on a big job there—remodeling three bathrooms and installing a sauna and hot tub—but I have a little time."

"Can you even do plumbing work right now? With your arm and all?" He wondered if he should give Cobb one more chance to take the money back.

"I've got guys working for me. These days, I let them deal with the pipes while I mostly do administrative stuff. So don't worry about me. Now let's get this crap off our faces and go grab a cup."

"Sounds good."

Cobb closed the bathroom door behind him, and Jason took a seat in the same chair in which he'd waited for his turn in the makeup chair. Through the doorway to the hall, he watched members of the crew carrying equipment out of the suite.

Jason heard water running behind the bathroom door, then another sound, one that surprised him. Cobb was whistling. Jason thought that if he'd been the one on Crackerjack's table, with the killer standing over him, whistling that stupid song, hammer in hand and torture on his mind . . . well, he'd never want to whistle again. But Cobb was washing up in there and whistling a tune Jason couldn't place.

*Tougher guy than I am,* he thought.

# CHAPTER TWENTY

Jason and Cobb crossed Arlington Street, then passed through a wrought-iron gate and into the Boston Public Garden where, it seemed, everything was in bloom and bursting with color. With the day as beautiful as it was, they decided to forgo a trip to one of the city's many Starbucks locations and walk through the Garden, where Jason knew they wouldn't find food vendors sullying the park's beauty, to buy coffee from a vendor on the adjacent Boston Common, where they would.

In the Garden, they strolled between beds of brilliant tulips—red, yellow, and orange—past a statue of George Washington astride a horse, and over a small bridge that spanned the four-acre pond. Passing beneath them was one of Boston's famous Swan Boats—a small passenger boat carved to look like a huge swan and powered by a young man at the back, pedaling as though he were on a bicycle. The Swan Boats were a quaint Boston attraction that dated back to the 1870s.

This walk would have been romantic if Jason were with Sophie, but he wasn't.

They left the Garden, crossed Charles Street, and entered the Boston Common, the oldest public park in America and Boston's answer to New York's Central Park.

"What'd you think of the interview?" Cobb asked.

Jason didn't think much of it, actually. He'd been uncomfortable through a lot of it, as Cobb recounted facts that Jason either remembered differently or couldn't remember at all. Then there was the awkward episode with the checks that left Jason feeling a little . . . unclean.

"I'm just glad it's over," he said, hoping to put an end to that line of discussion.

"I'm with you there."

Every now and then someone seemed to recognize them but gave them their privacy. After a few more minutes of walking and small talk, they still hadn't found anyone selling coffee.

"I could buy you a balloon," Jason said, nodding at an old man standing with a fistful of helium balloon strings in one hand and dollar bills in the other.

"I'd settle for a snow cone," Cobb replied as they reached a cart with an image on its side of a rainbow-colored snow cone.

Jason bought them each a cherry cone and they continued walking. As they passed a playground, Cobb nodded to a middle-aged man leaning against a tree, watching the children on the monkey bars.

"A guy like that," Cobb said, shaking his head, "hanging around a playground where he doesn't belong. He deserves to be strung up."

Jason looked more closely at the man as they passed. He could have merely been a father watching his child play, but maybe there was more to him, some darkness that Jason couldn't see. Perhaps he had no children of his own on the playground and liked to watch other people's kids at play while bad thoughts ran naked and wild through his mind. Maybe Cobb's radar was sharper than Jason's. He turned to Cobb to ask what had triggered his suspicion when he noticed that Cobb had stopped walking. Jason followed his gaze to a woman and a young girl not far away. The child was sitting on a tall stool. The woman stood in front of her, applying bright paint to her face. A kitten design. Cobb kept staring, and Jason realized that the sight might be causing unpleasant memories for him.

"Come on, Ian."

Cobb looked away from the face painter and over at him again. "Yeah. Let's keep going."

They strolled in silence for a few moments, with Jason unsure how to break it, before Cobb finally said, "Your hair looks a little redder out here in the sun."

*Again with the color of my hair.* "I'll take your word for it, I guess."

Cobb nodded, as if confirming the fact. Then he said, "I think we have a lot in common, you and me."

"Besides surviving a serial killer?"

"Yeah, besides that. You were in an accident that crippled your wife."

Jason hated that word, *crippled.*

"Well, as you heard a little while ago," Cobb went on, "my parents and youngest brother were in a car accident. Left my mother and brother dead and my father in what they call a permanent vegetative state."

"Yeah, I was sorry to hear that."

"And my other brother died in a crash just a few years ago."

"Sorry about that, too."

"Thanks. And I was sad to hear about your accident. Mind my asking how it happened?"

Jason didn't like to even think about the accident, much less talk about it. He looked away and said nothing.

"Sorry," Cobb said. "Don't mean to pry. Just thinking about all these things we have in common. Like . . . your son . . ."

"What about my son?"

"Well . . . I read in an article that he's got Down syndrome."

There were a lot of articles being written about Jason right now—about Cobb, too—and some delved into topics he'd rather remain private. But Max's Down syndrome wasn't one of them. "That's right," he said, smiling. "He's a really great kid. Along with my wife, he's the best thing that ever happened to me."

"Oh, I'm sure he is. It's just that . . . my youngest brother, Stevie, had Down syndrome. That's another thing we have in common, you and me. Stevie, he's the one that died eight years ago in the accident that killed my mother."

"Again, I'm sorry for your loss," Jason said because he couldn't think of anything else to say.

"Me, too." Cobb took a bite of his snow cone. Red syrup ran down his chin until he wiped it away with his sleeve, leaving what would surely be a stain on the light-blue fabric. "Johnny, my other brother, was a redhead . . . like you. You remind me a lot of him, if you don't mind my saying."

Ah, now it made a little sense. Not a lot, but maybe a little.

"Of course not."

"So you and I have a fair bit in common, right? Car accidents, Down syndrome, red hair . . ." He trailed off.

"Uh . . . I guess," Jason said. This was getting strange. "And again, there's the biggest thing of all . . . Crackerjack."

"Well, yeah, of course." After a pause, he added, "And there's more."

Jason didn't feel like hearing any more.

"I saw the way you looked at him," Cobb said, almost conspiratorially. "At Barton. After you killed him."

Jason said nothing.

"I saw the look in your eyes. You enjoyed it. You were glad he was dead."

Most of his time in Barton's stable was fuzzy, but Jason remembered very clearly standing over Barton's dead body, staring down with no remorse at the man he'd just killed. He had sensed Cobb watching him at the time and wondered what the man had seen on his face. At the time, he'd felt . . .

"I don't know that I enjoyed killing him," he said carefully, "but under the circumstances, I was definitely glad he was dead. Thrilled, in fact. It was either us or him who was going to end up that way, and I'm glad it wasn't us."

"Yeah, I was glad to see him die, too. See, that's what I mean. A lot in common."

Jason was ready for this little walk in the park to end. He looked at his watch. "Hey, Ian, it's getting late. Didn't you say you have a job to get to this afternoon?"

"In Tewksbury."

"Right, Tewksbury. And I need to call my agent. So I'm going to take off."

"Okay. Hey, you got a plumber you use?"

"Uh . . . no."

Cobb tossed what was left of his snow cone into a nearby trash can, then pulled a wallet from his back pocket and opened it. "If you ever need one, or . . . you know, you just want to talk about anything . . . here's my card." He handed Jason a business card. It was sticky from the snow cone.

"Thanks."

"Hell of a thing we went through together, huh, Jason?"

"Hell of a thing."

Cobb nodded once. "All right then."

He turned and started walking away. Jason felt unexpected relief the moment he was gone. And then . . .

The back of his neck tingled. Gooseflesh rose on his arms. His immediate instinct—without even knowing the cause of it—was to run like hell. His heart kicked at the inside of his chest as though it wanted to flee even if Jason didn't have the good sense to do so.

It took him a moment to realize the cause of these reactions. Cobb, who had gone only a dozen feet, had started to whistle that same nameless tune he'd whistled behind the bathroom door at the hotel. Only then, the door had largely muffled the sound. Out here in the open air, it carried clearly, and Jason was slammed with a brief, irrational feeling that Cobb would stop and turn around to wave goodbye, only Wallace Barton would be standing there instead.

*That's ridiculous,* Jason told himself. *Cobb likes to whistle. So what?*

Something made him take a few steps after Cobb to hear him better. Then he felt a coldness dripping down his spine . . . because Cobb's whistling, though growing fainter, also grew more familiar. Chillingly so.

A lot of people whistled, though, Jason reminded himself. Some were better at it than others. Some warbled sustained notes and others injected very little vibrato. Some blended their notes seamlessly together while others released them in tiny staccato bursts. Jason had never paid close attention to any of this before, but he knew that whistlers had distinct tones and styles.

And Ian Cobb's whistling struck a major chord with Jason. Because it was similar, too damned similar, to the whistling he'd heard in Wallace Barton's stable.

Hell, maybe more people whistled like that than he could possibly imagine. He wasn't much of a whistler himself, but if he were to whistle at that moment, perhaps he would sound a lot like Ian Cobb.

And Crackerjack.

Cobb had gone nearly fifty yards from where they'd said their goodbyes, and Jason had followed, staying a good twenty feet behind him. But if Cobb were to glance back, he'd see Jason immediately, which could be tough to explain. So he stopped and watched Cobb crest a small hill, then disappear behind it, whistling all the way.

# CHAPTER TWENTY-ONE

*Long day*, Lamar Briggs thought as he sank back into his favorite chair, a decade-old recliner with worn armrests, stained fabric, and a depression in the seat that, after years of evenings spent watching television from it, conformed perfectly to his backside. Beside him, his wife, Bonnie, had her chair reclined this evening, as usual, but Briggs didn't. He was sitting up, a notepad in his lap, a pen in his hand. The television across the room was tuned to *The Real Scoop*. While it was nearly eight-thirty at night, Briggs knew the segment they were watching had been taped earlier.

On the screen was Elaine Connors, on whom Briggs had a little crush, if he had to admit it—and he'd indeed had to admit it a few years ago because Bonnie could tell that he did and asked him about it directly, and he didn't care enough about the matter to lie. On TV, Connors had just said to Jason Swike and Ian Cobb, "Now, gentlemen, I have a surprise for you."

Briggs watched as Leonard Sanderson—father of Michael Sanderson, Crackerjack's fourth known victim—walked on-screen. Briggs had met Sanderson. As one of the detectives on his son's case, Briggs had spoken with him several times while his son was missing. Every time Briggs had heard the man say that he'd give up everything he owned—which was a hell of a lot—to bring his son home alive, Briggs had believed him, which was really saying something because Briggs rarely believed anyone with whom he spoke in connection with a case. And when Michael's body was eventually found, Sanderson's devastation was all too real.

Now there he was on television again, not pleading for his missing son's life but chatting with Elaine Connors and the two men who had been able to do what Michael Sanderson hadn't—survive their encounters with Wallace Barton. Briggs watched Connors introduce him to Swike and Cobb.

Over the next few moments, Sanderson thanked the men for what they did, stopping Crackerjack, then tried to give them each $100,000.

"You worked that case for a year," Bonnie said. "He hasn't offered you anything."

"Couldn't accept if he did," he said, while thinking the exact same thing. Not that he expected a gratuity in his line of work—though he wasn't above skimming a little here and there where he could on the job—but it was a little galling that he put all those hours into the case in return for nothing but his meager paycheck, while Swike and Cobb put a few days into it and were each being given a hundred grand.

"I know that," she said. "Would have been a nice gesture, though."

"Shh, I'm trying to listen."

Briggs watched Cobb give his half of the money to Swike, whom he said was the real hero. It wasn't the first time Cobb had said that. He must have felt strongly about it.

"Whoa," Bonnie said. "Talk about a gesture. The guy's a plumber and he gives away a hundred thousand dollars."

"Plumbers do just fine," he said. "Remember what we spent to fix the leaky shower?"

"Still, that's a lot of money to most people."

Briggs couldn't deny that. He watched Swike take the second check, looking a bit uncomfortable. Probably figured he should have tried to refuse the money like Cobb did and worried he now looked like he was trying to cash in on the whole thing. It looked a bit like that to Briggs, actually.

Cobb told Connors that he had no plans other than to return to his plumbing business, and Swike said he had a book deal in the works. That was interesting. Maybe Swike was cashing in, after all. Or, to view it less cynically, maybe he was just a writer who hadn't had a break in a while until the story of the year fell in his lap, giving him the chance to ply his trade and kick his stalling career in the ass.

Connors wrapped up the segment, and when a commercial for adult diapers came on, Briggs turned off the television. He looked down at the notepad on his knee.

"Good thing I wasn't watching that," Bonnie said.

He looked at her over his reading glasses, which he hadn't needed a few years ago. He'd tried bifocals last year but couldn't get used to them. "I'll turn it back on."

"Never mind. I have to take the pie out of the oven. Not that you deserve it."

She ruffled his short hair, which was far more than halfway to gray now, as she headed into the kitchen. Briggs smoothed his hair back down and scanned his handwritten notes.

> *J.S. clearheaded or drugged?*
> *Tackled W.B.?*
> *W.B. on top of J.S., facing him?*
> *Fought for hammer?*
> *Check location of hammer wounds.*
> *Which hand?*
> *Book deal for J.S.?*

"Iced tea?" Bonnie called from the kitchen.

"This late? You want me up all night?"

"Depends on how you mean it."

"You're a shameless tease," he called.

"Who says I'm teasing?"

Briggs leaned forward in his chair. In the kitchen, Bonnie was bent at the waist, taking the pie from the oven. She no longer had the body of a twenty-five-year-old, but neither did her body look fifty-nine years old, which it was. To Briggs, it looked somewhere in between, and for the most part, that was good enough for him these days. He watched the little sway in her hips as she carried the pie to the counter and placed it on a cooling rack.

She might have only been teasing, but maybe she wasn't. He hoped she wasn't. Actually, she better not have been, because now she'd put it in his head. Come to think of it, he'd make sure she wasn't.

Later, though. Until then . . .

He looked back down at his notes.

# CHAPTER TWENTY-TWO

Sophie turned off the television above her living-room fireplace and stared for a long moment at the blank screen. At last, she said, "Two hundred thousand dollars?"

Jason nodded. He was sitting at the end of the sofa, near her wheelchair. He could have reached out and held her hand if he thought it would have been welcome . . . which it wouldn't, of course. Not even a little. But still, she had invited him over to watch the interview. Other than the few minutes of news they'd watched the night he left the hospital, they hadn't watched television together since their separation.

"Just like that, he gave you two hundred thousand dollars?"

"Well, first it was only a hundred."

"Oh, is that all? *Only* a hundred."

"I didn't mean it like that."

"I know. It's incredible."

She looked over at him and there it was again—that look in her eyes. Not love, or anything close to it. It wasn't even affection. But whatever it was, it was *not* anger, or disappointment . . . or fear. And it made it easier for him to remember the way she used to look at him—which he liked to do sometimes—back before he lost her. When they used to make each other laugh. When she loved him. Before the night when she thought she saw darkness in him.

"We're really going to be okay, aren't we?" she asked.

"I think so."

She held his gaze a moment longer before looking away.

"Jason," she began, "we're still married because we needed your insurance plan. But now—"

"Okay if Max joins you?" Janice asked as she led her grandson into the room. For the first time in his life, Jason was glad to see his mother-in-law, who had agreed to distract Max during the interview broadcast so he wouldn't hear the disturbing subjects discussed. They had worked on a puzzle together in his room. Max really loved his puzzles.

"Hey, Max," Jason said. "Get over here."

The boy graced them all with that wonderful smile of his as he hurried across the room and jumped onto the couch beside his father.

"Grandma said you were on TV," Max said.

"I was."

"You're famous?"

"A little, I guess."

"If you're on TV, you're famous," the boy said. "Like Wile E. Coyote."

"Wile E. Coyote?" Jason said, feigning indignation. "Couldn't I at least be the Road Runner? Or better yet, Bugs Bunny?"

"Daffy Duck, maybe."

"What? You're dithpicable," Jason said in his best Daffy Duck voice, which made Max giggle.

"*You're* dithpicable," Max echoed.

"I'm not the dithpicable one here," Jason said, throwing his arms around his son and shaking him playfully. "Help me out here, Sophie. Who's the dithpicable one?"

Before she could answer, Janice said, "My vote is for Jason."

He paused and looked over at her. Then he smiled. She didn't smile back but he chose to believe it had been a joke, her way of joining in the fun. It probably wasn't, but what the hell?

"I think you're both dithpicable," Sophie chimed in with a Daffy Duck imitation that put Jason's to shame.

Hugging his son, with the woman he still loved so very much near him despite their troubles, the three of them laughing together like they hadn't in years, Jason smiled and realized, with amazement, that this was all made possible by his almost dying at the hands of a serial killer.

Then, uninvited and entirely unwelcome, a memory from that morning came to him. Though the hug continued, and Sophie and Max were still laughing, the beauty of the moment drained away for Jason as a thought started nibbling on his brain like a pesky rodent, a thought that had been circling him for most of the day.

In his mind, he cursed Ian Cobb and his damn whistling.

# CHAPTER TWENTY-THREE

Ian Cobb turned off the television on the wall opposite his father's bed and looked down at the old man. His rheumy eyes were open—a purely random occurrence since the accident—and staring at the ceiling. A line of drool ran from the side of his mouth to the pillowcase beneath his head. Ian grabbed a tissue from a box on the nightstand, wiped away the spittle, then dropped the tissue into a nearby trash can.

Returning to the chair by the head of the bed, he said, "What did you think, Dad? I was a little nervous and uncomfortable. Could you tell?"

Silence but for the *click, whir, hum* of the ventilator in the corner of the room.

"You know, you haven't said a thing since all this fuss began."

He stepped over to the ventilator.

"I'm feeling lonely right now, Dad. I could use a father-son chat."

The machine was equipped with an alarm that sounded if the person attached to it stopped breathing for some reason—for example, due to an equipment malfunction—for a preset length of time. For his father, the default setting was eight seconds. On a keypad, Ian navigated through the machine's functions, then entered a code increasing the setting to a full minute.

He sat back down and ran his fingers along the ridges of the blue tube that ran from his father's tracheal tube to the ventilator. It was his air-intake tube. The white tube was for exhalation of air. It didn't matter which Ian chose; either would produce the same result.

"So? What did you think?"

He grasped the blue tube in both hands and, with an easy, practiced twist, crimped it closed, stopping the flow of oxygen. A rattling sound escaped his father's throat. After a few seconds, Ian released the pressure on the tube.

"Thanks, Dad. I appreciate that."

He crimped the plastic tube again. Another stuttering wheeze issued from the old man before Ian let the air flow again.

"Yes, she was very pretty."

Ian cut off his father's air a third time. *Wheeze, rattle . . . wheeze . . . rattle . . . wheeze . . .* When the noise that slipped from the old man's throat became a prolonged squeak, like a door with rusty hinges slowly closing, he allowed the air to flow again.

"Like I said, I'm feeling lonely," Ian said. "Do you ever get lonely, lying here by yourself most of the time? Or have you totally closed up shop in there? Turned out the lights, locked up, and left for good? I hope not. I hope you're still in there, Dad, thinking . . . remembering . . . feeling everything."

He twisted the air tube closed again and listened for half a minute to the rasping sounds coming from his father. He wondered for the hundredth time, maybe the thousandth, if a few seconds either way mattered at all to Arthur Cobb.

"Yeah, Dad, since you asked, I guess it *is* good to hear that you're lonely. Because you deserve it. Neither one of us would be lonely if you'd listened to Mom that night."

Ian had heard the story from a few different people who were at the party that terrible night. His mother told his father that he'd had enough to drink. *One more for the road,* he had replied. Apparently, he'd said it three or four times.

He noticed his father wheezing. He hadn't even realized he was twisting the air tube again. He eased up on it.

"Oh, please. That same old story again? How can you even defend yourself? You didn't listen and now Mom is gone because of you. And so is Stevie. But you . . . you walked away from the accident. Okay, you didn't walk away, I guess, but you're still alive and they aren't. I miss them. Do you?"

Ian twisted the tube hard and listened to his father's ragged wheezing for a while before letting him breathe again.

"So how about it, Dad? Is this the night you're finally going to say you're sorry for taking Mom and Stevie from me? Or how about Johnny? Isn't it time you apologize for everything that happened to him . . . for allowing all of that to happen for all those years?"

He twisted the tube until Arthur Cobb's weak, sucking breaths mingled with the ventilator's shrill alarm. Sixty seconds went by fast. So did the next thirty. Well, they went by fast for Ian anyway.

"Really?" he finally said. "That's all you have to say? Pathetic."

He let the tube fall from his fingers and the air began to flow again. He walked over to the ventilator and changed the warning setting back to eight seconds.

"I really do hope you're still in there, Dad. *Feeling* things. Remembering everything."

And just in case he was, for years Ian had made sure his father had the best care money could buy. It was where most of his savings went, and where a huge chunk of his earnings continued to go, but it was worth it. Arthur Cobb wasn't going anywhere for a long time.

Ian dragged his chair back to its place against the wall and opened the door.

"I'm glad you liked seeing me on TV. Good night, Dad."

# CHAPTER TWENTY-FOUR

Jason sat at the desk in the corner of his living room, his fingers dancing across his computer keyboard. After leaving Sophie's earlier, he hadn't been able to get Ian Cobb—and therefore, the entire Crackerjack experience—out of his mind. Rather than sit in his apartment and obsess about it, he decided to put the intrusive thoughts to productive use and work on the book about his escape from captivity. To his mild surprise, the outline began to fall nicely into place. And, given that the media had already done a lot of the heavy lifting, unearthing mountains of information on Barton and his victims, including numerous photographs—all of which was available on the Internet—he didn't think he'd have a difficult time filling the pages when he began to write in earnest. He would have to interview Ian Cobb one day soon, of course, and though the guy's creepy vibe made Jason less than thrilled about having to spend any more time with him, he was more than willing to do so to get this book written.

In addition to the chapters about all of the people involved, of course, he'd have to write about his abduction itself—which wouldn't take long because, in his mind, it amounted to him walking to his car in a dark corner of the parking lot of a twenty-four-hour convenience store, then . . . nothing until he woke up.

And that was where he was running into problems. Days had passed in that stable where he did nothing but drift in and out of consciousness. Crippling hunger, acute thirst, drugs in his system—all had conspired to render his time in captivity hazy. How excited would the publishers throwing around big numbers be if they knew how little he could actually recall of the entire ordeal? He certainly hadn't told Howard. He remembered a few of the details of the fight with Barton, and he could always talk to Cobb and rewatch their interview with Elaine Connors to fill in some blanks, but there were still huge stretches of time—days even—when nothing much happened. Hardly riveting stuff. Jason had no choice: he was going to have to fib a little—though *embellish* sounded better in his head. He would rely on his skills as a novelist to sprinkle some fiction into this nonfiction book—maybe some actions he could claim to have taken to try to escape; possibly an episode he could concoct in which Crackerjack, unseen, taunted him, whistling to him, telling him exactly how he planned to torture him, which bones he would break first. The more Jason thought about it, the more enthusiastic he became about writing this book. If he was careful to keep things plausible, he could make his entire ordeal seem even more harrowing than it had been, which would make for far better reading . . . and greater numbers of books sold.

He had just started making notes about a fictitious event in which the masked Crackerjack stood in the shadows and gave Jason choices as to what design he would like to have painted on his face before he died when his door buzzer sounded. He glanced at a clock on the wall: 10:40 p.m. He hit the "Save" button on his computer, then walked to the intercom by the door.

"Yeah?"

A tinny voice came from the speaker. "Mr. Swike, it's Detective Briggs. Got a minute? I know it's late but I saw your light on up there."

It *was* late, and Jason hated to stop the flow when work was going well, but what could he do? He reminded himself that he'd eventually want to interview Briggs, after he came up with a list of questions, and he made a mental note to ask the detective about it before he left.

"I'll buzz you up."

In a few seconds, Briggs was at the door, which opened right into Jason's living room.

"Sorry to bother you, Mr. Swike."

"No problem. I was working anyway. And didn't I ask you to call me Jason?"

"Not yet."

"Well, be my guest." He shut the door behind Briggs and led him toward the only seating in the room other than his desk chair—a Salvation Army sofa and an armchair he'd found at the curb down the street and rescued mere minutes before the arrival of the garbage truck. He figured Briggs would prefer the armchair so he sat on the sofa. He was wrong, though; Briggs remained standing as his eyes casually roamed the room.

"What can I do for you, Detective?"

"I have a few more questions."

"I figured. Fire away."

"How's the book coming?"

"Which book is that?"

"The one about Crackerjack."

"You heard about that?"

"I saw your interview with Elaine Connors tonight."

Jason felt a prickle of sweat at his hairline.

"Is she that pretty in person?"

"I guess. Maybe a little older than she looks on TV, but she's definitely attractive."

Briggs took out his notebook. "Yeah, I watched the interview and just wanted to check a few things with you."

The bead of sweat trickled down Jason's forehead. He wiped it away while the detective looked down at his notes.

"When we spoke in the hospital," he began, "you said you were drugged—or at least felt drugged—a lot of the time you were there. Right?"

"I guess I said that."

"You were a bit sketchy on the details at the time."

"At the time, yeah, I suppose I was."

"But in the TV interview, you provided some details you hadn't given me."

"I didn't remember them at the time. I'd only just woken up."

"But your memory has gotten better since?"

Jason had to be careful here. Lying to the police was serious business. But so was selling books, at least if you wanted anyone to buy them. He was already on record, of sorts, on national television. And he planned to say even more in his book. If he told Briggs something different now, it could cost him in numerous ways down the road. Besides, he reminded himself again, only Wallace Barton could dispute his version of events, and without a séance, Barton wouldn't be talking.

"I've remembered a few things I'd forgotten."

"I guess you lost my card."

"I didn't know it mattered. Barton is dead, right?"

"Can't argue with that last part anyway."

"I guess I should have called, Detective. Sorry."

"Well, we're talking now anyway. So," he said, looking at his notes again, "you originally told me that Cobb tackled Barton on top of you, and Barton was on his back, and Cobb was on top."

"That's right."

"And Cobb was screaming for you to hit him with the hammer."

"Right. Which I did."

"Okay. But on TV you told a different story. That Barton pushed Cobb off and was about to hit him with the hammer, but you tackled him, pulling him back on top of you, and he dropped the hammer."

Actually Cobb had said that, and Jason hadn't disagreed. "Right."

"You remembered that since we spoke at the hospital?"

Jason nodded. Briggs nodded, too, and wrote something in his little book.

"Then Barton somehow turned around and was on top of you, looking down at you and choking you."

"That's right."

"And you were both fighting for the hammer?"

"Yeah. I'll be honest, Detective, I'm a little confused about why this all matters now, with Barton dead."

"Like I said at the hospital . . . big case here. Dotting i's and crossing t's." Another look at his notes. "So you won the battle for the hammer and you hit him."

"Right."

"How many times?"

What had he said yesterday? He wasn't certain.

"It was all happening really fast. I'm not sure. Two or three times, I think."

"Which hand were you holding the hammer in? I know you told me at the hospital but I don't have it in my notes."

Jason doubted that was the case. But that part of his ordeal he remembered well. He could still feel the hammer's smooth wooden handle in his palm.

"My right hand."

"And where'd you hit him?"

"In the head."

"I mean, where in the head?"

"The side. Around his temple, I guess."

"Which side, though? Left or right?"

Jason paused, sensing that the question was a rattlesnake coiled in the grass. The thing was, there was nothing he could do to avoid the strike. It wasn't like his answer could change the location of Barton's wounds.

"The right side of his head."

Briggs nodded and made a show of flipping through the pages of his little notebook, as if consulting things he'd written, though Jason had no doubt the man had memorized every fact of the case.

"Here's where I'm confused, Jason. If Barton is on top of you, facing you as he choked you, and you grabbed the hammer with your right hand and hit him, wouldn't the wounds have been on the left side of his head, not the right?"

Another bead of sweat rolled down Jason's forehead. He willed himself to keep from drawing attention to it by wiping it away, but he doubted that Briggs had failed to notice it.

"I'm not really sure, Detective. I must have grabbed the hammer in my left hand. Like I said, things are a bit hazy."

"I thought your memory was improving."

"Yeah, but not everything's clear yet. It may never be."

Briggs nodded, jotting down another note. Then he looked up and his eyes began to explore the room again, casually taking it in. When they fell on the computer screen, they stopped. He took a few steps closer and peered at the words there.

"This your book?"

Jason dabbed his forehead with his sleeve while Briggs was focused on the monitor.

"Just some random things. I haven't actually started writing yet."

The detective said nothing as his eyes scanned the words on the screen.

"I'm not really comfortable with people reading my works in progress, Detective. It's so unpolished at this point. A writer's ego, I guess."

"I don't remember you mentioning this," Briggs said as he read. "About Crackerjack asking you what design you wanted on your face when you died. Is this one of the things you only recently recalled?"

He was getting in deeper and deeper. But again, did it even matter with Barton dead? "Yeah."

"That must have been terrifying."

"It was."

"Anything else like this? Something you haven't yet told me?"

"I'm not sure. I don't think so."

"I bet as you write, more and more things are coming to you, right?"

Jason got the feeling that Briggs knew he was fabricating a little to ratchet up the drama for the book. He doubted the detective would care much about that. But the discrepancy concerning the location of the head wound might be a different matter. *But why should it be? Wasn't this case closed?*

"Yeah, now and then something new comes to me."

"New?"

"Well, not new . . . something I remember."

"I see. Well, I'd like you to let me know if you remember anything else, okay?" He slipped a business card from his pocket and placed it on the desk next to the computer. "In case you lost my card."

"I'll show you out."

"The door's right there, Jason. I think I can find my way. I'm a detective, after all."

He smiled and Jason thought of rattlesnakes again.

# CHAPTER TWENTY-FIVE

A few days passed, and Jason was eventually able to put Detective Briggs's visit out of his mind. He also began to forget that Ian Cobb's whistling sounded like Crackerjack's whistling. The day after hearing it, he'd searched online and listened to samples of people whistling, which weren't hard to find. Nothing is hard to find on the Internet. He listened to dozens of whistlers—focusing on the men—and there was indeed a wide variety of styles and tones. Some men sounded more like Crackerjack than others, and though probably none sounded as much like him as Cobb had, there were those who approached a similar technique, so maybe Cobb's whistling sounding a bit like a serial killer's whistling wasn't a big deal.

Other than the uncomfortable questioning from Briggs the night of the Elaine Connors interview, the five days since the show aired had been pretty good to Jason. Since his escape from Wallace Barton's stable, Sophie had allowed him to visit the house every day. And instead of waiting in the next room for Jason to leave as she used to do, she joined Max and him as they read books together and worked on puzzles. And, remarkably—given all they'd been through the last couple of years— they were even able to laugh now and then.

Things were progressing on the professional front, too. Two days ago, Harold had traveled from Los Angeles to New York to hold an auction for the rights to publish Jason's book about his Crackerjack experience. And just that morning he'd called to say that things had gone very, very well. The publishers loved the idea that Jason, a published mystery and crime novelist, had escaped from—and killed—a notorious serial killer who had murdered sixteen men after painting their faces like kids at a carnival. The winning bid was $500,000.

"They'll announce it once the contracts are finalized and the ink is dry on the signatures," Howard said. "Should be no more than a week, two at the most. Have you gotten started on an outline yet?"

"Yup. Making good progress." Other than visiting with Sophie and Max, he'd done little else but work on it. There was a lot at stake. He wanted to do it right.

"Written any chapters yet?"

"I'll probably start this weekend."

"Attaboy. Congratulations, Jason. This is a great deal."

"I know it is. And thanks, Howard."

"Thank me by writing a killer book so we can get you an even better deal next time."

"I don't plan on getting abducted by any more serial killers."

"Yeah, but if this book sells, they'll line up to bid on your next mystery."

He added that two studios were duking it out to option the film rights to the book. "We could get another couple hundred thousand for the option alone."

Before returning to his writing, Jason spent an hour pricing specialized vans loaded with adaptive equipment designed to allow people who used wheelchairs to operate the vehicle using only hand controls. For the first time since the accident, Sophie would be able to drive again. It was something he knew she'd dreamed about but had never hoped could become a reality. The price range of $50,000 to $100,000 didn't faze him.

That night, she invited him over for dinner—at Max's urging, she said, though he wanted to believe it was her idea—informing him that her mother had plans that evening and wouldn't be home. While Max watched TV, they did the dishes together. Other than the fact that Sophie was in a wheelchair, it felt a little like it did years ago, when they were together and happy. When the kitchen was clean, they sat at the table and he told her he was looking into buying her a customized van. He'd also looked into installing a stair lift that would take her up and down the stairs, giving her full access to her own home again. Finally, he said he wanted to buy her a state-of-the art, top-of-the-line motorized wheelchair.

"You don't have to do any of that, Jason. I could understand your wanting to give Max whatever you can, but you and I aren't . . ."

She trailed off.

"It's the least I can do, Soph."

She looked away and he knew what she was thinking. That it was the least he could do because the accident had been his fault. It wasn't what he meant, but it's what she was no doubt thinking. And *he* was the one behind the wheel that night, so she was probably right about that much . . . but not about Jason. She couldn't be. He was able to remember a lot of that night but, because of his head injury, very little of the accident itself . . . but still, he refused to believe *that*.

It had been raining, though the rain didn't have much to do with what had happened. The producer who had optioned the film rights to *The Drifter's Knife* was throwing a lavish party at the Ritz-Carlton in Boston. Famous Hollywood people with Boston connections were there. Jason and Sophie were there, too, rubbing elbows with the beautiful and famous while Janice babysat Max. And they drank and laughed and had a wonderful time . . . until the producer pulled Jason into a quiet corner and told him that he had decided not to make *The Drifter's*

*Knife* after all. Another project had just become available, one he'd had his eye on for a while, and time was a factor. It was possible, the producer said, that someone else would become interested in Jason's book in time. He hoped Jason understood.

And he did. All too well. *The Drifter's Knife* wouldn't make it to the big screen.

He didn't talk on the drive home. He'd told Sophie the bad news before they left the hotel, and she evidently sensed that he wasn't yet ready to talk more about it. As he drove, his mood darkened and festered, his mind a nest of snakes. *That* much he remembered.

It was late, nearly one in the morning. The rain was light but steady. There were no other cars in sight. No one around at all . . . no one but the man up ahead on the gravel shoulder, walking a bit erratically, probably drunk. Jason couldn't remember turning the wheel, or giving the car a little more gas . . .

That was what roused Sophie, she'd told him later. Her eyes had been closed, her head resting against the passenger window. The car started to swerve; the engine growled louder. She looked up, out through the windshield, and screamed Jason's name—he was glad he couldn't remember that part.

According to Sophie, she'd reached over and jerked the wheel, and the car swerved violently away from the man on the side of the road. Metal shrieked—somehow, Jason could recall the sound, though he remembered nothing else from those final moments—and the world slammed to a stop. He would learn that their car had missed the man but torn through a rusted guardrail and rolled down a small hill, coming to rest on its roof.

It was almost a week before they'd talked about *exactly* what happened, with Sophie lying in her hospital bed, her back broken, her legs useless. And when they finally talked about it, they argued.

"But I saw your eyes, Jason."

"You're wrong."

"You can't even remember."

"I must have been speeding up to pass him in case he stumbled into the road. I think I remember that he looked drunk or something, and I probably just wanted to get past him."

"You were heading right for him."

"It was late. I was tired. Maybe I was starting to doze off and—"

"You were wide awake and heading right for him."

"God, Sophie, how could you even say that?"

"Because I saw your eyes, Jason."

He looked away. Unconsciously, his hand ran to the bandage on his head. He was lucky, they told him. He'd suffered only a concussion and a wound requiring fourteen stitches to close. And, of course, the loss of his memory of those final, crucial seconds before the crash, up until the world came back to him in the ambulance later. But, he told himself, he didn't have to *remember* to know that he would never have hit that man on purpose.

"I saw your eyes," she repeated. After a brief pause, she added, "And it wasn't the first time I've wondered."

She might as well have slapped him. For a moment, he couldn't speak. "What does that mean?"

"Every now and then . . . when you'd get angry about something. Really angry. When our car broke down in Maine and that service guy gouged us for the repair. When you thought that couple on the beach looked funny at Max."

"Those times . . . I didn't . . . I wouldn't have . . ."

"Jason . . . I even wondered sometimes when I read your stories."

"What? You always said I'm a good writer."

"You are. But your ideas are so . . . dark. Where do they come from? What kind of mind comes up with such things?"

He shook his head. "You're wrong, Soph. Last week . . . on the road . . . You have to believe me. I never would have . . ." He trailed off. "Please believe me."

The way she'd looked at him at that moment—a way she'd never looked at him before . . . a way no man would want the woman he loved to look at him—shattered him into jagged pieces.

"I saw your face," she'd said simply. And because she couldn't walk away, she'd turned her face to the wall.

When she came home from rehab two months later and asked him to move out, he'd tried to convince her that things weren't what she thought . . . that *he* wasn't what she thought. She conceded that the night was dark and she'd gotten only a glimpse of his face before grabbing the wheel, so . . . who knows? But she still wanted him to move out. So he did.

"Jason?" Sophie said, snapping him forward two years, back into the present. "Are you listening? I said you really don't have to do all that for me. Special van, fancy wheelchair."

"I want to. And like I said. It's the least I can do."

She smiled ruefully. "I don't know what to say. Of course, we shouldn't buy anything like that until—"

"I agree. Not until Max starts on the Solizen. His appointment's in a few days, right?"

She nodded, and they struggled a bit to hold back their tears as they discussed a future with their son . . . a future that, only two weeks ago, they weren't sure they would have.

———

It was shortly before 8:00 p.m. when he left Sophie's house, less than five minutes after Janice got home, which was far from coincidental. As he was driving home, his cell phone rang.

"Hello?"

"Jason, it's me. Ian. Am I calling too late?"

Jason sighed. He didn't feel like talking to Cobb.

"No, it's fine. What's up?"

Cobb said nothing for a moment, and Jason wondered if they'd lost their connection. Finally, he heard, "Not much, I guess. Just wondering if . . . maybe we could . . ."

"Yeah?"

"I don't know . . . maybe we could grab a beer or something."

"Are you okay?"

"Oh, sure. Yeah. I just . . . I don't know . . . I wouldn't mind having someone to talk to right now."

Jason's inclination was to politely decline, but he remembered that Cobb wasn't married, that his mother and brothers had died in car accidents, and that his father was in a vegetative state. Perhaps he didn't have many people in his life to whom he could turn when he needed to talk. There was no doubt he'd been through something horrific; they both had. Maybe Cobb was really struggling with it. He'd certainly suffered physically far more than Jason had. And if he needed someone to talk to about it all, who better than the person with whom he had walked through the fire?

Jason sighed. He didn't want to talk to Cobb. Forget the fact that he sounded like a serial killer when he whistled, the guy was . . . well, he was just *off*. But like it or not, they were bound by their shared experience. They literally owed each other their lives. And after Cobb gave Jason his hundred thousand bucks, didn't Jason at least owe the man a beer? And if being a good person wasn't incentive enough, there was the fact that he wanted Cobb's cooperation when it came time to interview him for his book.

He glanced at the dashboard clock. Ben was working late tonight down in Boston and Jason had promised to meet him for a drink. He'd been so busy lately plugging away on the book and, when possible, spending time with Sophie and Max that he had declined every invitation to get together that Ben had extended, a fact Ben had used to imply, in mostly joking fashion, that Jason had grown too famous for his closest friend.

"Jason?"

He didn't have to meet Ben until 10:00 p.m., more than an hour and a half from now.

"I guess I have time for a quick drink."

———

They met at a hole in the wall in Salem called the Shark's Tooth, which had been providing beer and very little in the way of atmosphere to folks—mostly locals—for decades. No one seemed to like it much but they drank there enough to keep it in business. Rumor said it was little more than a front for some midlevel criminal's money-laundering and bookmaking activities, but Jason didn't know much about that, nor did he care. It wasn't like guys with bent noses sat around in fedoras and had you whacked if you looked at them wrong.

Cobb was already seated at the bar when Jason arrived, so he took a stool next to him. The bartender—a beefy guy well suited for slinging drinks in a place like the Shark's Tooth—slid a beer in front of Cobb, which he'd already ordered, and Jason ordered one for himself and threw a twenty-dollar bill onto the bar.

"For both," he said.

"Thanks," Cobb said, nodding to the beer.

"Least I could do. How you been?"

Cobb mumbled something under his breath. If Jason had to guess, it was probably "Okay."

"Long day?"

Cobb shrugged. "Long enough."

"Still on that job in . . . where was it? Tewksbury? What's that, an hour with traffic?"

Cobb nodded, and Jason wondered why the hell the man had said he felt like talking if he didn't plan on actually saying anything. He looked at Cobb's reflection in the mirror behind the bar. He was looking down into his beer. Then he glanced up and met Jason's gaze in the reflection, but he appeared to be looking through Jason rather than at him. His eyes were flat, almost lifeless. It seemed that the days since their interview hadn't been as kind to him as they had to Jason. Maybe he was just really tired, but he didn't look good at all. He probably should have been at home instead of at the Shark's Tooth.

"You okay, Ian?"

Cobb shrugged again. "Like I said, long day."

Jason decided he was done pulling teeth. If Cobb wanted to talk, he'd talk. If not, Jason was more than happy to finish his beer in silence, then hit the road. When Jason's glass was three-quarters empty and he could almost glimpse a light at the end of the tunnel, Cobb finally spoke.

"Disappointing day today."

"Yeah? Want to talk about it?"

Cobb shrugged again. "Just . . . not what I was hoping for."

"The job you're on not going well?"

"Job's fine. It's not that. It's . . . personal, I guess."

Jason waited for more, but that was all there was. "Listen, if you don't want to talk about it, that's fine. No problem." He drained the last of his beer. "I have to meet a friend in Boston in a little while anyway. Just let me know if—"

Cobb turned on his stool and looked at him directly for the first time tonight. "I want to, Jason. I want to talk to you about it. Nobody else would understand."

Jason nodded. "Okay, so talk. I'm listening."

Cobb looked back down into his beer, which he hadn't touched. "I'm not sure . . . I'm ready."

The man needed help, probably more than Jason could give. "Have you thought about seeing someone?"

"Like who?"

"Like a therapist."

Cobb looked at him directly again, and the previously lifeless eyes were alive now . . . alive and angry. "I don't need a therapist. That's not what I need at all. You think I asked you to meet me to hear *that* from you?" He took a long pull of beer, then brought his glass down hard on the bar. A few feet away, the bartender frowned.

"Ian, I'm sorry, but I have no idea what you want from me. I wish I did, but I don't. So if I'm not saying what you need to hear, maybe you can find someone who can."

"Nah, it has to be you," Cobb said. "Nobody else—at least nobody still in my life, and certainly no damned therapist—would understand. There's just . . . you and me . . . we have so much in common, and . . ."

*Again* with how much Cobb thought they had in common. Jason waited to see if he would finally be forthcoming about whatever the hell was bothering him, finally say something of substance, but he said no more. Jason was done. He hoped Cobb would still help him with the book when the time came, but if he refused, Jason could rely on the statements Cobb had made in *The Real Scoop* interview, along with his own patchy memory. He got up from his stool.

"You seem reluctant to talk about whatever's on your mind. And that's okay. I understand. I have to leave anyway. If you get to the point where you feel like talking about whatever's going on with you, actually talking, you have my number. Good night, Ian. Hope tomorrow's a better day."

He headed for the door, leaving Cobb at the bar hunched over his beer. He was halfway across the room when he thought he heard Cobb speak. It was low and mumbled, but it sounded a little like, "You spending the money yet?" But he wasn't sure. He stopped and looked back. Cobb hadn't turned around. Maybe he hadn't said anything after all. Jason looked for his eyes in the mirror, but they were gazing down into the depths of his beer.

He almost walked back to the bar. He almost said something he probably would have regretted. Instead, he pretended not to have heard—if indeed Cobb had spoken—and left the man to finish his drink alone.

# CHAPTER TWENTY-SIX

"I thought I saw a light on in here," Lieutenant McCuller said from the doorway of the conference room that, for nearly a year, had served as the nerve center of the Crackerjack task force.

Lamar Briggs was sitting at the table in the center of the room. Around him were several whiteboards on wheels with photographs taped to them—pictures of each of Crackerjack's victims and the locations where their bodies had been found; close-ups of wounds; shots of faces painted with garish colors and silly designs; pictures of people who had been persons of interest before Wallace Barton, who had never even been on the authorities' radar, was revealed as their perp. Beside the various photos were notes written in dry-erase marker or on note cards taped to the board. One entire whiteboard was now dedicated to Barton while another held photographs and notes about each of the six victims found buried behind his stable.

"The rest of the task force went home hours ago," McCuller said. He looked at his watch. "It's after nine thirty."

"Do we still even have a task force?"

At full strength, the task force had consisted of Briggs; Dusty Owens; Dennis Hutchins, another trooper from right here at 10 Federal Street in Salem, the main office of the state police in Essex County; a detective or trooper from each of the four counties where the killer's sixteen victims had been discovered; and a special agent of the FBI whom Briggs had invited to the party, looking for a psych profile and a little extra manpower. But with the suspect dead—because of two lucky citizens rather than through the efforts of the authorities—FBI Special Agent Eggers had disappeared without a trace, and the state police personnel from other jurisdictions had been assigned to other cases.

"There's still work to be done, LT," Briggs said. "Loose ends to tie up. We still haven't identified two of the victims we dug up the other day."

"Nobody's shutting you down yet, Lamar. Just saying that Owens left hours ago and I just saw Hutchins walk out. He has a pretty wife and two kids to get home to. And Owens has . . . what?"

"A fifteen-year-old cat his wife left behind when she walked out on him."

"Well," McCuller said, "somebody has to feed the thing, right?"

Briggs, with his eyes down on his notes, grunted noncommittally.

"So what is it you're working on here?" the lieutenant asked as he walked into the room and leaned against the table.

"I talked with Jason Swike the other day."

"And?"

"You happen to catch the interview he and Cobb gave on *The Real Scoop*?"

"I recorded it but my wife deleted it before I could watch it. Anything interesting?"

Referring to his notes a few times, Briggs went over his discussion with Swike in detail. Then he looked up and said, "Seems strange that he would forget which hand he held the hammer in, don't you think?"

"Maybe. But he was drugged at the time, right? And he'd had no food and barely any water for days. It's possible he doesn't remember things very well."

"That's what he tells me."

"Did you talk to the other guy? Cobb?"

"The morning after I talked to Swike. He said he couldn't remember."

"Nothing unusual there. There was a lot going on. And they were both drugged and fighting for their lives."

Briggs nodded but said nothing.

"What are you thinking?"

"I'm not sure what I'm thinking yet."

"I assume you're not worried about Cobb, because Barton busted him up quite a bit, right? Hard to believe—"

"Swike's the one that bothers me."

"What are you saying? That he could have been in on it with Barton? Because there's no doubt the guy hadn't eaten for days. And he'd barely had a drop to drink. He was dehydrated as hell. The docs confirmed all that, right?"

Briggs nodded slowly.

McCuller continued. "And Cobb hasn't said there were two bad guys working on him. After what Barton did to him, if Swike was in on it, why would Cobb protect him?" Briggs said nothing. "In fact, he's been saying the guy saved his life. Calling him a hero."

"Gave him a hundred thousand bucks, too."

"What?"

He told McCuller about Cobb giving Swike his half of the money that Leonard Sanderson offered them.

"That's sure as hell not something I'd do if Swike had been involved," the lieutenant said.

"Maybe he didn't know."

"Or maybe you're looking for something that isn't there."

Briggs shrugged. He almost mentioned Swike's book deal but chose to let the matter drop for now. He needed to keep thinking it through. "You're probably right."

McCuller walked to the door. "Look, if you're still hanging on to this in the morning, talk with Owens about it, see if he can talk you down. If he can't, come see me and I'll give it another try. Now go on home," he said over his shoulder as he left the room.

Briggs scanned his notes for another few moments, then allowed his eyes to wander over the photographs on the whiteboards before letting them come to rest on the picture of Jason Swike.

"What's the real scoop on you?"

# CHAPTER TWENTY-SEVEN

Jason sat at a table in the back of the Green Dragon Tavern, an historic pub in downtown Boston. It was one of his favorite places in the city. Lots of dark wood, little candle-shaped lamps on the walls, a display of authentic, antique weapons from the Revolutionary War hanging on the wall beside framed documents and artistic depictions of revolutionary activities and Colonial days. It had opened in 1657 and, during the time of the American Revolution, was a meeting place for the likes of such patriots as Samuel Adams and Paul Revere. Those were men who fought for something, who made a difference. And right in this place—which some scholars called the "headquarters of the revolution"—those great men had discussed their plans for resisting the tyrannical acts of the British Crown. Not that Jason was any American history scholar. He knew all of this because it was printed on the paper place mat in front of him. And though he couldn't vouch for the authenticity of the tavern's claims, who was he to doubt a place mat?

A waitress approached his table. She looked to be in her midtwenties, a few years younger than Jason, and though she was pretty, she looked tired. Maybe it was toward the end of a long shift.

"Something to drink?" she asked in a flat voice.

He ordered two pints of Guinness, one for him and one for Ben, who had texted to say he'd be at the tavern in two minutes.

Jason glanced around the room and imagined, as he did every single time he came here, Sam Adams and Paul Revere and a few other patriots huddled at a corner table, plotting their acts of courage and rebellion against the British Crown. His gaze fell on his waitress over at the bar. She was talking with the bartender, a bald guy with a thick neck and thick glasses. They were both looking back at him. A moment later she returned with the drinks and an expression on her face very different from the sleepy look she'd worn only moments ago.

"Here you go," she said with a little smile. Not flirtatious, just friendly.

"Okay if I run a tab?"

"Not tonight."

"Really?"

He was reaching for his wallet when she asked, "Are you who I think you are?"

He hesitated. "Probably."

"Thought so. Then tonight's on Eddie and me," she said, looking toward the bartender. Jason saw Eddie watching them. When their eyes met, the man nodded once before turning to a patron at the bar who was signaling for another round. "I can't promise you'll drink for free the next time you come in, but tonight, your money's no good here."

"Well, thanks very much . . ."

"Susan," she said.

"Thanks very much, Susan. I hope you'll let me tip when I leave."

"You sure as hell better."

She laughed and walked away, and as she did, Jason saw Ben approaching the table.

"Well, she sure seems to like you," he said as he took the chair across from Jason. "Looks promising."

"She was only being friendly. The drinks are free tonight, by the way."

"Well, that certainly *is* friendly. Let's order a keg to go."

Jason smiled.

"Then again, you can afford the keg. What are you up to now? Eight hundred fifty thousand or so?"

"You're counting?"

"Hell, yes. Two hundred thousand from that guy's father, half a million to write the book, another one fifty for the movie option. And that's not counting if the movie gets made or if they resurrect *The Drifter's Knife*. You order your Ferrari yet?"

"Not yet, but I priced a few customized vans for Sophie so she can start driving herself around and not rely on her mother. And a better wheelchair, too."

"Well, now I feel like a dick."

"And we're going to get Max started on that medication I've been telling you about. We'll be able to afford it now. It could literally save his life, Ben."

"Okay, you're just piling on now."

Jason smiled. "It's all true, though."

"Happy to hear it. And you and Sophie . . ."

"Are getting along okay. Nothing more. But I'm glad I'll be able to do more for her anyway. And for Max."

"You know something, Jason? It turns out you're a good man. Who knew?"

Jason wasn't so sure about that, but he was trying.

"You never said what you thought of my interview," he said. "How'd I do? Sophie said I was fine, but she might have just been saying that."

"I have no idea. I was watching a rerun of *The Simpsons*."

"You do love *The Simpsons*."

"Best show ever. But now that I think about it, I caught a little of the interview. You came off fine."

"I didn't look too . . . awkward? Hesitant?"

"I don't know. You looked thoughtful, I guess. You took your time to respond now and then. Nothing wrong with that, though. Not given what you went through."

Jason nodded and took his first sip of Guinness, then wiped the foam from his lips. Ben did the same.

"Your partner, though, Cobb? He looked a little uncomfortable at times."

"He's not my *partner*," Jason replied, remembering Cobb calling them a team for their escape. "We just happened to be two guys who . . ." He trailed off.

"Whoa, sorry I said it that way. I only meant—"

Jason cut him off. "Forget it. Sorry about that." He took another sip and looked away. And froze. A man was standing outside the tavern's window, looking in. Light from inside was insufficient to illuminate his features, leaving him in silhouette. But something about him . . .

"Cobb?"

Then the man was gone.

"Cobb?" Ben said. "What about him?"

"Hang on."

Jason hurried across the small pub. On the sidewalk outside, he looked up and down Marshall Street, but the man, whoever he was, was gone. Jason trotted to the corner but didn't see anyone resembling the man at the window.

Back at the table, Ben said, "What the hell was that?"

"I thought I saw Ian Cobb out there."

"Really?"

"Yeah."

"It probably wasn't him."

"Looked like him."

"Well, if it was him, so what?"

"He was looking in here."

"Again, so what?"

"But he didn't come inside."

"Maybe he wasn't thirsty." Ben squinted at him. "What's going on, Jason?"

"I don't know. Probably nothing."

"Let's have it," Ben said as he leaned back in his chair and crossed his arms.

For the next few minutes, Jason talked about his strange meeting with Cobb a little while ago, and about the whistling, and how Cobb kept insisting that he and Jason had so much in common.

When he finished, Ben asked, "So what are you saying?"

"I'm not sure."

"The guy whistled. So what? Everyone whistles."

"I never whistle. But that's not my point."

"I know, I know. His whistling sounded like Crackerjack's."

"*Exactly* like Crackerjack's."

"And he points out things you have in common. Is he right? Do you have things in common?"

Jason thought about it. Sure, both of their lives had been dramatically affected by tragic automobile accidents. And they both had loved ones with Down syndrome. And, of course, they both had been abducted by the same serial killer.

"I guess we do," he said. "A few things."

"Maybe he comes off a little creepy, Jason, but he just sounds like a lonely guy to me. He saw a few things you two have in common and latched on to them. Hearing this, I kind of feel sorry for him."

"What if that was him at the window just now?"

"Seems unlikely."

"But what if it was?"

"I'd probably feel even more sorry for him."

"It wouldn't seem strange to you? I just left him in a bar in Salem, and the next thing I know, he's standing outside a bar in Boston watching me? And when I see him, he runs?"

Instead of responding immediately, Ben took a sip of Guinness.

"Well?"

"*If* those things were true, it might seem a bit strange. *If* they were true. But Jason, are you positive it was him outside?"

"Positive? No."

"Are you even close to positive?"

Jason said nothing.

"Scale of one to ten. Be honest."

Jason thought for a moment, then admitted, "Three, I guess."

He took the last sip of his Guinness.

"Listen," Ben said. "I've known you a long time. I know the kind of imagination you have. You're cranking it up, thinking—what? That Ian Cobb might somehow really *be* Crackerjack? And why? Because he's a bit odd, is weirdly focused on things he believes you two have in common, and he whistles a certain way."

It did sound crazy, put like that.

"Think it through," Ben said. "The stable was on that guy's property, right? What was his name . . . Wallace Barton."

Jason nodded.

"And when the two of them crashed into your stall, Barton was the one wearing the mask."

Jason remained silent.

"And Cobb was the one with a pretty design painted on his face—butterflies, right?—just like Crackerjack's other victims."

Jason noticed that Ben had been keeping track of his points on his fingers. He added a fourth finger and said, "And when they landed on top of you, Cobb was begging you to help him, and Barton was fighting you for the hammer, right?"

It was right about there during the TV interview that Jason had started to fudge the facts and his memory became Swiss cheese, but he nodded anyway.

"And I saved the best for last. Let's not forget that Ian Cobb has a broken arm and several broken ribs. You think he did that to himself? Grabbed a hammer and smashed a bone in his own arm? Then broke his own ribs? Do you have any idea how hard that would be? What kind of person you'd have to be to do something like that? And according to you he was *whistling* while he did it? Sounds nuts, Jason."

"No one ever said Crackerjack was sane."

"Yeah, but you're the one who sounds crazy now."

He could imagine how all of that sounded to Ben. What he couldn't imagine was what it would take to shatter one's own bones with a hammer. And not just once but several times.

*One . . . two . . . three strikes, you're out!*

"It just doesn't make sense, Jason. If Cobb was really Crackerjack, and if Barton discovered him killing people in his stable, he wouldn't break his own bones, paint his own face, and have *you* kill Barton. He'd just kill the both of you. It's what he liked to do anyway."

Jason didn't have an answer for that. He hadn't gotten that far in his thinking.

"Listen, I don't just watch *The Simpsons*, Jason. I also watch a lot of crime shows, and they all seem to say the same thing: that most serial killers typically don't just stop killing. Some do, but most don't. They need it like a drug. They may try to give it up, but they usually end up doing it again. So if Cobb was really Crackerjack, why end it all when he didn't have to? It's not like the cops were closing in on him or anything."

Jason didn't respond. Susan showed up with a smile and two more beers, though neither of them had asked for another drink. He thanked her, and she was still smiling as she left.

"I think she definitely likes you," Ben said. "And you know what else I think? I think you went through a horrible experience not long ago, then spent the past several days reliving that experience to work on your book, then had an admittedly uncomfortable drink with Cobb tonight, and maybe . . ."

"Yeah?"

"Maybe you're just creeping yourself out. Thinking too much about all of this. You need a break from it."

"I've got a deadline. Or I will as soon as we sign the contracts. I want to get a jump on things."

"Okay. I get that. But how about *tonight* you forget about all of that? Forget about Ian Cobb, and let's enjoy the free drinks your flirty new friend is giving us. You can shift your overactive imagination back into hyperdrive tomorrow. Deal?"

Jason nodded. So they sat and chatted about Ben's job, the waitress, money, sports, and a few other mundane topics, all while Jason kept one eye on the window.

# CHAPTER TWENTY-EIGHT

It was nearly two in the morning. Jason had memorized every tiny crack and imperfection in the ceiling above his bed. Every time he closed his eyes to try to fall asleep, he saw that damn Ian Cobb–shaped silhouette looking in the window of the Green Dragon . . . only now, in Jason's head, in his bedroom in the middle of the night, Cobb's face was clearly visible behind the glass. He was staring at Jason. And he was whistling.

Perhaps Ben was right. Maybe Jason was spending too much time forcing himself to relive his days in Wallace Barton's stable. Sure, Cobb's behavior at the Shark's Tooth was a bit off-putting, but maybe he couldn't help it. Maybe his inability to express himself at the bar was the result of a social awkwardness that was the very reason he had no one else to talk to when he needed someone. He certainly seemed lonely. And why else would he cling so desperately to perceived commonalities he shared with Jason? He actually started to feel sorry for Cobb.

He was too wide awake to sleep, so he padded on bare feet into the living room, where he sank into the sofa in front of the TV. Late-night television often put him to sleep, and it wasn't long before his eyelids grew heavy. Almost on autopilot, he kept changing channels. ESPN became an infomercial, which became *Gilligan's Island*, which became a twenty-four-hour news station. He barely noticed the remote control slip from his fingers.

Then something on the TV snagged his attention. The word *Tewksbury* in a news story. The video footage on the screen showed an afternoon scene. A group of people, some in police uniform, were gathered near the brightly colored structures of a playground. A voice over the image said, "Though the police haven't released details, witnesses described a grisly scene. The body of a man, apparently murdered, hanging from the monkey bars in a local playground."

The image cut to a twentysomething woman in a light pullover. Earbuds hung around her neck.

"When I first saw him hanging there, I wanted to run away. But then I thought he might need help, you know, if he was still alive. So I got closer and saw that his eyes were open. But his face was purple. He was definitely dead. He was hanging there, and there was blood all down his face, and he had a . . . dent in his head or something. Like he'd smashed his head before hanging himself."

The woman on-screen was replaced by a well-coiffed reporter. This footage was shot at night, a bright light shining on the man's face and throwing illumination onto the now-empty playground behind him.

"For now, the authorities are withholding the victim's identity. Reporting live from Tewksbury, Massachusetts, I'm Christopher Rollins, Fox News."

Jason sat up.

A man with his head caved in.

In Tewksbury.

Where Cobb had visited a plumbing job yesterday.

*Is it possible that . . .*

He told himself to slow the hell down. This couldn't be the first murder ever committed in Tewksbury.

But Cobb just happened to be there yesterday.

*Okay, sure, Cobb was there, but so were tens of thousands of other people. And Cobb has a broken arm, for God's sake.*

Something Ben had said a few hours ago floated to the surface of his mind. It was something Jason had also read in numerous books while doing research for the villain in his first novel . . .

*Most serial killers don't stop killing until they're in prison or dead.*

*If Cobb is Crackerjack . . . he's going to kill again. He's going to kill again, because that's what serial killers do.*

Was he somewhere in the dark night even now, hunting again? Hell, was he watching Jason's apartment at that very moment? But no, why would he come after Jason now? He'd already *had* Jason as a captive; he could have killed him then, if that was what he wanted. But if Cobb really *was* Crackerjack, then . . .

He thought of the families of all the victims, who might have found some small measure of peace upon hearing of Wallace Barton's death, a peace that would be shattered when they learned that the murderer of their loved ones still lived and breathed.

In his savings account sat $200,000 given to him by a grieving father, money he'd have no choice but to return.

He thought of the book deal and the movie deals and how nothing had been agreed upon yet, no contracts signed so far, and likely wouldn't be if he hadn't actually killed Crackerjack. After all, no one wanted to pay him for the story of his escape. No, it was his escape *plus* his killing of the bad guy that people wanted to hear.

He thought about what it would mean to his family if all those financial opportunities disappeared. No potentially lifesaving miracle drug for Max. No customized van for Sophie. No financially secure future.

He thought of the way Sophie had looked at him since all of this began, since he had come home a hero. He didn't want her to stop looking at him that way. But how could she not? He wasn't the hero the media had made him out to be. And he wasn't his family's savior. He was the same man he'd been two weeks ago, only now he was unemployed. He was the same man he'd been the night of their car accident. To her, he was still whatever she believed him to be on that rain-slicked road.

But he was more than that, too, because he was also a liar. A self-aggrandizing, glory-seeking liar who had gone on national television and told a tall tale about his life-and-death, hand-to-hand battle with a serial killer . . . a story that, now that he thought of it, had conveniently been fed to him—in dramatically embellished form—by Ian Cobb, who just might be the killer himself. He didn't remember tackling Barton to the ground, the two of them fighting for the hammer. He remembered only Cobb and Barton landing on him, and Barton lying there while Cobb thrashed around above him and screamed for Jason to hit him with the hammer . . . which he did. He killed Wallace Barton. Who maybe . . . and this thought occurred to him only at that moment . . . was nothing more than another of Crackerjack's victims. Like Jason was. But what if . . .

He tried to remember whether Barton had actually moved when he was on top of Jason. Had he been conscious? *Maybe he was already dead,* he thought with faint hope. *Maybe Cobb had already killed him. Or maybe not. Maybe . . .*

Maybe Jason had killed an innocent man.

*What if I didn't end the reign of a serial killer? What if I murdered a man who may have been just another victim himself . . . and gave a twisted serial killer the perfect opportunity to ditch the public persona that had drawn so much attention over the past year so he could start all over again if he wanted?*

*And of course he'll want to. It's what serial killers do.*

"What do I do?" he asked the empty room.

*Call the cops. Call Detective Briggs and tell him . . .*

*Uh . . .*

*Tell him that Ian Cobb is Crackerjack because a man was strangled and bludgeoned in Tewksbury, where Cobb has been working lately . . . along with nearly thirty thousand other people? Also, he whistles a whole lot like Crackerjack, whom I heard when I was drugged and practically delirious from lack of food or water. And forget about his broken bones. Cobb is a bit socially awkward, so he must be a killer. Oh, and all that stuff I said on TV and when you interviewed me about how I fought Barton to the death . . . well, I might have been exaggerating a little. He might actually have been barely conscious when I killed him Or, I don't know, already dead.*

Would Briggs believe him?

Was Jason even certain about all of this? Was he *positive*? Positive enough to confess to lying in his statement to the police?

He thought there was a chance he might be right. That, somehow, despite his broken bones, Ian Cobb actually might be Crackerjack. But the evidence sure seemed to indicate that he was wrong. Sure, the Tewksbury victim's head was bashed in, but that wasn't an uncommon way to kill someone. And there was no face paint. And the body wasn't found in a remote dumpster or ditch; it was hanging from a set of monkey bars in a playground for all to see. None of that sounded like Crackerjack's handiwork.

He had to give it more thought. It was late. He was tired and not thinking clearly. If things looked the same to him in the morning, he'd call Briggs. If the worst-case scenario turned out to be true, if Cobb was really Crackerjack and had truly murdered someone that day, it wasn't likely he'd kill someone else before morning. Crackerjack went weeks, sometimes more than a month, between kills, so why would he suddenly decide to kill two people in one night? Jason had a few hours at least to work it through a bit more and decide whether he was right to be suspicious, or whether he was being ridiculously paranoid.

He closed his eyes to think better. He thought hard for as long as he could. It had been a long day, though, and in a little while he fell asleep. And he dreamed . . .

Of driving through the rain along a dark stretch of road . . . Sophie asleep beside him, her head resting against the passenger window . . . A man appearing in his headlights, walking on the shoulder of the road . . . the car swerving . . . Sophie awake now and screaming . . . the shrieking and rending of metal . . . and the night suddenly blacker than black.

# CHAPTER TWENTY-NINE

Ian Cobb sat on a small rocky outcropping at the edge of Black Joe's Pond, a small body of murky water in the Steer Swamp Conservation Area at the eastern end of Marblehead. The pond was named for "Black Joe" Brown, a freed slave, Revolutionary War veteran, and wealthy tavern owner whose drinking hole was the liveliest spot in town in the late eighteenth century. Fortunately for Cobb, the pond bearing his name centuries later was quiet, especially after 2:30 a.m. It was mostly surrounded by woods, and though there were houses in the area, none was close to Cobb's location.

The water rippled and shimmered in the moonlight. It was a peaceful sight, but Cobb was feeling far from at peace. He turned to the man sitting next to him.

"You've confirmed it," he said. "This isn't going to work for me."

The man said nothing.

"I hoped I was wrong. I tried this by myself earlier today . . ." He glanced at his watch. "Well, yesterday now, I guess . . . and it didn't work. I hoped you and your friend could help, that having company would help. But it hasn't."

The man remained silent.

"It's not your fault. Or your buddy's. You guys did your part. It's me. Other people do it by themselves all the time. But for me, it's just not going to work."

The man beside Cobb grunted into the duct tape secured tightly across his mouth. Tears ran from his eyes, mixing with the blood that dripped down his cheeks from where Cobb had sliced away his eyelids.

"Sorry I lied to you."

Before Cobb had let the men—gagged and bound with duct tape at the wrists—out of the back of his van, he had promised not to hurt them if they followed him through the woods. He'd pointed out that if he had wanted to cause them harm, he could have done so while they were unconscious in the vehicle. They had believed him—or, at the very least, acted with blind and desperate faith that he was telling the truth—and Cobb was spared the effort of having to carry them one by one through the trees to the lake.

He looked at his watch again: 2:40 a.m.

"It's getting late. I have to get a move on here, Isaac. I still have to sink the two of you in the water. And I'm thinking now that I may have to go break into someone's house before morning. But that's not your concern."

The man grunted again, loudly, and struggled in vain against the silver tape wrapped tightly around his wrists, and around his ankles now, too. His eyes looked wide in his panic but Cobb figured the effect was enhanced by his lack of eyelids.

"Calm down. I'll make this quick. Even quicker than I did with your friend."

Cobb glanced at the body of the other man lying on the rock not far away, his head resting bonelessly to the side, his neck broken. He still had his eyelids, though.

"I usually take more time with this kind of thing, but . . . well, like I said, this is just a no-go for me. Now, I just want to get it over with."

He stood, stepped over to the dead man, grabbed him by his feet, and dragged him into the water, a task made more difficult by the burlap sack filled with rocks that Cobb had tied around the body's waist. He pulled the corpse behind him as he walked out until he was chin-deep in the pond, ignoring the muck beneath his feet and the algae clinging to him, then let the rocks take the man to the bottom. Cobb knew this pond, knew how murky its water was. No one would find the bodies for a good while.

Back at the water's edge again, he found Isaac trying to roll away. A waste of energy. How far did he think he'd get? Cobb grabbed his ankles and dragged him, burlap bag of rocks and all, toward the pond. When water ran over the man's feet, he began to thrash.

"I'm not gonna drown you," Cobb said. "I've heard that's a horrible way to go. I'm gonna strangle you. I don't think that'll be as bad as drowning, but I obviously can't promise that."

Despite what he'd said about not being into it tonight, what he was itching to do was break every bone in Isaac's body, then crush his skull. But he couldn't. One bashed head in Massachusetts this week was enough, unless he wanted the world to wonder whether that Crackerjack was truly dead.

Eventually, he supposed, he would come up with some new signature to add to the bodies of the people he would kill, instead of bone breaking and face painting, something interesting and different. But for now, a simple strangulation would have to do.

He glanced again at his watch, which fortunately was water resistant.

"Man, I have to get a move on. Sorry about your eyelids, by the way. If you'd just kept your eyes open and watched me kill your friend like I said to, I wouldn't have had to do that. But I had to know, you understand? And now I do. It doesn't work for me by myself, and forcing someone to watch doesn't help, either."

He put his hands around the man's neck, thankful that the cast on his right arm didn't extend to his hand and affect his grip, and dug his thumbs into the windpipe. As he began to squeeze, he congratulated himself for his foresight in always keeping a spare set of clothes in his van. He didn't want to spend the next few hours soaking wet from dragging bodies into a pond, and he still had things to do before he could call it a night.

# CHAPTER THIRTY

Jason awoke to an insistent, annoyingly cheerful chiming. As he fumbled for his cell phone, he realized that he'd slept on the sofa. A moment later, on the phone's third ring, he remembered what he had been thinking about when he'd fallen asleep.

Should he call the police? Did he know enough? Was he certain enough? Either way, was he ready to give up everything? *Everything?*

The phone rang again and he found it down between the sofa cushions. He glanced at the display as he answered.

"Hi, Sophie."

"Jason . . . did I wake you? It's after ten."

"No . . . well, yeah. Late night for me. I was working on the new book," he lied.

"Oh, sorry. Can we talk for a minute, though?"

"Yeah, sure."

"It looks like we need a new furnace. And a new hot-water heater."

In his mind, he sighed. *We* used to mean Sophie, Max, and Jason. Now it meant Sophie, Max, and Janice.

"Mom's helping out as much as she can, as you know," Sophie went on, "but . . . well, we're looking at almost seven thousand dollars and she doesn't have that kind of money right now. I hate to ask . . ."

Rubbing sleep from his eyes, Jason said, "No problem, Soph. Of course I'll pay for the furnace and the water heater. Anything for you and Max. But are you sure you need new ones? I don't mind paying for them, but are they definitely necessary?"

"I brought in a plumber this morning. He's still here and he assures me they're necessary."

Faint alarm bells began to ring, and Jason felt that if he weren't so tired, he'd know why.

"What made you call a plumber in the first place?"

"No hot water this morning. Then we realized there was no heat, either."

He stood and stifled a yawn.

"So I called Ian Cobb."

Jason was wide awake now.

Sophie continued. "In the interview he said he's a plumber, and I knew from the news that he lives here on the North Shore. So I called him."

"Sophie, listen to me—"

"I figured we owed it to him to give him the job if he wanted it, right? After he gave us—well, after he gave you—all that money."

"Sophie, I don't want to scare—"

"Is that Jason?" It was Cobb's voice coming over the phone. Fainter than Sophie's. In the background. "Sorry to interrupt, but I overheard you. Is that you, Jason?" he called.

Jason felt as though he might crush the phone in his hand. "Is he right there, Sophie? Right now?"

"He just came into the kitchen."

"Is Max there, too?"

"He's in the living room. Why?"

"Can I talk to him?"

"Max?"

"No, Cobb. Can you put him on?"

"Sure."

A moment later, Cobb said, "Good morning, Jason."

He hesitated, unsure what to say. Should he tell Cobb that he'd better not harm Sophie or Max? Was he ready to accuse the man of being a murderer? Wouldn't it be stupid to do so while Cobb was in the house with his family and Jason was across town? Besides, was he even close to certain about that?

"Hey, Ian. So . . . we need a new furnace and hot-water heater, huh?"

"Sorry to say. I feel bad about it, too. It's not cheap and your wife seems so nice. She doesn't deserve this. Max is nice, too. He doesn't deserve this, either. Like you told me, he's a great kid."

Jason held his phone in the crook of his neck and dressed quickly in the same clothes he'd worn last night, which he'd left in a pile on a chair in the corner.

"Listen, Ian. I'm on my way over. Don't do anything until I get there, okay?"

A pause. "You don't trust me, Jason?"

"What's that?"

"You don't trust that you need a new furnace and hot-water heater? After what we went through together? After I gave you that money? You think I'd try to sell you something you don't need?"

Damn if the man didn't sound sincere, as though Jason had truly hurt his feelings.

"No, no, it's not that. I just want to discuss options. Maybe we should put in a bigger furnace . . . or one of those tankless water heaters."

Cobb was silent a moment. "Okay, see you when you get here. Want to talk to Sophie again?"

"Yeah."

He grabbed his keys and was out the door as Sophie returned to the line.

"Hey," she said.

He wanted to warn her but what would he say? He was far from sure that Cobb was a killer. Besides, if he warned Sophie and she did something to spook Cobb, who knew what the man might do?

"I'll be there in ten minutes. Stay away from . . ."

"From what?"

"The furnace. Stay away from it. Might be dangerous. Why don't you go sit with Max until I get there?"

"I couldn't leave Ian alone here in the kitchen. That would be rude. I'll see you soon."

The line went dead as Jason slipped behind the wheel of his Camry, fired up the engine, and punched the gas. Despite the cool midmorning air, sweat streamed from his every pore.

# CHAPTER THIRTY-ONE

Jason blew through a red light and two stop signs on his way to Sophie's house. He decided that if a cop saw him and threw on the lights and siren, he wouldn't even slow down until he got there. Once he'd seen that Sophie and Max were safe, the cop could arrest him if he wanted.

But he made it all the way to Sophie's with no more than some honks, a few dirty looks, and two middle fingers directed at him. He swung into the driveway, slammed on the brakes beside a white van, and bolted from the car. He threw open the front door and was greeted by Sophie rolling toward him down the hallway.

"You made record time," she said.

When Jason saw she was unharmed, relief washed over him in a wave that almost knocked him to his knees.

"Are you okay?" she asked. "You look—"

"Where's Max?"

"Max?"

"*Where is he, Sophie?*"

"In here, Daddy."

Jason slipped past Sophie's chair, crossed the foyer, and looked into the living room, where he saw Max and Ian Cobb kneeling side by side at the coffee table, piecing together a puzzle.

"I like your friend," Max said, smiling that gorgeous, sweetly innocent smile.

Jason wanted to scream. Was that a serial killer working on a puzzle with his precious son? Or was it just an average guy, a little socially awkward, a bit creepier than most, but otherwise not much different from everybody else?

Cobb held up a puzzle piece. "I think this one is part of the fire truck, Max. What do you think?"

"I don't know . . ." He took the piece from Cobb and, after a couple of failed attempts, pressed it into place where it belonged. "You're right," he exclaimed, clapping his hands. "Good job, Ian."

"Hey, you're the one who made it fit. You did the hard part."

"Ian, can I talk to you?" Jason said.

Cobb looked up. "Sure, come give us a hand. We've almost got the fire engine done."

"Maybe in the kitchen?"

Cobb hesitated. "Okay, Jason." To Max, he said, "Sorry, buddy. Your dad wants to talk to me. Can you handle the rest of this without me?"

Max frowned, then shot a reproachful look at Jason and said, "I guess so."

"Great. I'll check your progress before I leave."

He picked up a coffee mug from an end table and walked past Jason, through the foyer, heading toward the kitchen. Sophie started to roll after him but Jason said, "Can we have a few minutes, Soph?"

She stopped. "Everything okay?"

"I just want to talk with him alone for a little bit," he said quietly. "I want . . . to make sure he's okay with the idea of doing the work even though he gave me all that money. Feels a little funny to me."

"Maybe you should offer it back to him? You'd still have a hundred thousand dollars."

He didn't mention that he'd already done that, twice, and Cobb had refused both times.

"Exactly. That's what I plan to do. He might be more likely to accept if it's just the two of us."

She nodded and rolled herself back into the living room. Jason heard Max say, "Help me with the police car, Mommy."

When he entered the kitchen he found Cobb leaning against the counter, sipping his coffee. He didn't look well. Even worse than he had at the Shark's Tooth last night. Maybe he was just tired. He certainly had the appearance of a man who hadn't slept a wink the night before.

"You wanted to talk?" he asked.

Jason did. The problem was, he had no idea what to say. He racked his mind for options.

*Listen, it's a little awkward, your working for me after everything that happened, so maybe we should call a different plumber.*

Or . . .

*I know what you are. Stay the hell away from my family.*

Or . . .

*Your secret is safe with me if you just keep your distance.*

Or . . .

"How about I show you what's wrong in the basement?" Cobb asked, interrupting his thoughts. "We can start with that."

"Uh . . . sure."

Cobb walked over to the door in the corner of the kitchen and started down the stairs. Jason followed, thinking he'd seen this in a dozen movies, the good guy following the killer into a dark basement. That usually didn't end well for the good guy.

When they reached the bottom, Cobb started toward the furnace. As he walked, he began to whistle softly, very softly, and the hairs on the back of Jason's neck stood up. He was about to head back up to the kitchen on some pretense when Cobb abruptly turned, stepped close to him, and said, "Yes, Jason."

"Yes what?" Jason asked, backing up a step.

Cobb stepped close again, far inside Jason's personal space, and said, "That's the answer to the question you've been asking yourself. Yes, I'm Crackerjack."

And before Jason could react, a knife was at his throat.

# CHAPTER THIRTY-TWO

"Make a sound and I'll push this knife right through your neck. Understand, Jason?"

Jason nodded, feeling the tip of the blade poke his skin as he did. Cobb wasn't restraining him in any way. He wasn't backed up against a wall. There wasn't anything preventing him from jumping backward, out of striking range, and either running back up to the kitchen or attacking Cobb, who was a fair bit bigger than Jason but who had only one unbroken arm.

Nothing except the thought of his wife and child upstairs. The basement was chilly and damp, yet Jason was suddenly sweating.

"As you know," Cobb said, "a knife isn't really my weapon of choice, but I know how one works. You gonna stay calm?"

Jason nodded again, swallowed a lump in his throat the size of a charcoal briquette, and wondered if there was the slightest chance he'd be able to remain calm in this situation.

"I just wanna talk," Cobb said, "and it'll be a lot easier if I don't have to watch your every move, wondering if you're gonna try something stupid. And if you do, I'll have to hurt you . . . and if I hurt you I'll have to hurt your family next, and I'd rather not do any of that if I can avoid it. So I'm gonna tie you up, okay? There are some old kitchen chairs down here and some extension cords, so we should be in business."

"I can't let you tie me up. That'd be crazy."

*This whole scenario is crazy.*

"I'm not gonna hurt you, Jason. If I wanted to do that, I could've done it days ago, right?"

If he let Cobb bind him to a chair, he'd be helpless. And his wife and son would be at Cobb's mercy. *No way.*

"First of all," Cobb said, "you gotta calm down. I'm not trying to insult you, but you're breathing like a frightened bunny. Second: I get it. You're worried about Sophie and Max. But think about it. I could've already hurt them, too, if I'd wanted. Before Sophie even called you. So sit down so we can chat for a bit without me having to watch your every muscle twitch."

He was right. Jason had practically been panting. He took a deep breath, let it out slowly. Cobb was also right that he could have killed Jason back at the stable. And he could have murdered Sophie and Max before Jason even woke up that morning.

"Feeling better?" Cobb asked. "You look a little better." Jason took another deep breath and nodded. "Good. Now, you see my logic here, right?" After a moment, Jason nodded again. "Terrific. Grab one of those chairs, would you?"

Jason pulled a dusty wooden chair from a corner, ignored the cobwebs clinging to it, and dragged it into the middle of the basement. He looked at Cobb, who nodded to the chair. Reluctantly, he sat. As Cobb put the knife—which Jason now saw had a nasty-looking, six-inch serrated blade—into his back pocket, Jason felt a rising sense of panic followed instantly by a nearly overwhelming urge to lunge off the chair, drive Cobb to the ground, and go for the knife. But he fought the urge, remembering the reasons he had agreed to allow Cobb to tie him up in the first place. In moments, Cobb had used the extension cords to tie his hands behind his back and each of his ankles to one of the chair's legs.

"Just relax, Jason. We'll do a lot better here if you try to forget that you're tied up, that I have a knife, that I've killed a lot of people, and that your family is right upstairs. All of that will only distract you, and I want you to hear me out. Can you try to do that?"

"I don't have a choice anymore. Tell me again that you're not going to hurt my family, Cobb."

"It's *Cobb* now? What happened to *Ian*?"

Jason said nothing. Behind his back, his hands were clenched into fists so tight he thought he could feel blood trickling from his palms.

"Well, I'm still gonna call you Jason, okay?" He smiled cordially. "By now you may be thinking there's nothing actually wrong with your furnace and hot-water heater. But there is. Because I broke in here in the middle of the night and made sure of it. Nothing that can't be fixed, though."

The thought of Cobb sneaking around his house while his family slept nearby made Jason regret he'd let himself be tied up. He'd have gone after Cobb and not stopped fighting until one of them was dead, which probably would have been a bad idea, seeing as Cobb had killed something like sixteen people and Jason had killed only one.

Trying to remain outwardly calm, he said, "Sophie could have called any plumber in the area. How did you know she'd call you?"

"I didn't, not for sure. And if she hadn't, I'd have figured some other way to get your attention. But you told me last week that you don't have a plumber you regularly use, and I figured mine would be the first name she thought of. Besides, she'd feel like she owed me, given my generosity when I gave you all that money on national television. By the way, I can tell you how to fix the furnace and water heater. It's easy. Or you can call another plumber—I assume you won't want me to do it—but let me tell you, if they want to charge you more than an hour's labor, they're ripping you off. And I wouldn't put it past some plumbers. You have to be really careful who you let into your home, Jason. Some people just can't be trusted."

Jason shook his head but said nothing.

"You'd already figured out that *I* couldn't be trusted, am I right? You started having suspicions about me, didn't you?"

He shrugged.

"You were supposed to, you know. I wanted you to. That's why I started whistling when we were walking on the Common after the TV interview. I knew you'd hear me."

"The guy in Tewksbury . . . ," Jason began to ask, though he knew the answer.

"Yeah, I killed him. I *knew* you'd get it. I mentioned enough times that I was working a big job out there. I figured a murder there—along with my whistling—would start your gears turning. I hung him in the playground to make sure it made the news, thinking you might remember—"

Jason cut in, "When we were walking through the park, you said something about grown men loitering around playgrounds where they didn't belong . . . that they deserved to be strung up."

Cobb smiled. "Very good. I hoped you'd remember that. In case you didn't, though, I bashed his head in, too, so you'd know for sure it was me. By the way, I killed two other guys, too, just last night. Sunk them in a pond. Hey, did I ever thank you for that snow cone?"

*Two more guys? Dear God.*

Sophie's voice drifted down from the top of the basement stairs. "Jason, Max wants to know if he can join you and his new best friend down there."

Cobb smiled.

"No, Sophie," Jason said quickly, hoping she didn't notice the strain in his voice. "Don't do that. Please."

"Uh . . . okay."

"We've got the furnace open," Cobb called upstairs calmly. He winked at Jason. "It wouldn't be a good idea."

"Okay. I'll go deliver the bad news."

Tiny rivulets of sweat ran down Jason's forehead. "Listen, Cobb, how about you untie me and we can take this outside?"

"You want me out of the house," Cobb said. "I get it. I did it this way so you'd see the danger to your family. I needed you under control so we could talk. And that's all we're doing right now, right? Just talking." He chuckled. "Boy, I bet you never thought you'd be tied up by a serial killer again, did you? What are the odds?"

Jason couldn't come close to getting a read on the situation. Cobb didn't seem to want to kill him. As he'd said, he could have done that days ago.

"Why didn't you kill me at the stable?"

"I didn't want to."

"Why not?"

"You seem kind of eager for me to kill you."

"No, it's just . . . I'm wondering why you haven't, that's all."

"Because we're in this together now, Jason. We're a team."

# CHAPTER THIRTY-THREE

"We're a team?" Jason said. "What does that mean?"

Cobb saw the confusion on Jason's face. And he understood it. He was dumping a lot on him right now. He needed to be patient. He needed Jason to *understand.*

"We killed Wallace Barton together, didn't we?" Cobb said. "As a team. You see?"

"I don't see anything here."

Cobb had known this wouldn't be easy.

"Just tell me what the hell you want from me," Jason said.

Jason was getting a little bolder, Cobb noticed. "It's a little soon for that, I think. That's big-picture stuff. Bonus-round material. We'll get there in a few minutes. Let's stick to the qualifying round. You gotta have other questions. Like, maybe you're wondering how I was using Barton's stable without him knowing about it. Now, that's a great question. With an answer I think you'll find interesting. He actually *did* know about it." He paused for effect. "The fact is . . . he and I were working together."

"*Working* together?"

"Okay, okay, we killed people together. Is that better? Actually, *I* did the killing. That was my thing. He liked to watch. That was *his* thing."

"You were both Crackerjack?"

"I guess you could look at it like that. I did the kidnapping and the killing. He just gave me a nice, secluded place to do my work. And he watched."

He chose not to mention that sometimes—not every time, but now and then—when he had someone strapped to his table, when he was snapping a tibia or caving in a skull, he would look back at Wallace and see his brother Johnny there instead, in Wallace's place . . . Johnny, plain as day, sitting there with a small, satisfied smile on his face, watching his big brother work. One minute, Johnny would be dead and gone, as he had been for the past three years, and the next, he'd be right *there* again, right beside Cobb.

"You get off on killing," Jason said, "and Barton got off on watching."

Poor Jason looked both horrified and stunned. Again, Cobb understood. This was a lot to take in. He gave Jason a few seconds to process it.

"I didn't kill an innocent man," Jason finally said. "I killed a murderer . . . or his accomplice anyway." He thought for a moment. "But why, Cobb?"

"Why'd you kill him?"

"No, why do you do it?"

"Torture and kill people?"

"Yeah. Do you find it *fun?*" Jason asked, and he made no effort to hide the disgust in his voice. Yes, he was definitely growing bolder. "Is it arousing? What is it?"

Cobb thought for a moment. "You know what, Jason? This may surprise you, but I'm gonna tell you the truth. Something I've never told anyone. Not our victims. Not even Wallace. As for him, I have no idea why *he* did it. But I'll tell you why I do. And here it is: for whatever reason . . . it's the only thing that eases my pain."

"It eases your pain?"

"Right. It's the only thing. Believe me, I've tried others."

"Your pain? *Your* pain? What about the pain you cause other people? Your victims and their families? Is *your* pain the only one that matters?"

"It's the only one that matters to me. I know how that sounds, but it's true. It started out as my brother's pain, and when he died, it became mine."

"Your brother's pain?" Jason said. "What the . . . are you talking about physical pain?"

"Only a little," Cobb said, "but the truth is, physical pain isn't the worst kind."

"Your victims might disagree."

"It's emotional pain that does the most damage, pain deeper inside you than your bones. When you hurt really, really far down, where your true self is—now *that's* pain. When it's bad enough, it's way worse than anything I ever put anyone else through."

"And it was your brother's pain first?" Jason asked, and Cobb could see that he was having a hard time with this. "What the hell does that even mean?"

"Johnny suffered so much, carried it for so long, ever since he was a little boy—this . . . *thing* inside him. He had a name for it. His Inside Dark, he called it. And it was cruel as hell to him unless he gave it what it needed. Turns out it was even stronger than I could have imagined, too strong to just disappear when he died. It had to go somewhere, I guess, so it came to me. Now I carry it."

Jason looked as though he were about to say something but changed his mind. He also looked scared and more than ever like he wished he were anywhere but in that basement. Cobb knew this concept was a difficult one to grasp. He thought back to how it had started, when Johnny was alive.

"See, Johnny had broken a lot of bones as a boy," he said. "Walked with a really bad limp. Said he used to hurt all the time . . . except—and this part's really important—except when he witnessed someone else's pain. Somehow, for some reason, that pleased his inner darkness, which made Johnny feel better, too. I didn't understand it then, of course, but he was my brother. I would've done anything for him. If watching people get hurt made him feel better, well, I was willing to hurt people for him. He would have liked to help me with that, but he couldn't. He just wasn't up to it physically. So I'd do what had to be done while he watched."

"I don't understand how seeing other people getting injured would make him feel better. That's beyond crazy."

Cobb had thought the same thing at first, that what Johnny had endured at the hands of their Uncle Joe while their parents looked the other way had broken his mind. Cobb didn't care. Crazy or not, he'd do whatever his brother thought would help him. The thing was, it really *did* seem to help. After doing what they did, Johnny would stop complaining about the pain. His Inside Dark was satisfied, he'd say. And he'd be himself again, at least for a month or two. Then the pain would come back and he'd get depressed, and Cobb would know it was time. He'd know what his brother needed. And when they were done, Johnny would be smiling again. For a while, at least.

"We didn't kill anyone, you know. Not back then. Just knocked guys around a bit, stomped on some fingers, kicked in some teeth."

It went that way for a few years. Every couple of months the pain inside Johnny would get too bad and the two of them would make a trek to some bar in some other town and wait for some drunk to totter out to his car alone. Cobb would come up from behind, drop a hood over the guy's head, and start in. Johnny would watch, smiling and offering encouragement, until the guy lay broken on the ground. On the way home again, Johnny would seem buoyant, all the weight lifted from his shoulders.

And everything was fine until one night they picked the wrong guy. He hadn't been alone like they'd thought, merely a few seconds ahead of his buddies. But Cobb realized that too late; he had already started. Seeing his older brother in trouble, Johnny stepped in despite his physical limitations. By the time it was over and the four other guys were bloody heaps on the ground, Cobb had a broken wrist and a separated shoulder, and Johnny had a broken jaw, a broken arm, and six broken ribs—all bones that, among others, had been broken for him a decade earlier, some more than once. Cobb decided that he would never put his younger brother in that situation again. He said that if Johnny wanted to watch from then on, it would have to be from inside a locked car. But Johnny wouldn't have it. He wanted to hear it all, every blow; he *needed* to feel a part of it, even if he was several feet away. So Cobb decided that it had to stop altogether, for Johnny's own good. He refused to do it anymore, despite his brother's pleading. He told Johnny he'd have to find another way to make his pain go away. And he did. Three months later he drove his car into a concrete abutment. Not long after, Cobb began to feel the pain himself, way down deep. His brother's pain—his darkness—was in Cobb now.

"When he died," Cobb said, "it wasn't long before I knew something was terribly wrong with me. I thought I was just sad that my brother was gone, maybe feeling guilty, but soon I realized it was more than that. Far more. The emotional pain became physical. Deep inside. It was terrible. Eventually, I realized what it was, why I was hurting. It was Johnny's Inside Dark. Somehow, it ended up in me. And sometimes, my God, you wouldn't believe how bad it is. I don't blame him for . . . the way he died. It's agony."

"You can't catch pain like a cold, Cobb. It's not a virus."

"Except when he died, his hurt became mine. I don't know how to explain it. So I did the only thing I knew to do . . . the only thing that helped Johnny. I hurt people."

"And that made you feel better?" Jason asked. "That's just so wrong, Cobb."

"That's the thing, though. It didn't help. Not at first."

Even though he'd hurt people—sometimes badly—the pain wouldn't go away. Without Johnny there with him, at his side . . .

stomping on fingers and kicking in teeth didn't do for him what it used to do for his brother. It didn't silence the voice inside him. It didn't take away his pain. "It wasn't until Wallace took Johnny's place, watching and cheering me on, that I could take the edge off. You understand?"

Jason said nothing.

"I needed someone to watch me, to urge me on, or the pain wouldn't go away. I don't know why it works like that, but it does. And Wallace was happy to do that."

Jason scoffed. "How on earth did two nut bags like you and Barton even find each other?"

"Luck, I guess."

It didn't matter how they had met, only that when they did, Cobb knew instantly that Barton was a like-minded person, that he had interests and desires that most people would consider twisted. And his was a special deviancy. Cobb saw that immediately.

"Right away I could tell he'd be interested in what I was doing." Exactly *how* he had been so certain about Wallace wasn't Jason's business, not yet—hell, he'd never even told Wallace—but Jason would learn soon enough. "And I was right. He liked to watch me hurt other people, but eventually . . ."

"It wasn't enough just to hurt them," Jason finished for him.

Cobb said, "No . . . not enough."

They'd discovered that early, on just their fourth victim together. At first, they'd just beat guys up in dark parking lots, the way he and Johnny used to, leaving them broken but alive. But that fourth guy . . . They hadn't planned to kill him. Cobb was working away at him and Wallace, cheering like a rabid fan at a heavyweight fight, was enjoying himself, but when they were nearly finished, Cobb felt . . . unfulfilled. Worse, he still felt a terrific pain inside, like a knife twisting in his stomach. Purely on impulse, he'd picked up a rock and crushed the guy's skull. And suddenly, the agony that had been his constant companion for months, ever since Johnny had died, that knife in his gut, was little more than a toothache. He looked over at Wallace, worried about how he might react, but the man was grinning from ear to ear. After that, they brought their victims back to Wallace's stable. After that, there was no going back for either of them.

"It wasn't enough to merely cause people pain," Jason said. "You had to kill them, too? To make *your* pain go away?"

"What can I say? It works. For a while anyway."

Jason shook his head, disgusted and dumbfounded. "If you hurt most of the time, why not end it all? Why not just kill yourself? Like your brother obviously did."

For an instant, Cobb considered cutting Jason's throat. Maybe he'd gotten a little *too* bold. Thankfully, the urge passed. "I'm not going to kill myself," he said, "because I don't want to die. I don't know what's waiting for me when I do. If there's a heaven, I'm not getting in. And if there's a hell, I'm in no hurry to get there."

Jason looked horrified but he also seemed fascinated, which Cobb took as a good sign. "Why do you only do it to men? Why not women or children?"

"Wallace suggested we do it to a woman one time and I told him I had no interest in that, and he didn't really seem to care. All that mattered to him was that whoever we chose suffered. But me? I just never wanted to hurt women or children. I like kids. They're innocent, at least until they get older. And I like women, too. I respect them. And no, I'm not gay, and I wasn't sexually abused by a priest or anything. Those stereotypes are insulting to gay people, victims of clergy abuse, and serial killers. I just think that grown men are no better than animals. Take Wallace and me, for example."

"I'm guessing it was a man who hurt your brother. Broke a few of his bones."

"Broke *a lot* of his bones. It was our uncle."

"Did you kill him?"

"I wish. He died too soon. Not before he ruined Johnny's life, but before we could punish him for doing it."

"Let me guess: he was a face painter? Maybe a carny or something?"

"Ah, that." Cobb chuckled. "Nah, he was a cop. That's how he got away for so long with what he used to do—that and the fact that my father was a coward. But the face painting? That was mostly for kicks."

Cobb recalled the night they had thought of it, halfway through a second six-pack. They had talked about how a lot of famous serial killers had their little quirks, their calling cards, so they decided to come up with their own. Besides making it a little more interesting, they figured it would also provide a little cover, give the authorities something irrelevant to run down, a red herring to add to their psychological profiles. And while the cops were questioning carnival workers and amusement-park face painters, he and Wallace would be laughing at them.

"I did all the painting," Cobb said. "Wallace didn't have an artistic bone in his body, but I think I got pretty good at it." He smiled. "You know, Jason, it feels really good to talk about this with you."

"But won't you have to kill me now that I've heard all this? I'll know your secrets."

"I already told you. I don't want to kill you."

"How about my family?"

"I don't want to kill them, either."

Jason desperately looked like he wanted to believe him. "I just don't understand what we're doing here, Cobb. I don't understand anything. If things were so great with Barton, why stop? Why did you kill him?"

"You mean, why did *we* kill him?"

"Whatever."

"*We* killed him to save you, Jason. He wanted to kill you, like we killed all the others. It was the reason we took you, after all. Except, when it came time to do it, I didn't want to. Usually when we brought someone to the stable, we'd kill him the same day, maybe the next at the latest. But we kept you around for days while we argued about whether to break you and kill you or dump you somewhere unharmed. Wallace didn't understand why I didn't want to kill you. I wasn't so sure myself for a while, either."

"So what happened?"

"He finally got tired of waiting and said, 'Screw it, I'll kill him myself.' But I stopped him. He had no chance against me. I choked him unconscious. Then I had to choose. Him or you. I chose you . . . and just like that it was all over with him. Everything we'd been doing together was over. While he was unconscious, I painted my own face— the butterflies were nice, weren't they?—and broke my ulna with a hammer and then my ribs with a mini-sledge."

"Oh, my God . . ."

"Yeah, that hurt, I'm not gonna lie. But I had to make it impossible for anyone to think I could've been anything other than one of Crackerjack's victims. Think about it. Who the hell would do what I did to myself? Seriously. How crazy would I have to be?"

Jason seemed to have no answer to that, so Cobb continued.

"I stuck a mask on Wallace's head, and when he started to come around, I carried him to your stall—not easy to do with my broken arm—and dumped him on top of you. And you killed him."

Jason looked shaken. Cobb bent down and looked straight into his eyes.

"It's all over now, Jason. It's all gone. Crackerjack; the bone breaking; the nice, remote place to work in; my partner in crime. I gave it all up for you. So, in a way, you actually did kill Crackerjack."

"Not well enough, it seems."

"That's more true than you realize. Because here's the thing: I'm not gonna stop killing. I've already started up again, as you know. But those were just random kills. I'll want to go about it more organized, like before. I'll want to come up with a new signature, a new way to express myself. Like the face painting, only different."

Seeing the horror on Jason's face, Cobb couldn't suppress a small smile.

"Looks like when you killed Crackerjack, Jason, you gave birth to a new monster."

# CHAPTER THIRTY-FOUR

Jason didn't want to be doing this. He didn't want to be tied up any longer, talking to a murderer. He didn't want to keep wondering whether Cobb would honor his promise not to hurt Jason's family.

"You still haven't told me why I'm so special," Jason said. "Why you didn't kill me like Barton wanted, like you'd originally planned."

"I saw something in you."

Jason sucked in a sharp breath. Cobb's words slashed more deeply than his knife ever could. Those words . . . so similar to the ones he'd heard Sophie say.

"Saw something in me?" Fearing the answer, he asked, "Like what?"

Cobb looked at him for a long moment before nodding, almost imperceptibly, as though he had settled some internal debate and was about to divulge something important, then he shook his head slightly, apparently having changed his mind. "Like I told you the other day, we have a lot in common."

Jason remembered. He'd heard it last week as he'd strolled through the park, unknowingly in the company of an infamous serial killer— the things they had in common . . . family members with Down syndrome, automobile accidents, permanently disabled loved ones. And Cobb seemed fixated on the color of Jason's hair . . .

"I remember now," Jason said. "Your brother Johnny, you said he had red hair, right?"

"Like yours, but his was a little redder."

"I'm not your brother, you know."

"Seriously, Jason? Is that what you think? That I'm imagining that you're my brother, somehow back from the dead? Or perhaps he's inhabiting your body? Wow, you really do think I'm crazy."

"No, Cobb, it's obvious that you're perfectly sane."

Cobb regarded him for a moment, then laughed. "Well, I'm not *that* crazy. I don't think you're my dead brother. You just . . . remind me a lot of him, that's all. And you and I . . . hell, there's just a lot we have in common. And really, you're *so* much like him. I swear to God."

"And *that's* why you didn't kill me? I have reddish hair? We have a few things in common?"

Cobb shrugged. "I didn't notice your hair when I took you. And I didn't know about the other things at first. I stashed you at Wallace's place and was going to let you stew for a day or two—sometimes it's better for me that way, let the anticipation build a little—but then I started seeing stuff about you on the news. All the things we have in common. And with your hair, you just reminded me so much of Johnny—you really wouldn't believe it—and you've suffered so much already . . . the car crash, a crippled wife, a sick child . . . Johnny suffered a lot, too. So I sat in the stall next to yours and acted like another victim so we could talk a little. And soon, like I said . . . I saw something in you. Something like inside Johnny. And me."

Again with Cobb having seen *something* in him. When Sophie said that, he could deny it with confidence . . . maybe sometimes with a little more confidence than he felt. But when Cobb—a serial killer—said it . . . well, perhaps there was more to it than—

But *no*. Cobb was insane. Sophie? She was wrong; Jason had to believe that. But Cobb? He was just nuts. The guy had a *name* for his pain, for God's sake. And Jason was supposed to believe Cobb saw an Inside Dark in Jason, too? No way.

"I needed to get to know you better," Cobb said. "So I could decide once and for all if I wanted to break you into pieces, then kill you. And the more I learned about you, the more you made me think about my brother, about the way things were when he was alive . . . and the less I wanted to kill you."

"So help me out here, Cobb. You don't want to kill me, but you have to know that if you don't, I'll tell the police everything."

"That's refreshingly honest, Jason. It really is. Most people would lie about that to save their lives . . . say they won't tell a soul while planning to call the cops as soon as they get the chance. But I bet you've already thought that through a little and can see the problems with it. And in case you haven't, let me help you. All the evidence so far points to Barton—whom you killed, by the way—and none of it points to me."

"They'd find something if they looked hard enough."

"Nah. I was really, really careful. So it would be your word against mine . . . and you already gave your word to millions of television viewers that you fought Crackerjack to the death. That you and I, working together, escaped a notorious serial killer. If you change your story without any evidence to back you up, you'll just look foolish. Worse, you'll look like a liar."

"I'll take my chances."

"You might want to hear me out first. I hate to break it to you, but there's more."

*More?*

Cobb nodded. "Remember when I said that all of the evidence points to Barton?"

*Uh-oh.*

"Well, that's only the evidence they have so far," Cobb said. "But there's more of it out there, waiting to be found."

"Like what?"

"A more important question for you is *where*? See, the night we 'escaped' from the stable, while you were in the hospital, I visited your apartment. I had to go in the middle of the night because of all the media in front of your building, and I had to find a back way in, but it was easy enough getting inside. And I planted incriminating things. A lot of them. In places you'd never think to look, but where the cops sure as hell would. In your closet? Maybe. Behind utility access panels? Possibly. How about all the dark, secret places in the basement of the building? Maybe even buried in the little patch of ground out back? All good possibilities."

"No one would believe it."

"Really? In and around your building, and in your apartment itself, are paints and brushes, the same kind they found in the stable. And books on face painting. Pieces of clothing with blood from some of the victims on them. Personal things of theirs, too, like watches and jewelry, each with your fingerprints on them. All it'd take is an anonymous call from a nosy neighbor claiming to have seen you hiding things in one of the public places I mentioned, and once they found one little thing, they'd tear your world apart. "

"My fingerprints? How—"

"While you were unconscious in the stable."

"Damn it."

"Want a sample?"

"What do you mean?"

"Did you find the key yet?"

"What key?"

Cobb smiled. "You have your keys on you?"

He hesitated. "In my left front pocket."

"I don't mean to get too chummy here," Cobb said as he stuck his fingers into the pocket of Jason's jeans, then pulled out a ring with several keys on it, keys Jason knew well: to his car, to the front door of the building where he lived, to the door of his apartment, to Sophie's house, to the small padlock he kept at the gym he hadn't visited in months.

"Recognize this one?" Cobb asked, singling out a small silver key. "Did you even notice it?"

After a pause, he shook his head.

"Know what it opens?"

"No."

"Would you believe it opens a padlock that used to hang on the door of Barton's stable but is probably now in an evidence box in state police custody?"

*Damn.*

"That one was a freebie," Cobb said. "I don't need it. There are plenty more of these little bombs hidden in and around your home waiting to go off. Hey, for all you know, I rented a storage locker under your name and stuffed it full of dead bodies."

Jason closed his eyes.

"Look," Cobb continued, "you're screwed here. You're the one who killed Barton while I sat helplessly by, as you admitted on national television. You're the one with evidence against you just waiting for someone to point the cops to it. And I'd tell them that I'm starting to remember things about the night I was abducted, how there might have been two men. I'm sure you heard the same things I did on the news over the last few months—speculation that Crackerjack might have worked with a partner."

Jason had indeed heard rumblings about that. Some wondered how Crackerjack kept overpowering healthy men if he was working alone. Jason wasn't sure how seriously the authorities took the idea, but if Cobb raised it now, it wouldn't be coming out of left field.

"And who would the cops be more likely to believe was working with Wallace Barton?" Cobb asked. "You, with all of that evidence against you? Or me, with a broken arm and broken ribs and no evidence against me?"

Jason's chin sunk to his chest.

"What would Sophie say, Jason, if she learned you aren't the hero she thinks you are? Worse, that you might actually be a killer? And how about poor, grieving Leonard Sanderson, who gave you two hundred thousand dollars on national TV? I think he'd want that money back, don't you? And how about your book deal? Think that might fall through? It would be terrible to see all of that go up in smoke. I know how badly your family needs the money. Didn't I read somewhere that your son has some rare blood disease?"

Jason closed his eyes.

"I can see you're struggling with this," Cobb said. "Let me make it easier for you. I'll be leaving here in a little while. And I won't hurt you or your family. After I'm gone, though, if I even suspect you'll go to the cops about me, I'll kill Sophie and Max."

"You swore you wouldn't."

"I'm a murderer, Jason. I break people's bones for the hell of it. You think I'm worried about breaking a promise?"

He was numb. The book deal, gone. The movie deals, gone. All that money, gone. Max's expensive drug therapy, gone. The way Sophie had been looking at him lately . . . gone.

Also gone? Possibly his freedom, when the cops turned their attention to him.

Worst of all, Sophie and Max would be in danger.

Unless Jason kept his mouth shut. Unless he kept to himself that Ian Cobb was a serial killer with every intention of killing again.

# CHAPTER THIRTY-FIVE

While Jason pondered the impossible position in which he found himself, footsteps sounded on the stairs above them, the ones leading down from the second floor to the first. A moment later, Jason's mother-in-law called down into the basement.

"Sophie says you're still here, Mr. Cobb. Did you find something else wrong down there? Are we looking at ten thousand dollars now instead of seven?"

"No, ma'am," Cobb called up in a calm voice. "Just showing Jason everything down here. I want to make the situation clear to him. I need him to understand all the potential risks and costs."

"Hmm."

Above them, the sound of her footsteps marked her passage out of the kitchen.

"I had the chance to chat with your mother-in-law for a while this morning," Cobb said to Jason, "about the furnace. Lovely woman. Want me to kill her for you?"

"I'm through with this, Cobb. Want me to promise I won't tell the cops anything? Fine. You got it. I have no choice. If I say anything, my life is over. My family is in danger. So I'll keep my mouth shut. Are we done here?"

"Not quite."

"Then, damn it, tell me what the hell you want from me."

"Haven't you guessed?"

Actually, he had. He hoped he was wrong, but he suspected he wasn't. "I'm not going to be your new partner, Cobb."

Cobb cleared his throat. "Just think it through. We made a good team when we—"

"We're not a team."

"We have so much in common that—"

"Stop saying that."

Cobb took a breath. "I need to kill with someone. You killed my last partner. I need a new one now. I want it to be you. After we talked for a while in the stable, I could tell . . . well, like I said, when I looked at you I saw something . . . the same thing I saw in Barton and, well . . ." He trailed off.

"You saved me from Barton so I could take his place?" Jason asked.

"Not exactly. I saved you because I didn't want to kill you. I didn't think about it beyond that. The idea of your taking his place came to me later. I realized what I had first seen in you, what was making me want to keep you alive. And I just . . . I think you should consider . . ."

"There's a huge problem with your plan, Cobb. I'm not a killer."

"You killed Wallace."

"It was self-defense."

"I saw the look on your face after you did it, Jason. The look in your eyes. I *know* that look. I have it myself when I'm ready to kill. The same look Johnny and Wallace used to have when they watched me do bad things to people. You enjoyed it, Jason, the way it felt to put an end to another life. If you won't admit it to me, at least admit it to yourself."

*No.* Cobb had misread him. He may have been glad that Barton was dead—and maybe Cobb had seen that on his face—but only because it meant that he himself would survive. And Cobb, too, though he was less thrilled about that now. No, Cobb was wrong about Jason. He had to be. And so was Sophie. He needed to believe that. He *did* believe it.

"Thanks for the invitation, Cobb, but if you want to kill people, you're on your own."

"I don't *want* to be on my own. It doesn't work on my own. It's like . . . going on vacation by yourself. If you do it alone, there's no one to share it with. No one to talk about it with later."

"You're lonely? That's what this is all about? You kill because you're lonely? Get yourself a dog, for God's sake."

"Without someone to share it with, it's almost like it doesn't even happen. When it's over, it's like I only dreamed it. Like it wasn't real."

"It's real, Cobb. There are at least sixteen families out there, families of the men you killed, who could tell you how real it is."

"But it doesn't *feel* real. I hoped it would when I killed the guy in the park. But by the time I got home, it was already gone for me. Even when I watched it on the news I couldn't really remember it, not like I wanted to . . . not like I had been there myself. So I tried again, just to be sure. Like I told you, hours later I killed two *more* people. Before I killed the second guy, I made him watch me kill the first guy, hoping it would be like it was when Johnny watched me, or Wallace. But again . . . it did almost nothing for me. The pain came roaring back almost immediately."

He took a deep breath, then continued.

"The last three kills, without a willing partner, gave me a fraction— a tiny *fraction*—of the relief I need. Like I was dying of thirst but able to take only a sip of water. I need someone to do this with. I want that someone to be you." He sighed. "I didn't ask for this, Jason. It wasn't something I planned. Everything had been going along just fine. But then we took you and . . ." He trailed off, shaking his head. "I know you have it in you, Jason. I can see it."

"Did you ever consider that the reason you think you see this . . . *whatever* in me is because you think your brother had it, and I supposedly look so much like him?"

Cobb sighed as though he were trying to explain a simple math problem to a child who just wasn't getting it.

"You're obviously not sold on the idea yet," he said. "It's a lot to take in. I get that. So here's what I propose: We do it to one person together. Just one. Like a test. And you'll see what I mean about it. I think a part of you, something deep inside that you don't realize is there, will find it interesting. Even enjoyable. Like Wallace did. And Johnny. And pretty soon, I think you'll get hooked. I swear to God, Jason. I really do."

"I'll say it again: You're completely insane."

"Probably. But that doesn't make me wrong. And you never know until you try."

"I'm not going to kill an innocent person."

Cobb nodded. "I thought you might say that. So I have one more argument to make. Remember this: I'm not gonna stop killing. I may not enjoy it as much by myself, but I'm not gonna stop. Eventually I'll find someone to do it with me. But until I do, I'm definitely gonna keep killing on my own. And if I'm gonna do it anyway, it's not like your being involved would add to the number of murders in the world. I'm not even asking you to help. I don't need you to lift a finger. Just be there with me. Watch me. See what you think. If I'm wrong about you, if you don't have the interest after giving it a try, we'll go our separate ways. We both keep the secrets we'll share. Live and let live."

"Tell that to your victims."

Cobb chuckled. "Good one. At least think about it."

"No."

"I'm disappointed."

"You'll live," Jason said, wondering if that was true for him, too.

Cobb shook his head sadly. He sighed. "Guess we're done here, then."

He walked around behind Jason's chair, knelt down, and untied his hands. As soon as they were free, Jason tugged at the knots at his ankles until his legs were loose.

"So that's it, Cobb? You'll leave the house, leave my life, and leave us the hell alone?"

"If that's what you really want . . . which I don't think you do, down in your darkest places."

"Trust me. That's what I want."

Cobb frowned. "Okay then. But remember what I said about going to the police. I know how much you love your family. I'm sure you don't want to do anything to put them at risk for the kinds of things I would do to them. And I'm equally sure you don't want to go to prison."

"I don't."

"Okay then." He started for the stairs. "Seriously, I'll show you how to fix the damage I did to the furnace and water heater. Won't take a minute."

"I'll call another plumber."

Cobb shrugged. "You understand why I'm letting you live, don't you?"

Jason said nothing.

"It's because I still have hope for you. Maybe you just need some time. You'll think about it. You say you won't—you probably even truly believe you won't—but you will. I'm sure of it. Just like I was sure about Wallace. When you're ready, you know how to reach me."

"Just get the hell out, will you? And don't you speak to my wife or son on your way."

Cobb turned and climbed up the stairs. Jason followed him to the front door and closed it behind him, then locked it. He went into the living room, where his family was watching an animated show about talking trains. He wanted to grab his wife and son and hug them fiercely, but Sophie wouldn't want that. She wouldn't understand. So he held Max as tight as he could. After allowing the hug to go on for a long moment, the boy said, "Daddy, I can't see the TV."

Jason pulled away.

"Where's your friend?" Max asked. "He promised to say goodbye."

"He had to go."

"It's not nice to break a promise."

"He's not that nice a guy."

He felt Sophie watching him.

"Everything all right?" she asked.

"I want you to stay away from Ian Cobb, okay?"

"What happened downstairs?"

"Nothing. Promise me you'll stay away from him. That you won't let him in the house."

"Is it about the money? Didn't you offer to give it back to him?"

"That's not what he wanted."

"Then what—"

"Please, Sophie," he said sharply, but this time she didn't seem to take offense. "Please just do what I ask."

She regarded him for a moment. "What about the furnace and the hot-water heater?"

"I'll find someone else to fix it. I'll make some calls."

She frowned slightly but nodded. He stood to leave.

"Are you going to stay away from him, too?" she asked.

"That's my plan."

It wasn't much of a plan, though, and he knew it.

# CHAPTER THIRTY-SIX

For nearly four hours, Jason had been sitting in his Camry in the shade of a huge oak, three doors down from Sophie's house, watching and waiting. No sign of Cobb. Maybe there wouldn't be. Maybe, despite being a serial killer, the guy was as good as his word when he had promised to stay away from Jason's family. The problem was, there was no way to know for sure. So Jason began a stakeout during which he had nothing to do but think, which he did while keeping his eyes glued to his family's house.

The last thing he wanted to do was tell Sophie the truth. That he didn't stop Crackerjack. That he wasn't a hero. That all of the newfound hope they had for the future—most important, for Max's future—was in jeopardy.

He didn't want to tell her any of that. But the more he thought about it, the more he realized that he had no choice. It would be dangerous not to. So he fired up the Camry and drove down the block.

When Sophie opened her front door, he said, "We have to talk."

He slipped past her wheelchair and was heading into the living room when he saw Janice walking out of the kitchen.

"I need some time alone with Sophie, please," he said.

"It's my house, Jason, and if I want—"

"Actually, it's *my* house. Mine and Sophie's. We allow you to live here. So if I want some time alone with my wife, you're going to give it to me." She stared at him wide-eyed. "Please take Max to his room. We'll let you know when we're finished." She said nothing. "Please, Janice," he said as he turned away. "Just do it."

In the living room, Max was sitting on the sofa with a Curious George book in his lap. Jason sat beside him as Sophie rolled herself to a stop a few feet away.

"Hey there, Max," Jason said, "you curious little monkey. Do me a favor, will you?"

"Sure, Daddy."

"Go down to your room and spend a little time with Grandma. I think she's feeling lonely today."

"If she's the one who's lonely, how come that's a favor for you?"

Jason smiled. "Good question. You're not only a curious monkey, you're a smart one. I don't have a good answer for you. But would you do it anyway?"

"Sure."

He hopped off the sofa and left the room. Jason sat down in his place.

"What's going on, Jason?"

He found it hard to begin.

"Whatever it is you want to say, Jason, just say it."

"This isn't something I *want* to say. Believe me. You have no idea how badly I don't want to say it."

He told her almost everything: The little he truly remembered of his time in Wallace Barton's stable. The things he embellished in his television interview. The fact that Ian Cobb confessed a few hours ago, in the basement of this very house, to being Crackerjack. That Cobb had been partners with Barton. That he felt some strange connection to Jason that made him spare his life. That he felt a psychotic need to kill with a partner . . . and with Barton dead, he wanted Jason to fill that role. And that he'd planted incriminating evidence in Jason's apartment and building—indisputable evidence covered with Jason's fingerprints and the DNA of Crackerjack's victims to make sure he didn't go to the police.

As he spoke, Sophie's eyes grew wider and wider. Her mouth fell open. When he'd said all he had planned to say, she stared at him for a long moment, then asked very quietly, "Why would he think you would . . . join him?"

He looked away. He'd left that part out—that Cobb claimed to have seen . . . *something* in him.

"Because he's crazy."

He could feel Sophie's eyes on him. "And?" she asked.

"And what?" he replied, though he knew what she was after. "Was I interested? Was I tempted to take him up on it? Are you serious?"

She didn't answer. Instead, she looked hard into his eyes. After a moment, he turned away again. "Damn it, Sophie. Not this again. No. I wasn't the least bit tempted."

She was quiet for a few seconds. "Okay, so what did the police say?"

"I haven't called them."

"But you're going to, right?"

"He said he'd hurt you if I do. You and Max." He paused. "And besides, he'd just flip it around on me. Tell them that I'm the one Barton worked with, that I threatened him, saying that I'd kill him if he went to the police. And he's the one with the broken bones, remember? While I'm apparently the one with trophies from Crackerjack's victims hidden all over my apartment building. So not only would I put you in danger, but I'd throw suspicion on myself. Given all the circumstances, I just don't see how they'd believe me over him. My coming forward would both put you and Max in danger *and* probably land me in jail. What it *wouldn't* do is stop Ian Cobb."

"Then find the evidence he planted at your place first."

"That's what I plan to do as soon as I leave here, but how can I be sure I'll find it all? He says he put it in places I'd never suspect. And if he implicates me, all it would take is one thing I missed with my fingerprints and a victim's DNA on it to sink me."

"But if you don't call the police, he'll just keep doing . . . what he does, won't he?"

He decided not to tell her that Cobb had already killed three men since yesterday morning.

"I have to figure out a way to keep that from happening."

She looked at him, frowning. "How you are going to do that?"

He shrugged.

"You're not thinking about . . ."

"I don't know what I'm thinking."

"Killing him?" she asked. "Could you even *do* something like that? Haven't you been telling me for two years . . ." She shook her head. "You can't do that, Jason. It's dangerous and . . . you just shouldn't do anything like that. I'm not sure how I'd feel if you did it . . . if you actually *could* do it. You understand what I'm saying, right?"

He understood.

"I don't want you to open that door, Jason. There must be another way."

"There's no door, Sophie. I never wanted—" He shook his head, frustrated. "I don't *want* to kill anyone. I never have and I never will. Not even someone like Ian Cobb. I wish you'd just believe me."

She regarded him a moment longer. He couldn't tell what she was thinking. She obviously *wanted* to believe him.

"So what can you do, then?" she asked.

"I don't know yet. But hey, I write mysteries and crime novels—at least I used to. I should be able to come up with something."

They fell silent, lost in their own thoughts. He wondered if perhaps he shouldn't have reminded her that he was a crime writer. She was no doubt still troubled by that, still wondering about the inspiration for some of the more disturbing ideas that found their way into his books. And if he were being completely honest with himself, there had been moments since she first expressed her concern two years ago when he wondered that, too. Maybe it was simply because she had put the idea into his head . . . but were his black thoughts of murder and torture—the twisted actions of the killers and psychopaths he imagined—nothing more than grist for the story mill? Or could they be his own dark fantasies?

"Is it the money?" she finally asked. "Is that why you don't want to call the police? Because of the book deal and movie deal and—"

"No," he said firmly, though he wasn't being completely honest. He truly believed everything he'd said about why he couldn't go to the police—how it would put Max and her in danger *and* probably land him in prison, perhaps for the rest of his life. And while he rotted away behind bars, Cobb would be free to do whatever he wanted, go wherever he wanted, and start all over again . . . maybe in some new locale, with a new serial-killer persona, one to whom the media would give a shiny new nickname. But all of that aside, he had to admit that he didn't want to reveal to the world what he knew. He didn't want to lose everything they were now being offered. And though a part of him certainly wanted the book deal and the movie deal and a customized van for Sophie . . . most of all—and here he was confident he was being totally honest with himself—most of all he wanted to see Max get the expensive drug he needed to treat his blood disease. It meant more than anything, *anything*, to Jason.

"It's not the money, Sophie. And it's not my career. It's because of Max . . . and you."

"I wouldn't want you to take risks for me, but Max . . ."

"I know."

"But Jason, if Cobb kills again . . ."

She didn't complete the thought. She didn't have to.

"It will be on my head. I realize that. I have to make sure it doesn't happen."

"I'm scared," she said.

"Me, too." And he was, but panicking wouldn't help matters. "I won't let him hurt you, though. I promise."

She looked into his eyes, then nodded.

"To keep you safe, I need you and Max to slip out of town for a little while."

"How long?"

He shrugged.

"What about my mother?"

"She can go, too."

"She'd never agree. She'd want to call the police."

"If she does, they'd probably end up arresting me instead of Cobb." Sophie said nothing. "Which probably wouldn't trouble her a great deal, I suppose," he added. "It's probably better if she stays here. If Cobb drives by the house now and then, we don't want him to think nobody's home. It might alert him that something's up."

"You want to her to stay here? In danger?"

"I really don't think she's in any danger."

"Why not?"

He hesitated. "He probably wouldn't think that hurting her would . . . affect me enough." She frowned at him. "I think he could tell I'm not her biggest fan. But seriously, he wouldn't go after her. If he's going to try to hurt me, he'd do it through those I love the most. That's you and Max."

She thought for a moment, then nodded. A few minutes later she called her friend Geri, who lived in the small, picturesque town of Woodstock, Vermont. The two had met in college, become close, and when Sophie said she and Max needed to get away for a few days, Geri didn't hesitate to invite them to stay with her. She was a little curious as to the reason and voiced her suspicion that it had to do with Jason, and

Sophie let her think that she might be right. Given their separation, it was both plausible and easier that way.

Within a half hour they had packed suitcases for Sophie and Max and explained to Janice that Jason was using some of his newly acquired wealth to send her and Max to a fancy resort in New Hampshire for a few days.

Outside in front of the house, Jason scanned the street in both directions, looking for Cobb's white van. As he knew from when he'd arrived that morning, it bore the words COBB & SONS PLUMBING in bright red on its sides, with the first letter of SONS designed to look like a length of pipe in the shape of an *S*. It would have been easy to spot on this residential street. At the moment, it was nowhere in sight.

He hurried back into the house, then returned to the car with the two suitcases, which he stowed on one side of the back seat. The other side was for Max. The trunk would be for Sophie's wheelchair. When he turned toward the house again, Max was pushing Sophie down the ramp, though she was doing most of the work. He was the only one she allowed to push her anywhere. When they reached the car, he hopped into the back with his Curious George book and his favorite stuffed animal, a ragged black cat named Boo, while Jason helped Sophie make the transfer into the front passenger seat.

The trip took a little more than two and a half hours. The drive was pretty and the way through Woodstock was especially lovely. It was a beautiful little town, and Jason found himself wishing they were a real family again, heading for a bed-and-breakfast and some quality time together.

Geri's house was on the far side of town. She welcomed Sophie and Max warmly and regarded Jason curiously, maybe a little suspiciously, but without evident animosity. He knew she would grill Sophie later, and Sophie would tell the story they had concocted about needing some distance from her mother for a little while.

"I'm sorry I don't have a ramp," Geri said. "Once we get you inside, I'm afraid you'll be trapped in there until you leave."

"That's okay with me, as long as you don't mind."

Geri, who was recently divorced, said she was happy to have the company. She'd even taken a few vacation days from work to spend with her guests.

Sophie wheeled herself to the bottom of the porch stairs. There, she let Jason lift her from her chair. To ease his burden, she put an arm around his neck. It was the most physical contact they'd had since the accident. He hated the circumstances, but he had to admit that he liked the feeling of her in his arms.

He stood inside the foyer, cradling his wife and waiting for Geri to carry the wheelchair into the house. She placed it down, opened it, and Jason set his wife gently into the chair.

"Thank you," she said and wheeled off behind her friend, who led them into a living room.

"I have a guest room on the first floor here that will be perfect for you," Geri said. "Max can camp in there with you in a sleeping bag, or he can have his own room upstairs."

"I wanna camp with Mommy."

"Sleeping bag it is, then. But bedtime's not for hours, right, Max?"

"Right."

"Your mom says you like puzzles."

"I do!"

With a quick glance at Sophie, she said, "Well, I think we have a few in the other room. Let's go look for them."

She held out her hand. Max looked to his parents. Jason smiled, leaned down, and kissed the boy on top of his head.

"I love you, Max. I'll come get you and Mommy in a few days, okay? Now go with Geri and find the best puzzle in the house."

"I will!"

He took Geri's hand and Jason blinked away the beginnings of a tear as he watched his son walk away. He sensed Sophie looking at him and met her eyes.

"Have you decided yet what you're going to do to get out of this?" she asked.

"Not yet."

"You won't consider going to the police?"

"Not unless I absolutely have to. I'm hoping I'll think of something else instead."

"I'm worried, Jason."

"You and Max will be fine here."

"I'm worried for you. Be careful."

"I will."

"I mean it."

"I know you do."

"I want you to call so we know you're safe."

He nodded, then stood there for a moment, uncertain exactly how to make his exit. She made the decision for him by taking his hand, pulling him gently down toward her. When their faces were close, she tilted his face down and kissed him on the forehead.

He smiled slightly and took a last glance around the living room. His family seemed fine here but he was nonetheless loath to leave them. It couldn't be helped, though. There was nothing he could do about Ian Cobb from here. Whatever it was he was going to do, it had to be done back home.

Hopefully before Cobb killed again.

# CHAPTER THIRTY-SEVEN

As always, Carolyn appeared in the kitchen within mere seconds of Cobb's arrival home, almost as if she had teleported from upstairs. He didn't care. If she wanted to put the day with his father behind her and get on with her night, that was fine with him. He needed to talk to someone but it couldn't be her, so the sooner she was gone, the better. And with Wallace Barton dead and Jason Swike not yet interested in listening to his proposals, Ian was left with his vegetable of a father for conversation.

As soon as the door closed behind Carolyn, he thumped up the stairs, entered his father's room, and stalked over to the ventilator in the corner. His fingers stabbed at the machine's controls, completely disabling the alarm designed to sound when the patient ceases breathing.

"Hope you're feeling talkative tonight, Dad. We've got a lot to discuss."

No answer but the *whoosh, whir, click, whoosh* of the machine breathing for Arthur Cobb.

Ian dropped into the chair by the bed. His father stared sightlessly at the ceiling. Something white encrusted the corners of his mouth.

"Hector and Alan screwed up today," he said. "Installed the wrong pipes on a sauna job. Not up to code. I had to go and straighten things out. Lost us most of a day. I'll have to eat that cost, of course. God forbid I dock them for it, even though they should have known better."

He sighed, shaking his head. That wasn't what he really wanted to talk about.

"I killed three guys since I saw you last," he said. "Bludgeoned one, broke one guy's neck, and strangled the last one. And none of them did me any good. Can you believe it?"

He took the blue, ribbed intake tube leading from his father's tracheal tube to the ventilator and gave it a sharp twist. A moment later, the old man started to wheeze. After several seconds, Ian allowed the air to flow again.

"Don't lecture me," he said. "I had to do it. I had to see how it would be to kill by myself. And when that didn't work, I needed to see if it would help if someone watched me even though . . . he didn't want to. And it wasn't the same. It gave me no relief at all."

And he needed some of that relief now. It was overdue.

Another twist of the tube, more rusty wheezing from his father before Ian allowed the air to flow again.

"That's a fair question. The reason I let Wallace be killed even though I don't want to do this alone was that he wanted us to kill Jason . . . and I didn't want that."

Twist . . . *wheeeeeeze* . . .

"It's hard to explain, Dad, but ever since I took Jason, I haven't been able to stop thinking about him. If you met him, you'd see how much like Johnny he is. If I'd killed him, it would have felt like . . . killing Johnny. Like having him die all over again. His body was totally broken in the crash, Dad, remember? And remember all the bones of his that Uncle Joe broke when he was little? You must remember *that*. Well, the last thing I'd want to do is break Johnny's bones myself . . . kill him myself."

Twist . . . *wheeeeeeze* . . .

"Yes, I'm hurting. I'm almost always hurting. You know that. And it's getting bad now. This thing inside me is awake again, and it's angry. I know you don't believe in it, that you think I'm crazy, but you're not the one it's stabbing and burning and chewing up from the inside."

Twist . . . *wheeeeeeze* . . .

"Jason asked me the same thing and I'll tell you what I told him: I won't kill myself because I don't want to die. It's as simple as that."

Twist . . . *wheeeeeeze* . . .

"Now *that's* an excellent question. And yes, I do have a plan."

He told his father about his discussion with Jason, how he'd invited him to kill with him.

*Twist . . . wheeeeeeze . . . wheeeeeeze . . . wheeeeeeze . . .*

"Whoa, slow down. I know it was a bit risky. And he said no, of course. But he'll come around. You know how I know? The same way I knew that Wallace would join me. And I was right about him, wasn't I?"

Ian knew how strange it would sound to other people, but the pain inside him—the living pain that had taken up residence in his mind and body—recognized kindred spirits. Johnny had told him the same thing once, long ago. He'd said it was the reason he knew Ian would hurt people if he asked. His Inside Dark had told him so. It could see deep into Ian and knew that in the darkest corners of his mind, he wondered what it would be like to do bad things to people. And he'd been right. Johnny asked and Ian agreed. And when that black, shadowy thing later crept into Ian and began to torture him, and threatened to keep torturing him unless he tortured others, and whispered that Wallace Barton was secretly eager to be a part of what Ian did . . . Ian listened. And when he asked Wallace, the man didn't even hesitate.

And in the stable, when that same voice told Ian that Jason was a kindred spirit, too, Ian believed without a doubt. But Jason was resistant. So Ian was giving him time to come around.

Twist . . . *wheeeeeeze* . . .

"I haven't given that much thought yet. If he doesn't, I guess I'll have to do something about it. I'd rather not hurt his wife or son. You know how I feel about hurting women, Dad, and his little boy, Max . . . well, he's like Stevie was, so I don't want to hurt him, either. But I might *have* to hurt one of them, maybe both, if I'm going to get Jason to give my proposal some serious consideration. We'll see."

Twist . . . *wheeeeeeze* . . .

"Well, I guess if that doesn't work, I'll have to kill Jason after all. I don't want to—he reminds me so much of Johnny . . . I swear to God, Dad, you wouldn't believe it. But if he doesn't want to be my partner, that won't matter. I'll have no choice. He'll have to go."

Twist . . . *wheeeeeeze* . . .

"Ah, why the hell do you keep asking me the same questions when I give you the same answers every time? I keep telling you—I don't know if I'd be the way I am if you hadn't gotten drunk and crashed the car with Mom and Stevie in it. Or if you hadn't turned the other way every time Johnny came home from Uncle Joe's house with a broken bone or a fresh set of bruises."

Many times Ian had overheard his mother begging his father to confront Uncle Joe about it, but Arthur Cobb would only say that he didn't want to get his brother in trouble. And besides, he was a cop. No one would believe it. So he never said a word about what that bastard was doing to Johnny, to Arthur's own son.

"But I'll tell you what . . . if it wasn't for the things you did, or the things you should have done, I *probably* wouldn't be the way I am. So does that make you responsible for all the people I've killed? Hmmm . . . maybe it does. So how does that make you feel, you son of a bitch?"

He sat and listened to his father breathing through the machine. *Whoosh, whir, click, whoosh.*

"Suddenly not very chatty, are you? You make me sick."

He walked over to the ventilator and as he was resetting its alarm, his phone rang. Cobb recognized the number of his father's primary physician.

"Yes, Dr. Howe?"

"Good evening, Ian. Sorry to call so late. I just finished rounds and—"

"No problem."

"First of all, how are you? We haven't spoken since you—"

"I'm fine, Doctor. What's going on?" he asked, though he had a suspicion about the reason for the call.

"I'm glad you're okay. I watched the news, of course. It must have been . . ." He trailed off. "Anyway, I'm glad you're all right."

"What can I do for you?"

"Well, it's been a while since I've raised this subject . . ."

"Good, because I'm still not interested."

"Your father's condition—"

"I know."

"His situation isn't going to—"

"I know that, too."

"It wasn't that long ago that he went into cardiac arrest, if you'll recall. He would have passed away in relative peace if we'd had a DNR order in place. But because you didn't, Carolyn was able to resuscitate him and—"

"Well, it's a good thing I haven't signed a Do Not Resuscitate order then."

Howe's sigh was a bit overly dramatic, in Cobb's opinion.

"Ian, when I was last there, your father looked like he had lost some weight. I'm not sure he's getting—"

"Is he suffering?" Cobb asked, knowing he'd get the same frustrating answer as always.

"I don't know."

*Just once, can't you tell me that he is suffering? And horribly?*

"We're doing everything we can for him, aren't we, Doctor?" Ian asked. "We give him medicine and nutrients. We watch for infections and pneumonia. We adjust his position to prevent blood clots and cut down on bedsores, and when he gets sores anyway, we treat them. He gets massage and light physical therapy. I can't imagine what else we could be doing for him. He's getting the best care money can buy, isn't he?"

After another sigh, followed by a long pause, Dr. Howe said, "Ian, let me put it this way . . . would you want to live the way your father's living?"

"I'm not my father."

"He could survive for several more years like this, for God's sake. *Years.*"

"Terrific."

Still another exaggerated sigh. "If he were my own loved one, I would—"

"But he's not. He's my father, not yours. You make the decisions about his medical care, Dr. Howe. How to keep him alive. But whether we let him die? That's my call. And I say he lives. For as long as medical science and the expertise of you and the nurses I pay good money for make possible. I want him to outlive us all."

He ended the call quickly so he wouldn't have to listen to another of the man's theatrical sighs.

"We may have to find you a new doctor, Dad. This one's getting pushy."

*Whoosh, whir, click, whoosh.*

"You know what? I'm getting that creative feeling again. It's been a few days, hasn't it? I'll be right back."

He left the room, grabbed what he needed from the top shelf of the hall closet, and returned to his father's bedside.

"Even if I never paint another victim's face," he said as he set up his paints and brushes on his father's nightstand, "it would be a shame to let my talent go to waste. Besides, I think it might be therapeutic for me. If you'd rather I didn't, though, just say the word."

He waited through a long moment of silence but for the sound of machine-assisted breathing.

"Fantastic. So what'll it be tonight? A clown? Wait, I made you a clown last week. No . . . that was the week before. You were a puppy last week. What are you feeling like tonight? Oh, I know. This is perfect. How about a zombie?"

He opened a jar of light moss-green paint, picked up his largest brush, and got to work. Fifteen minutes later the old man looked far more like one of the undead than Arthur Cobb. *How appropriate,* Ian thought. He reminded himself to get up a little earlier in the morning to scrub his father's face clean, as always. He wondered, as he often did, how Carolyn or Rose would react if she showed up for her shift and found him with his face transformed by one of Ian's masterpieces.

"I honestly hope you can hear and understand everything I say," he said as he gathered up his paints and brushes. "That you've heard me talk about every man I've ever tortured and killed. And that you think it's all your fault. And Dad, I hope you live a hell of a long time with that belief. Pleasant dreams."

# CHAPTER THIRTY-EIGHT

Jason's apartment was trashed. Drawers open with their contents dumped onto desktops and counters. Sofa cushions on the floor. Closets emptied, the items he kept in them scattered across the carpet. Grates covering air vents had been removed and propped against the walls. His mattress lay half-on, half-off the bed.

He had spent most of the night tearing the place apart looking for evidence Cobb might have planted.

In his nightstand drawer, beside a watch that had belonged to his father, he'd found another watch, one he didn't recognize. He'd used a tissue to pick it up and put it in a plastic grocery bag.

On a closet shelf, in the middle of a stack of several shirts, was a blue golf shirt, neatly folded but without the crisp, clean feel and smell of an unworn garment. Jason couldn't remember if he owned a shirt like that. He might have but he wasn't sure. He also couldn't be certain if that was one of *his* hairs he saw near the collar. It might have been . . . but the hair looked like it might have been pure blond, lacking Jason's strawberry tint. The shirt went into the grocery bag with the watch.

Over the course of the rest of the night, Jason found a pair of dress shoes he didn't remember ever wearing and that appeared to be half a size too small for him. In his desk he discovered a pair of metal-framed eyeglasses even though he didn't wear glasses—and a brown speck on one of the lenses looked suspiciously like dried blood. In a drawer in the bathroom was a black plastic comb with several strands of long dark hair, just chock-full of DNA, snarled in its teeth. Hanging on a hook in the closet near the front door was a New York Jets baseball cap. Jason hated the Jets. Behind a grate in an air duct he found a man's wedding ring. Inside, the inscription read *Forever . . . Margaret.*

He consulted his watch. It was 6:45 a.m. With very few breaks, he'd searched his apartment for more than nine hours and found eight suspicious items, some he was pretty sure didn't belong to him and others that definitely didn't. What *hadn't* he found, though? Where hadn't he looked? And what items had he seen but simply not recognized as being suspect?

Cobb had mentioned planting face paints and brushes and even a book on the art of face painting, but Jason hadn't found those things. Had Cobb lied about them, or were they there somewhere and Jason had simply missed them? Had he missed other things as well?

He hadn't even started looking elsewhere in the building or on the grounds outside. He hadn't searched his car. There were countless places Cobb could have stashed items that could land Jason in prison for the remainder of his days.

He pulled out his cell phone and dialed a number.

Twenty minutes later, the door buzzer sounded. Jason pushed the "Talk" button.

"Yeah?"

Ben's voice came from the speaker. "I'm here."

Jason buzzed him in, then unlocked the front door and left it ajar. A few moments later, Ben stood in the doorway, his eyes surveying the wreckage of the apartment.

"Time to fire your maid," he said. His words and tone were glib but Jason could see that he was rattled by what he saw. "Are you all right?"

"You made good time. You said you were still dripping wet from your shower when I called."

"Your friend calls and says his life may be over, you tend not to dawdle. I'm not even wearing underwear. What happened here? Who did this?"

"I did."

"Okay, I'll bite. Why?"

"Because I'm freaking out, that's why. Things are really screwed up, Ben. And I don't know what the hell to do."

"Slow down. What's going on? Give me the short version."

"The short version is that I was right. Ian Cobb actually *is* Crackerjack. And he planted evidence here implicating me of being Crackerjack instead."

He blew out a shaky breath. Then another.

"Hmm," Ben said. "How about giving me the long version now."

It took several minutes, with numerous interruptions, but Jason finally got nearly all the story out. Essentially the same story he'd told to Sophie, only this time he didn't omit the fact that Cobb had already killed three more men since he and Jason "escaped" from captivity together.

When he was finished, Ben looked stunned.

"Things like this don't happen to people like us, Jason. In your books, they do. But not in the real world."

"No shit. What do I do, Ben? Tell me. What do I do?"

"Give me a minute. I'm still processing. You had a whole day with it, but you dropped it on me two minutes ago. Let me try to get my head around it." He thought for a long moment, then said, "Nope. Can't get my head around it. You're saying that because you remind him of his brother, because of these things he thinks you have in common, he wants you to become his partner? He'll thinks you agree to kill people with him?"

Jason hesitated. "He says he sees something in me." He didn't want to elaborate on that, didn't even want to think about it himself, so he quickly added, "He's totally nuts."

"As your lawyer, I have to advise you to call the police right away."

"You're not my lawyer."

"I'm *a* lawyer."

"But you're not my lawyer. You're not even a criminal lawyer. You do contracts."

"I took criminal courses in law school, though, and did an internship in the DA's office before my third year. And I think you should call the police."

"Would *you* do that? If you weren't sure you'd found all of the evidence that could implicate you as a serial killer?"

That shut Ben up.

"As a lawyer," Jason said, "what do you think of the evidence against me?"

Ben looked thoughtful but said nothing. Jason nodded as if his friend's silence supported his own position.

"And I haven't even mentioned that the lead detective on the case thinks I'm guilty of something."

"Of what?"

"I have no idea, but he keeps asking me questions and never seems satisfied with my answers."

"Yeah, he asked me a lot of questions about you, too."

"He definitely thinks I've been hiding something."

"Which you have."

"Exactly. But if I go to the cops with what I know, Detective Briggs will jump all over me. He's *dying* to find something on me. If he gets a whiff of the slightest shred of evidence against me, I'm history. It won't matter that I came forward and implicated Cobb. Briggs will focus on me."

"You don't know that. If you tell him that Cobb—"

"You mean the guy with the bones broken and the painted face?"

Ben opened his mouth but closed it again without saying a word.

"So let me ask you again, Ben. With everything you now know, if you were in my place, would *you* go to the police?"

Ben shook his head. "No, but I have to tell you that you should."

"So what *would* you do in my place? Seriously. I need to know what the hell to do. Because I'm going crazy here."

"Sophie and Max are safe where they are?"

"I think so. I really do."

Ben frowned, thinking. "You have to get Cobb out of the picture somehow."

"Obviously. But how?"

"I see only two options. The first is you get him arrested for something . . . something other than being a serial killer, I guess."

"Frame him for theft, something like that? That's a short-term fix at best. Even if he's convicted of whatever it is, he'll be out in two years and really pissed off. I need him out of my life for a lot longer than that."

"Okay, I agree. Try to stay calm, Jason. So . . . and I'm just spit-balling here . . . but there's only one other option I can see."

"Which is?"

"You know what it is."

Jason shook his head. "No, no, no, no, no. That's a terrible option."

"Shit, Jason, I didn't say it was a good option, just that it was the only other one I can think of if you want to get rid of Cobb. What other choice do you have?"

Jason ran his hands through his hair. He couldn't think clearly. Someone started pounding on the door and for a terrifying moment he thought it must be Ian Cobb, but then Jason realized that the sound was the blood pounding in his head.

"It sucks," Ben went on, "but I don't see any other way for you to be sure he's out of your life for good. Out of your family's life."

"I wouldn't even know how to do something like that."

"Dumber guys than you are able to figure it out."

"And they get caught."

"You're smarter than they are."

Jason backed up a few steps until he was against a wall, then slid to the floor. His chin dropped to his chest. After a long moment, he said, "Sophie . . . wouldn't want me to do that."

"That's not a shock."

Jason looked up. "She has a good reason." Unconsciously, he touched the slight depression on his head.

He'd never told Ben about what Sophie thought she'd seen in him the night of the accident, and apparently a few times before—the darkness she feared was inside him. He desperately wanted her to be wrong about him, *needed* her to be . . . but since that night, he wasn't always certain. Had she truly seen something in his eyes that night? Was it the same thing that Ian Cobb believed he saw in him now? Did Detective Briggs see it, too? Was that why he seemed so suspicious of Jason? And if Jason could even bring himself to kill Cobb in cold blood, assuring himself that it was the only way to save lives . . . could he be certain that would be the end of it? That he wouldn't want . . . more?

With all his heart, he didn't want to be like Cobb. He'd never wanted to hurt anyone. He couldn't remember what he was thinking just before his accident, but he refused to believe he could have intentionally run anyone over with a car. And he hadn't wanted to kill Wallace Barton, but he'd had no choice. It was self-defense, and it all happened so fast. And the way he'd felt after . . . when he stared down at Barton's body, knowing that *he* had killed him—well, that feeling could be attributed to the adrenaline coursing through his body. Couldn't it?

*He wasn't like Ian Cobb.* He *couldn't* be . . . not if he harbored the smallest hope his wife might one day look at him the way she used to, or close to it anyway.

"I'm not going to kill a man in cold blood," he said to Ben as he rose to his feet. "Sophie wouldn't . . . *I* don't want to do that. I can't."

Ben looked at him closely for a moment, as if noticing something about him for the first time, something he thought he probably should have noticed before. Or maybe Jason was imagining that. Finally, quietly, Ben said, "Even if that man is going to kill other people, which you know for a fact he is? In fact, he already *has*. And if you don't stop him, he's going to kill God only knows how many more?"

Jason took a deep breath. "What if I decided to try that . . . and I failed?" *Or, what if I succeeded . . . and I like it?* He turned away from that thought. "If I fail," he went on, "he could kill me, then go after Sophie and Max. Or, God forbid, what if he killed them and left me *alive?*"

"You have to get him out of the picture, Jason."

"You're a lawyer. You can't talk like that."

"I know, but I'm right."

"I know. So let's come up with a way to do that short of my committing first-degree murder."

They continued straightening up the apartment while they thought. They stuffed things back in drawers and cabinets and closets, and moved the furniture back where it belonged, and did it all while barely saying a word. After half an hour, Ben said, "Man, can't you hire someone to do this?"

Jason looked up from the pile of books he was returning to their shelves, over at Ben, who was in the kitchen putting canned goods and cereal boxes back into cabinets.

"That might be a good idea, Ben. I'll hire someone."

"Don't sweat it. I'll help. I was just joking."

"I wasn't."

Ben met his eyes. "Oh. Oh . . . you're right. That might be a good idea. But how the hell—"

"It's time for you to leave, Ben."

"Would you even know where to begin—"

"See you, buddy."

"I can't just—"

"You're a lawyer. You can't be around me right now." Jason glanced around the apartment, which looked nearly like it had before he had gone through it like a tornado last night. "Thanks for your help here. I've got the rest."

"Jason . . ."

"We don't know if Ian Cobb knows who you are, but if he does, you could be in danger. So keep your distance for a while. I don't want to see you. We can talk every few days, as usual, but no more than that. We don't want it to seem like there's anything going on here, in case . . . the cops ever look into my phone records."

"For how long?"

"Until I take care of this." Ben shook his head but before he could protest, Jason added, "I know you want to help me, but this is the way it has to be."

They looked at each other for a moment before Ben said, "I thought *I* was the cool one."

"Believe me, I'm scared out of my mind."

"You don't seem it all of a sudden."

"Just trying to keep it together. There's too much at stake for me to lose it. Now, seriously, you have to get out of here."

Ben sighed, then nodded. "Be careful. Call me when you can. And don't forget, I'll be there if you need anything at all." At the door, he turned. "And Jason? When this is all over . . . I want to be the cool one again."

Jason smiled.

When Ben was gone, Jason found the number for several local home-security companies. It was early in the morning, just after the start of business hours, so he hoped he'd find one with available appointments that day. It wasn't until the fifth company that he found one willing to give him an appointment in less than a week. SecureHome said they could do an estimate first thing tomorrow morning and, if Jason wanted, do the installation that afternoon. According to online community message boards, it was far from the best alarm company in the area—which was probably the reason they had next-day availability—but Jason was in no position to be a picky shopper. With the appointment scheduled, he called Janice and told her to be home at eighty-thirty the following morning to meet the technician.

"Why do we need a burglar alarm all of a sudden?" she asked.

"You haven't heard about the burglaries in your neighborhood lately?"

"No."

"Three houses in the last two weeks."

"I hadn't heard."

"It's true. And I want Sophie and Max to be safe." If she noticed that he hadn't mentioned her, she didn't let on.

"I'd just like to see someone try to get into the house when I'm home," she said.

Jason almost wished for the same thing . . . almost.

"Just be home at nine, okay?"

He hung up, then began the next phase of his plan, such as it was. If he couldn't risk trying to kill Ian Cobb himself—if he didn't *want* to be the one to kill him, which he needed to believe—then it was time to find someone else to do it.

# CHAPTER THIRTY-NINE

Not everyone knew how to hire a hit man. And, Jason figured, the world was almost certainly a better place that way. But he knew.

A few years ago, before his career as an author dried up, he had toyed around with a contract-killer story. His research had led him down some dark and disturbing avenues. He ultimately learned that there are, on the web, decentralized networks of data relay points used by people who crave anonymity—professional assassins among them—to interact and advertise their services and wares. People communicate through encrypted e-mail, never meeting or talking with one another. The information bounces from relay point to relay point, many times over, until the trail is nearly impossible to follow. Found an assassin who seems to suit your needs? Use an encryption key to send the details, a picture of the target; the make and model and, if possible, the license plate of his or her car; anything you know about the target's daily routines; and whatever else is asked for. Payment is made in bitcoin, and most of the hit men offer to complete the job within a few weeks, possibly a few months, depending on the target.

Months wouldn't work for Jason. Every day Cobb was walking free was a day he might kill somebody else. Still, he had to try. Maybe he'd get lucky. Maybe he'd find a killer with a sudden hole in his schedule, or one who liked a challenge.

To find someone, he had to trust the encryption technology employed by the bad guys. And he had to hope that none of them was an undercover cop posing as a contract killer.

After perusing the advertisements of several people claiming to be professional killers, he settled on the three that seemed, based on nothing more than gut instinct, least likely to be cops and most likely to be able to do the job quickly. Two of them offered to kill an "average citizen" for $20,000 while the third charged $25,000. The killers each had premiums for murdering famous people, which Jason supposed Ian Cobb might be considered now. If one of them was interested in the job, Jason would let him decide to which category Cobb belonged. After Leonard Sanderson's generosity, he could afford it either way.

He drafted e-mail queries to each of the self-proclaimed assassins, with particular emphasis on the need for speed. Then, hoping that he wasn't making a huge mistake, and that the encryption keys would shield him from prosecution if things went sideways, he put his finger on the "Send" button and . . .

He paused. He stared at the screen for several minutes, thinking about the moral implications of what he was about to do, and about what Sophie would think of it. What he would think of himself.

He sent the first e-mail, then the other two.

Then he waited. He told himself that he'd had no choice, that he would actually be saving lives. He tried to believe himself. And for the most part, he did, but he couldn't completely silence the whispers of doubt that echoed through the most remote corners of his mind. If Ian Cobb, wherever he was, knew what Jason had just done, would a small part of him have approved? Would he have smiled in triumph?

All three responses came within four hours, forcing Jason to give the hit men points for promptness. The first had arrived in ninety minutes and read, "Six weeks minimum. If interested, let me know." The second had come forty minutes later and was nearly identical but had shaved the time estimate to three weeks. A little more than an hour later, the third e-mail arrived. It read, *Can't guarantee success in less than a month. Respond if I can be of service.*

Jason needed to find a different way to rid the world of Ian Cobb. It was either Cobb or God only knew how many innocent people . . . men unlucky enough to cross Cobb's path . . . and even perhaps Sophie and Max.

So if he couldn't hire a hit man online, and he still didn't want to consider the possibility of going after Cobb himself—which not only would be dangerous as hell but would force Jason to do something he had sworn he'd never want to do—then he had to find a hit man another way. In the movies, one of the characters always seems to know a shady guy who knows someone willing to kill someone for money. But Jason didn't know anyone like that. He was on his own.

He sat down at his computer, barely able to fathom that he had come to be in this situation. He nudged the mouse, bringing the computer screen back to life, and opened his Internet browser. He was a little concerned about the search history he would be creating, but he hoped that, if he ever had need to explain it, the fact that he was a crime writer would help.

After a minute of staring at the blank search box, an idea came to him. He looked for stories about suspected contract killers and murderers for hire in Massachusetts, as well as Connecticut and New Hampshire, which weren't far away. Even limiting his search to the past five years, there were quite a few. Various people had tried to hire someone to kill their spouses, their spouses' lovers, their bosses, law-enforcement officials, and witnesses in legal proceedings. Jason ignored the stories about the convictions of defendants; he wasn't interested in someone behind bars. Instead, he looked for acquittals.

After half an hour he had found only two relatively recent stories about defendants who were acquitted after having been charged with the murder or attempted murder of someone in exchange for money. From the articles, it looked to Jason like one of the defendants might actually have been innocent. The other guy, though, Ronald Wheeler—whose two trials had ended in hung juries before the government decided not to risk swinging and missing a third time—seemed guilty as hell to Jason. Without going into detail, the story implied that Wheeler had walked on legal technicalities. The unsuccessful prosecutor seemed to agree with Jason about the defendant's guilt, as he was quoted as calling the result "a travesty of justice." Then again, they all said that when they lost.

Jason looked at Wheeler's picture on the screen. He didn't look like a hit man—at least not what Jason imagined a hit man would look like. No steely gaze or emotionless eyes. He looked like a real-estate agent, or maybe an accountant. It turned out, according to the article, that Wheeler was a loan officer at a local bank. He was alleged to have agreed to kill the cheating wife of a man who, in reality, was an unmarried undercover cop. They had settled on a price of $12,000.

Jason decided he would try to find Ronald Wheeler. He knew the man had lived in Lowell at the time of his arrest, and in no time he found an address for him there. He looked online for more about Wheeler, but found only his Facebook page, which was sparse. A couple of photos of him, alone in each one. A few innocuous posts. Nothing about him being a contract killer, but Jason hadn't expected that. Nothing he had seen, either on Facebook or in any of the articles about Wheeler's arrest or his trial, indicated that the man was married, which would probably make things easier for Jason. A computer search gave him the phone number of the bank where he had worked. He called and asked for Wheeler, intending to hang up before the man could come on the line, but was told that no one by that name worked there, which wasn't surprising. Being charged with attempted murder for hire probably didn't make for good job security at a bank, or many other places, for that matter. It was quite possible that Mr. Wheeler had fallen on hard times after his acquittal, which might also make things a little easier for Jason.

He glanced at his watch. Nearly 2:00 p.m. In a little while, he'd leave his apartment, unsure when—or if—he would return. Before he could leave, though, there was something he needed to do. Because he preferred to write at his desk, he used his desktop computer most of the time and his laptop only when he needed to work elsewhere for some reason. He transferred his entire catalog of digital family photos, a few thousand in all, as well as his entire file of documents—completed manuscripts, partial manuscripts, barely begun manuscripts, files of research notes, letters to and from agents and editors—from the desktop to his laptop. The files didn't take long; he wasn't terribly prolific. When that was complete, he downloaded a destructive reformatting program that would make hundreds of passes across his desktop's hard drive, scrubbing it cleaner and cleaner with every pass. In a few hours, no digital trace of Jason's recent interest in hit men should exist on it.

While his computer was getting its lobotomy, he packed a bag with clothing, toiletries, his laptop, his phone charger, and anything he thought he might need for the next week. He didn't feel safe in his apartment. He would have arranged for a security system to be installed there, too, but he didn't plan on living there in the long term, nor did he plan on being there in the short term, in case Ian Cobb came knocking. He'd stay in a motel until everything had been taken care of.

And to begin getting everything taken care of, he would seek out Ronald Wheeler, killer for hire.

# CHAPTER FORTY

Outside his apartment, Jason looked for Ian Cobb's van. He didn't see it, but a few cars were parked on the street and Cobb could have been in any one of them. He decided to drive close to each and look inside. He walked half a block to where he'd parked his Camry, popped the trunk, and tossed in the bag of evidence Cobb had planted in his apartment, at least what he could find. He was about to get behind the wheel when a thought struck him: Could Cobb have planted a GPS tracker on his car? Research for books he never ended up writing had told Jason that such things weren't hard to get these days. Would Cobb even think to do so? Jason had no idea what was going on in that psycho's head. Because he couldn't afford not to be a little paranoid, he decided to check the places he knew to be the most common spots to hide a tracker on a vehicle.

As he was examining the car, his cell phone rang. It was Sophie.

"It's me," she said. "Everything okay?"

"So far. How are you?"

"Worried. About you."

Despite the terrible circumstances, that was nice to hear.

"How's Max?"

"He's fine. There's not a puzzle undone in the whole house." She paused. "Have you heard from Ian Cobb again?"

"No."

"Have you decided how to handle things there?"

"I'm working on it."

"I've been thinking . . . could you frame him for a crime? Don't hurt anybody or anything, but maybe a burglary or something. If you do it right, and don't get caught, he could go to jail and be out of our lives for a few years, at least. And he won't be able to do . . . what he likes to do to other people."

He said nothing, not wanting to tell her that he'd already rejected that idea for a variety of reasons.

"I know it would only be a temporary fix," she said, "but a lot of things can happen in a few years. I almost hate to say this, but maybe something would happen to him in prison and we wouldn't have to worry about him. I've read about more than one serial killer being killed in prison by another inmate."

"That's a really good idea, Soph. That might work."

He didn't like lying to her, but he liked it better than telling her the truth at the moment.

As they spoke, he continued his examination of the area under the Camry's hood. So far he'd seen nothing that looked suspicious to his admittedly untrained eye.

"It wouldn't be easy," she said. "You'd have to come up with a really good plan. But I figured, like you said, you being a crime writer, you'd be able to think of something."

"I bet I can. I'll start thinking as soon as we hang up."

Sophie said nothing for a moment. He wondered if she wasn't buying into his act.

"Can I talk to Max?" he asked.

For the next few minutes, he checked the rest of the car for a tracker while he listened to Max talk about every one of the puzzles he had assembled, some with Sophie's help, some with Geri's, some with help from them both, and one, he proudly proclaimed, without anyone else's help at all.

"I love you, Max. Can you put Mommy back on?"

"Love you, too. Here she is."

When Sophie was back on the line, he said, "I'll call in a day or two."

"Be careful, Jason. What you're doing is dangerous. That man is . . . he's . . ."

"I know what he is. And I'll be careful."

They ended the call and Jason closed the hood. He was opening his driver's door when he heard a voice behind him.

"I caught you."

He turned and saw a dark sedan pulling up behind him, Detective Briggs's head leaning out the open window.

"Caught me?"

"Looks like you're heading out somewhere," Briggs said. "I've got a few questions. It would have been annoying if I didn't catch you."

Jason thought he heard something in the way he said that. A message? Was Briggs trying to be clever? Or was Jason being paranoid?

"Got a second?" Briggs asked.

"Sure."

*I'm just on my way to try to hire a hit man, but it can wait a few minutes.*

# CHAPTER FORTY-ONE

To Briggs, Swike looked guilty. Of something. He wasn't sure what it was, but Swike had the look that Briggs had seen a thousand times. Something in his expression. Like he'd been caught doing . . . something.

He climbed out of his sedan and walked up to Swike, who was standing next to his car. He took his little notepad from his pocket, clicked a ballpoint pen, and leaned casually against the Camry.

"Sorry to slow you down," he said. "Hope you weren't on your way to do something important."

Swike was clearly trying to look just as casual as he leaned against the front quarter panel and folded his arms.

"Nothing that won't keep."

Briggs had really grown to dislike Jason Swike. Both Dusty Owens and Bonnie believed it was because Briggs had put so much time into the case without being able to make a dent in it while Swike had lucked into escaping and killing Wallace Barton, which left Briggs without any credit and Swike draped in glory. It didn't help, they said, that Swike seemed to be cashing in pretty big while Briggs was nearing retirement with modest savings and what could only be considered, at best, a decent pension.

And they weren't wrong. Briggs had been a fairly honest cop over his long career. He could almost—but not quite—count on his fingers the number of times he had taken a bribe or skimmed money recovered at a crime scene. What was the most he'd ever gotten illicitly at any one time? Ten thousand bucks? What did it all add up to over the course of thirty-six years? Less than seventy thousand? Eighty at the most? For all the hours he'd put in? The bad guys he'd put away? That was nothing.

Did he resent Jason Swike? Hell, yes.

But that didn't mean there wasn't something off about the guy, something wrong with his story. Did Briggs actually suspect that Swike was a killer? He wasn't sure. Was it conceivable, though? Sure. He had thumbed through Swike's novel, *The Drifter's Knife*, which he'd found in a library. Some pretty twisted stuff in there. Did it require the mind of a psychopath to dream up those ideas? Unlikely, but it probably couldn't hurt. And maybe worse than the idea that Swike might have killed because he was psychotic was a thought that had been teasing Briggs for a few days now: maybe Swike was completely sane but killed anyway . . . to sell books, to resuscitate a drowning career as a crime writer.

"I've been thinking about this case," Briggs said.

"I keep assuming, with Barton dead, that there isn't much of a case anymore."

"Oh, sure, the bad guy's done, no doubt. But we still have to make sure everything wraps up neatly. Make sure our questions are answered. You write crime stories. You know what I'm talking about."

Swike nodded and Briggs saw that look again.

"I was thinking about the timing of everything," Briggs said.

"Timing?"

"Yeah. See, our profile of Crackerjack told us that something probably set him off not long before the first murders. Something traumatic. It's like that with a lot of serial killers."

"A trigger."

"Bingo," he said. "See, I knew you understood these things. A trigger. And we just couldn't find anything in Barton's recent past that might have acted as a trigger. I was surprised about that. You look hard enough, you could probably find something like that for almost anyone. You get fired, your wife cheats on you, whatever. For instance," he added, "take you."

"Me?"

"Sure. If I wanted to look for a trigger in your life—just as an example—something that happened a couple of years ago, shortly before Crackerjack killed his first victims, the ones we found buried behind Barton's stable, I'd say that maybe it was the trauma of the car accident that left your wife paralyzed from the waist down. You know, then you guys separated and everything. That happened right around then, didn't it? A little over two years ago?"

Swike kept his eyes straight ahead. "It did."

"I thought so. See, that's the kind of thing that could make a man snap. That kind of thing could make a man do evil, you know?"

"Almost anything could make a man snap, I suppose."

"Sure, sure. I've seen it plenty of times over the years, believe me. Our profile also says Crackerjack was probably a loner."

"Like Wallace Barton."

"Like Barton, yeah," Briggs said. "Definite loner there. Like you, too, right? I mean, after you and your wife split and you moved out, you spent a lot of time by yourself, didn't you? Especially in that first year? Alone in your little apartment, writing books nobody was buying. At least that's what your agent said. And a few of your neighbors. Your friend Ben Britton said you guys saw a lot less of each other for almost a year after the accident and your separation. He even said that, for a while there, you were something of a loner. His word, if you can believe it, not mine. And that's what everyone seems to be telling me, including your ex-wife."

"My wife."

"What's that?"

"Sophie's not my ex. She's still my wife. We never got a divorce. And let me ask you something—are you doing this same song and dance for Ian Cobb? Because he escaped from Crackerjack, just like I did."

"Sure, but Jason? The guy got busted up. Broken arm. Broken ribs. And he had his face painted like a schoolkid at a county fair. You? You got away without a scratch."

"Five days with no food and barely any water? I wasn't exactly having a picnic in that stable."

Briggs nodded. "I'm not saying you were having fun. But while you were supposedly held for days—which hadn't been Crackerjack's MO up to that point, by the way—Cobb got the business the same day he was taken. So why the difference there? What made you so special that he wanted to keep you around for a while? Seems odd to me."

Swike laughed but he was forcing it. "Are you implying that Wallace Barton wasn't Crackerjack and that *I* was?"

"I'm not implying that Barton wasn't Crackerjack," Briggs said without addressing the second part of Swike's question.

Swike made a scoffing sound.

"Now that you bring it up, though," Briggs added, "there *was* talk about Crackerjack maybe being two people. I'm sure you heard it."

"Sounds ridiculous."

"Seems plausible to me."

Swike shook his head. "There's nothing here, Detective. You can keep digging but I can't imagine what you're looking for. And you can keep rattling my cage but I'm not hiding anything, and I don't know why you think I am."

"Did I rattle you?"

"Just my cage. Me personally, I'm fine."

"Glad to hear it. How's the book coming?"

"Making progress."

"I'll have to buy a copy when it comes out."

"I'll autograph it for you."

"That would be great. See you around," he said as he walked away, back toward his car. He was doing literally what Lieutenant McCuller wished he would do figuratively: just walk away. Close the case down. Box it all up. *It's over,* the lieutenant had said more than once now. *The good guys won. Let it go.* Dusty was saying the same thing. So was Bonnie. Soon Briggs might have to listen to them.

But not yet.

# CHAPTER FORTY-TWO

Jason watched Briggs drive off and hoped that he was truly gone and not simply waiting around the corner to tail him, given that Jason was on his way to the house of a suspected contract killer. As he drove, he kept an eye on the rearview mirror for Briggs's car. And for Cobb's white van, just in case. After a quick stop at the bank right before it closed, where he withdrew $7,000 that might be a little difficult to explain later, he headed for Lowell, Massachusetts, not far from the New Hampshire border. Late-afternoon rush hour had begun, so he knew it would be slow going.

It took almost an hour and a half to get there. Ten minutes later, he found the address where he hoped Ronald Wheeler still lived. Jason parked two houses down, facing the little two-story house. On the passenger seat were several bottles of water—Poland Springs, not Dasani—a few granola bars, and an empty plastic milk jug, in case the stakeout lasted too long. He looked at his watch: 6:40 p.m.

It was nearly eight o'clock when a Honda SUV that had seen far better days turned a little too quickly into the driveway and came to a stop a bit crookedly. Jason watched, anxious, as the driver's door opened. Ronald Wheeler—or someone who looked a hell of a lot like the guy in the news story on the Internet—stepped out and walked with slow, heavy steps to his front door. He took a moment longer than he probably should have to unlock it, and Jason figured he had stayed until the bitter end of happy hour somewhere. Jason gave him a few minutes to get settled, then stepped out of his car, leaving the money behind, and walked to the house. He took a deep breath and, with a disturbingly shaky finger, rang the doorbell.

His heart thundered. The man inside this house was quite possibly a murderer. At the very least, he had once wanted to be.

Footsteps thumped inside; then the door opened. Ronald Wheeler—it was definitely him—looked fifteen years older than he had in the picture Jason had seen, a photo that had been taken only two years ago.

"Yeah?" Wheeler said. Jason could smell the whisky.

He had decided that approaching Wheeler at home and surprising him was best. That way he wouldn't have to worry about the man trying to record the conversation, either to protect himself or perhaps to try to blackmail Jason later. He'd also decided on a direct approach.

"Mr. Wheeler, I'm here to offer you a job." He hoped the man didn't notice the tremor in his voice.

"I already have a job. Who the hell are you?"

Wheeler wore stained denim coveralls, so whatever job he was holding down now wasn't an office position like the one he'd occupied before his arrest. Maybe he didn't mind that—office work wasn't for everyone—but then again, maybe he didn't like it one bit.

"I'm going to just lay it all out for you, Mr. Wheeler, and I hope you'll give me a chance to finish, because you're going to want to close the door in my face pretty soon." Wheeler said nothing, merely frowned, so Jason continued. "First, you need to know that I'm not a cop, and I can prove that beyond a doubt. I swear to you. And I really do have a job offer. Good money, tax-free."

"Sounds too good to be true, Officer," Wheeler said.

"I'm really not a cop. You don't recognize me?"

"Should I?"

"A lot of people do lately. You have a computer, Mr. Wheeler?"

"Of course I do."

"Go inside and Google the name Jason Swike. You'll see who I am and know I'm not a cop. I'll wait here."

Wheeler shook his head, as though Jason were an idiot, and pulled a smartphone from his pocket. He opened a browser and searched for Jason's name. A picture of Jason's face popped up. Wheeler looked from his phone to Jason's face and back again.

"What the hell is this?"

"You believe me now that I'm not a cop?"

"I heard about you. I know what you did. Says here you're a writer."

"And not a cop, right?"

"What do you want from me?"

The time had come. Jason took a breath. "I need you to kill someone for me."

There. He'd said it. No turning back now. He waited for the door to slam. Wheeler squinted at him. Finally, he said, "Is this a joke? If so, it ain't funny. Not at all."

"No joke."

Wheeler looked him up and down and Jason tried to keep his hands from shaking.

"I can't figure this out," Wheeler said. "I can't see the angle."

"There isn't one."

Wheeler looked past Jason toward the street, perhaps looking for cops crouching behind shrubs. "Is this legit?"

"It is." After Wheeler stared at him for another long moment, Jason said, "Why haven't you slammed the door on me yet?"

"Because I don't know how you chose me in particular—I guess you read about my trial or something—but I can't for the life of me see why you'd be here if you didn't really want someone killed. I just can't see it. You're taking a hell of a risk, you being famous and all."

"I'm telling you the truth. And yeah, I read about your acquittal online and figured you might, just might, have some experience in what I'm looking to have done. If not, then I made a big mistake coming here. But if so . . . well, I thought maybe you could help me out. I also figured maybe you could use some money."

"I could turn you in."

"No offense, but who'd believe you?" he asked, dismayed at the tiny nervous crack in his voice. "You being an accused contract killer and me being famous and all?"

"Good point. So why are you here? I know what you say you want done, but why are you here, on *my* porch?"

"Because I'm desperate." It wasn't the best negotiating tactic but he didn't know what to do, where to turn, if Wheeler refused the job. "I need this done and I need it done soon. And I don't know any other way to make that happen."

Wheeler studied him for several long seconds. Jason could almost hear the gears grinding away in the man's head, the rusty wheels turning as he tried to see all the angles.

"I just don't see why the hell you'd be here if you weren't on the up and up about this."

"I told you, I am."

Wheeler frowned at him for a second or two. "Well, you might as well come on in. I don't do the kind of thing you're looking to do, of course, and those charges against me were BS, but if you want to come in for a little while, I won't stop you."

There seemed to be a disconnect between Wheeler's words and the look in his eyes, so Jason followed him into the house, hoping Wheeler couldn't hear the conga beat in his chest. Like its owner, the place seemed to have fallen on hard times. The top of a wooden coffee table rested on three legs with a stack of books in place of the fourth. Against one wall was an entertainment center where a thirty-six-inch television occupied a space big enough for a sixty-inch set. Wheeler had apparently been forced to downsize.

"Take off your clothes," Wheeler said.

"What?"

"Not that I have something to hide, or that we'll be talking about anything illegal, but I don't like talking to some people unless I know they're not wearing a wire."

"And I'm not big on stripping for strangers."

"Suit yourself. You know where the door is."

He turned away.

"Wait a second," Jason said. "How about just down to my underwear?"

"Seriously? You got a tiny prick or something? What's the big deal?"

Jason sighed and slipped off his shirt. When he was completely naked, Wheeler gathered up his clothes and carried them into a bathroom. He closed the door on them and then, with Jason standing there stark naked and self-conscious as hell, his hands over his private parts, they discussed the job.

"Ian Cobb?" Wheeler eventually said. "The guy you escaped with, right?"

Jason nodded and expected the man to ask why he wanted Cobb killed. But Wheeler was more of a professional than he'd expected, because true professionals didn't ask those kinds of questions. They didn't care about your reasons for wanting someone dead. They cared only that you could pay and keep your mouth shut. All of which was frightening as hell.

"I don't want to go to jail," Wheeler said.

"I don't, either. I have just as much to lose as you do," he said, thinking that he probably had a lot more to lose than Wheeler did.

"But if I did go, I'd take you with me."

"Fair enough."

The man nodded, seemingly to himself. "How fast do you need it done?"

"As soon as possible. A day, two at the most."

"Whoa. That *is* soon. Makes it a lot trickier. Cost you more."

"Okay."

"A lot more."

"I hear you."

"Plus, this Cobb guy is as famous as you. Costs even more if you want a famous person killed."

Jason sighed. "How much?"

"Twenty thousand, half up front."

Jason could afford that these days, but he didn't want to cave too easily or Wheeler would get greedy and ask for more. Plus, he didn't have ten thousand with him.

"I'll give you ten thousand. Five up front."

"I'll do it for fifteen. Final offer. We both know you're desperate."

Jason had known that would come up again. "Seven up front. It's . . . all I brought with me."

They stared at each other for a moment, then Wheeler stuck out his hand. "Agreed," he said.

Jason kept his left hand over his privates and took the man's hand with his right. They shook, and it felt to Jason like he was closing a deal with the devil. Inside, he shuddered to think it was *that* easy to order the death of another human being. They might as well have been negotiating the sale of a pickup truck.

Wheeler retrieved Jason's clothes, and once he was dressed again, Jason went back to his car for the money, which he'd never actually touched with his bare fingers. Back inside, he tore open the small bank envelope and tipped the cash onto a table, pocketing the crumpled envelope.

"Now," Wheeler said, "what can you tell me about Cobb that will help me do the job?"

"Not much you can't find on the Internet. He owns a plumbing business. He has no wife or kids and his father's in a coma or something somewhere, so I assume he lives alone. Other than that, I don't know much about him personally. But a lot has been written about him. You should be able to find anything you need, including pictures of him, the name of his business, whatever. I'm sure I don't need to tell you how to do your job."

"No, you don't."

Jason nodded. He started to say something, then stopped. He started again before aborting a second time.

"Something to say?" Wheeler asked.

"You should know that Ian Cobb is . . . well, he's dangerous."

Wheeler squinted at him a long moment. "So am I."

"Really dangerous. You won't find that about him on the Internet, but take my word for it."

Wheeler nodded. "I hear you. I'm guessing this is why you came to me. Well, don't worry. Like I said, I can take care of myself. Just because I didn't go to jail for what they accused me of doesn't mean I was completely innocent . . . or that I hadn't done that kind of thing before. More than once. So don't worry about me. Just get the rest of the money."

Jason swallowed. The man had just confessed to multiple murders. "Okay. So how will I know when it's done?"

"You guys killed Crackerjack just two weeks ago. If Cobb dies, it'll be on the news, right? You'll hear about it."

"I really need it to happen soon."

"It will. I'll give it some thought tonight, but I might even call in sick tomorrow, check him out. If everything goes okay, if I get the chance . . . well, let's just say I'll finish the job as soon as I get an opening. Now, about the rest of my money. I'll expect it no more than two days after I do it. There's an empty flowerpot on a windowsill at the back of the house. Leave it in there. And do it during the day, when I'm not home."

"Okay."

"And from this moment on, we never see each other again. We never talk. We've never even met. You got me?"

"Works for me."

Wheeler held Jason's eyes for a good long moment before nodding, apparently satisfied with what he saw there. Then he asked Jason, "How do you know you can trust me?"

"I don't. But I need this done and I figure you need the money."

"Here's a more important question . . . how do *I* know I can trust *you*?"

"Because a lot of people know who I am and I have a lot to lose. Because I didn't even know who you were before this morning and have no reason on earth to try to set you up. And because I know that you don't mind killing people, and you probably sure as hell wouldn't mind killing me if I crossed you."

Wheeler nodded. "That's all true. Especially the last part."

Jason believed him.

In the car a short while later, he thought about all the people he had killed in his stories over the years. He'd shot some, strangled some, poisoned one, bludgeoned another, and drowned yet another. It had all been so easy, killing them on the page, putting glib lines of dialogue into the mouths of the characters doing the deeds. But this was different. This was real.

He could tell himself that he never would have hit that man on the road that horrible night, the last night Sophie could walk. He could tell himself with perfect honesty that he had killed Wallace Barton in what he thought was self-defense, and maybe convince himself that there wasn't a single part of him that found it exhilarating. But this? It was cold, calculated, premeditated murder of a real, living, breathing human being. And Jason had paid for it. It would be hard to forget that.

# CHAPTER FORTY-THREE

At the Sleep Easy Motel in Danvers, Massachusetts, Jason paid cash for a room for seven nights, hoping he wouldn't need it that long. It was the same motel in every television show and movie he'd ever seen. Same cheap furniture, tasteless curtains, and tissue-thin bedspread. But he didn't care. He only needed someplace to hide out that wasn't his apartment or Sophie's house . . . somewhere Cobb wouldn't find him, if he was even looking.

There wasn't much for him to do but stay out of Cobb's sight and wait to hear from Wheeler. Every few hours, to establish an alibi, he walked down to the small reception area on some pretense—asking about Wi-Fi, which the motel didn't offer; buying a newspaper from the lobby vending machine; asking directions to the nearest ATM. Each time, he made sure to chat with the clerk behind the desk—a gray-haired man whose hands shook gently with some sort of palsy. Figuring it might make him more memorable, he mentioned once or twice that he was an author writing a book there. As the hours passed, he made runs for fast food and bottles of water, always stopping by the reception desk and asking the clerk if he needed anything from the store.

In between alibi-establishing forays out of his room, he actually did try to work on his book, assuming there would still be a book deal after all of this. He kept finding, though, that the ability to concentrate was as far beyond his grasp as the power of telekinesis. His mind wandered unceasingly. At one point, he thought about Cobb's brother, the one who reminded Cobb so much of Jason. Curious, he called up a search engine on his laptop and typed in *John Cobb*.

The first few hits were for John D. Cobb, purportedly one of the most influential theologians of the twentieth century. Wrong John Cobb. The next John Cobb was a British race-car driver who died in the 1950s while trying to break the water speed record in a jet speedboat on Loch Ness, in Scotland. He hit an unexplained wake in the water, which, of course, many claimed had been caused by the famous monster of the lake. Interesting, but again, not the right John Cobb.

Jason limited his search to Massachusetts and soon found the John Cobb he was looking for. First, he found an obituary, which noted that John Kenneth Cobb of Beverly, Massachusetts, had died three years earlier at the age of twenty-nine. A graduate of Beverly High School, a photography enthusiast, and an amateur astronomer, John was survived by his batshit-crazy brother Ian. Beside the obituary's text was a photograph of John. Jason immediately understood why big brother Ian saw similarities between Jason and him. Looking at John's picture wasn't exactly like looking into a mirror, but the resemblance was considerable. Comparable facial structures and light complexion, same high cheekbones and square chin, similar eye shapes, and even though the picture was in black and white, Jason knew that John also had red hair. Yes, the resemblance was striking.

Next, Jason learned that Beverly High School yearbooks were available online. He found the book for John's graduation year and moments later found his photo, which, at a glance, Jason could have mistaken for his own yearbook picture. The photograph was where the similarities between the two ended, though. While Jason had played in rock bands in high school and hung out with the cool crowd, John had been a member of the astronomy and photography clubs.

He searched the Internet for mention of the fatal car crash but came up empty.

And that was all he found. A life that lasted twenty-nine years reduced to a few hundred words. A life remembered, it seemed, by no one but Ian Cobb.

The day passed quietly. The older clerk with the shaky hands was replaced by a younger man, nondescript but for the sideburns that reached down to his jawline, and Jason gave him the story about writing a book there. When he went out for coffee, he brought some back for the guy. Now and then he did try again to get some writing done but was too distracted. Somewhere, if all went well, a man would die soon, if he hadn't already, because Jason had paid for that to happen. It was a sobering thought. He didn't want to think about what Sophie would say if she knew.

Eventually, he turned on the cheap television sitting on the scarred surface of the cheap dresser and found a news station. He watched and waited. Sophie called to check in, and Jason told her that her plan to frame Cobb of something or other was progressing nicely. He didn't want to share the details with her, but it shouldn't be long, he said. He hadn't decided what he would tell her when Cobb ended up dead. He'd have to take his clue from whatever method Wheeler chose to kill him. If it looked like a suicide, which Jason had requested, it wouldn't be an issue. But if things got messy, Jason might have to spin a good yarn.

---

At just before 2:00 a.m., Jason was still awake, his tired eyes staring at the ceiling, when a call came on his cell phone. For a brief moment, little more than an instant, he hoped that Wheeler was calling with news that he had completed the job, but then remembered that the hit man wasn't going to call when the job was done. There was to be no more contact between them. Jason answered the call.

"Hello?"

"Hope I didn't wake you." It was Cobb, still very much alive. "I have someone here who wants to talk to you."

Cold iron pincers gripped his heart as he waited to hear Sophie's voice on the line. Instead, he heard someone grunting desperately, someone with a male voice. Wheeler?

"Wait a second," Cobb said. "Let me remove the tape."

Jason heard a ripping sound followed by a man's voice. *"Please help me. Pleeeeease."* The voice was strained and distorted by panic, but Jason didn't think he recognized it.

Cobb was back on the line. "That was Lyman J. Gooding. We met just a little while ago. He has a lovely home. And a pretty wife named Lauren. And twin girls named Kayla and Suzie. And he's really hoping his entire family doesn't die tonight. But that's up to you, Jason."

# CHAPTER FORTY-FOUR

"Are you there?" Cobb asked. "Did you hear what I said?"

Jason was too surprised by Cobb's call to think clearly. Who the hell was Lyman J. Gooding? Was it someone Jason should know?

"Jason?"

"I'm here."

"Oh, good. I thought I lost you."

"What are you doing, Cobb?"

"Right now? Sitting with Lyman in his living room."

*Oh, God.*

"Where are his wife and daughters you mentioned? Did you hurt them?"

"They're fine. They're in a bedroom, tied up with hoods over their heads."

"Why are you calling me?"

"To give you a chance to save an entire family, Jason. Well, most of it anyway."

"What do you mean?"

"I mean that Lyman is going to die tonight. That's a done deal. Nothing either of us can do about that now. But his family might die, too. You can prevent that from happening, though. All you gotta do is drive out to Lyman's house here in Chelmsford and watch me kill him, and I'll let the family go free."

*Oh, God.* "You won't let them go. They've seen your face."

"Not true. They were all asleep in their beds when I knocked them out one by one with chloroform. Tied them up before they even woke up. I'm sure they're scared, but I haven't hurt them. Yet."

In the background, Jason heard Gooding grunting again. Cobb must have slapped the tape back across his mouth.

"Now," Cobb said, "how about we give this thing a try? You and me together. You can't say you haven't thought about it. Remember . . . I know what's inside you."

"You're crazy."

"You can deny it to me, Jason, and to yourself, but you can't deny the thing inside you forever. But listen, if it helps, don't think about it as taking a life. Think about it as saving three. What do you say? Do you watch me kill Lyman, or do I murder poor Lauren, and little Kayla and Shelley?"

*Shelley?*

Jason frowned. Cobb had said *Shelley*, not *Suzie*, like he'd said earlier. Was it a slip of the tongue? He easily could have forgotten their names. No doubt he'd heard them for the first time only a short while ago. But then again . . .

"What do you say, Jason?"

He opened his laptop, which, thankfully, he had kept powered on, and searched the Internet for *Lyman J. Gooding* and *Chelmsford.* He got several hits, all apparently pertaining to the same man, including a year-old obituary for a Lauren Gooding.

"Are you even listening?" Cobb asked.

"I'm thinking. Give me a second. This is a lot to take in."

Jason skimmed the obit and learned that Lauren Gooding was survived by her husband, Lyman J. Gooding, and her sisters Rachel and Theresa. No mention of children.

"Lyman here is running out of time, Jason. What's it going to be? One death tonight or four?"

"If I came there," Jason said, stalling, "would I have to see the family? Because I don't think I could take that . . . seeing them, knowing I stood by while their husband and father was killed."

"They'll never even know you were here."

Jason clicked on another of the Google hits—the website of an architectural firm where Gooding worked. His picture popped up on the screen. He looked to be in his late fifties, a bit overweight with thinning hair, a professional smile on his lips, and a quirky little bow tie around his neck.

"Ticktock, Jason. I need an answer. Will you save an innocent woman and two innocent girls? Or let them be slaughtered like animals?"

Gooding was almost certainly going to die tonight. There was nothing Jason could do about that. But there were no children in peril. And his wife was already dead.

"Give me the address. I'll be there in an hour."

———

Jason was pacing in his motel room when his phone rang seventeen minutes later. It was Cobb's number again, which wasn't a good sign.

"Didn't I tell you what would happen if you called the cops on me, Jason?"

"I didn't tell anyone that you're Crackerjack. All I did was report a break-in at Gooding's address."

For five bucks, the clerk with the sideburns had let him use the phone at the reception desk. He hadn't buried his tracks very deeply if the police ever got curious about the 911 call, but he hadn't had a lot of time. At least he didn't use his own phone.

"Thankfully, Lyman and I were actually in my van down the block when we called you. The cops drove right past us."

"Is he . . ."

"Not yet. But soon. How did you know?"

"Googled it."

"What would you have done if he really did have a family?"

Jason wasn't sure. It was all he thought about as he'd walked laps around his motel room, until Cobb had called. He liked to think he would have done the right thing . . . whatever that was. But he had a family of his own to think about.

"At first," Cobb said, "I wondered why you would risk calling the cops, but then I realized that this wouldn't have been like calling them out of the blue and telling them that I'm Crackerjack. If you did that, you'd have to convince them to investigate me. And an investigation would take time. And during that time, you know I'd kill your family. But if they actually caught me in the act tonight, they wouldn't need convincing of anything. In fact, Crackerjack wouldn't even have to come up, right? They'd have me for Gooding's murder."

"It would only have been attempted murder if they got there in time."

"They wouldn't have. If there was even a small chance they might've caught me, I'd have killed Gooding first. And I bet you knew that, Jason. And you called the police anyway. Wow, it seems that in order to send me to prison, you were willing to sacrifice an innocent person."

Jason said nothing.

"See? You're not so different from me. Which means there's still hope for you."

Jason closed his eyes. Cobb was *wrong* about him.

"I'm not going to help you kill anyone, Cobb. And I'm not going to watch. So there's no point in trying anything like this again."

He waited for a reply but heard only silence for several moments. Then, Cobb started whistling. It was "Take Me Out to the Ball Game." Jason shivered.

"Listen, Ian, maybe you could just let Gooding go. If he promises—"

Cobb stopped whistling and said, "Don't be stupid. I can't do that. And Jason?"

He waited.

"That was strike one."

# CHAPTER FORTY-FIVE

For the rest of that first night at the motel, Jason barely slept. When he finally dozed off briefly, his sleep was fitful and haunted by dreams of Lyman Gooding's face as it looked on his company's website, only there was a huge gash in his neck between his bow tie and his chin. He never lost his professional smile, though, as blood ran down his shirt and his life seeped out with it.

The following morning was quiet. Jason tried to write now and then and watched a lot of the news, hoping he wouldn't see a story about the murder of a local architect named Lyman J. Gooding, and praying he *would* see a story about the death of local hero Ian Cobb. He did see a story about two Wenham men who were missing, last seen three nights earlier at a bar in Hamilton, and he wondered whether they were the men Cobb said he'd murdered.

Things turned a bit more interesting for Jason, unfortunately, when Detective Briggs called his cell in the midafternoon. His first thought, naturally, was that the call had to do with Gooding. He hoped it didn't.

"I swung by your place looking for you," Briggs said, "but you weren't there, so I decided to call. Got a few minutes to talk?"

"I'm writing at the moment, Detective, in a really good flow. Can it wait?"

"I don't want to inconvenience you. Tell me where you're working and I'll come to you."

*Nice try.* "I have some research to do at the Salem library anyway. Why don't we meet there? Say, half an hour?"

"Sure."

———

Their meeting didn't take long. Jason figured its purpose had been to make him sweat a bit. And it did. In an effort to dot his damn i's and cross his piece-of-shit t's, Briggs asked whether Jason could remember his whereabouts in the early morning hours on numerous specific dates, which he'd helpfully written down for him. Briggs didn't explain the significance of the dates. He didn't have to. They were the nights that Crackerjack's various victims had been abducted.

"I'll have to check my calendar and get back to you," he said, knowing that alibis were highly unlikely.

"That would be great. Hey, I don't suppose you know anything about a couple of missing guys from Wenham."

"Why would I?"

Briggs shrugged. "Just thought I'd ask. The North Shore used to be such a quiet corner of Massachusetts, didn't it? Since Crackerjack started up, though, it hasn't been nearly as quiet. The thing is, when you and Cobb killed that psycho, I figured we wouldn't have any more guys disappearing. But suddenly . . . two more this week, and that doesn't even count the guy who showed up dead in Tewksbury the other day, hanging from some monkey bars with his skull crushed. And we know Wallace Barton wasn't responsible for any of it, right?"

So Briggs didn't know anything about Lyman Gooding yet. Or if he did, he hadn't connected him to this case.

"Maybe the two missing guys hopped a flight to Atlantic City," Jason said. "Or they're off camping and forgot to call in sick."

"You're probably right. When you check your calendar for those dates, let me know."

For half an hour after the detective left, Jason hung around the library pretending to do research and trying to convince himself that Briggs would soon realize there was nothing to his suspicions and would finally leave Jason alone. On the drive back to the motel, he tried to determine whether he was being followed. He didn't think so.

Back at the Sleep Easy, he called Ben to check in.

"Jason? Is everything . . . is that book you were working on finished yet?"

*Very subtle.* "Not yet." He told Ben about his meeting with Briggs.

"That guy's been busy. He called me again at work this morning to ask another bunch of questions about you. I was going to call you later to tell you about it."

"What did he ask?"

"Everything about you. And I mean everything."

"Did he ask if I'm a serial killer?"

"Practically. Listen, a senior partner's calling on another line. I only have a minute before I'll have to call him back."

He told Jason he'd caught a huge project at work a few days ago—one of his firm's biggest clients was acquiring its top competitor's company, and the contract issues were numerous and thorny—so he was hunkered down at the office with a gaggle of other lawyers, all of them crashing on their office couches the past few nights, sleeping, eating, and breathing their client's impending deal.

"I'm looking forward to sleeping in my own bed tonight," he said. "Listen, I've gotta go, but I've been thinking about that book you're working on. You know the one I mean?"

"I know it."

"Are you sure there's nothing I can do to help you? It feels weird to me, going through my normal stuff while you're going through this."

"You can't stop your life while I try to get mine sorted out."

"Yeah, but you're not just sorting things out. You're dealing with—"

"Thanks, Ben. Seriously. But there's nothing you can do to help." Besides being true, he thought that it would be best, from a covering-his-ass standpoint, if as many things in his life as possible remained as normal as they could. That would leave fewer anomalies to explain to the police, should it ever come to that.

That night, he dreamed he was driving through a rainy night on a dark stretch of road, Sophie asleep in the seat beside him. A man suddenly loomed in his headlights and Jason calmly aimed the car straight for him. The man turned and Jason looked into the face of Lyman J. Gooding, who stood and smiled professionally until the car slammed into him, sending him flying through the dark. In the dream, Sophie woke up screaming and Jason said, "Don't worry, I'll take care of him." When he reached Gooding, lying twenty feet in front of the car, the man was a broken mess, jagged bones protruding from all over his body. Still, he never lost his smile. Jason knelt beside him and a hammer with a smooth wooden handle appeared like magic in his hand. "Finish him," someone said, and Jason looked up to see Ian Cobb standing a few feet away. Beside him stood Wallace Barton. And Cobb's brother Johnny was there, too. "You know you want to, Jason," Johnny said. "Right, Sophie?" And then Sophie was there. She was crying. And then two guys from Jason's high-school band who didn't seem to belong at all were there. Along with most of his former coworkers at Barker. And Jason's first-grade teacher—and first real crush—Ms. Willard, beside Jason's parents, who had just shown up. His mother said, "Why are you fighting it, Jason? Time to finally let your Inside Dark out." He shook his head. She was wrong about him. They all were. "I'm already dead," a voice said, and Jason looked down at Gooding. "You let me die once. You might as well kill me again." Jason didn't think they were right about him, but he was so very tired of fighting about it. He raised the hammer and brought it down hard. The wet crack almost drowned out Sophie's screams.

He woke up with her screams in his ears. It was hours before he fell asleep again.

———

The next day, his third at the Sleep Easy Motel, was uneventful. Still nothing on the news about Gooding, which meant either that his body hadn't yet been discovered or that his death wasn't newsworthy. And Jason didn't hear from Cobb or Briggs, which was a good thing. Less good was the fact that there had been no indication that Wheeler had been successful in his efforts.

As the hours passed, Jason tried to get some writing done but made little progress. That evening, he brought a Big Mac meal back for the clerk with the long sideburns. With the television on in the background—it was *always* on now—he tried to write another chapter of his book but the words kept blending into one another. Finally, after spending far too long staring at the word *muther* and wondering why spell-check kept insisting it was misspelled, he closed his laptop. He sat on the bed, his back against the headboard, and watched blurbs about local news stories scroll across the bottom of CNN.

At 8:00 p.m. he called to say good night to Sophie and Max. Around 3:00 a.m., he fell asleep. He tossed and turned and twisted his sheets into knots, sleeping well past noon the next day and far into the afternoon.

In a nightmare, he killed Lyman Gooding again.

# CHAPTER FORTY-SIX

Behind the wheel of his 2013 Ford Transit panel van—which he drove when he didn't want to travel in his conspicuous company vehicle—Cobb squinted through the windshield into the late-afternoon sun as he pulled into the lot of his fifth motel that afternoon. Having lived his entire life in nearby Beverly, only a few short miles from Jason Swike's hometown of Swampscott, he knew there weren't many motels in the area. He also knew that Jason was staying in one of them. And he knew the color of Jason's Camry and its license plate number. It wouldn't take long to find it, especially with Cobb having the luxury of owning his own business. While his employees were working the big job in Tewksbury, the boss was free to make finding Jason his sole occupation.

Fortunately, as expected, the list of local motels he'd called up on his smartphone wasn't extensive. He cruised through the lot without seeing a red Camry and pulled back onto the street, heading for the next motel on his list.

He had a fever. At least it sure as hell felt that way. It had been too long since he'd done what he needed to do. He'd killed, but not the right kind of killing. Not the kind that quieted the dark whispers. The four men he'd slain over the past two weeks had done next to nothing for him. He'd already been overdue for the right kind of killing when he'd taken Jason, but then he held off, let Jason go, and with Barton dead and Jason refusing to take his place, Cobb was unable to find relief. His pain was a knife inside him now, making it hard to breathe. His Inside Dark hadn't given him a moment's peace in weeks. And it was getting worse every day.

He wasn't stupid. Neither was he crazy enough to believe that his pain was actually in his stomach or his bones. Its cause wouldn't show up in an MRI or CAT scan. It was in his head. But isn't that where all pain truly is? Cut the connection between the shard of glass sticking out of your hand and the pain center in your brain and you wouldn't feel the glass, right? That it was all in his mind didn't make it any less real to him, any less agonizing to endure; he felt it nonetheless . . . and he found relief only when he did what he did, exactly as he needed to do it.

As he drove from motel to motel looking for Jason, his fever rose and the knife twisted inside him and he knew he needed to do it again—the right way—very soon.

# CHAPTER FORTY-SEVEN

Jason's fourth day at the Sleep Easy was feeling depressingly similar to his first three, only by now he had completely given up trying to write. Other than making an occasional appearance at the reception desk to establish his whereabouts, he did nothing but lie on the bed and watch the news. He drifted off to sleep for a few minutes at one point and had yet another nightmare about killing Lyman Gooding while Sophie screamed and Ian Cobb and a host of others watched—the horror movie that played with little variation every time he slept now.

He kept thinking of an Edgar Allan Poe story he'd read in high school—"The Tell-Tale Heart"—in which someone kills and dismembers an old man, stuffs the body parts under the floorboards, then goes nuts and confesses because he can't stop hearing the dead man's heart beating below him. Jason wondered if his sins—hiring a hit man, allowing an innocent man to be murdered—could be seen on his face. Surely, the motel clerks, the cashiers at McDonald's, the woman at the 7-Eleven register knew that he was guilty of something terrible. What Sophie thought she saw the night of the accident years ago—what Cobb, and possibly Briggs, saw when they looked at him now . . . hell, what Jason had begun to fear he might see in the mirror—was plain for all to see.

Late afternoon passed into early evening, and he began to dread the coming of yet another evening spent staring at the boob tube, waiting for a news story that never came, waiting for a night filled with long stretches of wakeful restlessness broken by snippets of sleep filled with nightmares of cold-blooded murder.

On his way to dinner, he left a message for Ben saying that he hoped the deal he was working on had gone through without a hitch. He ate in the dining room of a nearby Wendy's—because he was getting *really* tired of McDonald's—and on the way home he called Sophie, who said she was doing fine but thought that Geri might be getting a little tired of having company, even if she wouldn't admit it.

"I hope to take care of things here soon," Jason said.

"You're being safe?"

"I am."

"Okay. Here's Max."

While he was saying good night to his son—even though it was only 7:15 p.m., as Max was quick to point out, and his bedtime wasn't until eight o'clock, which he also made quite clear—Jason's phone vibrated in his hand, indicating that a text or an e-mail had come in. He would check it after his son finished telling him about the bumpy brown toad he'd found in Geri's backyard. Jason listened, smiling his first smile in three days, and ended the call as he pulled in to the lot of the Sleep Easy.

As he climbed the stairs to his room, he checked the text. It had come from a number he didn't recognize. It read, Balance due ASAP. It was signed simply RW.

Wheeler wasn't supposed to contact him. He had never even given the hit man his number, though phone numbers aren't terribly difficult to obtain. Sending the text was stupid and counter to their agreement and could cause serious trouble for Jason, but as he dug his room key from his pocket, he forgot the careless breach of protocol as the man's news started to sink in.

Was it really over?

Was Cobb really dead?

He stepped into his room and closed the door behind him.

"You had to be on the second floor?"

Jason spun toward the voice. On the far side of the room, a man wearing denim coveralls sat on a chair, a black hood over his head. His hands were behind his back as if they were bound. Beside him stood Ian Cobb, an ugly knife in his hand.

# CHAPTER FORTY-EIGHT

"Seriously, Jason, you couldn't be on the first floor?" Cobb said. "I had to lug this guy up all those stairs. I've got a broken arm, for God's sake."

Cobb's words were light and airy, almost playful, but his tone didn't match. His voice was flat and emotionless. And he looked different to Jason, even worse than the last time he'd seen him. His face was drawn; he looked like a wax figure that had begun, ever so slightly, to melt. His empty, glassy eyes added to the effect.

"I can see your mind racing," he said, "trying to decide what to do or say. Let's start by me telling you not to do or say anything that might get this guy killed, okay? At least not yet. Though I think we both know he deserves it, don't we?"

Jason had immediately recognized Ronald Wheeler's denim coveralls beneath the hooded head.

"Clever, texting me from his phone. Is he alive?" Jason asked, afraid of the answer.

"For now. Where the hell did you get this guy? I saw him coming a mile away."

He again took note of Cobb's appearance, the sunken cheeks and glazed-over eyes in a face devoid of emotion.

"You don't look good."

"Yeah, well, I've had a bad day. Disappointing. Someone tried to kill me. That hurt my feelings, Jason."

At first, Jason thought he was kidding in that twisted way that Cobb had, but the look on his face, his tone of voice . . . he actually seemed to be serious.

"Why are you here, Cobb?"

"To give you one more chance. The very last one."

"Because you want a partner."

"No, I *need* a partner. I can't explain it any better than I have. And don't start in with that *I'm not a killer* crap. We both know that's not true. Remember, I know what you have inside you. I may be the only person who does. I watched you kill Wallace without batting an eye. I saw your face after. No remorse. No regret. Just satisfaction, and though you might not have even known it was there, I saw naked desire . . . desire to do it again."

"Bullshit."

"Jason, you sent a hit man to murder me, which proves you're not above killing in the proper circumstances, right? But maybe you don't want to get your hands dirty. Fine. Hang back and watch me do it. Feed that thing inside you the way I feed mine. In a day or two, we'll talk about it, reminisce a little, see what you think of it then, after the beasts have been fed."

"Maybe I'm just not into killing people who don't deserve it."

"Every man I've ever met deserves it for one reason or another."

"In your twisted opinion."

"I'm the one with the knife. My opinion is the only one in the room that matters. And come to think of it, there is one person I know who doesn't deserve to die."

"Yeah? Who?"

"My father."

"Really? He's so special, did such a stellar job raising you, that he deserves to live?"

"You've got it wrong. He's a piece of garbage who doesn't deserve to live—but he's not living right now, not really, because he's a vegetable. What I *said*, though, was that he doesn't deserve to *die*. His doctor is begging me to let it happen. His nurses, too. They imply it's inhumane to keep him alive in the state he's in. And I agree. *That's the whole point.* I hope he's suffering, lying there in a state of endless mental torture. *That's* what I meant when I said he doesn't deserve to die. Death is too good for him."

Jason shook his head. *How do you respond to that kind of cruel insanity?* "Seriously," he said, "you look sick."

"Well, I feel sick. My brother's darkness, his pain—*my* pain now—it's like cancer. It's eating me. I need a release. And I need it to be the way it was, with Johnny and Wallace."

"I don't mean this to be an insult, I swear, but is there even a description in psychology books of what's wrong with you?"

"Actually, one of my early victims was a psychology minor in college. Before I killed him, I asked what he thought about me. He said my need to be watched while I kill demonstrates some form of exhibitionism. I guess that makes some sense."

"Yeah, well, I think he was just scratching the surface, Cobb. You need help."

"So help me."

"You know what I mean."

Cobb sighed. A sorrow came to his face so profound that Jason might have pitied him under almost any other circumstances. "Let's try something different."

Without taking his eyes off Jason, he opened the door behind him and reached into the bathroom. He tugged at something unseen and a man wearing only a black hood and a pair of saggy underwear shuffled into the room. His arms were bound in front of him with silver-gray duct tape. Jason heard his rapid, panicked breathing. Cobb gave him a small push and he stumbled forward three steps before bumping into the bed.

"Sit down," Cobb said.

He did as instructed. Cobb now stood with one hand on the shoulder of the man on the bed, and his other hand, the one holding the knife, resting on the shoulder of the hooded man in the chair. Jason noticed now that Cobb was wearing light-blue latex gloves.

Cobb pulled the hood off the man on the bed, revealing the terrified face of Ronald Wheeler. Tape covered his mouth. Tears streamed down his cheeks. Jason immediately looked at the hooded man in the denim coveralls. The back of his neck began to tingle.

"I think you should ask for your money back, Jason. What do you think we should do with him? Kill him?"

At that, Wheeler shook his head violently and tried to stand. Cobb pushed him back onto the bed.

"Let him go," Jason said.

"He'd turn both of us in to the police."

"No, he won't. He'd have to reveal his involvement, which he'd never do."

Wheeler nodded vigorously.

"Ah, why should we believe you?" Cobb asked, looking down at Wheeler. "You're a hit man, for God's sake."

"I believe him," Jason said.

"Well, I don't, so we're not letting him go. But let's move things along a bit."

With that, he tore the hood from the head of the other man. Even though Jason had begun to suspect it, his heart stuttered when he saw Ben there. His head was down. He was unconscious. Or was he . . .

"Tell me he's alive."

"Two for two," Cobb said. "It's your lucky night so far. I gave him a pretty hefty dose, so he'll sleep for a while yet."

Jason saw red. He took two quick steps forward, and in a flash the knife was at his friend's neck, the point making an indentation in the skin. It would take little more than a flick of Cobb's wrist to draw blood, barely more than that to slice the neck wide open. There was something in Cobb's eyes now, something resembling resignation, and Jason didn't doubt that he'd kill Ben. So he backed up two steps.

"Good decision," Cobb said.

"That *was* you outside the Green Dragon that night. You followed me there, then followed Ben home later."

"Yeah. I was lucky to find him home. I've checked his apartment every night for the past few days. This is the first night he's been home all week."

"This isn't necessary."

"Yeah, it is. You weren't interested in saving the life of strangers the other night, so I thought maybe you'd feel differently about saving the life of a friend. Here's how this is going to work: I'm going to cut Ronnie here into little pieces, and I'll tell you everything I plan to do as I go along—slice by slice, stab by stab—and if you don't watch me, I'll do it to your friend instead. Understand?"

*Holy hell.*

"You're going to force me to watch?" Jason said. "That's not going to work for you. You told me that. You need it to be voluntary."

Cobb brought the knife close to Wheeler's face, positioning the point just under the man's eye. A tear ran down the blade. "Maybe," he said, "but let's find out for sure."

# CHAPTER FORTY-NINE

"Okay," Cobb said, holding a fistful of Wheeler's hair with one hand and the knife with the other. "Here we go. Watch me cut out Ronnie's eye."

"I thought your thing was breaking bones," Jason said quickly, anything to keep Cobb talking instead of stabbing or slicing. "Because of Johnny, right? Your uncle breaking his bones?"

With his legs shaking, either from adrenaline or fear, Jason briefly—very briefly—considered trying again to rush Cobb. He'd go right for his knife hand. But the blade was sharp and would take only a second to do permanent damage, first to Wheeler and then, no doubt, to him. And then to Ben. He had no choice. So he looked away.

"Breaking bones?" Cobb said. "That *was* my thing, yeah. But if I want the world to keep thinking that Crackerjack is dead, I have no choice but to mix it up a bit. So maybe I'll try some things with cutlery and see how it goes. Now, eyes front please, Jason."

Jason kept looking away. His eyes found an ugly framed watercolor on the wall above the television. A street scene. He couldn't bring himself to watch Wheeler lose an eye.

"Maybe you didn't hear me. If you don't look, I'll do it to your sleeping buddy here instead. Now, watch me."

Reluctantly, Jason started to turn toward Cobb but, at the last moment, looked at the watercolor again.

"You're just not listening, Jason." Cobb's voice was louder now. A little agitated. On a hunch, Jason turned his head farther away.

"Damn it," Cobb said. "*Watch me.* You know you want to. The thing inside you wants to. Admit it."

As angry and frustrated as Cobb was getting, he hadn't cut anyone yet. That was interesting.

"You're wrong about me, Cobb. There's nothing inside me that wants to do or see these things. And there's nothing inside you. You're just crazy."

Cobb sucked in a deep breath. "Have it your way. Someone's about to lose an eye."

Jason's heart skipped a beat but he kept his eyes averted. It was the most difficult thing he'd ever done. He waited for a wet slicing sound. All he heard, though, were Cobb's deep breaths and Wheeler's little mewling sounds.

"Last chance, Jason."

"I'm not going to be your audience, Cobb. I'm not going to give you whatever it is you think you need from me."

He took a deep breath and walked toward the door. Remembering something Cobb had told him, he added a slight limp to his walk. Nothing obvious. Just a subtle hitch in his stride.

Cobb started to speak, faltered, then asked, "Where are you going?"

Remembering what he'd read about Johnny Cobb in his yearbook and obituary, Jason played another hunch and said, "Outside to look at the stars. I've always loved the stars."

He had reached the door and was halfway out when Cobb finally said, in a hushed voice, "What did you say?"

Without turning around, he replied, "I'm going out to look at the stars. There's no moon tonight and you can see more stars than usual." Doubling down on his hunch—perhaps tripling, at this point—he added, "Wish I had my high-speed camera. I bet it's a great sky for pictures."

Before Cobb could respond, Jason left the motel room, closing the door behind him.

Outside, he bent over at the waist, put his hands on his knees, and sucked in a huge lungful of air. When he blew it out his head felt light, as though it were floating inches above his body. What had he done? What was happening in the room behind him? He resisted the urge to peer between the window curtains. Instead, he walked a few feet away and sat with his back against the wall, his knees drawn up.

After what seemed an eternity but was certainly only a minute or two, the door opened. He looked over at Cobb as he closed the motel room door behind him. He had the knife in his hand. It wasn't bloody, but Cobb might have wiped it off after using it. He stood there, a dozen feet away. He looked beaten, defeated. He looked . . . sick, as though whatever pain he believed he felt truly *was* killing him from the inside. Jason wished it would get a move on and finish the job already.

"I hope you're not thinking of trying to attack me," Cobb said in a voice utterly without inflection. "You wouldn't stand a chance."

Jason had been thinking of doing exactly that. What stopped him was the thought of what could happen to Sophie and Max if he failed. And Ben, if he was still alive.

"Is he dead?" he asked a moment later.

"Ben? No, just sleeping a while longer. It took guts for you to walk out like that. How'd you know I wouldn't kill him?"

"I didn't. But there's no way I would have reached you in time to stop you. And I wasn't about to stay in the room while you did it. So I left." *And hoped like hell it wasn't a tragic mistake.* "Also, I know you need a willing audience."

He knew that Cobb could have killed Ben anyway in an attempt to scratch his murderous itch. Or maybe to teach Jason a lesson. But he suspected that Cobb still hoped he might come around to his way of thinking, and he would have to know that if he killed Ben, there was no chance in hell of that ever happening. So he'd gambled—with Ben's life—and, *thank God*, he won.

Cobb nodded thoughtfully but said nothing.

"What about Wheeler?" Jason asked.

"I did you a favor with him."

"He's alive?"

"What? No, I killed him. But I didn't use the knife. I broke his neck instead."

Jason closed his eyes and sighed. *Oh, God . . .*

"How is that a favor for me?"

"You're a pretty smart guy. You'll figure that out. But Jason, you have to admit . . . that one's on you."

He didn't even try to deny it.

Cobb leaned against the railing and looked up at the night sky. He let the smallest of smiles, rueful and sad, creep onto his face. "You're right. The stars are really out tonight."

He looked back at Jason, sitting there with his back against the motel wall.

"God, you look so much like Johnny. He loved the stars, too."

Jason knew that. And he knew that Cobb's brother had liked photography. He'd read both things on the Internet in Johnny's obituary and in his high-school yearbook. And Cobb himself had mentioned his brother's pronounced limp.

Cobb was looking at him, and for the first time tonight, there was something in his eyes. Jason didn't know what it was, but it was there. And now he seemed to be looking *at* Jason but also *through* him; though his eyes were on Jason's face, they were focused on something— or someone—else.

"I wish you could have met him," he finally said. "My brother. You would have liked him."

"I might have."

Cobb's eyes refocused on Jason.

"We're running out of time, Jason. We need closure soon. I wish you'd surrender to the thing inside you and give this a try. You know I'm not gonna stop what I'm doing whether you join me or not. I can't. But there's actually a chance I might kill *less* if you're with me on this. If I get more out of it each time I do it, the more pain it takes away, the less often I'll need it. You could actually be saving lives, Jason. So if you won't do it for yourself, do it for the people I *won't* kill because of you. Think about that, would you?"

Jason nodded, though he had no intention of giving the notion a nanosecond of consideration.

Cobb frowned and shook his head sadly. "I wish you hadn't tried to have me killed, Jason, but there's a silver lining in it. It seems like progress for you, don't you think? My brother would have—"

"*Stop it*," Jason snapped.

Cobb frowned.

"Just stop it, Cobb. I'm not your brother. I'm nothing like your brother."

The instinct that moments ago had told him to appear to be more like Johnny to rattle Cobb, to increase his sympathy for Jason, was now screaming at him to shut his mouth. But he couldn't. He'd had enough.

"I read about your brother. He was a geek in school. You say I would have liked him, but the truth is that if I'd known him, I probably would have ignored him."

Cobb took an unsteady step backward, looking as though he'd been slapped.

"But your hair . . . your face—"

"Yeah, I admit it, we look a lot alike. But that's where the similarities end."

"The car accidents—"

"Which one? The one where your brother drove into a wall to kill himself? Or the one where your father killed your mother and youngest brother and turned himself into a vegetable? You think we have something in common because we both suffered catastrophes we didn't deserve? Well, guess what? I *did* deserve mine. I wrecked my family."

Cobb shook his head. "What? No, that's not true. It was an accident. It wasn't your fault."

Jason had no intention of sharing the details of his family's misfortunes with Cobb. He certainly wasn't about to admit that Sophie might have seen the same monster inside Jason that Cobb believed he saw.

"Trust me, Cobb, it was my fault. So if you think that we have this bond, this connection, because forces beyond our control brought tragedy into our lives . . . well, you're just wrong."

Cobb backed up another step. He shook his head. He started to speak, then fell silent. Jason wondered if Cobb was finally starting to have doubts about him. Maybe he was wondering if the voice in his head was wrong. Jason wondered whether he should have listened to the voice in his own head imploring him not to say any of that, because if Cobb decided that Jason would never join him, he had no reason to keep him alive.

"I'm really tired," Jason said quickly. "Can you just leave?"

Cobb looked at him with sad eyes for a long moment. "Okay. I'm tired, too."

"Any chance you'll take the body with you?"

"That's your mess. You have to clean it up."

Jason nodded. He understood that and even saw the justness in it. He'd brought Wheeler into it.

"I have some thinking to do, I guess," Cobb said. "Can I give you a piece of advice, though? If you're hiding out from a serial killer, don't text your friend to tell him you're staying at a local motel."

Jason groaned inwardly. He thought he'd been so careful by not providing the name of the motel. He realized only now that there simply weren't many motels in the area.

"I've been trying so hard not to kill you, Jason. I just don't know how long I can keep trying."

"Are we done here?"

"For now. I hope you realize, though, this was a one-time free pass for your pal Ben. I may still have to kill him. Or your family. Or you. Unless you all stay out of my way. There's just no telling what I'll do if you don't."

Suddenly, Cobb's body snapped into motion as he lunged toward Jason, thrusting his arm as he came. The knife sliced the air beside Jason's cheek before Cobb sank it an inch into the wooden doorframe beside Jason's head. Jason hadn't even had time to react.

Cobb walked away. As he did, he began to whistle "Take Me Out to the Ball Game." He'd left behind the knife in the wood. Perhaps it was a show of contempt. Or a taunt. Or maybe even a challenge.

In Jason's opinion, though, it was a mistake.

Because Cobb was right. He could come after Jason or his loved ones at any time. Sophie and Max were safe at the moment, but they couldn't stay in hiding forever.

Cobb was still whistling as he neared the top of the stairs that led down to the parking lot. The song was an ice pick in Jason's ears. He hated Cobb's whistling. He hated that song. He hated that it was the last sound ever heard by Cobb's victims.

Of which there would be more. Innocent people. Maybe even Sophie or Max. Or Ben.

Unless Jason ended it now. He might never get a better chance.

He stood, grasped the handle of the knife, and worked it back and forth until it pulled free of the wood.

Cobb had almost reached the stairs.

Jason gripped the knife tightly and broke into a run, staying on the balls of his feet to mask his approach for as long as possible.

And in that moment, for the first time, he almost hoped he had an Inside Dark of his own lurking within him after all. If he did, it ran with him, claws extended and fangs bared.

# CHAPTER FIFTY

There were twenty feet between them at most, then only fifteen, and as he ran, Jason imagined where he would strike, exactly where he would plunge the blade into Cobb's body. As the distance between them shrank, he kept his eyes on Cobb's neck—the right side of it, actually, the place where he would sink the knife up to its hilt. He was flying now, nearly there, running as quietly as possible, and it didn't seem as though Cobb heard him coming—

But he did hear him. Because he spun at precisely the right moment, blocking Jason's strike with the cast on his right forearm. The knife flew from Jason's hand and skittered away. Jason took a wild swing with his left and missed by a mile. Then Cobb's hand was on his throat, squeezing, the sheer strength of it hard to believe. Jason thrashed his arms, and one of his elbows shattered a window. The crack was loud, the broken glass clattering and clinking to the cement surface of the walkway.

Cobb's hand never left Jason's throat as the killer pushed him back, slamming him into the railing, and still he pushed, bending Jason backward, crushing him against the railing, his upper body out over the parking lot now. Jason struggled, resisting as best he could, but Cobb was bigger and stronger, and Jason had spent far too many days in front of a computer instead of in a gym over the last few years. The pressure

Cobb exerted was unrelenting, and one by one Jason's vertebrae popped as though he were on a chiropractor's table, nothing breaking but everything straining to its limit. Soon, though, Jason knew . . . soon something *would* break. Or Cobb would crush his windpipe. Or he would succeed in pitching him over the railing, which might not kill him but could sure as hell put him in a wheelchair beside Sophie.

Maybe the thought of his wife gave him clarity in that wild moment—or maybe something dark and feral inside him issued an order—but he suddenly knew what to do.

As Cobb leaned into him, bending him back, choking the life out of him, Jason stopped throwing wild, ineffective punches and instead gripped the railing pressing into his lower back as tightly as he could. Then, for one final moment, he resisted with as much of his remaining strength as he could muster, forcing Cobb to lean into him even harder, and suddenly—

He pushed off the floor of the landing with both legs, launching himself *backward*, adding his own momentum to Cobb's, and they both tipped up and over the railing. Cobb slid headfirst past him as Jason hung on to the railing exactly as though his life depended on it. His left hand slipped but his right hung on. There was a painful, wrenching torque in his wrist and shoulder, but he didn't fall. From below came a loud thud. As Jason struggled to grab the railing with his other hand, he wondered how Cobb had fared in his fall to the pavement below.

Was he lying below with a broken neck?

Was he thumping back up the stairs even now to where Jason hung helpless?

That thought was a kick in the ass. He took a deep breath and somehow, from somewhere, found the strength to pull himself up and back over the railing. He looked down into the parking lot below and saw Cobb rising to his feet from the pavement. There was a shallow dent in the hood of Jason's Camry.

Cobb wasn't dead. Nor was his neck or back broken. He didn't look terribly hurt, in fact. He just looked . . . pissed off.

And he was heading for the stairs again. Jason looked around for the knife but didn't see it.

*"Hey,"* someone called. "What the hell's going on out here?"

The clerk with the sideburns was standing at the open door to the motel's reception area. Jason watched Cobb stop in his tracks and turn to look at the guy.

"Get inside, *fast,*" Jason yelled. "And call 911."

The clerk ducked back through the door.

Jason looked down at Cobb, who was staring back up at him now, the look in his eyes a messy blend of anger, confusion, hatred, and pain. He looked weary. And sick. Yet, to Jason, he still looked more than capable of unspeakable violence. Then Cobb's eyes shifted over to the door where the clerk had disappeared. Jason watched as he seemed to be debating whether to try to kill the clerk before he called 911 . . . calculating the odds, how much time it would take, wondering whether the clerk would be able to identify him if he were allowed to live. After a moment, his eyes drifted back up to Jason.

"Interesting advice, Jason . . . telling him to call the cops while you've got two guys up in your room, one of them dead and the other unconscious."

*Oh, shit.*

"Wonder how long until they get here. When they do, you're gonna have some explaining to do. There are different ways you could go. You could decide you've finally had enough and try to convince them I was Crackerjack all along. Maybe they'll keep their minds open about that. Maybe they'll try to ignore the evidence they'll definitely find against you, and the fact that there is none against me—and don't think your pal Ben can help you because he was unconscious before he even saw me coming tonight. Yeah, maybe the cops will listen to your crazy story, at least enough to investigate me while they keep you behind bars. In the meantime, though, where will Sophie and Max be while you're locked up? Will they be safe? I haven't even tried to find them yet, Jason. And police investigations take time . . . there are stakeouts and search warrants and questioning and all sorts of hoops to jump through before an arrest warrant is issued. How long can your family hide out? Not long enough, I think. And the second I realize that the cops have taken the slightest interest in me, I will gut your family like fish. First, I'll kill Max while Sophie watches helplessly from her wheelchair. I'll slice him open, then skin him. When I'm done, I'll do the same to her. Sure, the cops might catch me after, and you might even end up a hero after all for turning me in. But at what price?"

As Jason listened, he kept expecting to hear sirens at any moment.

"But there's another option, Jason."

"Yeah?"

"Sure. You can refuse to say a thing. Or, hell, say anything you want, as long as you keep me out of it. You'll go to prison for a long time, unless you find yourself one hell of a lawyer, but at least Sophie and Max will be alive. It's your choice."

He turned and started walking away across the parking lot, toward a panel truck parked in a remote corner, in the shadows of the trees bordering the motel on one side.

"Of course," he added over his shoulder, "if you want to try, maybe you can get away before the cops even show up. But that's your call." He opened the door of the truck. Before he climbed in, he called, "I guess this was strike two. I don't think you'll get a third one."

Jason sprinted back to his room.

How long *did* he have?

He ran to Ben first and knelt beside his chair. He put two fingers on his friend's neck and felt a pulse, steady and strong. A quick visual once-over and hands-on examination made him believe that Ben was physically unharmed but for what appeared to be a couple of angry little welts at the base of his neck, where it met his shoulder, similar to marks

Jason had on his chest when he first woke up in Wallace Barton's stable. Stun-gun marks. Nothing serious.

A mere glance at the mostly naked body on the bed was enough to tell him that Wheeler hadn't been as fortunate. He was sprawled across the bedspread, his eyes wide open, his head lying at an unnatural angle.

Cobb had been right. This death was on Jason.

*God . . .*

He had to get moving. In his mind, he heard a giant clock ticking. Soon, he would hear sirens, too, and they wouldn't be only in his head. There was so much to do and only seconds to do it. But he suddenly couldn't move.

Couldn't think.

Couldn't—

He took a deep breath. Then another. Then a third. Then he sprang into motion. He had to get Wheeler out of here. And Ben, too. He couldn't let his friend wake up in a strange motel room with no idea what had happened to him. It wasn't fair to Ben, and it would certainly raise some troublesome questions for both of them when the police arrived.

The dead body was the priority, though.

The ticking in Jason's head was almost deafening.

He rushed to the window, listening for sirens, looking for flashing lights. Nothing yet. He stepped out of his room. His was one of only two cars in the lot. The other was probably the clerk's. Thankfully, the Sleep Easy Motel was doing a slow business tonight.

Jason realized that the clerk might be looking out the window, waiting for the police. He couldn't have that right now.

He hurried to the phone, snatched up the receiver, and punched the zero button. A moment later, the clerk answered.

"Yeah?"

"I'm the guy who was just attacked," Jason said. "The guy who did it is still around here somewhere. If I were you, I'd hide until the cops get here. Do you have a back room?"

"There's an office."

"Get inside and lock it."

"Okay. Should I—"

*"Do it."*

He slammed the receiver into its cradle and hurried back to the dead man. Kneeling beside the bed, he dug his arms under the body and lifted, using his knees as much as possible. Then he swung the corpse onto his shoulder.

At the door, he snatched his car keys from the top of the dresser and paused, listening one last time for signs that the police were on the way. Nothing yet.

He took a breath, opened the door, and leaned his head out. Seeing no one, he stepped outside with Wheeler's body, utterly exposed, expecting to be seen by someone at any moment. But what choice did he have? He carried the corpse down the stairs, groaning under its weight and silently agreeing with Cobb that a first-floor room would have made this far easier. He stumbled once, and Wheeler's head hit the railing with a dull clang. Jason winced and kept going.

Somewhere across Danvers, sirens sounded.

He hurried over to his car, cursing the fact that the lighting in the parking lot was quite good. He hoped like hell he was right and no one was watching as he opened the trunk with the remote. As carefully as he could, he lowered Wheeler inside, then shut the lid as quietly as possible.

The sirens sounded closer.

He raced back up to his room. Inside, he moved quickly to Ben, knelt in front of his chair, tore tape from his wrists and ankles, and did the fireman's carry again. He pulled the door shut behind him and tramped down the stairs on legs that were turning to lead, holding on to Ben with one hand and relying on the strength of the handrail with the other. He yanked open the back door of his Camry and wrestled Ben's unconscious body across the back seat.

The sirens were definitely closer, mere blocks away now. No time to retrieve his laptop or other things from the room. He cursed as he started the car, then pulled out of the lot, forcing himself to drive calmly and just below the speed limit. Two blocks later he passed a police car heading in the direction of the motel.

He was in the clear for the moment, but Cobb was right: Eventually, he was going to have some explaining to do.

# CHAPTER FIFTY-ONE

As he drove, Jason kept one eye out for police cars and the other eye on the speedometer, trying very hard to maintain a speed three miles per hour below the limit. It would be extraordinarily bad to be pulled over right now. The unconscious man sprawled across the back seat would be difficult to explain. The dead one in the trunk would be even harder. And the small bag in the trunk, next to the dead body—the bag of things he'd found in his apartment that Cobb had planted there, things that had belonged to Crackerjack's victims and that surely had their DNA on them—would be downright impossible. He took out his phone and dialed Sophie's number, praying she hadn't decided to turn it off for the night. She answered on the second ring.

"Jason?"

"Did you tell your mother where you are?"

"Why? What's wrong?"

He should have led with something less alarming, but it was too late now.

"Sophie, did you tell your mother that you're staying with Geri? It's important."

"What happened, Jason?"

"Did you tell her?"

"No, I didn't."

"Are you sure?"

"Of course I am."

"So she has no idea? There's no way she could know?"

"No. We've spoken once a day, chatted for a bit. I've only let her say quick good nights to Max, claiming that he's been tired after long, full days."

He blew out a breath he hadn't been aware he was holding. She and Max were safe for now. Cobb couldn't possibly figure out where they were.

"Is Mom okay?" she asked. "Is she in danger?"

"No. I just thought maybe . . . no, she's not. She's fine. I promise."

After a long moment, she said, "So tell me what's going on then."

"I can't. Not right now." His mind flashed to the dead contract killer in his trunk. "I have something I have to take care of right away."

"It's almost midnight."

"I know. I'm sorry. I'll call you in the morning."

"You'll call me immediately after you take care of whatever you have to take care of."

He sighed. "Okay. I gotta go."

He hung up after nearly saying *I love you* by accident, then wished he'd said it anyway. What the hell?

It took a moment to get his bearings. At first, he'd simply wanted to get as far from the Sleep Easy Motel as possible. Eventually, though, he had to decide what to do with Wheeler's body. He thought about the nearby towns he had known so well growing up—Swampscott, where he was born, and Danvers, Beverly, Salem, Lynn—and realized he had to think about them differently now, see them with fresh eyes. In high school, his concerns had been where to go to hang out with friends or make out with girls. As he grew older, he thought about things like where to buy a new augur belt for a snow blower and which playgrounds would be fun for Max. Now he was forced to think about the best place to dispose of a corpse.

The town dump in Salem? Wasn't there one in Marblehead, too? How about one of the dumpsters behind the Stop & Shop?

The thing was, he had no idea where security cameras would be. This was the kind of thing most people looking to dispose of bodies probably considered ahead of time.

Eventually, it occurred to him what to do. And Cobb was right; he'd done him a favor breaking Wheeler's neck rather than slicing his throat and letting him bleed all over Jason's motel room.

Twenty-six minutes later, just before midnight, Jason was cruising down Ronald Wheeler's street in Lowell. Traffic had been nonexistent, given the lateness of the hour, and there were very few lights on in the houses on the street. Not a living soul in sight.

Jason backed into Wheeler's driveway, then stepped out of the car, closing the door quietly behind him. If Wheeler's body hadn't been nearly naked, he would have checked it for house keys. But unless the man carried them in a highly unusual place, Jason would have to find another way into the house. He hurried to the front porch and conducted a quick and ultimately fruitless search for a hidden key. He sighed and trotted quickly around to the back of the house, stepping through calf-high grass and over a rusted shovel. On a windowsill at the back of the house he saw the flowerpot in which he was supposed to leave $8,000 after Wheeler had killed Cobb.

At the back door, he tried the knob and found it locked. He picked up a rock and was about to break a window in the door as quietly as he could when he paused, stepped over to the flowerpot, and looked inside. And saw a key. Inside the house, he wiped the key vigorously with his shirt to obscure fingerprints before leaving it on a kitchen counter, then went back and did the same with the doorknob.

He hurried through the dark house and, at the front door, grasped the knob through his shirt and opened the door. He was starting to think he should have worn gloves. At the car outside, he popped the trunk and looked down at the body inside . . . and his legs almost gave out on him. This man was dead because of him. He had also certainly shed untold pieces of trace evidence and samples of his DNA inside the trunk. God help them both.

Without a lot of leverage, this part was going to be difficult. He bent over and worked his hands beneath the body and was concentrating so hard on his labor that he didn't hear movement behind him.

"What are you doing?"

He nearly cried out as he spun around to find Ben watching him with confusion in his sleepy eyes.

"Jason?"

"Ben," Jason began in a whisper, "I can explain . . . I think. Just not right now."

"What?"

"*Keep your voice down.* Please. I'll explain it all, but right now I really have to hurry."

Ben blinked groggily, looked down at the body in the trunk, then back up at Jason. He suddenly looked wide awake.

"Seriously, Ben, you should probably just get back in the car and wait for me."

Ben looked into the trunk again. "That's not Ian Cobb."

"No, it's not."

Ben looked at the dead man a moment longer. "You're going to be a while if I don't help you." He took hold of Wheeler's feet. "But I'll definitely need some answers once we get the hell out of here."

Jason nodded gratefully as he slid his hands under the dead man's shoulders. He whispered, "One, two, three," and together they lifted the body out of the trunk and shuffled up the short walkway, up three stairs to the porch, and into the house. Jason used his foot to nudge the door closed.

"I'm a lawyer," Ben said, sounding almost surprised, as if he'd just remembered. "If we get caught, I'll be disbarred. Two hundred thousand dollars in tuition down the toilet. Years of my life wasted."

"I'd worry more about the years of your life you'll waste in prison. Try not to touch anything."

"I already figured out that much. Who are we carrying?"

"Can I just tell you later?"

"Okay. What do we do with him?"

"I'm not sure. He's got a broken neck."

"Did you—? You know what? Just tell me later."

They stood in the foyer, looking around the dark house.

"The stairs," Jason said, nodding toward a flight of steps leading up to the second floor. "We'll position him at the bottom of the stairs, with his feet higher than his head."

"Like he fell and broke his neck."

"Exactly."

"Think it will fool people?"

"I'm hoping. He's not the kind of guy whose death is going to make many folks lose much sleep, especially the police."

"Why not?"

"He's a hit man."

"You know what? Don't bother telling me anything else. I don't want to know. Let's just hope you're right and no one looks too hard at this."

They dragged the body to the stairs and positioned it as realistically as possible.

"Looks terrific," Ben said. "Hey, I could sure use a beer. How about you? Ready to go?"

Jason followed Ben across the foyer. At the door, he resisted the urge to take a last look at the man who would still be alive if Jason had never knocked on his door.

# CHAPTER FIFTY-TWO

Ian Cobb stood in the dark living room of Sophie Swike's house, staring down at the older woman who had fallen asleep on the sofa with the television on. What was her name? Janet? No, Janice. He'd never been tempted to hurt a woman, but he'd really disliked this one when he met her. Still, it would be an unnecessary complication, one he should avoid if possible.

He and the woman were alone in the house, which was disappointing. He'd found empty beds in the two rooms down the hall, as well as the ones upstairs.

He realized he still had his lock picks in his hand, so he slipped them into their little leather case, then slid the case into his back pocket. He almost hadn't gotten the chance to use them. After he'd picked the deadbolt on the back door a little while ago, he was about to let himself in when he'd glanced into the dark kitchen and saw, on a nearby wall, a home-security panel that hadn't been there the first time he'd broken into this house. He cursed silently before noticing the green light on the panel, indicating that the system wasn't armed.

He eased himself into the armchair by the fireplace and watched the sleeping woman. He really didn't want to wake her and force her to divulge the whereabouts of her daughter and grandson. He honestly didn't like the idea of hurting a woman if he could avoid it, even this one, and he wasn't necessarily ready to deal with the complications that would arise from the torture and eventual death of Jason's mother-in-law.

How had he gotten here? What the hell had he *done*? Everything had been sailing along smoothly. He and Wallace had a good thing going . . . until they grabbed the wrong guy—a guy who looked so damn much like Johnny, and whose life had too many commonalities with Cobb's own to be ignored. A guy his inner voice told him was special. A guy with an Inside Dark of his own. If only Cobb could have ignored those whispers in his brain. If only he could have killed Jason and forgotten all about him. Everything would be as it had been. And Cobb wouldn't be in this damn situation.

He knew that Jason had to die. Still, it wouldn't be easy for Cobb to watch that happen. He remembered seeing Johnny's dead body after the accident. It had been cleaned and scrubbed but the damage done in the crash was horrendously evident. He couldn't stand seeing his brother that way, pale and dead and broken. Why the hell had he refused to keep doing what Johnny needed him to do to feel better? When Johnny drove himself into that concrete bridge, it might as well have been Cobb behind the wheel. He'd killed his younger brother. And now, he knew, he had no choice but to kill Jason.

With a last glance at the sleeping woman, Cobb stood and walked quietly into the kitchen, where he remembered from his last visit having seen a cordless phone on an answering machine base. He lifted the receiver, studied it for a moment, then pressed the "Menu" button and navigated to the call log. There were only six outgoing calls over the last few days, and all were to the same number with a 781 area code. In fact, almost every call as far back as Cobb looked was to that number. It told him two things: first, it was almost certainly Sophie's cell number, and second, that Janice needed to get a life. There were a few calls to other local numbers, but they were from the previous week, before

Sophie had whisked Max away to wherever she had taken him. Cobb then navigated to the incoming call log and saw a surprising number of calls from a multitude of area codes from around the country. Most had lasted only a few seconds, just long enough to leave a voice mail. Media calls, Cobb realized. Two numbers jumped out at him, though: Sophie's cell and a number with an 802 area code, which Cobb happened to know was the only one used in Vermont. There were two calls over the last couple of days from that second number, both coming in close to 8:00 p.m., and both lasting for several minutes—long enough for Janice to chat with her daughter a little before saying good night to her grandson.

Sophie should have stuck to her cell phone, Cobb thought with a satisfied smile, because if the 802 number was listed, it shouldn't be difficult to find an address to go along with it. On his smartphone, he called up a reverse white-pages website and entered the number. And there it was. An address in Woodstock, Vermont, for a Geraldine Hurd. Cobb opened Facebook on his phone, searched for a Geraldine Hurd in Vermont, and found a "Geri Hurd" in Woodstock. Fortunately, Geri didn't keep her friends private, and it took him only a moment to find Sophie Swike's name among them.

Cobb had no doubt he'd find Jason Swike's family in Woodstock, Vermont. He wasn't looking forward to killing a woman and a child, but he'd do whatever it took to make Jason come to him. And besides, it wasn't like he had a hard and fast rule against it. It was more of a guideline, really.

# CHAPTER FIFTY-THREE

On the drive back to Danvers, Jason explained everything to Ben, who needed a few minutes of silence to process the fact that he had been stunned into unconsciousness and held captive by a serial killer. The silence ended when he said, "So I'm clear on this, you just walked out and left me there?"

"You're alive, aren't you?"

"Lucky for you. What the hell am I wearing?" he asked, looking down at Wheeler's coveralls.

"Those belonged to . . . the guy we just left."

"How did I—"

"Cobb put you in them."

After a brief pause, Ben said, "Where are *my* clothes? That charcoal pinstripe suit was—ah, forget it." A moment later, he said, "Listen, I know I just helped you cover up a murder, but are you sure it isn't time to call the police?"

"Don't you think I'd call them if I *could*, Ben? If I thought it would do any good? You think I like wondering when Cobb will kill again, knowing that if he does it will be on *my* head? You think I wouldn't risk going to jail if it were only me I had to worry about? But it's not. Sophie and Max would be in danger."

He took a long breath. Ben waited him out.

"Besides, I'd probably be exposing my family for nothing. Why would the cops believe me? Detective Briggs is already convinced that I belong behind bars for *something*. And all the evidence points to *me*, not Cobb." Ben said nothing. "And I know what you must be thinking. I'm choosing my family over strangers. And you're right. I am."

Neither man spoke for a few seconds. "Okay," Ben finally said, "so that's a *no* on calling the police. Got it."

"So now I—"

The *ding* of his cell phone interrupted him. He pulled the phone from his pocket and saw that another text had arrived from Wheeler's phone even though Wheeler was lying dead at the bottom of his stairs at home. It was obviously from Cobb.

Then a thought struck Jason like a hammer blow. Cobb had sent multiple texts from Wheeler's phone, which meant that Jason's number was the last one contacted by it. Sure, Cobb had the phone with him, but if the cops looked into phone records, they'd certainly wonder why someone like Wheeler had texted Jason Swike close to the time he died.

*Damn it.* He had to hope that the cops truly weren't interested in delving too deeply into the death of acquitted killer-for-hire Ronald Wheeler. But the phone was yet another bit of leverage Cobb had over Jason.

And he now saw that more than merely a text had just arrived. A video accompanied the brief message, which read, The whole video is too long to send but you should get the drift from these few seconds.

Jason glanced back at the road to make sure he wasn't about to run off the highway, then started the video. It was less than half a minute long. At first, a tree filled the screen. Then the camera moved past the tree and slowly zoomed in on something not far away. Jason recognized the motel parking lot. On his little screen, Jason carried a mostly naked body down the stairs of a motel, then deposited it in the trunk of his car.

He realized that when Cobb had left the motel earlier, he must have parked around the corner and walked back to the parking lot through the trees.

From the passenger seat, Ben was leaning over and looking at the screen.

"Damn."

The phone rang in Jason's hand. He didn't need to look at the display to know who was calling.

*"What?"*

"I'm glad you got away before the cops arrived," Cobb said.

"What do you want?"

"You watch my little movie yet? I got better quality video than I'd hoped for. I assume it's more obvious than ever that you can't call the police."

Cobb had played him perfectly, knowing that Jason would have had little choice but to dispose of the body, and all Cobb had to do was record the event to add significantly to his leverage.

"Things got ugly between us, Jason."

"Things were always ugly, Cobb."

"True enough, I guess." He paused. "Even if I swear to leave you and your family alone, there's no chance you're going to look the other way and let me do what I do in peace, is there?"

"Every time I hear about another murder, or even a missing person, I'll wonder if it's another person dead because I didn't do something about you now. I can't live like that. My wife wouldn't let me live like that."

"You can't take the blame for what I do, Jason."

*I might have no choice, if you keep planting evidence to set me up,* he thought.

"I can't help it," he said. "We'd never feel safe."

Cobb was silent for a moment. "That's what I thought. I'm going to have to kill you. I didn't want to. I know you're not my brother, but . . .

I really felt something between us. Crazy, I know. But you've left me no choice. It's either you or me . . . and I think we both know how that comes out."

"You or me," Jason said. "Does that mean you'll keep Ben out of it from now on?"

Out of the corner of his eye, Jason saw Ben leaning toward him from the passenger seat, straining a little against his seat belt.

"If he keeps himself out of it," Cobb replied. "But when you're dead, if I suspect he's even considering saying anything to the cops about my involvement, I'll kill him. And if he has family—brothers, sisters, parents—I'll kill them, too. Tell him that."

"I will. How about *my* family? You'll leave them out of it, too?"

"Once you're gone, if Sophie keeps her mouth shut about me, I won't have to hurt her . . . or Max. Her mother, either. Deal?"

"Sophie will do whatever she has to do to protect Max, I promise you, even if that means letting my killer go free." He paused. "If you're the one still alive at the end, that is."

Cobb said nothing for a moment. Jason thought he heard him chuckle.

"I'm sorry it came to this, Jason," Cobb said after a moment. "As soon as I hang this phone up, I'm going to start thinking of you as just another guy. Just another future victim. Any connection between us will be cut. You understand? So watch your back."

"You, too."

Jason heard that chuckle again, or perhaps it was a sigh, right before Cobb disconnected.

He shook his head and looked over at Ben. "Cobb said—"

"I know. Your phone's loud. I could hear Cobb's half of the conversation, too."

Jason sighed. "I have to kill him myself. There's no other way."

"You mean *we* have to kill him."

"No, Ben. *I* have to kill him. Not you. You need to stay out of it."

"I'm already *in* it. Remember a little while ago when I helped you stage that dead guy's fake fall down the stairs?"

"Sorry about that."

"Don't be. Cobb brought me into this, not you."

"If you stay out of it, he'll leave you alone."

"You really believe that?"

He didn't know what to believe.

"Cobb made me a part of it," Ben said. "His mistake. Now he has to face both of us."

Jason looked over at his friend. "Is that seriously supposed to make me feel better?"

"You know it does. Admit it."

Jason let a small, weary smile slip through his defenses.

"You think he'll really leave Sophie and Max alone?" Ben asked.

"He'll know I told her everything, which means she could go to the cops at any time. No, he won't leave them alone. All the more reason for him to die."

"At least she's safe for now."

Jason's phone rang again. Assuming Cobb was calling him back, he answered without looking at the display.

"What now?"

"That's a nice phone manner you have, Jason."

"Janice? It's late." He glanced at the dashboard clock: 12:48 a.m. He thought of Sophie and Max and his heart began to race. "Is everything okay?"

"I'm sorry to call so late. I figured if you were asleep or something, the call would go to your voice mail."

"Are you all right?"

"I'm fine. I'm just wondering something. Is there any chance you were here earlier? Within the last hour or two?"

An unpleasant crawling sensation began at the base of Jason's neck and traveled swiftly down his arms and his spine.

"Why do you ask?"

"Well, Sophie and Max are away as you know, and you're the only other person with a key to the house."

"Janice, was someone in the house?"

"I'm not sure. I fell asleep in the living room a couple of hours ago. A few minutes ago I thought I heard something. A door closing maybe. Not loud, but whatever it was, it woke me up."

"But why do you think—"

"I'm coming to that. I was getting a glass of water to take up to bed when I noticed the kitchen phone off the base. But I always keep it on the base. Always. So I always know where to find it. And besides," she continued, "it *felt* like someone had been in the house. There was something in the air. A faint lingering odor maybe. Or just a *feeling*. That probably sounds silly to you."

"Wasn't the alarm on?"

"I hadn't set it yet. I was going to on my way upstairs."

"Janice, if you're worried about someone being in the house, maybe you should get out of there right away. Then call the police."

"There's no need for that. I figured you had been here and I wondered why, so I looked around the whole house to see what you might have been doing here. There's no one here. If someone was, he's gone now."

She'd never liked Jason all that much, he knew, and she liked him even less after the accident that left her daughter disabled—an accident for which she surely blamed him, and justifiably so—but God only knew what she thought he'd been doing there tonight. The important thing at the moment was that if Cobb had been there, he was gone now.

"Janice, please set the alarm right now."

"Do you think I'm in danger?"

"I don't," he said truthfully, "but you should be setting it anyway."

"You think someone was here?"

"Honestly, no," he lied. "Most likely you left the phone off the charger yourself—everyone makes mistakes, right?—and then spooked yourself into thinking someone had been there."

"I truly doubt—"

"I'm sorry, Janice, but I have to go. Good night." He ended the call.

"What was all that?" Ben asked.

He worked it through quickly. It was certainly possible Janice had merely left the phone off the base. But no, he felt sure Cobb had been there. Why? To get to Sophie and Max. But they weren't home. So why didn't he try to force their whereabouts out of Janice? He couldn't have known that she didn't know their true location. Yet he didn't even wake her. Why?

Because he didn't need to. He got the information some other way. The phone was off the hook. Call logs. He found Geri's number, then used it to learn her address.

"Jason? What are you thinking?"

"*Damn it.* He has a huge head start."

# CHAPTER FIFTY-FOUR

Jason was calling again. The second time in the past twenty minutes. And again, Cobb didn't answer. This time, though, Jason left a message.

"Cobb, I've been thinking about what you said. About us going our separate ways. About you leaving my family alone if I forget about you. Well, you win. I couldn't live with myself if anything happened to Sophie and Max. So I'm taking them away. Far away. Somewhere you'll never find us. Don't even bother trying. I've written about characters who need to disappear. I've researched the hell out of it. And I know how to do it. So forget about us, Cobb. And I'll try to forget about you. And when I read about a murder somewhere, I'll tell myself it couldn't have been you. I'll ask myself, what are the odds it was you? No way it was you. If I tell myself that enough times, maybe I'll start to believe it. Anyway, to hell with you, you son of a bitch."

Cobb didn't know what to make of the message. Was Jason telling the truth?

Probably not. He was simply panicking. That was good. He wouldn't think clearly if he was panicking.

And he had good reason to be nervous, Cobb thought as he drove slowly past Geri Hurd's house. Because there was no way Jason could have beaten Cobb here. And there were no signs of police activity. The windows were dark, as expected in the middle of the night. Everyone would be sleeping. That would make things easier.

Geri's house was the second in from the cross street, and Cobb parked around the corner. First he would secure the people inside; then he'd pull his van into the driveway and carry them out one by one. He switched his phone into silent mode and walked to Geri's house, staying in the shadows of the trees lining the street when he could. When he reached the house, he moved quickly toward the back, ducking below the level of the windows. He knelt at the back door and peered through one of its windows into the kitchen. He didn't see evidence of a security system or a dog and, with his lock picks, made quick work of both the dead bolt and the lock in the knob. He opened the door quietly, stepped into the dark kitchen, and took a moment to listen to the house. He heard nothing but the hum of the refrigerator.

His plan was simple. He'd tie up Sophie and Max and Sophie's friend, then call Jason and tell him to come save them. He'd ask how he could do that, and Cobb would agree to accept his life in exchange for theirs. Because Cobb was tired of this. Jason was never going to come around. That was obvious now. It was time to end it. If Jason wanted them to live, he would have to die. If he didn't agree to come, they were dead. If Cobb heard a siren or saw a cop car, they were dead.

Cobb would have to pretend to believe that Sophie would keep her mouth shut about his killing Jason in order to protect her son, and he would promise to let them go if Jason had the guts to do the right thing, if he loved his family enough to make the ultimate sacrifice for them.

It wasn't true, of course. Once they were all dead, Cobb would stage it like a murder-suicide. It wouldn't be difficult to believe: Jason, who never got over his wife leaving him and taking their son with her, goes postal. That kind of thing happened all the time.

Standing in the living room, lit only by the wan moonlight drifting in through the window, he looked down at an unfinished puzzle on the coffee table. He headed quietly for the hallway, figuring that Sophie had to be staying in a first-floor room. He slipped his stun gun from his pocket as he neared the first door. A bathroom. The next door down the hall was ajar. A glance revealed a sleeping bag on the floor beside a pullout sofa that had been made up and used as a bed. The sleeping bag was empty and the bedcovers on the pullout were in disarray.

*Damn it.*

He checked the rest of the house, finding it just as empty. Geri Hurd had almost certainly taken the Swikes wherever they were going, given that Sophie couldn't drive and there was no way Jason could have picked them up yet, not if he first wanted to dispose of the dead body Cobb had left him with, which he'd certainly want to do before reuniting with his family.

Cobb frowned. Had Jason somehow guessed that Cobb figured out where Sophie and Max were staying and was coming for them? Or had he simply planned to meet his family somewhere, as he claimed in his message, and Cobb had arrived after they'd left? Whichever the case, Cobb had no idea where to start looking for them. Given Jason's failure at hiding from him in a motel, it was doubtful he'd let his wife and son go to one. More likely, he'd meet up with them somewhere and they would disappear together, for a while at least. That would make them difficult to track down. Sure, Cobb would find them eventually, but until then, he'd have to look over his shoulder . . . for the cops, in case Jason grew tired of hiding out . . . and possibly even for Jason himself, if he ever recognized and embraced the darkness in him and decided to come after Cobb.

Cobb's eyes fell on a broken living room window, and a rock on the floor surrounded by shards of glass. Then he heard a siren not far away. Sophie—or, more likely, her friend—must have tossed the rock through the window from the outside as they left to make it seem as though someone had broken in, then called the cops, possibly posing as a neighbor.

Jason had gone all-in on this. He was planning to escape with his family—to hide out or start over or whatever he was planning—while at the same time hoping Cobb would be arrested for breaking and entering. It wouldn't land him behind bars for long, maybe only a year or two, but Jason probably figured that would be long enough for his family and him to disappear for good.

He was dead wrong, though.

The sirens were almost there. Cobb hurried through the house and was slipping out the back door and through the neighbor's yard as the police were banging on Geraldine Hurd's front door.

Down the street and around the corner, behind the wheel of his truck again, Cobb pulled away from the curb and left the neighborhood slowly, without passing the Hurd residence or the police. Moments later, he was on his way back to Massachusetts. He had two and a half hours to kill. He would spend that time thinking about the things he'd do to Jason when he caught him. Maybe he'd come up with something truly unique—unique and really painful. Something he'd want to try on others. Something that would earn him a snazzy new nickname from the media. Maybe Jason would become the first official murder committed by a new serial killer, one with a signature far more interesting than Crackerjack's face painting and bone breaking had been.

His body could never be found, of course. He had too much of a connection to Cobb. But he could be a good test subject, someone on whom Cobb could experiment before settling on a new method, something that might please the thing inside him.

Before he killed Jason, Cobb would have to remember to thank him for his sacrifice.

# CHAPTER FIFTY-FIVE

Jason's cell phone rang, and he almost punched his thumb through the display screen when he answered it.

"Sophie?"

"It's me. We're out."

Thank God. As soon as he'd realized that Cobb was likely going after his family, he'd called her and told her to get the hell out Geri Hurd's house. By his rough calculation, at that time of night, it would take Cobb less than two and a half hours to get there. Assuming he had gone right to Sophie's house in Swampscott after leaving the motel, then left immediately for Woodstock, he'd probably been less than thirty minutes away when Jason sounded the alarm. Considering that Sophie's physical limitations would slow their getaway, there had been no time to spare.

"Geri was able to get you all out of there?"

"She couldn't carry me down the porch stairs, but she helped me slide down them. We left Max in the house for that. I didn't want him to see."

Jason had never hated Cobb more than at that moment.

"We're heading to—"

"Don't tell me," he said quickly. "Don't go to a motel, but don't tell me where you're going. I don't want to know. Just in case . . ."

She didn't ask *Just in case what?* "Okay. But aren't you coming to meet us?"

He hesitated. "I would. I want to. But I have to . . . take care of things here."

"Which means . . ."

"It means I'll do what I have to do to take care of things here."

"If I wasn't in a damn wheelchair, Jason—"

"I know. I wouldn't want to be in Cobb's shoes if that were the case. Listen, do you still have Ben's number?"

"I think so. Yes, I'm sure I do."

She had to be terrified, but he couldn't tell from her remarkably steady voice.

"He left here a little while ago, on his way to you. Call him and tell him where to meet you. He'll stay with you until . . . it's all over."

"Which will be when?"

He had no idea. "No more than a few hours, I hope."

After a long pause, she asked, "You really can't go to the police?"

"I can't."

"Okay." He heard her take a deep breath. "Listen good to me now. I don't want you to get hurt." He was glad to hear that. "And I don't want Max to get hurt, either."

"Neither do I. So . . ."

"So you need to do whatever you have to do. You understand what I'm saying?"

After another moment of silence, he said, "I think so. Aren't you worried about . . ."

"A little. But you have to stop him. So do whatever you have to do. Just don't get hurt or killed." After a moment's pause, she added, "And if there *is* something . . . something inside you that . . . well, *use it* if you have to. Embrace it if it helps. Whatever it takes."

There wasn't much he could say to that, so he said nothing.

"But Jason? Just don't lose yourself, okay? You know what I mean?"

"I do. And don't worry, Soph. There isn't . . . I'm not—" He stopped himself. He was tired of their disagreement about this. "I won't," he said. "I swear." Just before he ended the call, on impulse, he added, "I love you, Soph."

A tiny pause, then, "Seriously, Jason? *Now?*"

"Sorry."

He disconnected and set his phone to silent mode. From the Camry's trunk he grabbed a tire iron, then he walked around the corner and down two blocks until he was standing across the street from Ian Cobb's house. It was a center entrance colonial, like most of the houses on the street. What struck Jason was how *normal* it looked. This was the house of an infamous serial killer, yet from the outside there was no clue as to the evil that lived within its walls.

The house looked dark from the street, which wasn't surprising. Cobb was almost certainly on his way back from Vermont at the moment and had no family but his father, who was lying in a facility someplace, no doubt, where medical professionals could care for him around the clock. There was no car in the driveway. A car was parked on the street between Cobb's house and the neighbor's to the right, but it obviously wasn't Cobb's or it would have been in his driveway.

Jason's plan was simple. He'd try to get inside, then do a quick search for anything linking him to Crackerjack, just in case, evidence he'd take with him when he left later. Then he'd wait for Cobb and kill him the second he entered the house. With any luck, it would look like a burglary gone tragically wrong.

Cobb had left him no viable alternative. Jason would have to ambush him and kill him. Cave his head in with the tire iron, which would be ugly and bloody but also dripping with poetic justice.

This wouldn't be easy. As much as Cobb deserved it, this would truly be murder in cold blood. Despite what had or hadn't gone through his mind the night of the car accident, something he would never know for sure . . . despite his killing Wallace Barton in self-defense . . . he had never truly imagined himself capable of something like this. But he needed to be.

He stood in the shadows, closed his eyes, and listened for a voice inside him, a voice urging him on, telling him that he was doing the right thing, the only thing he could do to save his family, to save countless others from Ian Cobb. He stood in the dark, looking inward, listening inward, hoping just a little to hear encouraging whispers, but terrified of hearing them, too.

He heard nothing. Did that mean there was no darkness inside him after all? Or was it simply staying out of this fight, perhaps waiting to see if Jason would prove himself worthy?

Crazy thoughts.

*Get your head in the game.*

He checked the time on his phone. If Cobb came straight home from Woodstock, he'd arrive less than two hours from now. He might take the time to check the Sleep Easy Motel, Jason's apartment, Sophie's house, and even Ben's apartment, but Jason doubted it. It would have been stupid for Jason to be in any of those places, and Cobb knew it. Either way, he'd come home eventually.

And Jason would be waiting for him.

First, though, he had to get into the house. If he had to, he'd break a window—one that Cobb wouldn't notice when he first arrived. The houses on either side of Cobb's were dark. The neighborhood was asleep. Jason moved quickly through the shadows, tire iron in hand, along the side of the house. At the back door, he peered into what looked like a mudroom and saw no alarm panel. Without much hope, he tried the doorknob, using the hand-through-the-shirt trick to avoid leaving fingerprints. To his surprise, the knob turned, and he pushed the door open.

Was he wrong? Maybe Cobb didn't go to Vermont at all. Maybe this was a trap. Could he be waiting inside, weapon in hand, like Jason had been planning to do?

He was about to find out.

# CHAPTER FIFTY-SIX

Jason stood in the mudroom of Cobb's house and listened. As expected, he heard nothing. After a moment, he started moving through the moonlit kitchen, toward the hallway. The sweat in his palm made the tire iron slip slightly in his grasp, and when he readjusted his grip the tool clanked against the kitchen table. If Cobb had been home, he probably would have heard—

Footsteps sounded above him. He froze. For too long, he froze. The footsteps were on the stairs now, and a light clicked on in the hallway.

"Mr. Cobb?"

A woman's voice. It came from near the bottom of the stairs. Jason had no choice but to duck through the doorway to his right, into a bathroom. A nightlight glowed from an outlet above the vanity. He pulled the door shut and locked it.

The footsteps stopped right outside the bathroom.

"Mr. Cobb?"

After a moment, Jason responded in a voice slightly deeper than his own, as close to Cobb's as he could make it. "Yeah?"

"Everything's fine here," the woman said. "I'm heading home now, if that's all right."

He said nothing.

"All right then?"

Again, imitating Cobb's voice as best he could for the length of a single syllable, he said, "Sure."

"Okay, then. See you tomorrow."

He heard footsteps fade away down the hall. A moment later, a door opened, then closed.

He'd been half-right. Cobb wasn't home. But somebody had been.

He opened the door and peered into the hallway. Empty. Outside, a car started. It must have been the one parked on the street.

Who was that woman?

She had come from upstairs. So Jason climbed the stairs. As he neared the top, he began to hear strange, rhythmic sounds. A whirring, then a sucking, followed by a click. Then the same pattern, over and over.

He paused at the first door and looked into what appeared to be a children's bedroom. A twin bed and a set of bunk beds. Pennants and posters on the wall. Sports trophies and stuffed animals. He knew that Cobb didn't have children, so seeing this made gooseflesh rise on his arms.

As he approached the second door, which stood open, the sounds grew louder and he recognized them for what they were. And then he was at the threshold, looking in at the pale, gaunt man in the bed, his stick-figure arms at his sides atop covers. Tubes ran from his throat to a machine in the corner, a ventilator. According to Cobb, his father had been like this for eight years.

It had never crossed Jason's mind that Cobb kept his incapacitated father here at home. He had assumed the man would be in a long-term-care facility. That must have been a nurse who left moments ago.

He couldn't imagine how much it cost Cobb to have his father live with him . . . if one could call what he was doing *living*. And Cobb had said he intended to keep his father alive for as long as medical science would allow, despite pleas for mercy from the old man's doctor. Jason shuddered. He had no idea what this man had done to Ian Cobb, what sins he had committed, but no one should be made to exist like this.

Jason felt a barely perceptible vibration in his pocket and pulled out his phone. Cobb was calling, using his own cell phone this time. Apparently, the police didn't find him at Geri's house. Jason considered letting the call go to voice mail, but after four rings, he answered.

"Where are you?" Cobb asked without preamble. "Where are *they*?"

"My family? Somewhere safe."

"For now. But not for long." Something was wrong with Cobb's speech. It was thick. And a little slurred. "That was the second time you tried to get me arrested."

"I said I wouldn't tell the cops about who you really are . . . *what* you really are. I never said I wouldn't call them at all."

As they talked, Jason stared at the face of Cobb's father, gray and drawn, his empty eyes staring sightlessly at the dark ceiling. He listened to the quiet *whir, hiss, click* of the ventilator, without which the man would suffocate and die.

"You cheated," Cobb said. "And it's going to cost you. It's going to cost you everything."

"What does that mean?"

"It means I'm done letting you jerk me around. I'm done listening to my brother's pain. You aren't worth it."

"God, you're nuts. You know what, Cobb? I'm done, too. I'm going to call the police and tell them everything."

"That's funny. That's exactly what I'm gonna do. I'll tell them how I'm starting to remember things I must have suppressed, about how you were working with Barton all along, how you were there when he broke my bones, and how *you* were the one who tackled him on top of *me*, then convinced me that I was wrong, that it was the other way around. Let's see which one of us they believe."

"I'll tell them—"

"Were you able to find all of the evidence I planted at your house?"

After a brief pause, he said, "Yes," though he doubted that was true.

"All twelve things?"

He'd found only eight, but assuming that Cobb was bluffing, he replied, "Actually, I found more than that."

"Well, I planted twenty-two. There's no way you found them all. Plus, I've got the video of you with the hit man's body. You're screwed, Jason."

It was sounding to Jason as though Cobb might be right about that.

"They'll arrest you," Cobb added. "And when they do, what will Sophie think of you? What will Max think of his daddy?"

Jason was still staring at Cobb's father.

"Jason?"

He checked the time. He probably had less than an hour now before Cobb would be home.

"Of course, it won't matter what they think because they won't be around for long. Once you're behind bars, they'll be easy pickings."

Jason spotted a box on the nightstand beside the bed. A powder-blue latex glove protruded from the top like a tissue poking out of a Kleenex box. Jason slipped a pair onto his hands.

"Enjoy your last night of freedom, Jason. And say goodbye to your family while you're at it."

"Wait."

After a pause, Cobb said, "Yeah?"

"You've got me by the balls. I have some thinking to do. I'll call you in the morning."

He hung up without another word. It was a gamble. Maybe Cobb would call the police, but he seriously doubted it. When his phone rang again, he ignored it and began to search the house, looking for any evidence Cobb might have kept that could tie him to Crackerjack's crimes. Twenty minutes later, he found a box behind a larger box on the top shelf of an upstairs closet. Inside were small jars of paint, a collection of delicate brushes, and a book on face painting.

A plan began to come to him. He put the box back and kept searching the house. Forty-six minutes later, when Cobb pulled into the driveway, Jason was back outside, watching from behind a tree down the block. He was ready.

Someone was going to die tonight. And Jason would be either a cold-blooded murderer or a victim. He wasn't thrilled about either option but knew which he was pulling for.

# CHAPTER FIFTY-SEVEN

Cobb had driven straight home from Vermont. There was no point checking the local places where Jason would likely hide out, because there was no way he'd be in any of them. He was smart enough not to make that mistake. He was undoubtedly holed up with his wife and son right now, somewhere Cobb wouldn't find tonight, trying to decide whether he should go on the run with Sophie and Max, or take his chances and go to the police. Would he call Cobb in the morning as he said he would? Maybe. Was Cobb ready to call the police himself? Absolutely. Unless he decided to try to trick Jason into revealing his whereabouts, in which case he'd kill him. Either way, it could wait until morning.

He was bone tired.

He left his van in the driveway and entered the house through the mudroom, as always.

The last time he'd felt this low was right after Johnny died. Nothing had gone as he'd hoped the past couple of weeks. Everything was shit.

Deep inside him, the pain he had inherited from his brother chewed on his bones. With clawed fingers it plucked tendons and sinew like harp strings, each tug sending another ripple of ache through him.

Even now he felt his pain scratching at the inside of his skull. God, how he hurt.

He had a fever. No doubt. It must have been 103 degrees. Maybe higher.

Jason would love to see Cobb this way.

And Cobb would love to see Jason at that moment, too. He'd kill him without a moment's hesitation, despite his resemblance to Johnny, despite all the things that had forged a bond between them. He could have killed *anyone* at that moment. In fact, he'd have to be careful to control himself when Carolyn—

Where was Carolyn?

She was usually thumping down the stairs by the time he reached the kitchen table. The other night she had even stood outside the bathroom and said good night, not even giving him time to take a piss in peace.

She must have dozed off by his father's bed. It had happened before. Cobb didn't give a damn. The old man certainly never seemed to care.

He trudged up the stairs on weary legs, each step more difficult than the last.

Was he dying? It felt like he was dying.

When he had almost reached the second floor, the doorbell rang. Cobb didn't have to check his watch to know that it was nearly three-thirty in the morning. And he wouldn't have to look through the peep-hole to know that Jason Swike was at the door.

He descended the stairs again, returned to the kitchen, and grabbed his stun gun from the counter, where he'd left it beside his car keys.

The doorbell rang again. He opened it a few inches and peered through the crack.

"I thought you were going to call me in the morning," he said.

"I said I had some thinking to do," Jason said. "I just finished doing it."

"Show me your hands."

Jason raised two empty hands.

"Now turn in place, slowly."

He did. No gun that Cobb could see. That was the only thing that would have concerned him. He could handle anything else. He opened the door all the way.

"I have a proposition for you," Jason said.

"I'm all ears."

He stepped aside and Jason walked past. He lowered his hands and Cobb let him. After Cobb shut the door, he said, "Gotta frisk you."

"Be my guest."

He did and came up empty.

"You here to try to talk me out of telling the police the truth about you?" Cobb asked.

"You mean telling them lies about me."

"You say *to-may-to*, I say *to-mah-to*. But now that you're here, I'll probably just kill you."

Jason opened his mouth to respond, then shut it again, frowning. He studied Cobb's face. "Man, you look half-dead."

Of course he did. The pain was squatting on its haunches up in his head now, poking at the backs of his eyeballs.

"Inside Dark," he said, but realized he might have said it only in his mind. "Is that why you're here? To sacrifice yourself? You let me kill you and I'll leave your family alone? And maybe they'll get to keep some of the money you've made? Something like that?"

Jason shook his head. "No, I'm not here to die. I'm here to make a deal." He looked Cobb dead in the eye. "I'm ready to watch you kill someone."

# CHAPTER FIFTY-EIGHT

"You're lying," Cobb said. "This is a trick."

"No trick," Jason said. "No lie. We need to end this. I've figured out a way to do it that will work for us both."

Cobb nodded but seemed barely interested in the conversation. Jason couldn't believe how badly the man was sweating.

"You need to kill someone," Jason said. "And you need me to watch. And from the looks of you, you need to do it soon. Very soon. I don't know how much of this is in your head, but you sure as hell look like you have one foot in the grave yourself, so apparently this has to happen fast, I'm guessing."

Cobb didn't disagree. He said nothing.

"Well," Jason continued, "I'm ready. Here's what I propose: In the morning, we go wherever your father is staying and I watch while you kill him. Make it look natural. If they question how it happened, I'll back you up. But here's the important part . . . we both record the entire thing on our phones so we each have evidence against the other. That way, neither one of us can ever go to the cops without implicating himself in a premeditated murder. After it's done, you'll feel better and we'll go our separate ways, each armed with the means to destroy the other . . . and ourselves. Mutual assured destruction."

Cobb's face twitched. He seemed to be working it through in his head.

"I don't want my father to die," he finally said. "I told you that. I want him to keep suffering."

"From what you also told me, he's old and broken and practically dead anyway. That's why I chose him. It's the only way I'll do it. I don't want to watch you kill a young, healthy man. But your father . . . you should have let him die a long time ago. I think I could live with that. And who knows? You might be right. Maybe I won't find it as . . . objectionable as I think I will. Maybe I'll find it . . . interesting." After a brief pause, he added, "Maybe there's a voice in my head whispering to me right now, telling me to give in."

Cobb chewed on it some more. Then he shook his head.

"My father has to live, Jason. He has to live with what he's done."

"But he's not really living now, from what you told me. From what his doctors have been telling you. He's not aware of anything happening around him. You need to kill, Cobb, with me watching, and you need to do it *soon*. And admit it, after all your father did? After what he allowed to happen to Johnny? Wouldn't you enjoy killing him? Pulling the plug and watching him gasp for air like a goldfish out of its bowl?"

Cobb took a deep breath. Then another. "Then what? Then I'm all alone."

"Then you find someone else, like you said. Someone like Barton. It probably won't take long. There are plenty of others like you out there. Spend an hour on the Internet and you'll find a dozen."

"And you? What if you *do* find it 'objectionable'?"

"I'll take my family far from here and try to forget all about you."

"I thought you said you couldn't do that."

"I'll do anything to protect my wife and son." He let Cobb think for a moment. "And you never know, I might give in to some sort of . . . Inside Dark, after all."

Cobb closed his eyes and thought for a long moment. After several seconds, his lips started to move as he spoke silently to himself . . . or maybe to his dead brother. Jason watched, unsure which way this was going to go. It was entirely possible that Cobb would use his stun gun to put Jason at his mercy . . . of which he had none.

Then he opened his eyes and said, "We don't have to go anywhere. My father's upstairs."

# CHAPTER FIFTY-NINE

Jason followed Cobb up to the father's room. As he entered, he made a show of looking around, taking in the room as if seeing it for the first time. He let his eyes land on Cobb's father, whose own eyes were open and staring at the empty white ceiling.

"Jason, meet Dad," Cobb said. "Dad, this is Jason. Here's here to watch me put you down like a crippled dog."

"Mind if I sit?" Jason asked, nodding to the chair next to the bed.

Cobb shrugged. He was looking down at the old man. "Can't decide if I should pull the plug and disable the backup battery, or just yank the tube from his throat and put it back on after he's dead."

"Let's take out our phones."

Cobb looked up, almost in surprise, as if he'd forgotten Jason was there. He took his phone from his pocket.

"Now," Jason said, "we both record the . . . event. You'll have your evidence against me and I'll have mine against you."

Cobb nodded and worked on his phone. "I'm using video," he said, smiling an ugly smile. "I'll want to watch this a few hundred times."

He positioned his phone on the nightstand on the opposite side of the bed, which put Jason in the background of the scene.

"Recording," Cobb announced.

"Me, too," Jason lied, holding his phone up as though shooting a video. "Now, for the sake of posterity, I'll admit that I'm here voluntarily, and the camera can see that I'm not restrained in any way, but once you start, Cobb, I'd rather just watch, okay? Don't try to make me a part of it. I'm willing to watch but I won't pretend to enjoy it."

"Whatever."

Jason started an audio recording as Cobb looked down at the pale, gray man on the bed, at the father he was about to kill, and Jason was surprised to see absolutely nothing in his eyes.

"Well, Dad," Cobb said, "off to Hell you go. You ready, Johnny?" he asked, looking Jason's way.

"You mean Jason."

"Here we go," Cobb said as he unwound tape from around the tracheostomy site, where the tubes from the ventilator attached to the old man's throat. Then he disconnected the tubes. The old man wheezed. A ragged breath stuttered out of him. Then another, followed by more wheezing. Jason tried to ignore it. He tried to tell himself that he was engaging in an act of mercy.

With no sign of emotion, Cobb watched his father dying. After several seconds of silence but for the sound of the old man struggling for breath, Jason asked, "How does it feel, Cobb? Killing your father?"

"I thought you weren't going to talk."

On the bed, the old man's wheezing was growing quieter. After another few seconds, Jason asked, "Are you getting the same rush you got when you killed all those guys as Crackerjack?"

"It's not the same, no. It's not as good. But whatever it is, you're ruining it for me, Johnny, so shut up."

*Johnny* again. Jason curled his fingers around the edges of the seat of his chair. As he watched Arthur Cobb dying, he prayed he wouldn't hear a voice in his head . . . cooing or chuckling or sighing with satisfaction. If he was going to do this, he wanted to do it alone, without anything inside him urging him on.

"I'm just wondering," he said, "were you tempted to paint his face before killing him? Like all the others."

Arthur Cobb's breaths were getting weaker and weaker, farther and farther apart. Jason tried to tune them out.

"I told you to shut up," Cobb said. "Let me get whatever enjoyment I can from this, then I'll deal with you."

"Deal with me? What does that mean?"

Cobb tore his eyes from the sight of his dying father and focused on Jason. There was something *now* in his previously emotionless eyes, and it was scary as hell.

*"Just shut up."*

Cobb began making his way around the bed. He was standing straighter. He looked stronger. It seemed as though pulling the plug on his father had energized him, as if his father's dying breaths were breathing new life into him. Jason reached under the seat of his chair and loosened what he had taped there earlier.

"What do you mean you'll deal with me?" he asked.

Cobb cleared the foot of the bed and continued toward Jason. From a back pocket he pulled a device Jason recognized as a stun gun. "You aren't Johnny," Cobb said. "You're nothing like Johnny. And since you won't shut up, I guess you'll find out right now how I'll deal with you."

As Cobb neared him, looking really big and royally pissed off, Jason wondered if his plan might have been a huge mistake.

# CHAPTER SIXTY

Cobb was already feeling stronger than he had in weeks. His son of a bitch of a father was dying, and Jason was right: it felt good. In his head, he could feel the dark thing inside him shriveling up and slinking off to a quiet, shadowy corner of his mind. His fever seemed to be almost gone. Another miracle cure, like all the times before.

A few feet away, Jason was cowering in his seat. He seemed to know what was coming. Now that Cobb was thinking more clearly, this mutually assured destruction idea was ludicrous. He couldn't let Jason leave the house with evidence of Cobb's crimes. He couldn't let Jason leave the house alive at all. He would never agree to partner with Cobb. He had to die.

He was about to lunge the last two feet and jam the stun gun against Jason's chest when Jason surprised him by lunging from his chair first, thrusting his arm as he came. Cobb saw a glint of metal in his hand—a small knife, probably—and Cobb swung his right arm, the one in the cast, knocking Jason's hand and then connecting with the side of his head. The blow sent Jason sprawling and his weapon flying. Unfortunately, the stun gun slipped from Cobb's hand and bounced away.

"You almost got me there, Jason."

Jason rose to his feet, looking a bit dazed. Cobb wasn't sure where he'd gotten a weapon. It hadn't been on him when Cobb had frisked him. Then he remembered hearing a faint tearing sound, like tape ripping, as Jason leaped from his seat. He must have been in the house earlier and secured something under the chair. Which meant that this had all been part of some plan . . . except for Cobb avoiding his weapon and disarming him. And, of course, the painful death he was about to suffer.

"Yeah, you almost got me," Cobb said, "but it was a swing and a miss. I guess that was strike three."

"I guess so."

"This is where it ends."

"Yup."

They stared each other down. Both had lost their weapons, which tilted things dramatically in Cobb's favor. He was a lot bigger. And stronger. And he stood between Jason and the door. He liked his chances. A lot. For the hell of it, just to mess with Jason, he began to whistle.

"Take Me Out to the Ball Game," of course.

Suddenly, Jason dove toward Cobb's feet—for the fallen knife, Cobb figured. Rather than risk losing a crucial second looking for the weapon himself, Cobb dropped on top of Jason. If he could just get his good arm around Jason's neck . . .

But the bastard was twisting and bucking and making it difficult . . .

Soon, though, size and strength won out and Jason was on his back with Cobb on top of him. Even with his arm in a cast, he knew Jason didn't stand a chance. He closed his good hand around Jason's throat and began to squeeze. Jason clawed at the fingers at his neck with one hand while his other flopped around the floor, no doubt searching for the knife he'd dropped. All Cobb had to do was finish squeezing the breath from him before he found it.

Even in that moment, the irony of the situation wasn't lost on Cobb—they were in roughly the same positions in which Jason and Barton had been in their fabricated version of the story, the one they had told the world in their television interview . . . Jason on his back, his hand scrabbling for a weapon while a killer sat atop him, choking the life out of him. This time, though, it was real. This time, Jason would die. His eyes were already rolling lazily in their sockets.

Suddenly, Cobb felt a small, stinging pain in his leg. He squeezed harder. Jason's eyes were starting to close . . .

But so were Cobb's now . . .

He felt strangely weak. His fingers slipped from Jason's throat. When Jason pushed up against him, he nearly fell on his side.

Jason scrabbled away and stood uneasily. Using the wall for support, Cobb lurched clumsily to his feet.

Jason backed up a step.

Pointless, Cobb thought. The room wasn't that big. There was nowhere to go. And Cobb couldn't see the knife in either of Jason's hands, which left him defenseless. He took a step forward and Jason took another step backward, watching him warily.

"We're just wasting time now," Cobb said. His tongue felt funny.

He took another step and Jason backed up farther, bumping into the bed behind him. Cobb wondered how he could walk backward so well without tripping over the waves in the carpet, rippling as they were, like the surface of an unquiet lake. Cobb's own steps were unsteady in the waves.

Then he was sinking, sinking into the carpet. It was already up to his knees. He looked down. No, he wasn't sinking into the carpet. He was kneeling *on* it. Something was sticking out of his leg, a few inches above his knee. Was it the knife? No, it wasn't. There never had been a knife. Only this . . . thing. It looked vaguely familiar. What was it? And why on earth would he choose to kneel now? It seemed like a terrible time to be kneeling.

# CHAPTER SIXTY-ONE

Jason took a moment to catch his breath as he watched Cobb kneeling unsteadily on the floor, the hypodermic needle and syringe sticking out of his thigh. Jason had been lucky. His first strike was supposed to catch Cobb by surprise. It was supposed to land cleanly. Instead, things had gotten dangerously dicey.

His search of the house earlier had been fruitful. He hadn't found anything he recognized as evidence that could tie him to the Crackerjack crimes, but he *had* found syringes, hypodermic needles, and vials of some drug. Not wanting to add anything suspicious to the search history on his smartphone in case anyone looked later, he used a desktop computer he found in a downstairs office—from which Cobb had clearly operated his plumbing business—to conduct a quick web search. It didn't take long to learn that the drug was a sedative used by veterinarians that, due to its rising use in the production of recreational drugs, wasn't hard to find on the street, which was probably where Cobb obtained it. It was likely what Cobb had used to knock people out after initially taking them down with a stun gun. As for whatever he had drugged Jason with in his water bottles at the stable, there were several prescription insomnia medications in his medicine cabinet that could have done the trick. Apparently, Cobb didn't sleep well.

Cobb swayed a little from side to side on his knees but didn't fall over unconscious, which was what Jason had expected him to do. Jason looked at the syringe sticking out of Cobb's leg and noticed that he hadn't depressed the plunger all the way. Apparently, he'd given him a big enough dose to dope him up, but not enough to kill him. The dose he had meant to administer—the killing dose, according to his quick and dirty research—was still in the syringe.

Jason took a careful step closer and looked into Cobb's glassy eyes, then exhaled with relief. He spotted his cell phone on the floor, picked it up, and stopped the audio recording, nearly dropping the phone as he did. He clenched his hands into fists to quiet the tremors in them.

"Damn it," Cobb said in a thick voice. He sounded drunk. From his knees he watched Jason, moving only his eyes. "Didn't have to be like this," he added. At least that was what Jason thought he said. It was difficult to understand him.

"If you think that, you're even crazier than I thought. Of course it had to be like this."

"You gonna kill me?"

"Yeah. No choice. Can you move?"

Cobb seemed to try, then said, "No," and Jason believed him. Still, he was wary as he approached, half expecting him to lunge at him like the slasher at the end of a horror flick, after everyone thinks he's dead. He patted Cobb's pockets and found a cell phone. He knew that Cobb's was on the nightstand recording everything, so this must have been Ronald Wheeler's.

"I'll get rid of this one."

"There are . . . phone records," Cobb slurred.

"If they care enough to look, which I doubt they will for Wheeler, especially when it looks like he died in a household accident, breaking his neck falling down the stairs."

It was time to start moving quickly. He turned toward the bed—letting his eyes rest only briefly on Cobb's father, who Jason chose to believe looked peaceful in death—and snapped on a pair of the baby-blue latex gloves from the box on the nightstand.

"What are you doing?" Cobb asked, sounding half-asleep now. His eyes were nearly closed.

"Covering my tracks."

First, he deleted the video Cobb had just recorded. Second, he got rid of the one Cobb had sent earlier of Jason stuffing Wheeler's dead body into the trunk of his car. Third, he deleted the voice message he had left Cobb a short while ago.

Cobb was still on his knees, still swaying from side to side. "Mom . . . ," he said, his eyes closed now. Was he hallucinating? "Mom . . . sang to me . . . when I was little." Maybe he was talking to Jason, but he might have been talking to himself. "Stevie used to smile . . . a lot." A faint trace of a smile appeared on Cobb's lips before fading quickly. "Johnny used to hurt . . . all the time . . ." The remembrances were oddly intimate and Jason almost felt guilty hearing them. "And my dad . . ."

He opened his eyes a crack. "My dad . . . you made me kill him . . . an innocent man . . . at least to you." A strange sound burbled from his throat and Jason realized he was chuckling. "We aren't . . . so different after all."

"You're wrong about me. You have been from the start."

"But my father . . ."

"Was an act of mercy."

Cobb nodded, his head bobbing loosely. "Maybe . . . but now you're gonna kill me . . . not mercy . . . cold-blooded murder . . ."

Jason said nothing.

"Your morals." Cobb made that burbling laugh sound again. "Where are they now?"

Jason didn't answer.

"If you kill me," Cobb said as his eyes slip closed again, "I win."

Maybe he was right. Or maybe Jason simply needed to end this once and for all.

"Congratulations," he said with a shrug. "You win."

He leaned down suddenly, grasped the syringe sticking out of Cobb's leg, and depressed the plunger the rest of the way, injecting the remainder of the horse tranquilizer. As he did, he let out a yell, mostly to drown out any howl of triumph that might have—just *might have*—echoed from a dark corner of his mind.

His research had been accurate. Over the next few minutes, Cobb died as Jason watched.

# CHAPTER SIXTY-TWO

It was over. And Jason was still standing. He allowed himself a minute to process all that had happened, then got to work. He'd planned it out ahead of time. Earlier, he'd retrieved from his trunk the items Cobb had planted in his apartment, as least the ones he could find—he was thankful he'd never touched any of them with his bare fingers—and put them into Cobb's box of face-painting supplies, which he left on the floor of the hallway closet with the door ajar. It couldn't be missed. Then he listened to the audio recording he'd made of Cobb's murder of his father and the aftermath and decided that he didn't need to trim it. There was nothing there to contradict the version of events Jason would tell the police later.

Next, he stuffed Wheeler's cell phone into one of the latex gloves and stomped on it several times, shattering it into pieces. Then he made sure that Cobb's fingerprints were on the syringe, and on the duct tape that Jason had found earlier in a kitchen drawer. He wound it around his own wrists, not too tightly, then twisted it and stretched it until it looked as though he had been able to free himself. He slipped one hand out of the loop. He took off the gloves, stuffed them into the other glove, the one containing the smashed phone, and took the little bundle downstairs.

He hurried through the house and out the back door, and when he felt confident that no one was watching from a neighbor's window, he slipped through the shadows and dropped the glove down a storm drain on the street.

Soon he was back upstairs again, steeling himself for what would come next. When everything looked right, he retrieved Cobb's stun gun from where it had skittered under the bed. On its side was printed 500,000 VOLTS. He pressed the power button for half a second and heard the deep thrumming crackle, saw a tiny thread of blue-white lightning arc between the prongs. The power in the little device was frightening.

He lay on the floor, took a steadying breath, then touched the weapon's prongs to his bare neck as he thumbed the power button. It had been a quick test, no more than a fraction of a second long, but God, how it *hurt*. A stabbing, burning shock. The contact had been far too short to incapacitate him, even briefly, but hopefully it had left burn marks. That was the point, after all. In case it hadn't, he steeled himself and did it again, pushing it against the side of his neck, holding it for a full second. As he did, fire lit up his insides. Pins and needles shot through his entire body before he dropped the stun gun involuntarily.

For several moments—he wasn't sure how long—he lay motionless. His neck ached. His muscles ached. At last he reached up and touched two tender welts on his neck. Perfect.

He sat up, with effort. He wiped his fingerprints from the stun gun, then pressed Cobb's dead fingers to it to add his prints to the device before dropping it by Cobb's body. Slowly, he stood and found himself relatively steady on his feet. He pulled the syringe from Cobb's leg and added a tiny bit of the tranquilizer from the vial he had stashed in the nightstand. The Internet had told him how much, based on his weight, might be enough to put him to sleep. He cut that dose by half, just to be safe. All he wanted was for the drug to be in his blood for a while, and for a needle mark to be visible on his skin.

Using his phone, he called 911. Weakly, he said, "Please . . . help me. He's down but I don't know if he's dead. He may still kill me . . . hurry . . ."

He decided not to leave Cobb's address as he dropped the phone to the floor without disconnecting the call. It felt more realistic that way. The cops would probably triangulate the signal or something. If not, he'd call 911 again when he woke up in a little while.

He knelt beside Cobb, stuck the syringe into the side of his own bicep, and injected himself with the tranquilizer. He yanked the needle from his arm and closed his fist around the syringe. When the drug kicked in a few seconds later, he fell over sideways, imagining that it would look very natural when the cops eventually found him.

His last conscious thought was that it was over. It was finally over.

# CHAPTER SIXTY-THREE

A little after 5:00 a.m., the police found Jason lying barely conscious across Ian Cobb's dead body, an empty syringe clutched in one hand. His cell phone was on the floor beside his other hand, where a loose, twisted loop of duct tape encircled the wrist. An EMT checked him over thoroughly and declared him uninjured. A half hour later, when State Police Detective Lamar Briggs arrived, looking—in Jason's opinion—tired and cranky, Jason was wide awake.

Later, the two men sat at the table in Cobb's kitchen, Briggs looking even crankier than when he'd arrived. He also looked skeptical as he flipped through his little notebook, scanning the pages he had filled with notes for the past hour while Jason had answered his questions.

"That's a hell of a story," Briggs said, sitting back.

Jason nodded.

"Tell it to me again."

"Which part?"

"All of it. Start with the motel."

Jason sighed and recounted the story he had already spun about being asleep at the motel where he'd been staying while doing some writing, and getting a call from Cobb, who sounded desperate and maybe a little crazy. He'd had enough of his father, couldn't take the old man anymore, and frankly, Cobb admitted, his mind hadn't been right ever since he'd been taken by Crackerjack two weeks ago. He kept having nightmares—*God*, the nightmares. He really wanted to talk.

"So I told him to come to the motel."

"Remind me why you were staying there."

"I told you, I'm kicking around a story that takes place in a motel. I wanted to really get the feel for it. Soak it in."

"I thought you were writing a book about Crackerjack."

"The motel book will be after that one, but I wanted to get some thoughts down while the idea is fresh." He shrugged. "A writer has to follow his muse, you know? Strike while the iron is hot."

Briggs frowned. Actually, he hadn't stopped frowning since he'd gotten there.

"And what did Cobb want to talk about when he showed up?"

"It was hard to tell. He wasn't very coherent."

"Was he drunk? High?"

"Like I told you already, I don't know. He just seemed . . . off."

"And he attacked you."

"Not really. I feel like you're not listening at all. I stepped out onto the landing with him and he got a bit belligerent, and when I put my hand on his shoulder and asked if he was okay, he pushed me back."

"Into another room's window," Briggs said, consulting his notes.

"Right."

"What about the knife?"

"The knife?"

"We found a knife at the motel."

Briggs had left that out the first time they'd gone through this.

"Yeah, he showed me a knife. I talked him into giving it to me, which he did peacefully. I don't remember where I left it."

Briggs looked dubious. "Then he peacefully pushed you into a window?"

"Well, no, that wasn't very peaceful. It was just a knee-jerk reaction, I think, after I touched his shoulder."

"And you pushed him back and he fell over the balcony."

Jason nodded. "I didn't mean to push him that hard. Just a knee-jerk reaction of my own, I guess. Luckily, he wasn't hurt."

"Yeah, you were both lucky, I guess . . . until he tried to kill you later, of course. Tell me that part again."

Jason sighed, shook his head wearily, just for show, and began. "After he left, I got in my car and drove away. So when he called—"

"Why'd you leave the motel?"

"In case he came back. Things hadn't gone so well the first time he was there."

"So when he called later and said, 'Hey, pal, sorry I attacked you. Wanna come over for a beer and some Cheetos?' you said, 'Sure,' and headed right over?"

"He seemed to have calmed down. But he also seemed . . . depressed."

"So off you went. In the middle of the night. After he'd already attacked you."

"I didn't think of it as him having attacked me. It was just . . . a misunderstanding. I thought maybe he really needed someone to talk to. I thought I could help him."

"Why'd he call you? Had you two become bosom buddies in the two weeks you'd known each other?"

"Not really. We met at a bar for a drink one time. Talked on the phone a few times. He had me over for a beer one night," he added, in case his fingerprints or DNA showed up somewhere else in the house.

"Yet you're the one he called in his moment of crisis."

Jason shrugged. "I don't think he had many friends. And given what we'd been through together—or what I believed we'd been through—I figured maybe he thought I was the only one who might understand whatever was bothering him tonight."

Briggs nodded and flipped forward a couple of pages in his note-book. "So when he asked you to come over, sounding all depressed, and after attacking you earlier, it didn't occur to you to call the police?"

"I honestly didn't think he was dangerous—to me or to anyone else, including himself. I thought he was just feeling really down. He'd been through a lot, or so I thought. I didn't yet know that he was . . ."

"Crackerjack?" Briggs said.

"Right. How could I possibly have known that?"

"Good question."

At Briggs's prompting, Jason continued his fiction—about Cobb subduing him with a stun gun, binding him with tape, and admitting he had been Crackerjack all along.

"Why would he do all of that?"

"I already told you all this, Detective."

"You're a spellbinding storyteller, Jason. I want to hear it again."

Jason sighed. "He said he was tired of it all. Tired of pretending. Tired of taking care of his father. Apparently, his old man had abused Ian's brother when they were younger, so he decided it was time to kill him."

"After all those years of keeping him at home, paying a fortune in medical care, he finally just up and decides to kill Daddy?"

"I can't explain it. But remember, by that time, I was taped in a chair and he was threatening to kill us all—first his father, then me, then himself—so it's obvious he wasn't thinking rationally."

"Why kill you?"

"Like I already told you, he said I was 'the one that got away.'"

"From Crackerjack. Because Ian Cobb confessed to you that he and Wallace Barton were working together, and you were the one that got away."

"I assume that's what he meant."

Briggs leaned forward in his chair, his elbows on the table. "See? Right there is where you lose me, Jason. Because you've been saying all along that he helped you escape in the first place, two weeks ago. So why would he want to kill you tonight?"

Jason told that part of the story again, about their escape from Wallace Barton's stable, adding that Cobb had revealed just tonight that he had decided not to kill him back then—decided to help him escape, in fact—because he reminded Cobb so much of his younger brother, Johnny.

"I haven't seen any pictures of his brother yet," Jason lied, "but he said we looked a lot alike." He knew that Briggs would eventually see photos of Johnny Cobb, if he hadn't already, and wouldn't fail to see the strong resemblance between them.

"I still don't understand, though, Jason. Why would he want to kill you tonight? If he saved you because you looked so much like his brother, why decide to kill you? What changed?"

Jason shrugged. "All I can say is that he clearly wasn't well. He was obviously . . ."

"Crazy?" Briggs finished for him.

"I'd say that's about right, wouldn't you?"

The rest of the story, which Jason had concocted a few hours ago, was easy. While Cobb was watching his father die, Jason was busy trying to get his hands free of the tape. He succeeded just as Cobb was approaching, and they fought. Somehow, even though he was groggy from the drug, Jason got his hands on the syringe of horse tranquilizer, which was on the nightstand, and managed to stick Cobb with it.

"The next thing I remember, a policeman was asking if I was okay. I think I managed to make a recording of some of this, by the way. On my phone."

Briggs regarded him in silence for a moment. "Yeah, I listened to it."

"So you heard how it all happened then."

"I'm not sure what I heard."

Jason knew the recording supported his version of events. He also knew that must have pissed off Briggs.

"And how the hell did you manage to make a recording anyway?" Briggs asked. "Your hands were taped. And how did you even still have a phone? He didn't take it from you?"

"Like I keep saying, he wasn't in his right mind. He was sloppy, I guess. Didn't even ask if I had a phone. Didn't tape my hands well enough. He was in pretty rough shape."

"Why didn't you dial 911?"

"I was trying to work the phone without him seeing, keeping it hidden. I could barely see what I was doing. I was lucky just to get the audio-recording app open. Hey, when do I get my phone back?"

Briggs shook his head in disbelief as he closed his notebook and sat back in his chair. "I've gotta tell you, this whole thing stinks."

"I know," Jason said, nodding sadly. "It's a shame. Two men dead."

"That's not what I'm saying. I'm saying that this stinks. It smells all wrong."

"Meaning what?"

"Meaning that I think you're lying."

Jason tried to look shocked. "About what?"

"I don't know. Maybe everything."

Overconfidence is dangerous for a criminal, Jason knew. And there are a thousand ways to screw up. The smallest detail overlooked could send a murderer to prison for life. He did a lightning-quick rundown in his mind and couldn't see where Briggs would be able to bring him down.

"I don't know what you're talking about, Detective. I've been as helpful as I can be. I've told you everything I can remember. So if you don't have any more questions for me tonight, can I go home? It's been a long night. Don't forget, I was almost killed a little while ago."

Briggs eyed him for a moment. Jason figured that he wanted to say something like, *I'll figure it out eventually. And when I do, your ass is mine.* Instead, in a voice dripping with contempt, he said, "I bet this will make a great ending for your book. A second escape, this time from the second half of a serial-killing team. Very exciting finish. Probably help you sell a lot more copies."

"You might be right," Jason said. Then, in what was a complete and utter lie, he added, "I hadn't thought about that."

# CHAPTER SIXTY-FOUR

Jason Swike's book—*The End of Broken Bones*—came out eleven months later. Briggs had already read it from cover to cover. He even annotated numerous passages in the margins with thoughts of his own, various questions that occurred to him and suspicions he had. And now he stood in line at a Boston bookstore that specialized in mystery and crime books, waiting for the celebrated author to sign his copy of the bestseller.

After twenty minutes, hardcover in hand, he reached the table where Jason Swike sat, pen at the ready. On the wall behind him hung a banner depicting the image of the book's cover, along with a question printed in bold red script: *What Drives a Person to Kill?*

"So tell me," Briggs said, "what *does* drive a person to kill?"

Swike, who was checking his watch, looked up. "Detective," he said with mild surprise. "It's been a while."

It had been nearly six months, in fact, since they had seen each other, ever since the day Lieutenant McCuller told Briggs to stop obsessing over the Crackerjack case trying to find something that wasn't there. Briggs's protests that something wasn't right about Jason Swike fell repeatedly on deaf ears. His attempt to obtain a warrant for Swike's and Cobb's cell-phone records that final night were unsuccessful. They had Cobb's phone itself, of course, but nothing on it seemed suspicious. Besides, men were no longer turning up around Massachusetts with broken bodies and painted faces. The bad guy, Wallace Barton—against whom the evidence was both overwhelming and incontrovertible—was deep in the dirt. The district attorney was happy. The public was happy. Case closed. As for Ian Cobb's death, nothing contradicted Swike's story about that. "Leave it all alone and work the cases that actually need working," the lieutenant had ordered.

"Want me to sign this?" Swike asked, reaching across the table and taking the book from Briggs's hand. "I didn't know you were a fan."

"Not sure I'd call myself that, but I definitely think you're someone to keep my eye on."

Swike seemed to consider that a moment, then opened the book and poised his pen above one of the first pages. "So, to whom should I make it out?"

"Just sign your name."

He did, then stuck a custom bookmark between the pages, closed the cover, and handed the book back to Briggs.

Ignoring the long line of people behind him, Briggs said, "*New York Times* Bestseller List, huh? Where is it at the moment? Number nine?"

"Down to twelve. Peaked at sixth on the list, which was fine with me."

"I hear they're shooting the movie right now."

Briggs had read in the *Globe* that Hollywood had cast an A-list star—he couldn't remember which one—to play Swike in the film.

"Should be in theaters early next year," Jason said.

"And did I read something about another movie, based on an old novel of yours?"

Swike smiled. "Well, it's not definite yet, but my agent thinks Paramount will give it the green light any day now."

Briggs nodded. Someone behind him coughed impatiently. "The *Globe* article also said you got a big deal for two more books."

"Novels, not true crime like this one. I'm probably three-quarters of the way through the first one."

"Congratulations. Looks like this whole Crackerjack thing worked out well for you."

"It was a nightmare," Swike said. "But I guess I've been pretty lucky since."

"Lucky. Sure."

The murmurs and grumbling behind Briggs were getting louder.

"I'm retiring in four months," he said. "Gonna have a lot of free time on my hands."

"You should find a hobby. Write a book, maybe."

"I already have a hobby all planned. *You're* going to be my hobby, Jason. I made a copy of the entire Crackerjack case file—which could get me in trouble if they ever found out, but what the hell? I've got a recording of your television interview, too. And I have this book you wrote, of course. I'm going to go over it all, again and again, for as long as I have to, until I find whatever it is you're hiding."

"I'm not hiding anything, Detective, but . . . whatever fills your day." He could not have failed to notice the growing unhappiness in the line behind Briggs, yet he refused to look impatient, to rush Briggs in any way. He simply sat and waited.

Finally, Briggs said, "Thanks for the autograph."

"Thanks for the twenty-two bucks you paid for the book. Take care, Detective."

Briggs walked away, ignoring the dirty looks as he passed dozens of people who, like him, had shelled out for Swike's book. They would probably all pay to see the movie, too . . . and read his other books, and see the movies based on those . . .

And Swike would get a cut of every one of those dollars.

As he promised, Briggs was going to keep at it. He would comb through the entire case file again, as often as needed. He would watch the TV interview over and over. He would read the book from cover to cover as many times as he needed. Lieutenant McCuller may have ordered Detective Lamar Briggs to close the case and walk away, but he couldn't make private citizen Briggs do so.

In fact, maybe Briggs would move his retirement up a month or two. He couldn't wait to get started.

# CHAPTER SIXTY-FIVE

Jason watched Briggs disappear in the crowd and wondered exactly what the detective suspected him of and whether he'd ever find evidence of it. He didn't think so. Still, he might not sleep as well knowing that Briggs might never stop chewing on the case, like an ornery dog with an old shoe. And maybe that was what Briggs wanted. Maybe it was the best he could hope for. A small victory.

He signed a book for another fan—a real one, this time—as Sophie zoomed up in her "hot rod," as she called it. A top-of-the-line electric wheelchair. All it was missing, she said, was a rocket launcher. At her side was Max. Sophie had driven the two of them herself to Jason's book signing in her customized van, also woefully lacking in rocket launchers, she'd noted, but not much else.

"Was that Detective Briggs?" she asked as Jason took a copy of his book from another reader, signed it, and returned it with a smile.

"It was."

"Big fan?"

"*Big* might not be the right word for it."

*Fan* wasn't, either.

Max asked, "Are all these people here to see you, Daddy?"

"They are," Jason said.

"I'm glad I don't have to stand in line to see you."

"Not you, pal. Never. And nobody here realizes it, but they came to see Mommy, too."

"They did?"

"Sure. They're here about my book, aren't they?"

"Yeah."

"And who drew the picture on the cover?"

"Mommy."

"Well, there you go. And she's gonna do the cover for my next book, too." He looked at Sophie. "Right?"

"If I'm not too busy," she said with a smile.

"Of course."

"Because I have another job lined up."

"I think you mentioned that."

"And two more after that. Did I mention *that*?" she asked, still smiling. "They're really piling up, but I'll see if I can fit you in."

"I guess that's all I can ask for." Literally, it seemed. For while everything was coming up roses professionally for both Jason and Sophie, personally—at least from his perspective—things could have been better. But they also could have been far worse. He hadn't had to kill anyone in almost a year. Even better, no one was trying to kill him. Best of all, Max had been on Solizen for ten months and the test results so far had been extraordinarily encouraging. There was every reason to hope that the treatment would give him a better, healthier, longer life—a life virtually undiminished by his rare disease.

His relationship with Sophie was better than it had been since the accident and their subsequent separation. Things weren't the way Jason wanted them to be, and they might never be, but the two of them had arrived at a place that had seemed beyond the horizon not long ago, before Crackerjack had turned their lives upside down. They were friends again, which was a start. Without expressly asking whether he had indeed embraced some sort of inner darkness when he faced Cobb,

Sophie asked how he'd felt about killing him, and he'd assured her that he hadn't enjoyed it one iota. It had been necessary but regrettable, he'd said. He'd have given anything to have been able to resolve things differently, he'd told her. And as he'd said all that, she had watched his eyes closely. In the end, she seemed satisfied with whatever she'd seen there. He was glad. He truly didn't know what she *would* see—whether there was something crouching in a shadowy place in his mind, an Inside Dark waiting for him to be ready to listen to it. He hoped like hell that wasn't the case. He even talked to a therapist about it twice a month now. And he prayed about it every night. And if someday he heard a voice answering that prayer . . . well, he hoped it would belong to God and not . . . something else.

A little less than a year ago he had personally killed two men, both of whom had been cruel and psychotic murderers who didn't deserve the blessing of life, so he wasn't troubled by that. He had also played a significant part in the killing of another man, but no matter what Arthur Cobb had done in his past, he hadn't deserved the punishment of continued life in the state he was in, so Jason wasn't bothered by his own role in that death, either. Finally, he shared some of the moral responsibility, to varying degrees, for the murders Cobb committed after Jason learned the truth about him, including those of Lyman Gooding, whose body had yet to be found, and Ronald Wheeler, whose death was deemed accidental. But after intense soul-searching, he decided that those deaths were far more appropriately a burden on Cobb's soul than his own.

He signed another copy of his book for another happy fan and looked at the long line of people standing behind her. At his side, his wife and son looked at the same line. Sophie was smiling, and Max was impressed that people wanted to meet his famous father.

Briggs had been right . . . the whole Crackerjack thing had worked out pretty well for Jason Swike.

# ACKNOWLEDGMENTS

First and deepest thanks go to my wife, Colleen, who makes my writing life possible and the rest of my life spectacular. Thanks also to my sons for being who they are and for never letting me forget what it's all about.

I am also indebted to Michael Bourret, my agent at Dystel, Goderich & Bourret LLC, for all that he does for me and for my books; David Downing, for his insight, honesty, and editorial eagle eye; and Gracie Doyle, Liz Pearsons, Sarah Shaw, and every single member of the team at Thomas & Mercer, all of whom work hard to bring my books to life.

Thanks to Heidi Kujda and good friends Stephen Karasawa and Daniel Suarez for information on which I relied in the writing of this book. Their help made my job easier and the book better.

Many, many thanks to my family and friends far and wide for their continuing and unwavering support, interest, and enthusiasm.

Final, heartfelt gratitude is reserved for my readers, whom I cannot thank enough for spending time with my books and for reaching out to me through my website and Facebook and Twitter to let me know that they enjoy what I do. It means the world to me.

# ABOUT THE AUTHOR

James Hankins's novels of suspense include *The Prettiest One*, *Shady Cross*, *Brothers and Bones*, *Jack of Spades*, and *Drawn*. Each of his books has become an Amazon #1 bestseller, and *Brothers and Bones* was named to the *Kirkus Reviews* list of Best Books of 2013. Hankins lives north of Boston with his wife and sons and can be reached through his website, www.jameshankinsbooks.com; on Twitter @James_Hankins_; and on Facebook at www.facebook.com/JamesHankinsAuthorPage.